W9-BXX-848

PRAISE FOR

No One Is Here Except All of Us

"Fantastical and ambitious . . . infused with faith in the power of storytelling . . . Light and tenderness persevere—in a shining moon, in a candle still aglow, in a mother's embrace of her child."
—*The New York Times Book Review*

"Debut novelist Ausubel casts a vibrant, dreamlike spell in this tale of a remote Romanian village whose citizens try to save themselves from the Holocaust by reinventing their own history." —*Marie Claire*

"Romanian Jews in 1939 reinvent their own reality in this inspiring novel about the power of community and imagination."
—*O, The Oprah Magazine*

"Ramona Ausubel's debut, *No One Is Here Except All of Us*, captures the magical group-think of a Romanian village that retreats into an imaginary reality at the outbreak of war." —*Vogue*

"*No One Is Here Except All of Us* contains so many achingly beautiful passages, it's as if language itself is continually striving to be a refuge. . . . If a book can be said to have a consciousness, the consciousness here is infinitely tender and soulful, magical and true. It's the kind of God we wish for." —*San Francisco Chronicle*

"An absorbing and unpredictable novel that manages to encompass a wide geographic and emotional range. . . . Ausubel's original voice combines fresh, clear observation and Old Testament grandeur."
—*The New Yorker*

"A special work of the imagination, an original gift, dark and light, and Ramona Ausubel colors it all with a glowing wisdom."
—Ron Carlson, author of *Five Skies*

"Ramona Ausubel's first novel, *No One Is Here Except All of Us*, is a poetic fable about a part of history after which some people say poetry is an obscenity. . . . Ausubel's fablelike tone is effective in creating a sensation of tale and dream. For conveying the full horror of the events surrounding the Holocaust, it is less so, but this isn't what she's trying to do. Instead, she is comfortable reshaping, in a safe time and place, stories that were handed to her, using her rhetorical and narrative skill to create something that can be carried without cutting the one who carries it."   —*Minneapolis Star Tribune*

"In her debut novel, *No One Is Here Except All of Us*, Ramona Ausubel breaks new ground, with a unique prose style that weaves a classic immigrant tale into a world of dreams. The town of Zalischik and its citizens rewrite their own story, filling it with magic, hope, and a determination to find new ways to begin in the face of destruction."   —Hannah Tinti, author of *The Good Thief*

"Here is a world created out of the most curious and beautiful remnants of our own: opera, suitcases, letters, rivers, daughters, strangers, and shovels. Ramona Ausubel cracks open the very idea of a book and fills its shell with a thing glimmering, thrilling, and new."
    —Samantha Hunt, author of *The Invention of Everything Else*

"Beautifully written and alive in story, fascinating characters, and place. You can't help but compare Ausubel's book to García Márquez, with her fantastic vision of history and invention, the small village dreaming the vast world, but she is her own new fresh voice."   —Brad Watson, author of *The Heaven of Mercury*

"A wise, compassionate book that even in its darkest turns uplifts."
    —Christine Schutt, author of *Florida* and *All Souls*

No One Is Here Except All of Us

RAMONA AUSUBEL

RIVERHEAD BOOKS

New York

RIVERHEAD BOOKS
An imprint of Penguin Random House LLC
375 Hudson Street
New York, New York 10014

Copyright © 2012 by Ramona Ausubel
Penguin supports copyright. Copyright fuels creativity, encourages diverse voices,
promotes free speech, and creates a vibrant culture. Thank you for buying an authorized
edition of this book and for complying with copyright laws by not reproducing, scanning, or
distributing any part of it in any form without permission. You are supporting writers and
allowing Penguin to continue to publish books for every reader.

The Library of Congress has catalogued the Riverhead hardcover edition as follows:

Ausubel, Ramona.
No one is here except all of us / Ramona Ausubel
p. cm.
ISBN 9781594487941
1. World War, 1939–1945—Romania—Fiction.   2. Jews—Romania—Fiction.
3. Imagination—Fiction.   I. Title.
PS3601.U868 N6   2012   2011046846

First Riverhead hardcover edition: February 2012
First Riverhead trade paperback edition: February 2013
Riverhead trade paperback ISBN: 9781594486494

Printed in the United States of America
10 9 8 7 6 5 4 3

Cover design © gray318
Book design by Amanda Dewey

This is a work of fiction. Names, characters, places, and incidents either are the product of
the author's imagination or are used fictitiously, and any resemblance to actual persons,
living or dead, businesses, companies, events, or locales is entirely coincidental.

To my grandmothers, Anne and Alice,
who told me their stories and left enough room
for me to imagine my way inside

· I ·

Dear Chaya,

I am sitting with you on my lap, by the window. There are ice crystals on the glass. If I put my ear close enough I can almost hear them cracking and growing. It's not snowing now, but it has been all morning. Even though you have only been alive a few days, your story, our story, started a long time ago. Ours is a story I know, both the parts I saw with my eyes and the parts I did not. This kind of knowing comes from somewhere in my bones, somewhere in my heart. Someday, your children will ask what happened, and you will tell a new version, and this way, the story will keep living. The truth is in the telling.

It began in 1939, at the northern edge of Romania, on a small peninsula cupped by a muddy river. The days then were still and peaceful. Morning was for kneading bread, milking cows. We brought babies up to our lips. The baker had loaves in the oven in time for them to come out again when we were hungry for lunch. Children added, divided and multiplied numbers and got pats on the head for it. The banker counted rolls of coins and locked them away. The greengrocer filled his shelves with cabbages picked by the cabbage picker and potatoes pulled by teenage boys out of the earthy plots behind old women's houses. The old women liked to watch the muscles on the boys' arms pop into life, strands of a knot.

Nine families called the valley our home. In each direction beyond the cultivated hills were mountains dark with pine. We never thought of the river as anything but ours, though its name on maps was Dniester. Our village was complete and so were our lives within it; our ghosts were quiet under the earth and we were quiet above it.

Our lives belonged to this place—we did not want to move them elsewhere, even though we knew that, in another country not so far away, a man with a square mustache wanted to remake the world. People like us were forced to register all wealth and property. Passports were stamped with a large red J. A curfew was set. It was a new chapter of an old story. Somewhere, a temple exploded in flames. Czechoslovakia was seized, Warsaw. People like us were gathered in ghettos. All men were Israel and all women Sarah.

"They will surely stop this," we said. "The worst is over," we surmised. "Someone always wants to tell you it's the end of the world."

We did not remember a time when there was no impending war, when there was no hatred or persecution. No pogroms, no army conscription. Maybe, when the world began, everything had been clean and pure. We had a story about a man and a woman and a few beautiful days in a garden, but none of us in the village remembered such a time. Our species might have growled at each other or spit into our palms. We might have rolled around on the thin-skinned earth, touched each other's closed eyelids or kneeled down at the pairs of footprints we were leaving everywhere. However life on earth started, we continued on until we forgot, time batting us with its paws and leaving the gristled meat of each day at our doorstep, while we headed out into the spinning world. For us, it was always the first time the particular baby had been born, the first time he shook his pickled little fists in the air. It was always the first today. . . .

BEFORE

One Friday evening, the sun hung heavy and waiting to drain, syrupy, into the wheat fields. Men walked home carrying evidence of the day—a scythe, a leather satchel full of needle-nose tools, a roll of receipts, a bag of cabbages, an empty lunch box. At the door, children like me had scrubbed cheeks that looked like juicy, pluckable fruit. "Shabbat shalom," we children said to our fathers. "Good Sabbath," the fathers said. On the table, a lace cloth. On the lace cloth, covered pots. "Shabbat shalom," the wives of husbands said through kisses.

At my house, a chicken leg cooked until meat fell off the bone into the soup. My brother had just carried wood inside before sundown and I was trying to figure out if winter clouds were frozen, or only the snow falling from them. My sister held a piece of cotton over the fingertip she had pricked with her sewing needle. This led the three of us to our favorite game—comparing wounds, the souvenirs of childhood. Moishe, the oldest at thirteen, had a bloom on the back of his calf from swimming into a log in the river. Regina, a year younger than Moishe and a year older than me, let a drop of deep red needle-pricked blood fall into her opposite palm. From a game of chase, I could boast a long branch-scratch across my cheek. Our skin was one map divided into three pages, the territory of our joy marked therein.

My mother twisted the fringe on the tablecloth into a knot that would not hold. She was reading a book about a futureless, midwinter love affair between two young Russians—a bright-cheeked boy about to enter the Czar's army and a beautiful, stupid girl. My mother frowned at the lovers because she knew they were doomed. She took it as a personal offense that they believed in something so hopeless. With each turn of the page, she twisted her hair faster.

"I hope he doesn't die until spring," she said. "She's too dumb to survive that kind of cold with a broken heart on top of it."

My father was not home yet, and the room was like a painting we had made for him. When the knob turned and he had had a chance to take the scene in, we fell back into action—Mother stood up and stirred the soup while the three of us children raced to show our father the evidence that we, too, had been alive all day long—blood on the cloth, firewood piled neatly and a question about the birth of snow.

"The most beautiful woman in the world," my father said, his lips pressed to my mother's hand. The room was rich with the smell of supper, and I placed one soft, old napkin at each of our places.

In our village, all of us—mothers and fathers, grandparents and children, uncles and great-aunts, the butcher, baker, saddlemaker, cobbler, wheat cutter, cabbage farmer—stood in circles around our tables and lit candles while we blanketed the room in prayer. All at once, we tugged at soft braids of bread, which gave way.

I walked to weekly prayers holding my father's hand in a drenching rain. The villagers nodded and smiled to each other, trying to appreciate our place on the turning earth. We concerned ourselves not with the world's many terrors, but with the most mundane of details. My mother said to my crazy aunt Kayla, "This is some kind of rain," and, "Glad I brought the wash in last night." She did not think, *I wonder if this storm will last for the rest of our lives.*

Kayla said, "Another day in paradise," and took the black top hat off my uncle Hersh's head to shake away rainwater pooling in the brim.

There was an old story that the prophet Elijah was responsible for rain and thunder—his only distraction while he waited for the great and terrible day of the Lord. "Yeah, yeah, we hear you," the baker said to the heavens.

Our village was too small for a proper temple—just over a hundred people—but we made do with the healer's house. In his kitchen: the women and children, quiet, watching rain gather strength out the window. I took note of the puddles forming, wishing I was outside jumping in them, delightedly dirtying everything my mother had scrubbed clean. The mothers had gently stretched the rules of the Sabbath over the years to allow them to do small, easy work while they listened to the service. Several were mending socks, several were knitting. Aunt Kayla had a half-finished needle-point picturing a basketful of bubble-gum-pink babies wrapped in a pale blue blanket. The babies did not have eyes yet, neither did they have hands. Blind little monsters. Next to Kayla, whose envy seeped out of her like slime, the banker's rounded, pregnant wife tucked a sweater between her shoulder and head and closed her eyes. At her feet, her eldest son, Igor, herded his little brothers and sisters into a tidy circle, distributed toy teacups around and pretended to fill them up.

In the sitting room the men prepared to stoke the coals of faith. But the healer fidgeted. A newspaper in his pocket rustled when he took it out. "There's something we need to discuss," he said nervously. "Before we start." He unrolled it on the floor. WAR. 11 am, SEPTEMBER 3rd, 1939, it said across the front. The butcher turned from picking dried blood out of his nails. The skinny, bespectacled jeweler thumbed his pocket watch. The greengrocer patted his slippery, bald head. The barber read the words out loud, a crack splitting his voice.

"It's our day of rest," the widow said, indignant.

"This was weeks ago already," the healer said softly. He took a folded square of newsprint from his vest pocket. He opened it, and it bloomed like a flower. He began to read. "The Jewish people ought to be exterminated root and branch. Then the plague of pests would have disappeared in Poland at one stroke."

Sure that I did not understand what this meant, I refrained from tugging on my mother's skirt because her shock-white face frightened me. The mothers who had been mending socks were no longer diving the needle in and out. The tip-tapping of knitting needles had stopped. The banker's wife still slept peacefully, while her children drew closer to her ankles, Igor trying all the time to cheer them up, offering pretend cookies to dip into their tea.

I could not see my uncle Hersh, but I recognized his voice. "Surely this cannot continue. Surely it will be stopped."

"I have a brother in America who says they will not let Germany win the war," the jeweler said.

"We are a forty-day walk from Iaşi, and two weeks to Lvov. We are safe here," the baker said.

"Chernowitz is only forty-seven kilometers," the healer said.

The quiet that followed was desperate, starving, rabid. No one moved. We were a houseful of statues, discarded for imperfections. Waiting to be broken to pieces and thrown into the river. *What if I die?* I said to myself. *What if I don't grow up?* Even when I repeated this, I did not believe it could be true. My pink hands, my scratched cheek, my brown dress mended in three places— none of these seemed to be disappearing. They were solid and real, indisputable. What force could talk them out of existence?

My mother absently took my braids in her hand and held them like reins. I wished I could gallop her out of this fearful place, faster than the wind, to safety. We remained in the healer's kitchen, and danger crept around us like a salamander. The banker's wife woke up and swatted at her eleven children, huddled close, like a woman keeping flies off the pie. "Mother," Igor said. "We are in trouble." She rested her hands on her big belly and glared at him, her eyes blistering with heat. Do not betray me, the eyes said. Do not wake me from my slumber.

We were completely dumbstruck. Our hearts were racing, but we did not know what to do.

The healer moved his pointer finger across the flaking leather cover of the big book in his lap. He had cracked that spine ten thousand times. The rest of his body fixed, he opened his mouth and started to read. He began at the beginning, his words running over us, a familiar river.

> *In the beginning God created the heavens and the earth. Now the earth was astonishingly empty, and darkness was on the face of the deep, and the spirit of God was hovering over the face of the waters.*
>
> *And God said, "Let there be light," and there was light.*
>
> *And God saw the light, that it was good; and God divided the light from the darkness.*
>
> *And God called the light Day, and the darkness He called Night. And there was evening and there was morning, one day.*

His voice replaced the blood in my veins. Outside, the rain turned to sheets. Streams began to run over the cobbled streets.

> *And God called the dry land Earth, and the gathering together of the waters called He Seas; and God saw that it was good.*

And God said: "Let the earth put forth grass, herb yielding seed, and fruit-tree bearing fruit after its kind, wherein is the seed thereof, upon the earth." And it was so.

And then, as if she had gathered us for her audience, a silver airplane passed, grinding her big propeller at the sky. My mother released my braids, which fell palm-warmed onto my neck. Our faces, pressed to the panes, froze in silence. The young boys seared the shape in their minds so they could draw it later. The girls were not so susceptible to the spell and saw a shiny menace. Moishe shot me an exuberant, shocked look. Regina wrung her hands out. The airplane was low, but the sound of it was not. Igor did not have enough hands to cover the eyes of all ten of his siblings. He shielded the youngest ones and soothed the rest.

I imagined what the world might look like from so high. I thought the pilot would have seen three concentric circles. First, the brown, churning water—the circle of our river around us; inside that, the quilt squares of our fields, which were turned dirt, newly planted seeds, the bright green carpet of a field just beginning to come to life, fences mended or falling down into the soft new grass, humped haystacks, our cattle herd, our sheep herd, our goats, bare birch trees pointing straight into the heavens; and in the center, in the heart, our cobbled and dirt streets, our red-tiled and gray-shingled roofs radiating out from the town square with its statue of a long-dead war hero in the middle. In each storefront, promises were being made—the butcher's window with a freshly killed lamb hanging on a hook, the greengrocer's with a basket of a deep red beets and a tub of onions, the barber's empty chair and glinting scissors, the healer's pharmacy full of brown glass bottles with handwritten labels, the jeweler's gold chains strung around a black velvet neck.

We watched the airplane fly away into the gray and come back again, the approach rattling our veins. I followed with my eyes as it turned over the mountains on the other side of the river. Then my ears were punched out with a thundering, time-stopping boom and the crackling silence afterward. The memory of that sound circled us while the airplane glinted and disappeared into the clouds.

We waited, itchy, for everything around us to erupt in flames. For the surface of the earth to shatter. For the airplane to come back and drop an ending on our peninsula. The sky did not clear to let us see whether smoke was rising from the other side of the mountains. The rain put out any fires. Silence, that fat hand, slapped away all my questions.

People started to shout. The banker's eleven children yelled questions at each other, at their mother, who was awake but did not stand up from her chair. The word *war* popped like bubbles on my father's tongue. The word *death* came after. Forgiveness was begged for. The sky was pummeled with apologies and the ground was pummeled with rain. I thought about everything a person could drop from up high: pigs, logs, bricks. A letter stating YOU ARE DEAD. I knew the word *bomb*, but I had never seen one go off. My mother was silent, except for the grip of her fingers around mine. My hand fit completely, like a seed, inside hers. It must have been the very same sky as before, but it looked emptied out, lightless.

The barrier between the kitchen and sitting room fell. Men

and women mixed, husbands and wives held each other. Children tried to insert themselves into the embrace.

The river rose, rain crashed down, and the sound of all that water jumbled our words. We heard *glove* when someone said *love*. We heard *yarn* for *harm* and *bread* for *God*. We were like a windstorm, whipping ourselves dizzy, going nowhere.

There was no point in guessing how many minutes or days before another propeller cut our sky into billowing blue shreds. We began, first in our feet, then in our legs—those rootless stumps—in our sloshing guts and our clamoring hearts, to feel we were being abandoned on this island. The sinking island. Why were we not running downstream with all the rainwater? Why were we standing here, dumb as flags stuck into the earth, when everything that could escape was escaping?

The healer sat down on the floor. He opened the book and began again, his voice loud and sure.

> And God said, "Let there be a firmament in the midst of the waters, and let it divide the waters from the waters." And God said: "Let there be lights in the firmament of the heaven to divide the day from the night; and let them be for signs, and for seasons, and for days and years."

The healer's voice turned scratchy and he started to cough. I could not tell the meaning of the tears that streamed down his face. My father handed him a worn handkerchief, and the healer wiped his face.

I closed the door and went to the threshold between the

kitchen and the sitting room. "Please keep reading," I said. He forced the words out.

> And God created the great sea monsters, and every living creature that crawls, with which the waters swarmed, according to their kind, and every winged fowl, according to its kind, and God saw that it was good.
> And the Lord God formed from the earth every beast of the field and every fowl of the heavens, and He brought it to man to see what he would call it, and whatever the man called each living thing, that was its name.

My father considered me. His brown eyes were gray in the light. His beard was wiry and ragged-looking, his hands stubby. We all stood still. We watched the mountains where smoke still did not rise, where the silver flyer did not circle back. The blast already seemed like a dream, meaningless and impossible.

Wheat blew against the ground in surrender. The sky flattened, the cottonwoods slapped leaves against leaves. The rain kept coming and we kept watching it come. The froth-white river tumbled all of her stones.

> And a mist ascended from the earth and watered the entire surface of the ground.

After hours of waiting for the airplane to return, after the rain quieted to a soft dust, under the palm of a cool pink sky, our river sounded like our river again and we crept out to see what the world looked like now that it was coming apart. The air was thick with the scent of soaked sheep. Our feet stuck in the mud, our clothes caught on blown branches. We stood in the wind-combed wheat above the river. The mountains where the explosion had taken place looked no different from how they ever had. The sky was the sky, vast and prickling with light.

The riverbanks were alive with slapping fish. Beached and afraid, they curled up like question marks. "Something to save," I said, grateful, and I began to gather the fish in my skirt. I walked carefully, the mud slippery and deep, my skinny white legs browning, my socks falling down, until I threw open my bundle in one shining, silver delivery. Back in the water, the fish flicked their tails and disappeared. Everyone joined in, filling dresses and pants pockets and arms with slipping, flapping fish. The fish, stronger than they looked, swam out of our hands and made us laugh. We chased them, saying, "We won't hurt you. We're trying to take you home."

As we worked, the banks stopped glimmering with the jewels of trout, but the river receded to offer other treasures. I picked up the spout of a teapot, filled with silt. The front half of a piano smiled with its teeth punched out. The butcher found a gentlemen's wool hat with a ribbon around it. From the muck we pulled two bowls, one jewelry box full of mud, a doll with no legs, a matted sweater, some cut logs, a hand-drawn map of the summer constellations smudged but readable, and a woman. A woman—hair, teeth, feet, fingers all. And she was alive.

THE BEGINNING
OF THE WORLD

The healer's living room walls were painted bright yellow, and the windows were trimmed with blue. He had a huge bookshelf reaching all the way to the ceiling. I could read the titles: *Engravings from Specimens of Morbid Parts, The Medical and Surgical History of the War, A Lecture to Young Men on Chastity Intended for the Serious Consideration of Parents and Guardians, The Science of Life; Or, Self-Preservation.*

Today was no longer a day of rest. God was going to have to forgive us because it was not our fault. The healer boiled several pots of water for tea over the woodstove. The damp wood whined. The healer took everything out of his cupboards—some stale cake, half a loaf of bread, a honeycomb, a jar of last summer's apples. We dried the woman from the river, the wet and battered stranger, with thread-worn rags. "What happened?" we kept asking, and she kept shaking her head.

"Who are you?" my mother asked while she cleaned the mud out from between the woman's toes, wrapped her in blankets. Igor served her real tea in a toy teacup, which she drank in doll-size sips. No one said the word *prophet*, but everyone thought it.

She said, "The plums fell behind me and broke open bloody."

Wind howled in the trees. It was something alive, something hungry. We drew closer still, felt each other's warm skin as she whispered, "The living taken by their necks like puppies, and yelping that way, too."

"By water?" we asked. "By the terrible river?"

"The river saved me. I couldn't run anymore. My feet were bleeding. The river carried me away. The river made me into a stranger."

"Now you are safe. Now you are *our* stranger," I said. She began to cry.

"The soldiers were allowed to do whatever they wanted to us for twenty-four hours," she said. "A reward for them, a punishment for us. They cut off my mother's breasts and my sister's ears. They lit my husband's beard on fire."

We leaned on each other in our huddle. Night's gluttonous arms gathered everything living, everything dead. Outside, the gawking houses and the grabbing trees. Every wall could easily become a window, every roof a wide-open path to God.

The stranger stopped speaking. Her breathing changed and then she howled like a lost dog. Her voice became full and enormous, rattling off the walls. We were rattled, not only by the stranger's howl, but also by the desperate seas of her eyes, the map of cuts all over her arms and chest. The flood of her voice was like the flood of water, sudden and determined, sweeping up everything in its path.

"Do you need to be hidden?" I asked.

"What's left to hide from?" the stranger asked back.

In the silence of that moment, our hearts kept us alive without asking if they should.

"Everyone is gone?" I asked.

"Everyone," the stranger said.

"Everyone's children?" Igor asked, focusing on his crop of siblings.

An old woman said, "I want to lie down," and another old woman offered her lap and brushed her fingers through the threads of hair, warm and tangled.

We lit a few lanterns because we had lost all the light from outside.

Someone pushed a cup of soup toward the stranger, tapped the rim with the spoon to say, *Is this something we can offer you?*

The stranger took a small sip of soup from the bowl and then passed it along. We each put our lips to it so that they got a little coating of the hot liquid on them and then passed, wanting it to come back around to her still full. "Thank you," we said, "it's delicious." And we were happy when it did come to her and she took full bites this time, filling the spoon and then pulling it clean from her mouth.

+ + +

The moment we were in was a hinge—the past swung on one side, the future on the other. Everything that had ever happened led us here, from the very first day onward.

Ours was a migrating people even in the beginning. The first man and the first woman, set out into the unknown world. Fields were tilled and lambs were born. Begets were begotten, and begotten again. A tribe of luthiers, a tribe of forgers. Winemakers, plowers, sons and daughters.

Out the people went, fruitful, multiplying as they were told. The earth felt the padding of human feet. The tribes divided, God visited in dreams, in deserts, promised land to the ones he had grown to like. Men erected stones as markers, sacrificed calves. All the while, they told the story back: In the beginning there was a beautiful garden, and we were cast out of it, and we began again.

Twice we built huge, beautiful temples to recognize God and everything he had given us. Twice, they were destroyed.

The second temple, like the first, contained a chamber of knives, a chamber of oils and wines, a chamber of lepers, a chamber of wood. The gates were named for Music, Light, Sacrifice, Women, Water and Flames. The structure was made of white marble, rimmed with gold, and it stood for hundreds of years, and our people lived in the valley beneath. It would not be true to call that time peaceful, but from a distance, from this far away, we had allowed ourselves to dream of those days, because the next thing that happened was, an army appeared on the horizon, a swarm of men, sunlight glinting from their helmets, and we did not win the battle. We began to walk away in a million different directions: some went into the olive-green hills, some climbed over the mountains, some crossed the seas. Dunes collapsed under our feet. We slept in the bellies of creaky ships, disembarked onto unknown soil. All the while, we told the stories back, and they kept us alive as a people. Our bodies might have survived without them, but not our hearts.

We began again and again, across the face of the earth.

On a remote island there lived a powerful king with a hundred and fifty thousand subjects armed with sharp spears. The king rode a leopard and his men rode fearsome steeds that feasted on cooked mutton and drank only wine. These men were our great-great-great-great-grandparents. As they brushed their horses' oil-black manes the king told a story: Once, God tested the faith of our Abraham by asking him to sacrifice his eldest son, and because that man took his boy to the top of the mountain and raised a knife over his neck, God knows that we are true.

In the city of Mecca, our great-great-greats settled down. They refused to eat meat and filled their plates instead with peas, butter, sugar and fruits. They lived in roofless houses and wore silk robes bedecked in long strands of pearls. While they stirred a spiced stew, the mothers told a story: Once, to a faithful man, God said, "Among man, only you are worthy of my creation. Build yourself a very good boat. Use cypress wood and sap, and take two of every living creature with you." After days and days and days, rain and rain and rain, after weeks and weeks and weeks of floating: a dove with an olive branch in her beak. And the man stepped onto the land, and every toothy, beaked, trunked, whiskered creature with them, and the world, the whole world, was new.

In Ethiopia, the Jews received a strange gift. How it arrived, we do not know—the old men said it was a many-sailed ship; the old women said it traveled inside the belly of a whale; the bachelors believed a griffin carried it over the sea; the whores swore it was the fat hand of God himself. In any case, onto the desert walked a savage who had no head; his eyes and mouth were set in his breast. He wore forty clear sapphires. With him came a note from a place called Calicut.

Dear Brothers, We are on the other side of the ocean, but we have not forgotten you. We are always your family. The paper was embossed with an elephant and a tiger.

The Jews of Ethiopia sent a rowboat with six messengers, two spotted goats, a Torah scroll, the paw of a lion and a letter: *Dear Brothers, Thank you for the headless savage. He is the most beautiful we have ever seen. We do not know you, but we love you.* With the savage chained up beside them, those who stayed told a story: Once, we were slaves in Pharaoh's land, but we escaped. The sea parted, the commandments were given, and we began again on the other side of the desert.

The rowboat bobbled along for weeks until, nearing a foreign shore, a storm ground the craft to splinters and our great-greats were washed to shore by the waves, their Torah scroll destroyed. Over time, they forgot all the prayers but one, which they repeated on every occasion. At weddings they said, "The Lord is One." At circumcisions, "The Lord is One." They cut the orange in half, broke a coconut or two. They killed a rooster and said, "The Lord is One."

In the Caucasus Mountains, high above the Caspian Sea, our great-grandmothers went to the well wearing veils and cloaks in colors as bright as flowers. They carried water jugs on their heads and smoked long pipes. The older women belonged to a special league of mourners. Families of the dead hired the women to fall down in misery, pound their fists on the frozen earth, wail until all ears, including God's, rang with the sound of what was lost. In the dark, after their tears had salted everything, they said, "Once, after a lifetime of childlessness, Sarah became pregnant at ninety years old, and what did she do? She laughed."

In Spain, the queen said to our great-grandparents, "Please, open businesses and lend money." And then, a little while later, she said, "Look at you with your bills and coins. You are dirty, and I want you out." So our great-grandparents changed their hair, hid their candelabra in the closet and nailed crosses to the wall, though their beliefs had not changed. They became Señor Henríquez, Señora Estrada. They drew maps, joined voyages across the world, traded for Inca gold and Amazon women. Sometimes they were safe and sometimes they were rounded up and killed. Sometimes they were in the king's care and sometimes they were at the end of his dagger. They prayed, they worked, they escaped.

Someone said, "You are dirty and strange and I want you out," and our people crossed the river. There they were told, "Your kind are not welcome here," and they switchbacked the mountains. At the top of the highest peak, the locals crossed their arms and shook their heads and our great-great-grandparents continued on.

For hundreds of years: a little peace, the weeks marked with ritual, with work. Babies born, circumcised, feasts eaten, an extra place setting at the table for the prophet, weddings conducted, temples lit with lamps. Great-greats became greats became grandparents. They said, "This is the day the Lord has made. Let us rejoice and be glad in it."

And then an accusation in Bucharest, another in Sofia—Jews Sacrifice Christian Child for Ritual Purposes—and the mobs tore doors down, emptied the houses of valuables and killed the leaders, burned those who retreated into the synagogue. The survivors packed up again, went deeper into the mountains, settled down, marked the weeks. Life was like a parenthesis between catastrophes. Each time, they had to decide which to rebuild first—the temple or the cemetery. The stories of terror came from every direction. Cossacks in the north, our citizenship revoked in the south. The cities were not safe, the towns were worse. One ruler expelled all the Jews across the Danube, but when the Ottomans on the other side turned them back, the ruler said, "Oh, just drown them," and that is exactly what his men did.

And so, the little group, our heavy-headed and tired grandparents, the few to survive the latest pogrom, walked with their pairs of goats, sheep, dogs and horses for forty-one days from the town of Iaşi through Bukovina. The grandparents brought languages and coins from all the places everyone had lived—Spanish pesetas, Italian lire, Austro-Hungarian kronen, Polish zlotys, pieces of Ottoman silver, Yugoslavian copper, ancient Syrian gold and new Russian paper. They had German curse words, Polish love songs, English poems, Hebrew prayers and Yiddish scoldings. They had wandered and traded, wandered and traded, and they had been filled up with words.

They passed hamlets and hovels, Gypsy encampments and many roads that would have taken them back to the city. The rolling hills were bright green and dotted with yellow wildflowers and green pines, brooks and meadows. Even in pain and heartbreak, the grandparents commented on the beauty. For the last six days, descending the far side of the Carpathian Mountains, they saw no one. They passed through the scar of an old forest fire. In front of the grandparents twisted the muddy Dniester River, and in the oxbow below they saw the first village in nearly a week. It would have been an island if not for the road just wide enough for a cart at the opposite end.

The grandparents crossed an old bridge, two by two. The instant the last of them had crossed—goat herder and two goats—the bridge sagged below the surface and snapped in the middle. They were here to stay. There was a small wooden sign, and in white paint the name of the village: Zalischik. And on this almost-island, there were empty, falling-down stone houses. It was a left-over place, a forgotten place, and the grandparents looked at it and thought, Forgotten, yes, let us be forgotten. Let us be alone. They saw fallow fields and plenty of water for irrigating, an old granary and a deep well. The emptiers had already completed their mission here—the Jews and Gypsies had been expelled, taken care of. The map marked with an X, done. The circle of land was theirs to settle, a new world. They put their heads down, turned the earth, and began to plant seeds there.

For twenty years, they lived like forgotten people. They were a long way from any other villages, and farther still from any cities. The only way they knew they were alive was by repeating the stories again and again: the first man and the first woman, the great flood, the plague of frogs, the plague of blood, the plague of darkness. All the stories were stories of wandering, of being lost, of starting again. Meanwhile, the grandparents repaired the fallen-down walls, stopped up holes in the roofs, replaced missing street cobbles and stuffed all the mattresses with dried hay and horsehair.

My mother and father were born. My uncle and aunt. The banker, butcher, widow, greengrocer, future wives and husbands. They grew up, learned to tie their shoes, mend a curtain, harvest potatoes, tally the month's ledger. They were taught all the languages everyone knew—the whole world on their tongues. They got married and had children of their own. Their parents began to grow weak and forgetful. On a sunny spring afternoon, my mother's parents decided to go for a swim in the river, and their soft old bodies were not strong enough for the current, and they were carried away. A funeral was held in the cabbage field, and prayers were repeated. The healer told a story: Once, in the depths of despair, the prophet Ezekiel was carried to a field of old, dry bones, and Ezekiel spoke the name of the Lord, and the bones rose up, and skin covered them, and they were alive again. Always, another beginning.

Every few weeks, a man would come to deliver a piece of mail sent from a brother, sister or cousin in a faraway place. The letters contained news of births and deaths, pogroms and survivals, escapes and resettlings. Each spring and each fall, a few men would pack the cart with provisions to trade—lambs, turnips, cabbages, wool sweaters and socks knit by mothers and grandmothers, saddles hammered together—and set out into the world. Two weeks later, the cart would return with different provisions—sturdy canvas sacks, cotton pants for the men and cotton dresses for the women, wooden toys for the children, glass bottles for keeping milk, wooden buckets for storing butter, the sprout of an apple tree, ready to be planted, and a newspaper.

From this, the grandparents knew that a war began, raged, quieted. There were photographs of jagged shards of bombed-out buildings in Germany and tired Austro-Hungarian soldiers in Sarajevo. The grandparents recognized the places, having been to many of them. All the while, on their near-island, the days did not change. They kept repeating to themselves one word: *forgotten*. We remember the story, they thought, but let the story not remember us. Let us hide here until we are safe. And we had been, until now.

The healer cracked his knuckles and let his head hang heavy toward his chest. "No one in this room remembers learning to set fire to houses?" Regina asked.

We all shook our heads.

The old man who used to cut our hair wondered if perhaps we should start at the beginning and try to figure out where things went wrong: the same careful logic of hunting down a lost key. "This morning," a teenage boy tried, "I woke up and nothing was different. I ate breakfast and watched a crow hop across the grass."

"Yesterday morning," the weaver's mother said, "I arranged all the cups in the house by size and nested them perfectly in the cupboard."

"Three weeks ago today I turned forty-one and I gave myself a pair of gold earrings to celebrate," said the widow who lived at the edge of the village.

"I remember," said the jeweler. "They looked pretty on you."

"Last night, like every night, I dreamed I had a baby," Aunt Kayla said.

"Last night, like every night, I dreamed you forgave me," Hersh said under his breath.

The stranger swayed gently back and forth, a branch in the wind. I kept looking at her, waiting for her to say or do something. For a long time, all she did was listen.

We could remember many things about this year, and many about the year before, but no one could figure out the long ago.

"When we first arrived on the earth, did we like to swim right away?" I wondered. "Or did we have to learn to like to swim?"

We wished someone had made a drawing of that first human swimming. We wished someone had made a drawing of the scared ones, huddled on the shore. We must have been awkward and funny to watch, lumbering out in the dark, trying to find our way back to the holes where we slept. And it was only a guess that we slept in holes—it was possible we used to be better at climbing trees and maybe we had beautiful nests in all the crooks made out of tangles of our own hair.

"No," the banker insisted, "God created man in His image and the garden was perfect and we were naked but we weren't ashamed, and then there was the tree of knowledge and the snake, and the apple."

"That's just part of the story," the widow said, licking her lips.

"We might have had wings first," I said.

"We might have eaten nectar," the banker's wife said, smiling.

"We might have been able to talk to deer or eagles. We might have been much better at loving," Uncle Hersh said.

"But what if we've always been the way we are? What if we have always been scared and mean and beautiful exactly like this?" I asked. "Good and evil, banishment." The stranger's cloudy eyes rested on my face. Their sorrow was so deep and wet and they chilled me.

We covered our faces and we cried.

"What else is going to float down that river?" my mother asked. Elsewhere, the rest of the world, unfolded like a giant map in front of us. All the other villages along the river, all the mountains, all the seas, all the cities. What had been blown up? What had been saved?

"I have a brother in America," the jeweler said again. "Maybe we should go there. Run away."

"The English and Americans are turning ships away. We're too late," the healer told him. On our map, the light of those faraway countries was snuffed out, leaving two great big, dark holes.

"We could go to Warsaw," the butcher said. The healer drew an X over each eye with his fingertip. Poland turned dark.

"France has sometimes been friendly. Or Turkey?"

The healer's eyes looked as if they were sinking into his head. As if they were too tired to stay afloat any longer. "We would have to cross all those other borders." Romania fell into shadow, Bulgaria, Hungary. Elsewhere might not exist after all.

The widow rolled her eyes. "Don't you get it?" she asked. "We are dead men. We are through."

"We are in the precise center of this continent," my father whispered. "We are marooned."

"And we are the plague," the healer said, his eyes closed. Our tiny peninsula, a pinhead on the big map, was soon the only lit spot. Everything, everywhere, everyone else—extinguished.

"Should we build a wall? A barricade?" the greengrocer wondered.

"With what? Mud and cabbage?" his wife mocked.

I was in a room full of grown-ups who had no idea what to do. None of them. We were completely lost and helpless and my heartbeat turned irregular and I had to close my eyes and concentrate on breathing.

Just then, the stranger's voice came clear and strong, "We start over."

"We already tried. We can't remember how we got where we are," Igor reminded her.

"That's not what she means," I said, surprised to understand exactly. "She means, once upon a time, tomorrow was the first day of the world. The very, very first. The earth was unformed and void, and darkness was upon the face of the deep." My heart continued to flutter like a bird caught in a chimney.

And the stranger looked up at me and her gaze was so sharp that everything else in the room came to a perfect stop. She took my hand and held it for a long moment. The feel of her palm was like worn leather, thick and sturdy. "Land is limited—the space around us occupied, but no one can limit belief," she said. The stranger looked around the room. "We need a story," she told the villagers, but she was looking at me. "When there is nothing left to do, and there is nowhere else to go, the world begins again."

"No one exists but us and God?" I added tentatively. "Everything is still to come?"

She let her eyelids fall shut and nodded. I could see her eyelashes darken as she began to cry.

The moon that night was a cut in the sky and our slippery eyes reflected it. Could we put our hands out and hold back the rush of time? All the things we had invented—the wheeled, the wound-up, the pulleyed—now irrelevant? The others peered at the stranger in her battered body. They listened for the shriek of thieves at our door, for wild, sharp-toothed animals. They listened for the raving river but could not even hear it slither past.

What they did was so simple: they nodded. The stranger and I nodded back.

Before this blistered world caught up with us, we nodded. Before the wreckage of a hundred broken cities landed on our banks, before we were swept away to some faraway sea, before the sky filled with silver wings and everything below turned to fire, before the tiny candle flame of our home, the last flickering light on the map was put out, we nodded. Desperation to believe joined the terror still thrumming in our chests. If we wanted to survive in this story, we had to tell it that way. We swallowed hard and waited for a reaction from the heavens. At that exact moment, while the rain turned all the leaves outside into tiny drums, made landfall and twisted its way to the river, while the animals huddled in the barn, while the slender moon stood as a reminder of light amidst its opposite, right then, nothing happened. The earth did not shake us off.

We were alone there, floating on a sea of black emptiness—all the chapters unwritten.

"The beginning of the perfect world," I said.

"The beginning," the stranger repeated. "The world that is beautiful. Let there be chickens. Let there be trees. Let there be us. Let there be safe places to stay the night."

"Let there be rest for older brothers," Igor said.

"Let there be love," the jeweler said.

"Be fruitful and multiply," Kayla said, smiling.

"And what of the things I remember?" my mother asked.

"You don't," the stranger said with her eyes closed and seeping. "There are no such things as dead children. No such thing as burned up." Those girls with their pockets full of eggs were not dead, had not lived, had never been born, had never grown inside of the stranger's body. She had never been a mother.

"It's the night before the world begins," I said. "Everything is getting ready. Everything is waiting to be alive."

We lay down on our sides. We listened to what had not begun.

We did not see the rain flood our cemetery and dig the bones of our ancestors up. We did not see their ghosts climb into our trees, onto our roofs, into our beds. Nor did we hear the ghosts of the stranger's children begin to leak out of their bodies and into the mountain air full with the sharp pepper of wet pine needles. We did not hear the squeal of the radio in the airplane as the pilot made his way home. We did not see the person on the other end of the radio draw up notes about the flight, the tested bomb. We did not hear our river slip across thousands of miles—through cities feverish with lost wars, and villages trying to stay quiet and unnoticed; through fields of sunflowers, fields of wheat, apple and plum orchards; alongside vegetable gardens, pastures, train tracks and front doors where mothers dangled the feet of their perfect new babies in the river, both of them smiling because the water was cold, while fire in the house promised heat. Until the river finally met, with a desperate, gleeful rush, the ocean.

In the dark of a room that did not exist yet, a yellow room with a swinging pendulum of a gas lantern in the center of the ceiling, with the red coals of a fire slowly going out and rain sheeting the windows, a room that was absolutely quiet and shielded from even whispers of life outside—hunting, searching life, all the world's armies fading into the distance—my village and I curled up on the floor. We had refused to give up hope, and though we all knew that no incarnation of the world had ever been safe for us, no matter how beautifully God had tried to build it, we allowed ourselves to believe in this one. Perhaps, we hoped, at the last possible moment, we had made something perfect.

I began to speak. *And God said, "Let there be lights in the firmament of the heaven to divide the day from the night; and let them be for signs, and for seasons, and for days and years."* We held hands, we hummed, we listened, we prayed. Some people put their lips together. We let the spit from our mouths dry in crusts on the curve of shoulders. It did not matter whose shoulder or whose mouth. We were a pile of unborn babies together, rolling in the knots of one another's limbs, being kissed and caught and found. *And let the lights in the firmament of heaven give light upon the earth.*

And we hoped that it would be good.

THE FIRST DAY

The sun broke through the clouds and rolled up over us like it knew the whole plan. Rain continued and an arc of color spread across our sky. We voted to keep living in the houses we had already built and to keep being married to the people we were married to. There were those who protested this, who proposed we gather in the square and pair off anew, tallest to shortest. There were those who thought it would be better to put the stupid with the smart to even things out and those who thought we should try to put the smart with the smart and hope for true genius.

"But I love my wife," my father said.

"How do you know? Today is the first day—you have never seen her before today. What if you hate her by tonight?" the banker asked.

My father regarded my mother's mossy brown eyes. "I have a feeling," he said. "A very strong feeling." He winked.

The chicken farmer argued that we woke up in the morning and this is how it was—we were born into the world in pairs. This convinced us. Only two people decided otherwise: with a nod, the barber's wife and the sheep shearer's wife traded husbands. They patted on the back the ones they had come with, and said, "Nothing personal, sweetness, it's just better this way." Those two wives shook hands with each other as they traded positions, stood now with men they hoped to love better, longer. The men were wide-eyed, a little heartbroken to be abandoned this way and a little thrilled to be taken up by new, unexplored bosoms. The stranger's eyelids fell closed. I wished I knew whether she wanted to be assigned a mate or permitted to be alone. I caught the jeweler watching her, but she did not look up.

"What about God?" my brother Moishe asked. "Is he the same?"

I thought about God's view down onto the stranger's village, the Romanian soldiers unsheathing their knives and reloading their guns. Had he seen all of that? Had he always known that he would not stop it?

We glanced around, quiet, listening.

"We just arrived here, right? The world just started," Igor said. "Maybe he told us exactly what to do."

"I didn't hear anything," my brother said, and my father patted him on the head. I began to wonder if God would be angry with us for doing away with his creation and starting again. I suggested we write a letter in explanation and ask for his blessing.

Dear God,

We did not start again because it wasn't beautiful before.
The world we make will be much smaller and less glorious
than the one you made. Ours will have none of the strange,
wild animals—no elephants or tigers, no parrots or blue frogs.
It will have none of the exotic spices, no sea, no lakes. We are
content to accept this small circle of land as our entire universe,
so long as we are safe here.

I was worried that we weren't offering anything. "What would God want from us, to prove our love?" I asked. The butcher suggested sacrificing a goat, the banker suggested charity. I thought maybe God was simply lonely, by himself for all eternity at the top of the sky. "Maybe he just wants to be told a good story," I said. And that is what we promised to give him.

If we were going to have God, then we were going to need a temple for Him. The greatest temple ever built. The shape of that place, the glory of it, kept us talking for hours. So that the room would be flooded with the very first light of day, huge windows would face east. And others west, because the day's end is sometimes even more spectacular than its beginning. My sister wanted to have a small pool to throw things into. The healer wanted to have a hole in the roof to leave a way in for the dead. The two oldest men wanted to cover the floor in soft feathers so we could pray lying down. Igor suggested there be someone to watch the children.

The second thing God did after inventing the earth was to

invent the heavens. We had made the earth, and now we would make the sky. We would paint constellations on the ceiling of the temple, white against a background of blackest blue. The temple rose high above us, a misty vision so sparkling and grand we felt drunk. How could our God not fall in love with us?

"It sounds handsome," my mother said. "Gold and all that. But the world started again because we wanted a safer place. A more deliberate place. How do we make sure we don't forget that? How will we keep track of the story? Wasn't that going to be our big offering?"

Several people sulked—they were having fun sculpting great ivory balustrades and now they had to deal with the microscopic machinery of meaning. The mist of the temple dispersed and the room became quiet.

The chicken farmer figured we could write down the things we did each day. The jeweler pointed out that we might end up with a very complete accounting of the minutiae without ever knowing what happened in any bigger sense. Laundry would be on record but not faith. The stranger was braiding the fringe from the blanket around her shoulders. She looked up from this task and gave the slightest nod to the jeweler, whose face turned red.

Igor thought we should interview one another.

I wondered if we should gather each week and write the story of what had taken place.

"We write down everyone's prayers," the stranger said. "Someone listens."

"We might miss some of the events," the banker said.

"I vote that this world is about hopes more than events," my mother breathed. And so it would be. We voted to build a comfortable chair and a desk for the recorder to sit at, and we agreed that one of us would be there to listen, quietly writing down every prayer each of us uttered. There would be no interruption, no answers or questions.

"And what if we pray when we are in our kitchens or walking in the snow?" we wondered.

"We should listen to one another even then. If you hear a prayer, write it down and take it to the temple. We can have a box to put them in."

"I think we need all the languages," I said, thinking of the Russian my father sometimes spoke, the German the butcher carried on in, the Spanish, the Yiddish, the Italian, the Romanian, the Hebrew. "If praying is how we keep track, we should have a lot of words to wish with."

"As long as we forget where they came from," the stranger said. I promised I already had.

"Do we need protections?" my brother asked. "Do we need a wall or a shield?"

"No," I corrected. "We are the only thing that exists. Us and God."

We were tired by the time it grew dark. It was our first day and we had done a lot. But we had not thought ahead to this moment when the sky turned purple and we were hungry and wanted sleep. Should we stay together in the healer's house? Should we go back to the houses we had been born owning? Some decided to sleep outside in the drizzle, curled up in the bright cold. Others wanted to sleep better, to have a feather pillow and a wall keeping the bugs out. The ones who had been born with loves wanted to love. To make use of their skin and their fingers. To celebrate their good fortune at being alive in this historic moment, at being the first of our kind, at being warm and leggy and full of good ideas.

The jeweler invited the stranger to stay with him that night. As we walked out of the healer's house, I took the stranger's hand and stood on tiptoe to whisper into her ear. "Will you please help me to get it right?" Speaking to her felt like calling across a wide canyon to a faraway speck of a person. She squeezed my fingers twice, then released.

At his house, the jeweler cleared silver clippings and needle-nose pliers from his softest rug. He brought out a stack of moth-eaten blankets, which had not been draped over a sleeping body for years. They had once, in another world, belonged to his mother. She and his father had both died underneath them, and since then he had kept them hidden. Tonight they belonged to a deathless world, and they would not blanket the stranger in sadness, but simply blanket her in blankets. The jeweler felt a wave wash over his heart, foamy and soft. He felt soothed. Loneliness was hushed by the sound of water breaking across the shore. The stranger stretched out and rested her head on a pillow. In the dark, she looked to the jeweler like a cave he wanted to crawl into. Lightless, yes, but peaceful and cool.

My parents scurried us three children home and put us quickly to bed. In the scratchy, wooly dark I could smell my own breath. I felt perfectly alone, happily alone. I was proud. Nothing could shake this feeling—not even the image of the stranger, seated in the chair, braiding the blanket's fringe, her gaze fallen to the surface of the unknown sea she drifted upon. I squeezed my eyes shut tight and smiled, because everyone was playing the game. Here we were in the first night on earth. In my cave, I could say that as a fact—the first night on earth—and this made me grin so wide I could practically hear it.

THE SECOND DAY

Our house was made of wood, the roof shingled. It had a big room with two beds—one for our parents and one for us. The floor was covered in worn rugs and the woodstove had a deep layer of ash. We had a table and a stack of pots, pans and bowls. We had a beautiful old box full of silverware that we never used because it was too nice. I did not own anything—everything I had was shared. The soft baby blanket we children had each used, the pencils and paper, the marbles, the scissors.

On the second morning of the world, my mother ladled cabbage into everyone's bowls. My father kissed her on the forehead, and Moishe teased, "The most beautiful woman in the world."

"How do you know what I'm going to say?" our father said, smiling. "It's not the same world as before."

"There *is* no before," said Regina, joining in.

"The most beautiful woman in the *new* world," I said, patting my mother on the knee.

"That's right," my father said.

"The luckiest woman. The most beautiful family," my mother corrected. In the seconds of silence that followed, the room was electric with happiness. The most beautiful family could feel it pop on our tongues, in our ears.

My mother went out into the market with all the women who carried their baskets and their lists. They squeezed the tomatoes, smelled the melons, peeled the husks back from the corn to check for bugs. They eyed plucked, hanging chickens, passed the chocolate squares and peppermint sticks without a thought. Women left the shops with the tinking sound of a bell hung in the doorway. At home they took the pins out and let their children brush their hair, let us create messy braids.

My father had been born with the job of picking cabbages. In the field he worked, the muscles in his huge arms like raw chickens. His skin was dark and cracked as if ready to split open and reveal the slick pink pulsing and twitching beneath. As he worked that day, rainwater falling into his eyes, he told stories to himself about how good he was at his job. "Mister Vladimir," he said to himself, "you have no idea how talented you are at farming cabbages. Truly, no one has ever known them as you do."

In his fantasy, if the money started rolling in, he thought he would buy himself a fine hat and a coal-black coat and the same for his three children. His fields would be so huge, so populated with cabbages, and he would build a house right in the middle of them,

the rows radiating out from it. The cabbages would smile, knowing smiles, their rooty bodies lodged in the earth with only their
brainless skulls to look around, appreciating what luck they had to
grow in such a nice field, to be harvested by such strong hands. My
father would nod back at them, thanking them for the compliment. "No, really," he would reply, "I'm the lucky one. I couldn't do
it without you."

As the men walked home at the end of the day, my father
among them, they thought about the wives they had come into the
world with, the long brown waves of hair, blond curls, the silk of it.
In their minds, the hair would cover them completely. Impossible
amounts of it falling from the heads of women, making seas and
nests and beds. They snarled and snorted home, tugging at their
own rough beards.

But my parents had a secret. My mother was glowingly, shin-
ingly bald. Her hair had disappeared in a matter of a few weeks
when she was a teenager and she had worn a wig every day since. It
was not the fact that my father fell in love with her, but that he did
not fall out again when he saw her uncovered head that made her
trust him implicitly.

Because the world was new, people were sizing themselves up,
taking stock of what they had and what they lacked. Most families
in Zalischik had just about enough, but we all assumed that the
rest had more, and in some respects, we were right. Some had more
money, some had more sex, and some had more babies. My mother
had more cabbage. There were cabbages all over the house. There

were cabbages in bowls on the table. There were cabbages in a bowl under my parents' bed. There were cabbages on the shelves next to our basket of leftover balls of yarn and the box of pencils. There were cabbages in the washbasin that had to be taken out when someone needed to clean the dishes or wash her face. There were cabbages in the bassinet, since the house was babyless now. And of course there were always cabbages in the pot, cooking.

My mother stirred them at the end of the second day, her children and husband drawing each other on the floor and laughing. "I am not nearly that ugly!" my father said, laughing at Moishe's picture. "Look at my nose and look at this man's nose!" Regina and I could hardly breathe through our laughter. I drew our father with twice the nose my brother had drawn and presented it to my sister, who rolled backward and held her stomach. Our mother watched the show while she stirred, ladled and set dishes on the table.

"Supper," she said, plinking the edge of a bowl with a spoon.

"Somebody say a prayer," our father instructed, while he spread my napkin over my legs. He took out a slip of paper to write down the prayer, which would be folded into a square and deposited in the box.

"Bless Dad's nose, bless the soup, bless the family, bless the world," I said.

"Amen," the rest of them echoed, and we dipped our spoons.

In the light of morning, the jeweler asked, "Tea?" and the stranger said, "I don't know." The stranger wanted to offer her thanks, but could not find the strength. "Thank you for coming to stay with me," the jeweler said. "I have been alone a long time." The stranger managed to meet his eye for a second before it began to hurt, like looking into a bright light. The jeweler squirmed as he tried to think of something to talk about. With no history, conversations were harder to start. "It's raining," he finally said, as if she had not been aware.

"I'm sorry," she told him.

"For what?" he asked, but she continued to stare into the distance. "You have nothing to be sorry for." Please be happy, he thought, but he had no way to explain, even to himself, his affection for her, for the peculiar presence of her. He did not understand the stranger at all, but that seemed to have no bearing on his feelings. "You are like a shell," he said. "A seashell. Hollow but beautiful."

"Hollow." She nodded. He steeped the tea, pulled the basket of dripping leaves from the cup and put it in the washbasin. He stirred in sugar and cream and handed the steaming cup to the stranger. To his surprise, she reached out, took it from him, wrapped her hands around it. Gratitude filled them both silently up.

For the rest of the day they sat not far from each other, gazing out the window at the light shifting almost imperceptibly. The jeweler added logs to the woodstove and prepared things to eat: buttered bread, canned apples, slices of cheese. He boiled and poured water, washed the cups when they were empty. "I like beets," the jeweler said, wanting to talk. The stranger did not look at him, but he felt her absorb this fact. "I think they are perfect," he continued, because he wanted her to know him even while he could not think of anything important to say. "This cushion," he said, holding up a stained yellow thing, "means nothing to me. I

don't know where it came from. I wouldn't miss it if it were gone."
The stranger listened, he knew she did, whether or not she acknowl-
edged it. While the jeweler talked, they sat there and let themselves be objects on which dust might settle, air might brush past,
light could play.

That night, the stranger did not sleep. She could feel her veins
fighting to keep blood moving despite there being no apparent reason to do so. The pumping in her chest was a labor, a wheeze. What
dark room had she washed up into? What lost place was this that
had, at the sight of her, reset the clocks and begun anew? The first
day she had felt like a ghost, like a dead person. As night wore on
and dawn seeped into the room, she saw the endless days ahead
lined up, waiting to be lived in. None of them would let her politely
decline to attend, claiming illness or devastation. She could not
avoid being alive for one rotation here and there. She had watched
her husband's face catch on fire and seen her children led out into
the woods where a thousand gunshots rang out. Why did I survive
it? she wondered. It was so simple—she had hidden behind the
woodshed. She peeked out, dumbstruck, the scene before her
impossible to believe.

There had been so many chances for her to die that day, but she
alone was to see what the future held. Still, alive was not what she
felt. Scooped out, maybe. Like a woman whose innards have been
removed, unwound and lain down as a bed for her. When the jeweler, not knowing she was awake, tiptoed outside sleepily in the
baby-pink dawn light of the third day of the world, she thought of
tucking his form into the empty space of her body, giving him a
warm nest there, letting what she was missing become a place for

another person to rest. *I pray for*, she said, but could not name what was missing to a God she had not met. *I pray*, she said, and it was true.

When the jeweler returned and lifted the envelope of blankets on his bed to climb inside, she said, "Thank you for being nearby." The jeweler, shocked to hear her voice, came over and, crouching at her side, cupped his hand over her shoulder and took a turn being speechless. It hardly mattered, because she understood what he meant: emptiness could be so dense as to develop its own gravity. A planet forming out of the whirling dust of a void. Two planets, orbiting.

THE THIRD DAY

On the third morning of the world, my uncle Hersh, the saddlemaker, knocked on our big blue door. We children were lying on the floor by the window reading a book I had sneaked from one world to the other. Our father was out in the fields, gathering globes, and our mother put her knife down next to the ribboned green leaves.

Uncle Hersh shook his wet coat out and laid it across the back of a chair. "I have to say something right away before I lose my nerve. You have some children and we have none."

"You want some tea?" my mother asked. "You want some cabbage?"

She set him up at the table with a steaming bowl.

"I'm sorry. I'm terribly, horribly sorry and I haven't even said anything yet." He closed his eyes. The next words were spit out, like bitter grapeseeds. "Kayla wants a child, now that the world is starting over."

"She always wanted a child," my mother said.

"But now it's the beginning," Hersh told her. "Right now. She believes. Everything is ahead of us—who will Kayla and I send out into the new world? Who will carry our memories on for us when we die? How will I survive another lifetime of disappointing my wife?" He spoke quickly, the sentences memorized and practiced.

Years that did not matter now, that did not even exist, had been filled with fruitless trying. Hersh was strong and smelled of leather and oil, and had money stashed in all the cracks in his walls. He had big feet and big hands and the eyebrows of a man three times his age. His teeth were a strong fence. But at night, under the covers, he was useless.

At first my aunt and uncle had meant it when they took their clothes off and lay with nothing between them. Kayla had fixed her hair in a bun pinned with part of a turtle's shell and she managed to meet his eyes and she prayed and she liked how it felt. He loved how it felt and he was excited, very excited, to see what he would produce. He thought for sure there would be quadruplets right away, if not quintuplets or sextuplets and whatever came after that. It seemed impossible that thousands of babies would not come storming from his wife's body. "I'm sorry, my sweet," he practiced saying, "to put you through all that birth-giving. I cannot help it."

After the first months with no babies, Hersh had begun to feel confused. Where could they be? Kayla displayed no promising lump. He considered returning her to her parents. "This wife is not working," he would say.

Kayla's baby-hunger was a heat source, cooking her from the inside. After many baby-empty years, Kayla's mind had corroded from unfulfilled desire. My uncle got up in the mornings, kissed her, told her she was his darling, and went to work. He hammered and nailed and molded. He tanned the leather and cut the leather and sewed the leather with smaller strips of leather. There was nothing else for him to do. My aunt spent her entire day lying on the very unsoft wood floor of their large kitchen. The black stove smirked at her, the table legs and the chairs turned away. Her sewing box, bursting with pins, appeared like an open, laughing mouth. She saw no reason to stand up. She looked like a splayed-out star, her head resting on a stack of worn-out cookbooks.

She stared at the heavens, which she had to imagine beyond the low ceiling. She knew where all the spiders lived, and watched them string shimmering threads from beam to beam. She clicked her tongue. She saw babies sitting on all available surfaces. Babies on clouds, babies lolling about on the face of the sun, singed and singing. Kayla saw babies on her kitchen table, babies on the chairs, babies under the floorboards, the walls filled with them, stacked up on top of one another, standing on one another's shoulders. Her house was a house made of them, her own body was a body made of them, her legs were three babies each, her belly was four babies.

Then the world began again. Nothing had ever happened before. No failed attempts, no hopeful week or two followed by a terrible spot of blood. That first night, when my aunt and uncle lay down on their horsehair mattress, between the sheet and the quilt

Kayla's mother had made for her girl when she was married, they cried into each other's skin. "We have another chance now," she said. "Maybe in the new world it will be possible." But Hersh was sure that several days later he would hold her again while she disappeared with sorrow, her empty womb shaking like a rattle. They made love anyway and he let her believe in it. The smile she gave him was so crisp and pure, so unmuddied by sadness and disappointment that Hersh started to cry. "Yes," Kayla said, "I can feel it, too. We're going to have a baby." All Hersh wished for was to have his wife back.

He said, "Walk outside with me and look at the world." The two of them went shoeless to the doorstep. Their toes were blind and fragile on the stones. Around Hersh and Kayla, the trees were shooting buds out of all their pointed ends.

"You will always be enough for me," Hersh told his wife, but she waved him off.

"There is more to hope for." He rubbed his eyes and tried to make the word *hope* not mean despair. *Hope*, he said to himself, wiggling it with his tongue like a loose tooth.

In our kitchen, Uncle Hersh's hands trembled.

"Will you be helping out in the new temple?" my mother asked.

"Kayla really believes," Hersh told her. "I think I can save her. I think she'll be herself again." Hersh had found some courage, some trust in his reason for coming. His voice was full of determination.

"Have you made a saddle yet in the new world?"

"All those years felt like drowning. It felt like watching my wife sink to the bottom of the sea."

"You want some more tea?" my mother asked, polishing the handle of the teapot with her thumb.

"I'm sorry. I wish I could do this myself. You have no idea."

My siblings and I did not speak or move. Our eyes met for tiny seconds before we looked away again, not wanting to see our own scared faces reflected back.

Hersh paused. "I don't want you to think about it, I just want you to say yes."

"You want to buy one of my children?" My mother's face was flat and still.

"We can become parents, which you will still be. She will be happy."

"It's a she you want?"

"I wouldn't ask for your son. She can learn to cook everything. She can be taught to read and to write."

My mother explained that her children were not babies and already knew those things, even little Lena knew those things. "She's small for her age, but she's smart for her age, too." From across the room, hearing her say my name made me itch. Moishe, Regina and I had stopped turning the pages of the book we had been reading—an encyclopedia of dog breeds. We had been on the Australian shepherd page. The animal was frozen, staring at us with one blue eye, one brown.

"I'm going to beg you every single day for the rest of time. The entire world is yet to come and we'll never be part of it. Kayla will die and I'll die and that will be all. Do you understand?" He began to cry. "It will never matter that we existed."

"Help," my mother said.

"We all have the right to love something more than ourselves," Hersh said quietly. "We all have the right to die of sorrow when something happens to our babies."

"You want my daughter so you can lose her?" my mother asked.

"I want your daughter so I can keep from losing her. So I can break my fingers if it helps her. So I can bury my face in her hair when I sing to her. So my wife does not turn to dust. Give us hope. Perl, my sister, give us something to pray for."

My mother looked at the heads rolling everywhere in the house. Two cabbages were resting against the big blue door, like dogs waiting to go out. I could tell that our mother's own head was thick, filled up with mud. The mud wrapped its big, suffocating arms around every logical thought.

"Come back tomorrow," my mother said.

I ran out the door and down the street. My feet smacked the puddles hard. I thought about running away forever, except that the whole point was to be home. I spotted my father in the square near the statue of the long-dead war hero with a bunch of other rain-wet men. I wrapped my arms around my father's leg. He looked at me in confusion, but then patted my head and said hello. He did not know that a deal was under way to sell one of his children. The men, having finished their lunches but unready to return to work, were arguing over the fate of a typewriter. Around us, people walked from shop to shop, carrying baskets and bags of supplies. There were weak fingers of light coming through the spaces between buildings. The baker held the old black typewriter, tapping the S key with his ring finger. Should this be part of the new world? Should it be thrown to the bottom of the river, as the butcher suggested? Should it be stomped to bits and sprinkled over the tomato gardens? Should it be encased in glass and viewed as a museum object— evidence of an unknown time? Or should it be what the barber said it was—a clacking record keeper, inherited and benign?

People snarled, angry about the disagreement. "A lot of fuss over a few buttons," the barber said.

"How are we supposed to know *what* to do?" the jeweler cried.

"Starting over is starting over," the butcher spat as he stamped a boot-shaped puddle into the mud.

"Is it better to give the next generations the opportunity to invent new things, or is it better to provide them with the tools that were here when we arrived?" my father asked.

Igor said, "We'll take whatever we can get."

The typewriter was only one of the items in question. People disagreed about cash registers and hammers. If we threw out our hair ribbons, should we keep our shoelaces? What about our buttons and watches? "We have not gone *back* in time," the baker said, "we have gone somewhere in time that no one has ever *been*. A brand-new place. Those watches cannot keep track of this place any better than a hairbrush could. We need to get rid of the watches." He put the typewriter down on the ground, took his black felted-wool hat off and shook the rain out of it.

The barber agreed. "He's right. This hat is a new world hat

now, just as my eyes are new world eyes. But time roots us to the old world—time must never have existed before. Everything depends on that."

All the glass faces stared back from a wheelbarrow in the middle of the square, ticking down hours that we denied even existed. The watch killers followed the cart past the butcher shop, the bakery, the bank, the candy store, six houses, four wet dogs, a row of white rosebushes, to the path through the cabbage field toward the river. The river garbled, and the rain tickled our foreheads and the backs of our hands as the men tossed our watches one at a time into the rocky blue. The past and the impending future were buried together like a pair of stillborn twins. The typewriter went in too, but not before the barber could kneel on the bank of the river and type the word *goodbye*. The watch chains made snaky chimes as they hit the water. We did not see a single watch or clock stop ticking; we did not see those faces crack and fill with liquid.

On shore, all we saw was a time-empty cart with a big wooden wheel. No markers of what approached or what had been. No counting up or counting down. Igor looked worried, aware of the vast emptiness ahead of him, the land of the uninvented. The jeweler's eyes were panes of glass, easy to see through. In his mind was a man with a row of glinting needle-tipped tools and a pocket watch, its chest open and its metal heart revealed. The man, who had once been the jeweler's father, was a lost ghost now and all of time silent at the bottom of the river. "Well, that's one thing done," said the jeweler, chewing his knuckles and hoping that he could support himself with wedding rings and child-size lockets alone. And what was to ensure that those would not be cast out? "Let there be wedding rings and child-size lockets," the jeweler muttered. He remembered the small radio, which had kept him company for thousands of evenings since his parents died and his brother had gone off to seek his fortune. Now those people had been banished from existence, the past no longer a place. He was sure that radio too would be eliminated, but not if no one knew of it. The jeweler planned to hide it under the rotting floorboards of the old barn, where it would be safe.

I gazed out at the unchanged river and hoped we remembered to save more than we gave away. Already, cash registers and horse plows were named as traitors. Bicycles would be blacklisted, non-blank books. Anything with a wheel or a switch would soon sink to the bottom of the river, where the mud would hold it prisoner, shut it up.

The group looked up at the cloud-hidden sun, which had sunk to the side a little, making short shadows at our feet—small gray versions of ourselves who accompanied us back to town and shivered every time we crossed the mottled light of elm trees.

Living in the new world would not turn out to be that different from living in the old one. We had to survive with only the food we could grow and make ourselves, and the clothes we could knit or sew from fabric we already had. If a dish broke, there was no replacing it. But we found that it was not difficult. We had plenty of stuff. There were many bags of flour in everyone's cellars, the cows and goats gave enough milk for us all to drink and make cheese with. As long as they kept reproducing, we could slaughter an animal every few weeks without diminishing the herd. Instead of trading with other villages, we traded with one another. Someone always had more forks than he needed, but not enough butter. One woman was always willing to offer a big bowl of soup and a loaf of bread if another woman would watch the children for a few hours. There was not enough chocolate, but we had a lot of sugar to make cakes. Beyond any accounting, we had the feeling of abundance—our world brimmed over.

What disappeared completely, no leftovers, no crumbs, was news. For us, there was no outside world.

My mother served bowls of cabbage soup that evening. She put out the spoons. We children sucked and slurped, the whole room full of the sounds of our mouths, trying to create too much noise to talk over.

Our mother said, "Regina is going to go and live with her uncle and aunt." I hated myself for the relief I felt when my name was not the one spoken.

"What uncle and aunt?" our father asked, his eyes full of sharp surprise.

My mother explained with as much confidence as she could lie with that Regina would get music lessons and be a star. But mostly that she would be Hersh and Kayla's child.

"How did you choose me?" Regina asked. The words were as thin and sharp as ice breaking.

"Your brother was here?"

"She will come to love them."

"Regina is mine," our father said.

Regina looked around her. She was sitting at her own kitchen table, her own brother and little sister, her own mother and her own father and her own feet and her own hands. This was her table—the legs, the surface, the dents and edges. This was her wide, foot-polished floor. She now felt an overwhelming allegiance to the white enamel washbowl she had never thought much about before. And above all else, the cabbage soup—the smell of her life, the taste of it. "I will be their child?" she asked.

"We're all of us starting over," our mother said. "The world is new. Everyone deserves to love something more than themselves." The reasons, so passionate when Hersh had said them, were no better than soggy bread in Perl's mouth. Her face flushed with blood. "Hope," she tried, not knowing the meaning just then.

Our father gripped the table. "You gave away our daughter?"

His wife shook her head no and said, "Yes." She said, "They have a piano. And the horses she'll ride, and the bed of her own?"

Silently, Regina, as if in answer to her mother's questions, put her hands into the bowl of cabbage soup, both hands, and began washing them in the warm mush, wringing them together. "What are you doing?" my father asked. I understood—this was the last supper of my sister's known life. The soup, the same soup we had eaten every day, was a bath drawn of our mother, our home. Regina washed her hands in that broth as if it could bless her, make her permanent, mark her as part of this and no other family. We watched the dripping juice go up her arms.

We sat there for a moment, dumb. Then I put my own hands in my soup and washed. My mother dipped her fingers. My father and Moishe joined. Our dozens of fingers grabbed and wrung and squirmed. We rubbed the hot liquid up to our elbows. The skin came back pink from the heat, pulsing from the heat. Whether or not the soup had been holy before, we made it so. We were baptized together, a family born of cabbage.

"We're just learning how to live here," our mother said. "Everything is a guess."

I felt faint, like paper dissolving in water. "We are sorry for everything we will do wrong," I said, not knowing on whose behalf I was speaking.

"Sorry is only the beginning," our father told us.

THE FOURTH DAY

Since architecture was completely new to us, everyone felt proud of our early ideas for the temple—it seemed this came naturally. We would build up on the northern edge of the village, near the little spit of land that would have connected us to the rest of the planet had such a place existed. The main room would have a fifty-foot ceiling, vaulted. It would be a place for all the volumes we would write about the world, starting now and going on into the centuries. Leather bound, gilded edges, wrapped in a piece of red silk. The shelves, we figured: ebony. How do we know ebony? we wondered. We were born that way, and since we knew, we thought we should make use of that knowledge. Black wood bookshelves filled with the History of the World, and above, the vaulted ceiling painted with the constellations of the summer sky. Each of us would be his own planet in the middle of the universe.

We had many pages of drawings, measurements, lists of supplies needed. We would all have to contribute and we all would.

"The stranger is amazing," the jeweler said to the butcher and the baker.

"She's kind of odd. I find her a little scary," the baker said. This was nonsense, absurd to the jeweler. What further loveliness could have been included in a woman?

"She is the best listener." He sighed. "She listens and listens. Which gave me an idea . . ."

We voted yes on the jeweler's proposal to station the stranger in the square as the interim recorder. She was neutral and she was the one who had thought of the idea to keep track of prayers in the first place. When the baker had knocked on the jeweler's door to request the stranger's approval, the jeweler retrieved her from the rocking chair with pride. She was to be the one. She would have the honor. "I found you a really good job," he told her. "I think you are going to be great at it."

We gave her a thick stack of paper, a nice fountain pen and a well of ink. "Do we know about ink?" the healer had asked. We have to, the butcher thought. There are things that do not need inventing—that just are. Blood and skin, ink and paper.

We strung a gray-and-white striped blanket up to keep the rain away. We had the stranger sit with her back to the square and anyone who came to pray so that he or she would not feel self-conscious. The stranger sat down and waited, hearing the voiceless quiet of this particular day for the first time in her life. It was good to have something to fill the time, for the days ahead not to be gusting, empty wind. For hours, no one brought her a prayer, so she brought herself some. "I pray that I do not disappoint you." Her back began to ache against the chair, her feet were cold and damp. Doubt was a worm wriggling on the ground beside her, but the stranger stepped on it, leaving nothing but a pink smear on the stones.

I was the first to pray. "I pray for good and peace and enough of everything."

"Hello, my fellow storyteller," the stranger said to me.

I wanted to ask her something about herself. I wanted to make that small human trade—one truth from my life for one truth from hers. The reservoir was shallow, just a few days behind us. My question was too big and too small at the same time. "Are you all right?"

I heard her fill her lungs. I heard someone's heels mark the distance between one destination and the next. She said, "Something was rustling around outside in the night, and at daybreak there were three small mounds of newly turned dirt. A fat gray bird used them to bathe, ducking and shivering as if the earth were water."

"If I help stir the batter, I am allowed to lick the spoon," I said, not knowing whether I wanted this to mean something.

The stranger's laugh was a short gust of warm air. "That's a good trade."

My uncle's proposal flashed in my head like a struck match. I did not want anyone to get traded, but I could not bring myself to utter that prayer, since giving voice to the idea only made it feel more real. Instead I prayed for unexceptional, everyday mercy, and the stranger's pen scratched it down.

✦ ✦ ✦

The jeweler, like a nervous parent, spied on us from behind the statue of the long-dead war hero. He sauntered past with a cup of tea, as if he just happened to be passing by with exactly what she needed. As I left, a line of others wandered up to take my place.

"I pray that we do a respectable job on this world. I pray that my Jonah is the tallest boy in town. I pray that I am more tomorrow than I am today. I pray that we discover riches hidden under our bed."

"I pray that my house never sinks into the ground. I pray that my knee begins to hurt less and that I can once again help my mother into her bed at night. I pray that my wife is more beautiful tomorrow than she is today. I pray that the earth spills over with food."

"I pray for the sick to get well. I pray that what we build remains forever. I pray for money, which I'll take very good care of."

"I pray that my mother appreciates how hard I try to take care of everyone."

"I pray for money, for money, for money. And for baby boys."

"Do you remember me?" a small voice asked the stranger.

"What?"

"Do you?"

The stranger knew her daughter's high rasp, the softness in her r's. This was not a voice that could be mistaken. Without turning, she reached her arm around to touch her girl. Her trembling fingers opened. What her hand found was wood—the chair's cold leg, the empty seat.

"No," the stranger said to all the nothing around her. "I do not remember you."

My uncle the saddlemaker and his wife knocked on the door with the whole soggy afternoon around them, the whites of their teeth shining in it.

"You came," my mother said, her words a drooped flag on a windless day.

"We brought some cakes," Aunt Kayla offered, beaming, her big teeth a sloppy white smear. "For everyone. To share." Her eyes were too bright. Fiery.

My father wanted the visitors to know that he had given his approval. That of course his wife had not been able to make a decision without him. Words, nothing more than dressed-up nerves, rolled out of his mouth. Hersh's coat had a fur collar, which he petted in slow, meaningful strokes. Regina was standing with my brother and me, hoping not to be recognized. But she had the nicest dress and the flattest hair and the cleanest cheeks. There was no question which child was for sale.

Aunt Kayla put her hand on Regina's head and smoothed the light brown waves of hair. "Nice hair," she said, as if starting a list, but she did not seem convinced by it yet. Hersh agreed. "Nice bluish eyes," he added. They nodded together. I looked at her hair and her eyes, never having noticed either before. I felt sorry about this, that only now as she was leaving did I appreciate her.

"Nice nose," I said, wanting suddenly to complete the list of my sister, before it was too late. "Nice ears, nice legs, nice mouth, nice forehead, nice teeth," I said.

"I guess," Hersh said, "I guess it's time to go." He put his two first fingers under his sister's chin and lifted her face up. "Thank you," he said. "Perl. Thank you forever. We will do everything that has ever been done well, only better."

Kayla scooted closer and closer to the big blue door, as if it might suddenly vanish and leave them with no exit, no way to complete the miracle.

The whole knot of people moved outside to watch the departure. There were some magpies around and a few early flies out in the wet cold, but they were silent in this moment. A gust of wind shook water out of the trees, a cool mist. I watched my father kick a rock back and forth in the mud between his dingy leather boots. I watched my mother adjust her long black dress and Regina's white lace collar. We took turns hugging her, and I licked my own chin and watched out of the corners of my eyes. I saw my mother sneak one glance, the girl turning from her daughter into her niece as she went, her old wool coat swishing, and waves of hair catching light. Black boots turning the mud.

That night, my father rolled over to his wife. He put his hands on her bare head. He held them there, not polishing the surface, just holding.

"Now we really are in a new world," he said.

"We have enough," my mother said, which was not a statement but a prayer. She wondered whether she should write it down.

"Oh, help!" our father suddenly cried, loud enough to wake Moishe and me. He picked up a cabbage from the floor and threw it as hard as he could against the far wall, where it splashed open. My mother beckoned all three of us. She held us against her chest, my father crying and my brother and I stunned cold. She whispered into our hair, "You are reasons to live. You are enough to survive for." I grew older and heavier then, my mother's love bigger than my own small body could hold. Her love would hang on to my ankles and wrists on every journey I would ever have to take, even if she was the one who sent me on it. My mother's heart beat, oblivious to the upended universe around it. Everything goes on, it said. That is the best we can hope for.

THE FIFTH DAY

The stranger was welcomed into all of our homes. The butcher gave her the nicest pieces of herb-roasted chicken and the biggest squares of chocolate left in the universe. The banker's wife made Igor wash the stranger's socks every day in the river while the other children rubbed her feet with oil. She was very quiet, but always smiled at us when we offered her something.

"I'm not God," she kept telling us.

"Of course not," the banker's wife said, "but here is a candied orange rind. And here is another glass of fresh milk. And Igor will give you his own pillow, which will bring you sweet dreams."

"I will?" asked Igor quietly.

Even while we knew that she was a person like any of us and not God, or probably not God since none of us had any idea who

God was or was not, she did suddenly seem important and useful. At least, we said, if we treat her well she will get the prayers right. A person who was upset might copy down a request for a new cow as a request for a new plow. A person who was angry might switch what one asked with what another asked, and old women would become pregnant with twin sons while young women died quick and easy deaths.

"Do you want to trade off as recorders?" the stranger asked. But we liked having her do it and, now that we thought about it, it seemed risky to pray to each other, risky to air all our wishes to people who knew each other well, especially well, we admired, for having met only five days earlier.

The healer told her, "You are better at it. You are brilliant. We are nothing more than weak little rats next to you." She was homeless otherwise, childless. Everyone she knew was dead. Did she have a better option than to be our recorder? Should we feel bad about this? the healer wondered. But he decided that it was right—our stranger had come to us like an angel and we would go ahead and accept her as one.

"I am just an emptiness," she said.

The jeweler told her, "You are a resting place."

The dust of morning light started to get into the house, and my remaining family members and I woke up to see ourselves surrounded by scattered green heads. Our own eyes were red, our numbers diminished, with only four days of life under our belts. My parents were visibly heavy with the weight of a lost daughter.

My mother stood up, rubbed her eyes, opened the curtains and felt the emptiness double, triple, grow hungry. Life, the day ahead, the chores, the stove, the firewood, looked exactly the same as they had before Regina left. The world did not respect my mother's situation enough to transform itself in recognition of this day. She watched her husband eat some cabbage soup and put his boots on. He kissed her on the forehead before he left for the day. There was nothing to say.

Moishe and I washed our faces with harsh lemon-smelling soap that made my skin feel shrunken. Everyone was whole except our mother, whose bald head was shining against the daylight. My brother and I looked for the wig together, picking up quilts and peering into shoes, while our mother sat at the table, a polished crystal ball. I found the wig, looking like something dead under a pile of cabbages near the basket of dirty clothes. I picked it up, combed through it with my fingers. My mother did not put it on, but tucked it in the crook of her arm as though it were an animal. "No more secrets," she said, stroking it absentmindedly for a moment, then stood up and settled it on one of the cabbages on the counter. The cabbage, all dressed up with no place to go, stared blindly out at the room.

At the door, a knock. I opened it, shrieked when Regina was on the other side. Regina with her suitcase. Regina with her nicest dress and her white lace collar, soggy now with rainwater. Maybe we would be whole again. Behind her were Aunt Kayla and Uncle Hersh. My mother, still in her nightgown, straightened her spine. Her head picked up the light from all directions.

"My daughter," she said, taking Regina's hand and kneading it like bread.

"She is not what we had in mind," Uncle Hersh said quickly, looking to his wife for approval, his voice shaky and uncertain.

"Your daughter?" my mother asked.

"*Your* daughter," Kayla corrected. "She's too big. Her feet, her hands. Too big. We hadn't remembered how big she was. It is not a good match for us," she said sternly. "We want to be a different kind of parents." Kayla stepped forward and took my hand. "Young Lena," she said. "My Lena. Smallest of all, Lena." Kayla examined my fingers, their puffy knuckles, their delicate reach. She put my palm up against her own. She smiled at her husband. "Look at what a difference there is. She is so much smaller."

I felt like an open window through which anything might blow. Regina looked at the hands attached to her wrists as if for the first time. These hands were big enough to make her unlovable, but big enough to save her, too.

My mother closed her eyes and took the suitcase from the floor. She handed it to me. "You have everything you need," she told me. "You are my reason to live. You are everyone's reason to live. Look how many people you can save." My heart went on and on inside the empty cavern of my body. *There is no way this is actually happening. This cannot be*, my brain yowled.

Hersh looked at my mother with his red, unslept eyes. "You have no idea," he said, but she stopped him.

"Just go," she said. "Take my daughter. Your daughter. Our daughter."

I thought for the first time in my life about my body—what was inside, what was outside, what was strong and what was weak. I did not know whether my good knees were thanks to my father. I did not know that I had my mother's strong stomach and dry skin. My thick ankles were Vlad's, and my sinewy calves Perl's. My long, thin back came from my maternal grandmother, who died young and in love and unexpectedly from a disease no one could name. My collarbone, like my great-great-great-grandfather's, was weapon sharp. A line of great-aunts and great-uncles had passed along the blond fuzz now dusting my face like early snow, and the radiating red cheeks beneath were thanks to a fiery streak always present on my father's side, in the women especially. I was not old enough to tell whether I would carry myself heavy and low like my mother or high and light like my father.

Grandma Elka, Grandpa Sig, Aunt Rose, Aunt Esther and my mother's twin uncles Noah and Noah (who were told apart by their beards if not their names) were enshrined in my body. They did not spare their pointy elbows, deep belly buttons, pink skin, doughy earlobes, hard noses, flat feet, long second toes or propensity to go wandering until the sun slipped out of view; they gave me everything they had. All the ghosts gathered around me. "You have us," I heard them say. "You are us. We are your blood, your muscles, your bones."

In the doorway, Perl looked into my eyes, eyes a color never before seen in our family—a crisp weedy green my body had invented just for me. "You will always be you," my mother said.

Any legacy I pass down is mostly imagined, because on that day in the gurgling newness of the world, I began again for the second time that week. Would I grow like a seedpod sprung open a mile from my home? Or did everything owe itself to what had been, even if it hadn't?

The anger I felt dammed itself up when I looked at Regina. I had been complicit when she was the one given away. I had not hidden her in the forest or built a basket of reeds in which she might float away. I had loved her and wished her well, but I had let her go all the same. Now that it was my turn, I knew there was no one in the world to drag me back home. There was no little sister to trade me in for. I had invented a world—now all that was left was surviving it.

I refused to walk, and Hersh picked me up in his arms and carried me through the rain, which washed me down so that when we arrived at the door and Hersh stamped the mud from his polished black boots I was a new girl in a new life, dripping my old self onto the rug.

THE SIXTH DAY

In the syrup of late night, on the sixth day of the world, the butcher, banker and the barber's wife made their way out to the stranger's post with lanterns to ask for things they had forgotten to ask for in daylight. It would be nice to stop the dead old world from trying to sneak into this one. Good to look ahead to winter and hope for enough snow to wet the fields but not enough to chill our bones. When they got there, our stranger was gone. Her striped blanket was sagging and wet, the four sticks supporting it leaning into each other. Her chair was still footed to the cobblestones, but now the only thing in it was a pool of rainwater, milky with moonlight.

They finally found her lying on her side on the jeweler's floor, the jeweler watching her from the other side of the room while she drew a picture of two children with the charcoal of a burned log.

The faces looked back at her, bloodless and wrong, and she tried to make them righter by fuzzing the lines, and in this way they slowly disappeared into black dust blown across the floor by our stranger's breath.

The small group of seekers knocked on the door. They said, "Where were you? We need you." They shook their umbrellas out onto the jeweler's floor.

"I was here," she told them. "I am here."

Their prayers had turned to complaints. They began to list the strange ailments they had developed, revealing that, in spite of a new world, all the old anxiety had stayed alive and well. "I have terrible leg cramps. Could a demon be living in there?" the barber's wife asked.

"Every night I get a fever for exactly one hour," the banker said.

"Everything looks blue to me. Everything looks like dusk," said the butcher.

"I can't remember my own name sometimes. I can't remember who I am," the barber's wife added.

The stranger listened. She had no way to heal these people. She suggested, as kindly as possible, that maybe in the morning they could consult the healer.

"But we still have to pray. I'm serious about not being able to find you. I think you need to stay put," the banker said.

"If you don't mind," others added.

"We'll bring blankets for you. We'll pray for many warm blankets for you. In fact, we promise that every prayer we say for ourselves will also be a prayer for you."

The jeweler wanted to tape their mouths shut. He wanted to

roll them down a mountainside. He wanted to light them on fire. Before he could even perform the meager task of opening his mouth to object, the stranger was being led outside, preparing to give herself completely over.

In my new room there was a reddish wood dresser and a bed made up tight with a pink-and-green-flowered blanket. There was a silver music box on the dresser and a wicker basket for dirty clothes. There were six wooden hangers on a rod, waiting to display the shells of dresses and coats. My aunt and uncle sat on the bed next to me, the girl who used to be the youngest daughter of the cabbage picker but was now the only daughter of the saddle-maker.

"So," Kayla said, "you live here now. This is your bed, and that is your dresser. You can put your things in it. And on it. That is your music box. It plays music." I opened it and it plinked a song I had never heard before. This day was many things, but real was not one of them.

"It's a song about bullfighting," Hersh told me.

"Bullfighting?" I asked. This was not happening. It could not be.

"A man fights a bull, with a cape," he tried. "Like this," and he held up by imaginary corners a cape, which he dodged and waved.

"Stop doing that," Kayla told him. "That is *not* a good place to start."

"We were dancing," he said. I stood completely still.

"You can unpack in peace," Kayla said. "We leave you to it."

I opened the suitcase, a square leather thing with two sturdy brass buckles, and took out the dresses folded inside. One was yellow checks and the other was a solid, faded blue. The dresses belonged to my sister and were too big for me. I remembered seeing her wear them many times—while digging for earthworms, teaching Moishe and me a song, helping my mother carry full bags home from the shops. Underneath them was a note: *Dear Regina, This is how I love you. You will know that someday if you do not know it now. I will always miss you.—Your   Perl.* Between the two words in the signature there was a large space where the word *Mother* might have been, or the word *Aunt*, but instead the space was inhabited by a clean, bright hole. I put the note in the bottom of the drawer, the bottom of the drawer it had been in that morning when it had spoken to the correct child. The dresses had been unpacked yesterday by Regina, put away just as they were being put away now, and then carefully folded back up again. "She was just here," I whispered to myself. "My sister was just in this room." That was a fact; my own presence here was much harder to believe.

I walked over to the bed, pulled the covers back and kneeled on the floor. I put my face to the bed and tried to smell my sister there on the rough cotton sheets. Tried to smell her sleep the night before, what must have been an uneasy sleep. I tried to smell her dreams. Was she happy to be here? Was she glad she would get to be an opera star? In the morning, when she was told she was not the desired one, was she sorry? The bed smelled clean, undreamed in. Kayla was hardly gone a minute when she returned to fetch me. "Come out and be my daughter," she said.

I sat down in between my aunt and uncle on a hard red velvet couch. They placed a crystal bowl full of candy on my lap, brightly colored packages piled high. Kayla touched my hair, examined my scalp, ringed my ankle with her fingers.

Kayla noted that her new daughter would have to be fattened up. She said, "Life gets better from here." I noted that my aunt did not need fattening at all, that her ankles came over her short leather shoes like bread over the top of its pan. I noticed how her wedding ring divided her finger into two distinct provinces. Hersh, on the other hand, was rangy. Everything about him was tall—even his earlobes looked stretched. His forehead was an expanse and his chin looked curious and adventuresome, as if it might wander off his face into the great, unknown mountains.

Hersh asked me where they should start and I shook my head.

"Well, do you want to know about your grandparents? Do you want to know about your great-grandparents? Do you want to know about when I was a boy?"

"And what about me?" said Kayla. "I have a *lot* to tell you, too."

"So, tell," I said, carefully unwrapping a yellow candy and rolling it in my mouth. I remember vividly how much each motion of my hand mattered to me that day. I could reach, I could pick up, I could unwrap. The rest of the world was dizzy, but these things were known. I sucked the candy hard, and a sharp edge cut my tongue. The taste of lemon mixed with the taste of blood.

Hersh started to tell me about his parents, who were silk traders from the sea. He was excited and proud to show my ancestry off to me, but I reminded him that those had always been my grandparents. Hersh looked disappointed. Here he had given me a gift and I said I already had the same thing in another color. I tried again. "Thank you," I said politely with a small nod. How was I the one trying to offer comfort? I looked at the room with all its upholstered furniture and oil paintings. The woodstove had a ceramic horse standing stately and ready to gallop atop it. The rug at my feet was soft and richly colored with a repeating pattern of square deer. Everything in the room looked important and breakable.

"Your father is in the saddle business, did you know?" Kayla asked.

"My father?"

"Hersh here, your father." Kayla took my little hand and placed it on Hersh's knee. His pants were scratchy under my palm. "You should be proud of him. He is a very great man."

"I see," I said.

"Can you say it for me? 'I am proud of my father.'"

"I am proud of my father," I said, picturing a man in a cabbage field, but looking at a man with a pair of glasses glinting around his eyes and a mustache that hid the dark holes leading into his long nose.

THE SEVENTH DAY

On the seventh day, we rested. Men put their feet up and looked out the window at the rain that had not stopped falling. Children ate honey on slices of bread. Mothers rubbed a little butter on their dry heels. We looked back at our first week of life, our plans and accomplishments, and most of us felt proud. The trees applauded with their green, green leaves.

The stranger, prayer-ready and shivering, tapped her foot in the mud puddle below her rootless chair. The jeweler brought her bread for breakfast and cheese for lunch. He brought her tea on the hour every hour and dried her feet with an old towel.

When Hersh and Kayla collapsed in a parenthood-induced nap, I slipped out the door and went to the stranger. "Help," I said first. "Help," I said again. She waited for my prayer. I asked, "Is this real? Am I still me?"

"You know that smell, when you put your nose up to a pine tree?" I told her I did, perfectly. "No matter how long it has been, you always will. Like you are storing part of that tree in your own body." Was this a gift or a sacrifice? Had I given up my entire body to storing a sliver of every single object on earth? I said that I hoped there was a little room left for myself, just a small cave somewhere between the imprinted feel of walking across wet grass and the precise tension of an apple giving way under a knife. "You are thinking of it wrong," she comforted. "Everything stays true. You are yourself, no matter how much you have to change."

Until a long time later, until I was a mother myself, until I lost everything, until it found me back, I did not believe the stranger's words. *Everything stays true.* Now I know that. Now, it's all I know. And knowing it saves my life again every time I wake up.

That night, I stood up in my lightless room. Blackness seeped into anything with an opening. I pulled the drawer handle and let the dark inside and released the smell of crushed rose petals and dust. I opened the music box and let it sing to the darkness, the darkness got in close to that little spinning dancer. I took the note out and lit a candle to see it by. *Dear Regina, Dear Regina, Dear Regina.* Outside my window, the tree branches pointed me in all the wrong directions. They yelled to me, branch by branch, *this way, up, come in, turn back.* I ripped *Dear Regina* off the note and tore it into bits. I undid the lock on the window and pushed the two sides apart. Cold air and a mist of rain swept across my face. I threw the shreds of my sister's name out the window, where the moon made them glow and the endless rain smashed them into the earth. I closed the window. *This is how I love you,* the note said to no one in particular.

I took the note and put it under my pillow. I tried again to smell my sister on that pillow and could not. I tried to smell myself on that pillow and could not. I rubbed my body against the rough cotton sheets, turned around and around in the bed. I spit up and down it. Rubbed the spit in. This time, my nose pressed to the sheets, the bed was full of my own mouth's bitter scent. It was small, but it was proof of my miserable existence. I fell asleep imagining the note growing under my pillow, growing into a tree, branching out into the room, outgrowing the ceiling, outgrowing the reborn world. If I could climb it, I might reach a place high above the cloud cover of this weary, cold sorrow.

· II ·

INTRODUCING:
EVERYTHING

I t is a beautiful day," the saddlemaker said to me. "We have a
daughter and she is you and the day is just waiting for us." His
thin fingers whispered across mine.

I was far, far away, having left only one thing behind: my body.
I put on the mask of a smile.

On the stove a pot boiled furiously. Something salty foamed
down the sides. "I think the water is boiling," I said. Kayla did not
so much as turn around to look. She explained that my father was
going to work but not to worry because this would be the most
beautiful day of my life so far. And tomorrow would be an even
better day—and forever after, on like that. Kayla was so excited
she choked on her tea. Her big face turned red while she coughed.
She kept trying to excuse herself, but all she could manage to get
out was "Ex, ex, ex."

Hersh stood up to pat her on the back. "Hush," he told her. Kayla blew her nose and wiped her cheeks, striped by tears.

"Can I hold you on my lap?" Kayla asked me through a cough. "Can you be my baby?" My blood stopped. My fingers tingled with the loss of it.

"Do as your mother asks." Hersh nodded, but I could tell he was worried. He tipped me out of my chair and lifted me up. "The pot is boiling over," I said, this time meaning my heart. "Thank you," he said, smiling back. He placed me on Kayla's doughy lap, where I was awkward and too big, where my legs had no place to fall and my head rolled around.

"This beautiful baby is my baby," Kayla said, trying to rock me, pressing me into her large breasts. Her face was still splotchy from her coughing fit. "Say coo. Say goo. Like a baby." I was quiet. "She doesn't want to talk, my baby doesn't want to talk. She just wants me to hold her in my arms, because I'm her mother and I love her the most out of anyone in the world and she knows that."

Someone began banging on the door. My heart leapt. My true parents, come to take me back. But when Hersh opened the door, I could see from the shined and pointy shoes that this was no savior. It was the widow, taller than any man in the village and with a voice that sanded down your ears. Her body was all legs. She was like two old trees that had grown together in a brief love affair. Her arms were stiff branches and were always being waved around.

"We have no time to waste. This child might already be too old to teach. Look at her—you can tell just by looking at her that she can't sing. She can't sing one note. I might as well give up now."

"I'm paying you," Kayla reminded her. "I am paying you to *teach* her to sing. She is going to be a star."

"*She's* teaching me to sing?"

"I'm a saint. I'm doing God's work in this farce of a world. He will bless me and love me," the widow said to herself.

It had never occurred to either my aunt or uncle that I might need some sort of talent. They had gathered their gold coins together, enough to pay for the lessons, and these coins were polished and shining and it seemed impossible that they would not transfer themselves into notes as golden, as bright, as beautiful as the coins themselves.

"Wait. Do we know about opera?" Hersh had asked his wife, not wanting to break the rules of a world that had provided them with their dearest wish.

"I know about the opera," Kayla insisted. "Look, I don't have time to waste. My daughter has to learn to sing immediately if she is to have a chance. Immediately."

Alone together in the sitting room, the widow said to me, "You have very little chance of doing well." The red velvet couch looked child-size under her.

I said, "I don't know anything." It was the truest statement I had ever uttered. I was sitting on a chair opposite her, watching her cross and uncross her tremendous legs.

"You're telling me."

The widow put the leather case she had been carrying down on the rug next to her chair and took three things out of it: a bottle of vodka, a large glass and a stick.

"Okay," she said to me, "go ahead and sing some notes."

"Some notes?"

"Sing a song, sing anything. Make noise with your mouth." She poured herself a glass of vodka and sat back, crossed her feet at the ankles and drank. "That is good," she said to her glass, "that is wonderful." She looked at the child in front of her, picked up her stick and waved it up and down. "Sing! La-la-la!"

I creaked out a few notes, low to high, and the widow said, "That was terrible. Again," and I creaked out a few more notes, high to low, and the widow said, "That was terrible. Again," and I tried again, and again until the widow said, "I do not deserve this," and laid her head back against the high back of the couch and fell asleep. The stick reclined on her lap like a pet, like a loyal kitten, and she kept her hands over it lovingly while she snored. I sat down on the floor and waited. I petted the rug. I looked at the shadow where a grandfather clock must have stood, its shape darker than the rest of the sun-faded green wallpaper. I imagined that clock filling with slime at the bottom of the river. I listened to the absence of my own song. Dogs barked and howled in the distance, cries they did not have to learn and practice but knew automatically, just by being alive as dogs.

In the evening Hersh came home and we forked dark bread and dark meat while Hersh and Kayla drank dark wine. I ate little and spoke less. Hersh hoped I would soon not look so stunned. He asked me, "Do you like chocolate? Do you like cake? Do you like cookies? Do you like kittens? Do you like horses?" in a stream, which I answered all at once—"Everyone likes those things."

"Then name one thing only you like," Hersh said.

I thought about it. "I don't know," I said, meaning it.

"For example, many people like babies, but don't like mud . . . or rain."

"I do like all those things."

"Well, then you must be a happy girl." Hersh laughed with a wave to the wet windowpane. "Very happy!" I took stock of how I felt in that moment, a half-eaten piece of meat on my plate, my feet in a pair of socks, sitting in a chair too tall for my toes to touch the strange new floor. All the mud was outside or trapped in the tread of shoes at the front door, while the only rain I could see was hanging limply on the glass. Was this what very happy felt like?

Kayla put down her wineglass, empty, and interrupted the conversation. "Can Lena sit on my lap?" she asked.

"Again?" Hersh asked.

"She is my baby."

"I'm not a baby," I said. "I'm eleven, going on twelve."

Kayla picked me up, sat back down and began trying to shrink me by curling each limb up. I felt like a bug, tucked into itself. My feet, pressed into her leg, made a dent in that dough. Kayla's eyes narrowed. "You are the smallest. No one is smaller than you. That means you are the baby. I will make you be . . ."

Hersh interrupted his wife with a desperate stroking of her shoulder. "Hey," he said. "We are really lucky. Let's be careful. Plus, a baby isn't in voice lessons yet," Hersh said, trying to reason.

"You're right!" Kayla hollered. "How could we have been so stupid?" She laughed and rocked her baby girl. "We have a lot to learn about being parents," she whispered into my soft hair.

Hersh had to think carefully. His darling had not snapped

back into sanity now that she was a mother. She had snapped into something, but it wasn't that. He met my eye and I knew he wanted to tell me he was hoping to save us both. If I followed along, perhaps I would be spared. He built his first fatherly strategy, saying, "I have a feeling this baby is going to grow very fast." Here we were again, trying to save ourselves by telling a story. "Pretty soon I bet she will be as big as a one-year-old, not long after that as big as a two-year-old. She's a very unusual child." He looked at his wife with her oversize load. "Don't you think she'll grow quickly, my dear? Don't you think she's a prodigy? A prodigy at growing?"

"Could we be so blessed?" Kayla was not looking at her husband. She stared into my eyes as if the rest of the world had dried up around her. If Hersh had become a dead balloon of skin on the floor right then, she hardly would have noticed. But his voice seemed to filter into her like light. In this way, he offered his wife a deal—I could be a baby, a crying, drooling, helpless baby, but not for long. Every few weeks I would gain a year. Hersh wanted to catch me up with myself quickly so that the eleven-year-old they had adopted could soon be the girl they lived with and loved. He hoped sanity, reason, would be there to meet them then. He did not see how seriously his wife would take the proposition—the weeks that would continue to represent years, past when I should have slowed way down, aging as everyone else did, the change invisible from one day to the next.

"A prodigy!" Kayla glowed. "We are so lucky to be her parents. Where can we show her off?" Hersh begged me silently to comply. Just for a while, his eyes said. Before you know it, the upside-down world will right itself.

✦ ✦ ✦

For my debut, Kayla dressed me in a green velvet frock with a frilly collar and new pointy leather shoes that laced up the ankle. She clipped a string of delicate pearls around her own neck and another around mine. For the first time in her life, she put a ribbon in her daughter's hair. Hersh wrapped a soft gray blanket around me and held the whole cocoon in his arms.

"Here we go," Hersh said shakily, twisting the cold brass doorknob. The seam between the walls of their house and the rest of creation was a puddle my new parents had to leap over. The rain had softened to a mist that tickled my face. "This is our baby," Hersh said to each person they passed. "Please forgive me."

"She was born perfect," Kayla said.

"Oh?" the villagers asked. They studied me. I could not defend or save myself.

"We are trying to believe," Hersh said. "We are trying, in general." The heartsoreness the villagers felt when they looked at Hersh was a bruise whose origin they could not remember. He looked unprepared not only for the demands his love would make, but for his own endless desire to fill them. A happy wife is a happy life, the grandparents used to say. This kind of devotion tested that theory. The villagers examined me, this new version of me, and they thought I looked all right. The world was new, and there would be many surprises, wouldn't there? Isn't the fun of telling a story that you don't know what will happen?

"She's very, very beautiful," they said. "She's big."

That was it. If I tossed a rope out, no one was going to drag me back to shore. I bobbed out there in the depths and the villagers settled on picnic blankets, waiting to see what would happen next.

My new parents and I walked circles around our village, past windows trimmed with white, past flowerbeds turned and ready for new bulbs, past the few remaining stakes of an old fence, rotting and covered in vines. They walked until the round cobblestones had worn Hersh and Kayla's feet into crescents, until they were soaked and their eyes stung with dirty mist, until Kayla's hair began to fall out from its precise twist. There was little light left to see by and Hersh was tired from holding the sixty-pound infant. But they kept walking. And the longer they walked, the more they both felt the sting of being parents. Of loving something so much that their organs were crushed under the pressure. Their eyes were slimy with love, their throats were dry with it, and their bodies were purposeless except to protect the new life.

Crushed but safe in my uncle's arms, I did not cry or beg to go home, either my real home or my new one. I did not insist upon my own age or otherwise chew my way out of the cocoon Kayla and Hersh had me in. I said a very small prayer, a prayer for the right thing to happen, and then I closed my eyes, and in the arms of the man who would be my father forever after, I went soft, but I did not sleep.

Kayla said they would have to show me everything or I wouldn't know what it was.

"Should we take her to the river?" Hersh asked.

Kayla thought for a moment. "The river!" She laughed. "She doesn't even know what a river is!" Hersh laughed with her. "Can you imagine what that must be like, not to know?" they said. They looked into my eyes, foggy and wet. Hersh shifted me in his arms.

"Do we tell her or do we keep it secret?" Kayla suddenly asked.

"Once she knows she will never not know again," Hersh said.

"Let's keep it secret. Let's not tell her everything yet." They danced in the street, celebrating every unspoken fact of the torn and blooming world. Every iris and daisy and gravestone was theirs to give to their daughter when they saw fit. And before that, my eyes were as useless to me as river rocks.

"I want to nurse her—I bet she is hungry," Kayla said.

Hersh stopped short. "I don't know."

"What do you mean, you don't know? What kind of father are you? Are you the kind of father who starves his children?" Kayla sat down at the edge of the road and undid the long string of buttons on her top. "Close your eyes," she said to Hersh. My eyes were already closed and I kept them that way. I did not open them even for one short glance. Kayla took me to her substantial breast. She put the point of the nipple into my mouth. I tried not to cry, but was unsuccessful. If Kayla had looked down she would have seen that the only liquids being transferred between us were tears.

In the darkness, folded tightly into bed, the whole mysterious world was wrapped around me. Its wooden houses with their pointed roofs, the old bare trees out front, the wheelbarrow, the woodpile, the haystack. Shop windows and signs in those windows advertising jars of clover honey and bags of flour, and footprints in the mud leading to the doorway, and then leading back out through the mud again. The mud, which was a mixture of dirt and water, water that fell from the sky—what a miracle that was, to be there when it was falling, out of nowhere, no one in charge of it—down and down onto anything it could hit, onto any warm or cold or sharp or soft or lost or found thing, roaming or sitting dead still, mouth agape, swallowing whatever it was given.

And then, *ping*. Just like that. The sound of something hitting my window. I opened it, and the stranger's cloaked face was there. I had wanted it to be my mother. I wanted that worse and harder than anything. "Once upon a time," she began without saying hello, "there was a beautiful baby, but the problem was that two different women claimed to be her mother. They fought bitterly, but neither one would give in, so eventually someone called the king, who proposed a solution: he would cut the baby in half and give one part to each woman. One woman agreed, the other said that she would rather give up her half to ensure the child remain whole. That was how the king knew she was the real mother."

"So, can I go home then?" I asked.

"Your body has to live here, but your heart can live wherever you like."

"I get cut in half after all?"

"I'm so sorry," she said, already turning around.

My stomach churned with confusion and hunger both. Even if breast milk had come out, I was not a baby. I sneaked into the kitchen but found little to eat. I tore the meat off a small bone left in the icebox, put it under my nightdress and took it to my room to chew on in the moonlight. Someone must have seen me, because the next night, they left a loaf of bread and a large piece of cheese out for me, as if I were a rare, wild animal they wanted to befriend. There was a note: *I almost remember who you are and I definitely love you.—Father.*

Did I remember who I was? Not well, not really. I made a list of everything I knew. *River, mud, corners, mother, father, sister, brother, cabbage, rain, hair, arms, mountains, farm, hands, yesterday, tomorrow, kiss, meat, plates, tongues, eyes, bed, roof, tree, hunger.* Everything I wrote made me think of four other things. I wrote and wrote until the list took up the whole page, until it was black with markings. Out in the world dogs kept howling back and forth to each other, not in trained operatic voices but high, rough ones. *Spit, babies, snot, spoon, death, dogs, saddle, horse, rain, anger, howl.*

I sent a dream to my parents across town. I was sure that it reached them, that at the exact same time we all three saw the scene together: I jumped, did a somersault, whistled, snapped my fingers—anything I could do to make them clap, and they wanted to, they wanted to laugh and cheer, but they could not. They were mute. But they found they could throw their voices into other people's mouths. They could make Kayla and Hersh say, "Beautiful, wonderful girl, look at how much you know. We are dizzy with love for you."

In the morning, Kayla was hanging over me like a burning sun. "Hello?" she whispered. "You don't want to cry for me?" Kayla asked. "Don't you want to miss me when I'm in the other room?" Dutifully, I did my best to summon sadness into my eyes. I thought of the sound of frogs coming to life in puddles outside the window of my old life, singing for a few wet, warm nights before they were silent and I would go outside to find their dry, flat forms strewn out over ground. I thought about my old father's clatter when he woke and stood to look outside at the waiting day, while my old mother watched him quietly until he said, "Beautiful out there," and she asked him to describe the clouds to her.

"She's crying for me," Kayla called to Hersh. "Oh, my little girl needs me so much."

The old world seemed to have left us alone. No one had floated by in a boat, trying to sell us a canteen made from a sheep's stomach. No Gypsies had passed through, rattling their wine bottles and singing their songs. Was it because we had succeeded? Because the new world was real? Perhaps. Or maybe it was because, day by day, there were fewer and fewer people left in the countryside. We had not seen the Official Gazette, which published thirty-two laws, thirty-one decrees and seventeen government resolutions against us. We did not see crosses drawn on all the doorways where Christians lived, while Jewish men were made to dig huge trenches in the cemetery. The world was emptied. Anyone who thought about it would have assumed we were long dead or on our way to death. We were forgotten and we were lost and, because of that, the world we made was allowed to go on.

Meanwhile, the healer saw patients all day. People whose anxiety about the old, the new, the broken and the saved was manifested in strange physical afflictions. The healer's medical knowledge was sorely tested, but he knew that in most cases, all he had to do was provide a confident answer. It mattered very little what the contents of that answer were.

For demon-caused leg cramps, wear an amulet with three hairs from the bad leg and one underfeather of a sparrow.

For nighttime fever, catch an ant carrying a leaf and place it in a copper tube. Cover and shake the tube, saying, "What thou carriest on me, that I carry on thee."

For fear of ghosts, place four beetles in a pot and pour some good wine over them. Boil for one hour and drink each morning for nine days.

If you forget your own name, if you cannot remember who you are, take your shirt off and drop it down the chimney. Then bury it at a crossroads.

For heartsickness of the unending variety, befriend a dove. Do not catch it, not even so that you can set it free. Just get down on the ground with bread crumbs on your chest and wait for it to find you interesting.

When we asked our stranger never to leave the square, we had not counted on months of gray weather. Some of the time the rain was heavy, like buckets had been upturned. Sometimes it was soft and sometimes it was just a deep, thick mist. Our water tanks filled up and overflowed and we had to shovel the mud out from in front of our doorways, but the village never floated away, even though it seemed some days like it might. Just when the streets started to become rivers, the rain would turn to mist, the streams would subside, and we would go about our lives under a blanket of fog.

Meanwhile, our stranger sat in the square. She had the coats we gave her and we even built her a little canopy out of a cowskin, which was waterproof, where the blanket had not been. This seemed very smart and kind of us. We sat there with her and asked for the health of our babies and the health of our parents and enough dry wood to keep the house warm, and our stranger wrote these things down for us, her fingers red and her boots soaked through. After praying, everyone went home and wrapped our hands around warm cups of tea, dried our socks by the fire. We had figured a day or two of this weather, a week, two weeks. But on it went.

At night, the stranger came to my window. The hugeness of what was happening was impossible to express, so we worked in a smaller currency. We traded tiny, observed facts. "The chipmunks look like they are enjoying life," she said.

"Sometimes, when the water begins to boil, I put my face into the steam until it starts to hurt."

"Some of us are happier than others."

"I like it when I can feel myself falling asleep."

"The days are getting shorter and shorter."

"I am afraid of not being myself anymore. I feel like I'm disappearing or something."

"Yes," she said. "I know what you mean."

The jeweler's cheeks were sallow with worry. He had stopped sleeping, and ate only what the stranger left on the plates he brought to her. He was angry with her for being so obedient. If only she had insisted, told the villagers that she would sit during the day but come home—home to his house—at night. After a lifetime of waiting, a companion had appeared out of the heavens for him, dropped down like a gift from God, and been taken away by the petty selfishness of other people.

Most villagers were not aware of his discontent. We were busy worrying about the rain and our own morning-till-nights. Our houses were full of hanging clothes, which left puddles underneath themselves. When we wanted to leave our houses to walk to the shops or work, we made our way along the line of garments, feeling each one, looking for the driest, but nothing was dry. We smelled like drenched sheep all the time, our necks itchy under wet scarves.

Some people began to notice that our stranger was not writing as vigorously as she had been. The jeweler peeked over her shoulder and discovered a soggy list:

Money
Love
Health (mother, father, children, spouse, self, others)
Sex
A Son
Winning the bet

Next to each of these was a series of notches, one for each time one of us asked for the thing. Money had two rows of lines. We prayed for the health of ourselves more often than the health of our spouses but less often than the health of our parents. Sex was less requested, probably because we were shy, but almost all of us wanted to win the bet. The final category, the one that made us feel terrible, was this: A prayer that what happened to the stranger does not happen to me. Even with the safety of Creation between us and that story, many of us, dozens, had sat down on that old wooden chair and wished out loud that our stranger's stolen life, her lost children, her mutilated mother remain only hers. That she alone sit out in the falling sky and record our hopeful lives for us.

The jeweler told us what he had seen. He made the rounds from house to house to say that we were leaving our stranger outside in bad weather under a cowskin and telling her how grateful we were to be better off than she was. He told everyone he insisted she sleep in the house from now on. "Also, peace is not even on the list," he said. "Not one of us has prayed for peace."

"Yes, but it's only temporary. We're building her a palace. We're praying for peace when we pray for all the other things. We want money because we want peace, right?" the banker tried nervously to reason, while he popped a nut out of its shell and licked the crystals of salt from his fingers. The banker was leaning against his doorframe, each polished button on his vest reflecting the jeweler's face back at him, distorted and clownish.

"I think we could stand to pray for what we really want, then. But in the meantime, we haven't built the palace yet and our stranger is freezing."

"Many nights we invite her into our homes and rub her feet. Has she forgotten?" The banker tossed his shells into a puddle, where most sank but one floated—a boat big enough to save nothing.

"We are already so used to having a miracle with us that now she's soaking wet and we don't care to dry her off."

Shame was a feeling that arrived all at once. The villagers had gotten away with everything so far. The stranger was like a communal pet and everyone figured she was lucky to have been adopted by us, to have the square, safe and clean, to live in. Now that our selfishness had been pointed out, we figured we did not deserve even one good thing on the earth.

So the village agreed to take another vote. Most of us did not want to turn our own house into the temple, even temporarily, even when the idea was floated that it must be a very godly thing to do. Where would we say the thing that was too private, too quiet a desire to bring even to the ears of God?

"I would do it," the jeweler said, trying to sound as if he had only thought of this now. As if he had not racked his brain for a way to come home to the stranger each evening.

"Nah," the old men agreed. "Too small. Too full of junk." The jeweler bit his cheek.

"I could add a room," he tried.

"It's not really fair, anyway. What if you get closer to God than the rest of us? We don't want any special privileges," the banker said.

The jeweler was jittering. So taken had he been with the image he had sprung of the stranger in the low light of every evening for the rest of their lives, seated at the window with a book on her lap.

"What about the barn?" the butcher asked. "I'm sure the animals wouldn't mind."

"You'd choose the barn over my house?" the jeweler mumbled, his forehead turning red with shame.

The barn did not smell like a house of God, it smelled like the house of goats—their buttery oil and their stamping hooves and interested mouths. The horses swished their tails and looked at us with eyes that seemed to be melting. The chickens tucked themselves into their nests or walked nervously around.

"Welcome to the holy temple," we joked, kicking shit and hay. Our stranger dried off with some rags we had brought and sat down against the wall. "Thank you," she said. "This is better."

The jeweler got to work making the stranger's bed and setting up a pile of carefully folded shirts from his own closet for her to wear. He thought ahead to the day he would come to switch them out—clean for dirty—only his plan was not to wash the ones she had worn, but to ball them up and sleep on them.

The rest of us took stock of the big room. At the far end, the animals had their quarters: shelves for the dozen chickens, a pen for two horses. The four goats walked freely around. Heavy-coated sheep were left outside, their oily wool beaded with rainwater. We smelled them when the wind shifted. Small windows, probably never washed, ringed the walls. Floorboards creaked with every step, and the high ceiling was festooned with ribbons of dust, like a celebration planned by ghosts and spiders. My first parents and I found reasons to silently brush up against each other, and when we did our skin felt lit up. I was still supposed to be a baby, and could not tell them about the family-shaped hole in my chest.

The greengrocer and the weaver moved the crumbling piano into the barn from the healer's house, where it had sat since we had dragged it up from the river, its chest full of the other washed-up things. The piano smiled on. The weaver pinned the map of the summer sky to the wall above it. We had a temple. We were happy, in spite of the lack of ebony, of leather, of soaring arches.

Igor apologized for keeping our stranger out in the rain. My mother—Perl, I told myself to call her, the name she was given by her mother, the name she was called by everyone except her children, which I no longer was—apologized to the stranger for telling her we were glad not to have suffered as she had.

"I'm glad you didn't suffer that way, too," our stranger told her. "But thank you for saying sorry."

The animals chewed and shuffled, nosed at the hay. It seemed we were already moving too quickly. We were at the beginning of time just days ago and already we were apologizing. We thought it would be years before we would have had to start saying sorry. Perl and I knew the truth before the rest, that if hope was the first feeling, regret was the second or third.

"Can I say a prayer, and will someone else record it?" the stranger asked. Perl took out her notebook. "I pray that I am empty enough to hold you all," the stranger said.

"You are," Moishe said. "Enough, I mean. You have to be. You are the reason we believe." It was exactly what I would have said if I could speak.

"I will try. I pray." Perl scribbled it all down and ripped the page out. She folded it carefully up and handed it over, like a secret we knew but wanted to keep anyway.

"I wonder how many terrible things we do to each other every day?" the healer asked. Hersh looked at me, apologizing with every part of his face. Kayla's eyes were clear, regretless.

"For one," the chicken farmer said, "people sneak in and steal the eggs."

"Children leave their toys out for me to trip on," the baker's mother said.

"I wish that people would remember my name," added the man whose name no one could remember, even now.

"No one ever comes to check on me," whispered an old woman who was no one's grandmother or mother or friend. "No one knows if I'm even alive."

The old man with only one eye asked if we could start over yet again and this time do it really, really right. Much better than the first—or second, someone corrected—time. Everyone else agreed that we could not. The butcher thought we could try to grow up more slowly, more carefully, and the baker promised to check on the old woman every Saturday, at least. The children said they would stop stealing the eggs, which they admitted were never eaten, only crushed for the joy of it in their pink hands. Most of us said we were sorry, except the ones who insisted they had done nothing wrong. The rest of us said sorry on their behalf, which made them angry, so we said sorry to them, too. I made my apologies silently.

"You have a beautiful world," the stranger said. "Have you appreciated it?" Had anyone even gone down the river at night to go swimming? Had anyone closed his eyes and paid attention to the smell of the rain? Did we love everything wonderful around us? Had we kissed the old women on the tops of their warm heads? The children on their sticky cheeks? "We are trying very hard to be good," Igor said.

"Yes, we really are trying," the jeweler said.

The stranger asked, "How will we look after the new world? You don't get to keep things unless you take care of them."

"Let's divide the jobs up," the once wheat cutter, now silver polisher suggested. After some discussion and several small arguments, we decided on a system. The rain ran her fingers down the windows of the barn and the animals got used to our company as we designated committees of appreciation.

The Committee for the Appreciation of the River. The Committee for the Appreciation of the Grass. Committees for the Appreciation of Our Village, the Way We Build Our Houses, the Way We Feed the Dogs, the Way We Care for the Wounded, the Way We Slaughter the Cows. The Committee for Treating All Ailments, which consisted only of the healer. The Committee for the Appreciation of the Barn Which Is Also the House of God. The Committee for What We Have and Where We Have It. The Committee for the Appreciation of Our Stranger, the Recorder. The Committee Against Using the Rain as an Excuse to Be Unkind. And of course, the Committee for Apologies.

We tore up the plans for the temple with the library and the ebony bookshelves and promised to appreciate the barn. The jeweler took the two bowls and the hat out from inside the piano. The hat he wore, floppy and mold-green. The bowls he threw to the ground, where they smashed. Old women covered their eyes.

"What are you *doing?*" they asked.

"These are our stars," the jeweler told us, smiling along with the piano. "One piece at a time, we build the sky. Everything broken becomes whole again."

He was thrilled to see the stranger smile at him. The children, especially the banker's lot, were thrilled that the most dutiful thing they could do was to go home and break things. The grandparents were thrilled to see the children hopping up and down with excitement having something to do with God, although the children did not think of it that way.

When the rain turned to mist and wrapped us in foggy arms, we made tiles. Outside each house, the sound of smashing porcelain plates and bowls rang out. We smashed on rocks, mostly, and on logs, too. We sang as we smashed. We smashed and gathered the pieces. The colors we put into baskets for the sky and the whites we put into baskets for the stars.

Our heavens waited there, broken and unassembled.

THE BOOK OF DOORWAYS

The world was cooperative in her remaking. As the rest of the continent's towns and villages were emptied out, ours grew more and more peaceful. But, unknown to us, the new world also had a helper. A pair of human hands to sweep the dust off our threshold.

As afternoons slunk away, the stranger went for her walk. We knew she walked, but we did not ask her why or where. It never occurred to us that it was anything but a pleasant stroll: fresh air, birdsong. She followed the path to the river, listening to woodpeckers drill their way home. Listening to the rain, our constant friend. Mud and clay, snapped branches and feathers made her path. The feathers put her in mind of mother birds out to gather food for their helpless, bald young, nest bound and hungry. Hawks and eagles, prowling for baby swallows; mother swallows prowling for worms. Who eats first is all that matters. The stranger felt like a hunter, a village full of wide-eyed, hairless babies at her back, as helpless as anything on earth, trusting in a safe world made only for them, for no reason except the story was told that way. But she was not a hunter who brought things back, she was the opposite—her job was to keep the worms out. To catch the prey, but then bury it in the tree roots rather than bring it home in her beak.

The stranger patrolled the edge of our world where river met land, and the tendon that kept our peninsula from becoming an island. It was there, in the now overgrown brushwoods between us and everything else, where the stranger went each evening—the rest of us eating a meal with our families—to keep the gate. She was protecting us, but also herself. The new world had saved her life—the least she could do was protect it.

Behind her was the cupped palm of our spit of land; in front the flat, pale arm and the body—enormous and complete—beyond. No mountains marked an edge in this direction, no horizon except the spilling away of the earth itself. A birch forest was a troop of tall spirits in the distance. Fields were watered by our river, siphoned off as veins. Where the road used to lead from our village out, now thorns, blackberries, weeds and young oaks stopped up the hole. They were a thick seal, as resolute as every other resident. But hard as they might have tried to block the way, the stranger knew a path through to the other side. Her arms were scratched by brambles trying to talk her out of leaving. Cuts stung and bled—shining drops, the precious treasure of the body, dug up.

The stranger sat on the other side on a stump. She waited.

Nothing had burst into flame when she had crossed over. No bolt of lightning, no chasm. She wiped her cuts with the hem of her dress. The sky was still blue above her, but it was rusted like a forgotten tool all around the edges. Stars popped through. Another day wilted away in front of her eyes. Up the road, a shadow, a figure, like a hole in the landscape. As it came closer, it earned a nose and a beard. Eyes reflecting the last of the day's light. It turned into a man, and in his hand, a bag.

"Madam," the man said, close enough to have a scent, bitter as stepped-on milkweed, "good evening to you."

"Good evening," the stranger said.

"Beautiful out," said the man, panting, tired from his journey. He sat on the ground next to the stranger's stump, looped his arms around his knees. The man and the stranger looked out, and the earth provided facts to be conversed over. The stranger noted the temperature, which was cool but comfortable, and the man commented that it always seemed to be raining when he came. "Mmm," the stranger sighed, "wet here."

"Helpful for growing," the man told her. She nodded. The sky turned purple, which was a beautiful thing just then, and the stranger memorized the color. "You don't get flooding?" The stranger shook her head. She did not mention the high water that had carried her here. "I suppose it drains to the river." The man looked at the stranger and asked her, "Is anyone else here? Are you all alone?"

"In a way," she half lied. She did not want to admit to an outsider that a whole healthy village existed there. "Anything for me?" the stranger asked, knowing he would not have come if the answer was no. The man opened two brass buckles on his leather bag and held up several pieces of paper to the dying light. He squinted at each one, shuffling them to the back of the pile until he found what he was looking for, and handed the letter to the stranger.

"That's all."

MORDECAI GLASSMAN, the envelope demanded. Take me to Mordecai Glassman.

"Thank you," the stranger said, shaking the man's hand. He did not look like he wanted to stand up. The walk, the dark, the cold settling in. "I can't invite you to stay. I'm sorry. I have to send you home."

They batted politeness back and forth while the thorns were waiting for the stranger, vengeful.

The stranger made pools each time her feet sank into the riverbank. She rolled the letter into a tube, looked through. A particular grouping of stars. A shadowy willow grove on the other side of the river. She smelled the letter, but detected nothing of the forbidden place it tried to import. No cinnamon or myrrh. No churned butter, pine smoke, mutton stew. The stranger heard the long-lost wind chimes of a child's voice tink through her head: *Why is this night different from all other nights?* The stranger did not have to think long before she had the answer—because tonight, under the whole world's sky, she was not going to allow the rain and mud to destroy the letter unread, buried in the flower patch behind the barn with many others. Tonight, the stranger was going to read the message, carried by the man in his bag, from another planet.

It had not been a decision she had weighed. The stranger did not deliberate. From the first day of the world, when she had sneaked off to patrol the borders, and every day after, whether mail came or mail did not, the stranger understood that she would peek behind the curtain once. Because she was human? Because she was flawed? Because she was strong enough to know something about the truth? None of these. Because, she thought, one of the letters was going to matter. She would need to know the contents to keep order in the new world. Which one, she hoped, was going to be clear when she held it.

On a wet, rotting log, with the help of the trustworthy moon, the stranger split the seal.

Dear Mordecai,

   I have not heard from you for a long time. We are worried about you. Why don't you come to stay with us until you get on your feet? We could send you some money for passage. People say Antonescu is as bad as Hitler. The Americans think we will win the war, but I don't know. I wish you would not wait to find out. Esther sends her love. The boys are doing well in school. We bought a new icebox. Please, brother, come to where it is safe. Please answer, no matter what. I'm going crazy not knowing if you're all right.

Yours truly, Isaac

Her first thought was: Wrong letter. She stuffed it back into the envelope and pressed the flap, but it did not seal. She realized that she had expected the letter to be for her. That Mordecai

Glassman was only the name on the front, but inside she would find clear instructions for her personal care of the village. Straight from the mouth of God. The stranger did not know who Mordecai was. Of course she knew him, because she knew everyone in the village, knew everything they hoped for and worried about and every prayer they had uttered. But she did not know their names. She addressed them by the jobs they did.

The stranger could suddenly feel this brother, this Isaac, come out from inside a curtain's great folds and stand on what felt now like a darkened stage. How big our creation had seemed before, how entire, only one small opening to keep shut, one river to dredge for trespassing objects—a watch that reappears mangled on the sand, the leg of a faraway, unknowable chair. Now it was a wooden platform, a puppet theater, with every seat empty. Isaac was real, somewhere. He thought about his brother, the potential children with their running noses and flattened hair. The door our village had built, opened and walked through only existed for us— to the rest of the world the only likely explanation for our silence was that we were dead. Not re-created, not wrapped in the wisps of clouds summoned from the sky just for us, but shot, drowned, worm-eaten, dismembered. Extinguished, just as we thought they had been. Mordecai, whoever he was—baker, butcher, jeweler— may not have been one of a hundred-and-some small gods, stirring the pot of the world. He may have been nothing bigger than a faraway someone's brother, the whole of their love for each other passed back and forth on thin sheets of paper. A man, two men, fifty men. Their bodies breaking down, bending a little closer to the beckoning ground with each swoop of the sun.

"Is that true?" the stranger asked a God who was official on the books but had never bothered to assure her he was listening. "Are we nothing but heel skin and blisters? Traveling a straight line to the end of our lives?" She flipped a black rock with a belt of white quartz in her hand. Tossed it one palm to the other. God was mute. What if that's the flaw? she wondered. He's up there on his glorious perch, eagle-eyed and all-knowing, unable to communicate but for his doughy fists shaken at the air, while we knock into the furniture, throw rocks through the windows, punch each other in the stomach, leave our new babies untended on the edge of the ravine.

Rather than feel pity for this helpless, voiceless God, the stranger hated him just then. If he could not solve his problem, how were the stupid, mush-brained ants on the ground supposed to solve theirs? As she grimaced and sighed, the stranger was folding the letter from faraway Isaac. She made one pointed end, and then another; she made a flat bottom, a space inside for a tiny person to sit. A boat. "Pray we will," she said. "Because you never know. But still." She put her fingertips in the hull of the small craft. "This might be utterly stupid," the stranger said to her shut-lipped God, "and maybe that's our specialty, us humans, but I made a promise to these people. We made a promise, we made a world, together. I am going to serve them. If it's an angel they want me to be, I'll look as winged as I can."

The Germans are everywhere, the child's chiming voice sang. *Americans say we will win the war, but I don't know. Come to where it's safe.*

"What would we do? Pack up everything in the world and start walking?" the stranger asked the darkness. "Mordecai's brother surely will not house us all, wherever he lives." The sky was feverish with stars by now. "We are in the middle of a project. We are trying to do the right thing. What if the safest place we can be is on our river-wrapped island?" She sharpened all the boat's creases. "Have your wars," she said. "We'll stay here and be peaceful." To bury this letter like the unread others would have felt like an attempt to deny it, like a counterargument. The letter did not feel dangerous to the stranger. It was just a misplacement, a stray. Sometimes a fish gets stranded on the riverbank, but with luck, someone is there to toss it back into its right place.

The stranger knelt by the water and placed Isaac and Mordecai's boat on the fluttering surface. The boat nodded at her, *Yes yes yes*, then shook its head, *Never mind*. "Conviction. That's the hardest part," the stranger agreed with the boat. But in a minute, the vessel found its steadiness, and it used the light of the risen moon to stay traceable as it sailed straight out of the known world. Just like that, slipping through the gauze, and ceasing to exist. If there ever was an Isaac, he had brought his hat to his heart and bowed for the empty seats; he had exited stage left and fallen into the darkness.

The barn by lamplight that night was the same as the barn by lamplight every other night. The letter had changed nothing. The idea that it ever could have seemed stupid to the stranger. It was as meaningless as our village's bones will be, unearthed a million years after we finally fall to rest. The stranger still planned to keep guard, to bury the mail, to throw intrepid debris back into the river, but she was glad to let the curtain fall back over the stage, to believe that ours was the only world, despite any evidence to the contrary. In that little paper ship, the stranger had sent all the questions we might have asked away. In its wake: quiet, for a thousand days.

Truth belongs to the place where it lives, like a plant, she thought. That the mountains are spiny with beech trees does not make the valley's foot-soft grasses jealous. That one world is at war does nothing to interrupt the patient churning of peaceful years someplace far away.

THE BOOK OF SONGS

In my new life, Kayla, wanting the sweet candy of progress, prodded me by pointing to herself and saying the word *Mother* over and over. In front of Hersh and Kayla were the ravaged remains of a lamb's leg. In front of me was a bowl of mashed peas—food for a toothless little girl. I looked at the peas and realized that I no longer found them strange. Stupid human, I thought, stupid animal. Don't you see how awful this is? But I had simply done what we all do every day: gotten used to how things were. I watched Kayla chirping, "Mother, mother, mother," and knew that whenever I was ready I could parrot the word back, perfect and crisp. I liked knowing this. It was a treasure I could hoard, and hoard I did until my new aunt began to give up on me.

"Sometimes I think we should take her to the healer," Kayla

told Hersh. "What if she has some kind of problem?" She served herself a new glob of potatoes.

I bounced in my chair, trying to look like a baby who was, at this very instant, growing a little. I wiggled my patent leather shoes. If nothing else, I felt I had earned some acclaim for my performance. Disappointment was so pervasive in my life that I could hardly sort it from any other feeling. Yet I had not considered that Kayla could ever be disappointed in *me*. Was there something I had forgotten to give up? Some sacrifice I had missed the opportunity to make?

"She doesn't have any problems. She's learning," Hersh said.

I bounced and shook my fists. I tried to make my face sweet and unknowing.

Kayla frowned. I bounced. Kayla rolled her eyes. "That's all she does all day."

I looked Kayla straight in the eye and said, "Mother!" Kayla's hand flew to her heart. She wiped the tears from her cheek, replacing them with a delicate smear of potato. She looked at Hersh and shook her head. That Kayla had food on her cheek and did not know it made me strangely sad. Growing up saves a person none of the tiny humiliations. Forgetting my supposed age, I reached out with my napkin to clean it, but she slapped my hand, as if I were a fly.

"Yes!" she cried. "Yes! That's me! Mother! Me!" Then, not wanting to perform unless it was going to be a standing ovation, I turned to Hersh and smiled my big, toothy smile and said, "Father!" Hersh in turn put his hand on his heart and wiped the tear from his eye and shook his head and said, "Yes! That's me! Father! I'm your father!" I bounced in my chair, receiving the accolades.

"Bullfight!" I yelled. "Fire! River! Hunger!"

"Oh, she is learning so much!" Hersh exclaimed.

"Too much! Too much!" Kayla yelled, covering her ears. "I want to be the only words she knows for now. Where did she learn all those other horrible words?"

I cast my eyes to the ground and stopped talking. "She's sorry," Hersh said. "She's too smart for her own good. That's what happens when we don't teach her ourselves. She'll learn all the wrong things."

"Mother! Mother! Father! Mother!" I tried.

"She's so sorry," Hersh said again.

Kayla cried that she wanted my world to be small so that they could keep track of it. "I can protect her from six or ten things. I don't know if I can protect her from seven hundred or four million things."

"We teach her to protect *herself*," he tried. "That is our only job in the world."

"Mother," I said quietly. "Father."

Kayla sobbed as if her daughter had died. Hersh whispered to her what a privilege it was to get to pass the world down, the world as they saw it. In any order, with any particular meaning. "We could teach her that the trash can is the most beautiful of things— or the sapling or the butter knives. She will always live in the world we give her."

Kayla blew her nose into Hersh's sleeve. "It's so hard to be a mother," she told him. "I had no idea how much I would be asked to give away. Just as I have gotten to know her one way, I have to see her grow into something else. How much am I supposed to bear?"

Hersh's chair squeaked when he pushed it out to rest a hand on the broad expanse of his wife's back. "A few minutes ago you were telling me she was too slow."

"Being a mother is impossible," Kayla cried. "*Impossible*. Every single part breaks my heart." Being a daughter was so hard that I had not considered anything in the future could match it. If I made it through this, I had expected to be safe. But the world was busy inventing new ways to sacrifice every day. A lifetime of them. A heavy stone sank to the bottom of my stomach.

Hersh said to his wife, "Come with me into the day. Let's show our beautiful girl where she lives. Just us, her mother and her father, her very own parents. One thing at a time."

My uncle took me into his spidery arms. Kayla popped open her big black umbrella, which turned the rain into a percussion instrument, a drumbeat building up to the revelation of the world. On the street, Hersh said, "This is a street. You have seen it before but you wouldn't have known what to think of it. We use it to get from one place to another. We carry the rocks from the mountains and we lay them down to walk on. The horses walk on them, the bugs walk on them, the people."

"A bug, a mountain, a rock, a person—you're naming things that she does not know. She can't understand anything you're saying," Kayla scolded.

"A rock," he started, and knelt down, put his hands on the street.

"This is a rock. My hand is touching a rock. This is a hand. Fingers, these are fingers. To touch is when you put one thing against another thing." He touched me on the arm. "This is touching," he said.

I nodded. "Touching," I repeated obediently.

We had made it no farther than the first corner of the first street closest to our home, and still we were surrounded by so much that it was almost impossible to know where to begin.

"You haven't said about the mountains or the horses," Kayla prodded.

"The mountains are huge mounds of the earth. The earth is everything, the earth is the earth. The horses are what make us a living, because people, that's us, we like to ride on the horses to get places. We go on the horses on the streets and end up somewhere new. I make the saddles so that it's easier to ride. The saddle is made of leather, which is the skin of another animal. Not the skin of a horse, because that would be cruel, but the skin of a cow."

"Where do people go on the horses?" Kayla asked.

"The mountains maybe, the sea. The sea is where the rivers go, the rivers are what feed the sea. The sea is hungry for the rivers. The people do not live in the sea. We like to visit it, to go inside, but cannot live there. It's because of air. Air is what we breathe." He breathed loudly to demonstrate. "Like that. That is breathing. We have to do it or we die. Dying is the end, maybe. It's either the end or the beginning. It always happens, even if you are very good."

"Hersh?" Kayla asked. "I think it's too much. We don't have to tell her the bad things yet." But he kept on, he could not keep anything a secret anymore.

"When you die you do not breathe. When you do not breathe

you die. If you were to jump into the river and swim for a very long time until you got tired, you would start to sink down, and when you could not keep your head up in the air anymore, you would take water into your body and that would be the end of the breathing. You would sink to the bottom. The bottom, the dirt, is the last place to go."

I nodded at Hersh in understanding. "The bottom," I said. This was something I felt I understood. It felt good to be given back the words with which to describe my world. Like being paid. I imagined all the conversations I would be able to have with my new words.

"Please stop," Kayla begged.

"But flowers and trees grow out of the dirt. It's what makes all other life possible. It's the earth, the earth which is everything."

As Hersh talked we all slumped lower. We did not stand straight, but felt the weight of all the words, of all the things, of the ways all the things were the same and different from all the other things. Nothing was safe. Nothing was free from a name or a place in the world. If we wanted to start naming, we would have to never stop.

"When you say Mother it means Kayla. When I say Mother it means a woman who is dead. She died but I did not die yet. I have to keep living, to take care of you. No one has a choice about this. We do not decide when we die."

We slumped so low we had no choice but to sit on the side of the road, in a puddle under a willow tree. We leaned against one another. Kayla put her head on Hersh's shoulder, I put my head in Kayla's lap, Hersh leaned down to the ground. Kayla did not protest anymore, she just listened half-eared to the accounting. Hersh kept talking quietly, lost in the maze. And I kept exact track, trying to remember what I was allowed to know now.

"A choice is what your mother and I made when we had you. We asked for you. To ask is when you say please. To say is to use your mouth to make words. Words are what we say. We is all of us. We are all we."

We lay back on the ground. We put our heads on the stones, the stones from the mountains, the mountains from the earth. The earth from the bottom. All of it soaked with rain, puddles tugging the fabric of our clothes.

"God is also what we all are. God is more than anything. More is more. Anything is God. There is no way to say God without saying Everything."

The rain hit us on our skin. The stones rounded our backs. The calling of a dog was answered by the calling of another dog. We closed our eyes and Hersh and Kayla did not say words for a long time. They breathed. All that happened was everything.

"I give up," Kayla said, closing her eyes. "There is too much."

"We have time," Hersh told her.

"We have nothing. We need help. Hire all the teachers you can so Lena knows how to protect herself against every awful thing in the world. This child will never grow up if we don't."

I closed my eyes and prepared for the next wave to cover me.

The Committee for What We Have and Where We Have It was made up of the barber, the greengrocer and the greengrocer's wife—who had appointed herself an auditor because she insisted any accuracy in her husband's work was due to luck, not diligence.

The Committee for What We Have and Where We Have It found that some people were coming up short. Without outsiders to sell his jewelry to, the jeweler was struggling. The banker's piles of coins were smaller because money was not being saved up but constantly traded. Yet when the jeweler proposed he learn to help grow and harvest wheat instead of repair watches and set gems in gold, we hated the idea. What good was a little town without a friendly, nearsighted man from whom to purchase gifts to mark the moments of our lives? Women refused to imagine their days without that window display to dream over, and men had a hard time knowing how else they might express their ongoing devotion. While it was true that nothing new entered our village—no money, no clothes, no fruit—nothing left it, either. The plants offered new seeds, and evidently enough sunlight filtered through the clouds, because the plants kept growing. It would be sufficient for all of us, if we managed it right. We voted to pay everyone enough in bread, in meat, in milk, to continue to do the jobs they were put in our town to do. Instead of money, we traded goods. The banker's job began to include keeping track of IOUs—for this pair of earrings made of rubies, which the greengrocer wanted for his wife, he would deliver a basketful of vegetables at the start of each week for three months. For the service of making sure everything was fair, the banker was given a little of what everyone else earned.

Once they had catalogued and remedied shortfalls, the Committee for What We Have and Where We Have It set to work on a map. They paced the edges of our village, feet one in front of the other, toe to heel in a jagged circle. Their finding was that it took 10,034 of the barber's feet to circle the village. That number tickled us. A total, an exact and complete measure of the space we occupied. We asked the Committee for What We Have and Where We Have It to measure more. The banker was found to have the biggest house but the smallest windows. The chicken farmer had the smallest house but the tallest door.

When they had measured everything big and logged it, the jeweler, whose whole life had been lived based on miniature objects, begged them to find a way of measuring things that were small. They devised two new lengths of measurement: the length of the barber's left first finger, and the full moon of his thumbnail. The Committee for What We Have and Where We Have It grew tired of being chased with unmeasured brooms, butter dishes, baby shoes. They voted among themselves on a rule to measure things only at the start of each month when the moon was new. The rest of the time they would draw a map of the village and keep an inventory of all our belongings. At the end of one week of counting they showed us the first list.

Zalischik, Population: 102
Baby Shoes: 53 (26 pairs, 1 single)
Spoons: 478
Forks: 498
Full-Grown Trees: 190
Vegetable Gardens: 49
Houses: 22

Barns: 1

Doors: 61

Windows: 208

Wedding Dresses: 25

Strangers: 1

Horses: 2

Chickens: 50

Cows: 41

Sheep: 179

Goats: 137

Rivers: 1

Precious Gems: 32

Fake Gems: 299

Shovels: 109

Once the physical things were counted, we wanted a census of the rest of our lives. After some time, the Committee for What We Have and Where We Have It marched out of the back of the greengrocer's store where they met, and posted a new list on the statue of the long-dead war hero in the middle of the town square. The greengrocer's wife said, "The list is too long to post. Here are your top ten. No further items will be added at this time." We crowded around to read it.

Overbearing Mothers-in-Law: 11

Regrets in Matters of Love: 1,987

Regrets in the Matters of Money: 200

Secret Crushes: 6

Overdue Apologies: 712

Objects Believed to Be Lucky, but Not Proven to Be
So: 353

Objects Proven to Be Lucky: 3

Refutes to That Proof: 4

Concerns of Being Forgotten: 102

Recurring Dreams of an Explicit Nature, Treasured
but Never Told: 42

At Kayla's insistence, time sped up. Over the next months, I learned to crawl over the knotted wood floor and then to walk. Hersh and Kayla set themselves up on chairs at opposite ends of the kitchen and sent me back and forth like a ball. I wobbled a little for them. They gasped and giggled and grabbed at me. They took me into their arms when I made it, triumphant, and kissed me on each swath of skin. I was spoon-fed potatoes, mashed carefully, chunkless. I was never again given my aunt's dry breast. At the end of each day I said my small prayer for the right thing to happen, and I told my real mother and father, "This is how I love you." I was marching in the right direction, back toward my true self. I knew I would not get all the way there—even at eleven and a half, I would still be living in the wrong house—but progress was progress.

I learned to eat with a fork. I learned to tie a shoe. I learned the difference between a palomino and a cricket. I learned to write my name and the word *love*. I learned to take my napkin from the table and unwrap it on my lap. The music teacher was rehired. The barber's sister was hired to teach me how to walk with several books stacked on my head, because my mother had heard this was important. The house was a flood of learning and teaching. If there was a thing that you could learn to do, I had a teacher for it. Kayla wanted me to learn languages, even when Hersh reminded her that other languages might have come from other places, and there were no such things. "I don't care where they came from or didn't," Kayla said. "People know words, and I want Lena to know them, too." I already had a lot of Russian and Polish, and so it was that the jeweler began to teach me English, the butcher drew flash cards for me in German, Hersh taught me the fundamentals of Italian, and the sheep shearer set out to make me understand French.

Kayla sat at the table every morning with a list of all the lessons she needed to teach me about love and loss and God and potatoes and churning butter and crushing pepper and washing decent linens and better linens. Lessons about making lace, covering a wound, throwing a ball and untangling a knot. I needed to know how to pray well, how to sit straight, how to write a heartfelt condolence letter and a gracious invitation. I had to become proficient at keeping clean, mending a dress, buttering my bread like a lady and knowing which cuts of meat were which.

Kayla filled hundreds of sheets of paper this way, papers that gathered in the house like snow, dusting everything at first and then getting swept into corners or under the furniture, where they sat in banks waiting their turn. Kayla scolded herself for time lost coddling and swooning when she should have been teaching. Hersh tried to remind her how much she loved being the mother of a baby, how sweet those days had been. He did not say how hard he had worked to make such sweetness possible, and how much he himself had loved it, too.

True to the original deal, every few weeks was a year of my life: I was four, I was eight, I was ten again. We had little birthday parties, Kayla's and Hersh's faces aglow with time's miraculous passage.

But it did not stop as Hersh had planned.

Kayla rushed me along, right past myself. I was eleven, and then I was twelve. I was thirteen. I was suddenly meant to be complete. At night I peered into the oval-shaped mirror that hung above my dresser. I saw my face, which was pinkish, surrounded by dark brown curly hair. I looked unremarkable to myself. Like a person, a girl, no one in particular. Day by day, I checked for differences, and to my surprise, they started showing up. The same freckles on my forehead, but a different shape to my jaw. The same inward slant to my front teeth, but a new pitch in my voice. I climbed on a chair and took the mirror down, its cool frame in my hands, and passed it down my body so I could see what my chest looked like, my belly, my legs. I found the long, straight line of a girl was curving a bit, rounding at the hips. Strands of hair had begun to appear. My nipples peered tentatively out, bigger and softer than before.

That night, I spit all over the bed again. I rubbed it in. "I am alive here," I said to myself. "I know what I know." I tried to smell myself on the pillow—my hair had been there, I could tell. There were strands left, long brown snakes reclining. "Bullfight, rain, horse, saddle, hunger, hair, life," I said to myself, trying to hold all of it. But it wasn't those things I worried about forgetting—those things were presented to me each day, a list of activities and lessons and facts about the world. What I could feel slipping off me was my original life. Even while I aged at impossible speeds, the years piling up around me day by day, I could feel myself getting smaller, getting thinner, losing words, losing the memory of my real house and my real family and the smell of cabbage in the kitchen. "Cabbage," I said, "cabbage, cabbage, cabbage, cabbage."

I wrote the word down on my list, underlined it. "My house smells like cabbage. My house is one room. My mother is not my mother. My father is not my father. Is this how I love them? Am I alive in this place?" It was getting easier and easier to think of them as Perl and Vlad, the way everyone else did. For this I pinched myself hard on the arm until my nails left two moons.

Mine was an instant decision. I did not think about what would happen after, or how long before someone dragged me back. I was going home. I would sleep the night in my old bed with my old family around, and I did not care what happened next. I put my shoes on and slipped out the back door. I pressed my fists to my eyes for a minute, and when they came away the shimmer of darkness moved aside to reveal a milky, moonlit path toward home. My nightgown fluttered. It was not raining at that moment but the town had its misty coat on. I felt wonderful, walking alone in the right direction.

My cheeks filled with blood when I saw the house, and then the door. The door with its brass handle, wet under my hand. But when I turned it, my hand only slipped. The door was locked. I repeated it to myself in disbelief. "The door is locked." Had one of my parents always slid that latch, keeping me and the others safe inside? Now I was one of the people being kept out. I put my ear against the wood but I could not hear my family inside. I did not knock. I had wanted to appear there, to slip back in unnoticed. Not to be asked inside like a guest. I lay down on the stoop and listened to the breeze flip a dead leaf over and over across the ground. It was a treeless leaf, an orphan, caught on an instant breeze. Something invisible carried it. I kissed the brass doorknob on the big blue door, and I stood up to go.

I was truly no longer the cabbage picker's youngest daughter. They had locked the door behind me. In order to grow, to become the Lena that my new parents invented, I ate my way through the stale heels of bread and dry bits of cake under the bed, left over from my days as a hungry baby. I even ate the ants, who feasted despite imminent danger. I felt them walking the hills of my tongue, trudging through the wet cave. I stopped chewing and paid attention to their needle-feet. I swallowed them whole. I thought of them in my stomach, continuing to eat, the food prechewed for them, readily enjoyable. I ate the food until it pushed out against me. I ate the food until it hurt. I closed my eyes, full of bread and ants. From outside came the sound of dogs howling to track each other in the dark, calling out the difference between one dog's home and the other's. Inside the room, exhausted, I tried to stretch out the hours of peaceful night before the sun threw light down on me again, woke me up into another day of growing.

The next morning, I sneaked out early and went on two missions. First, I visited the stranger. "Do I survive this?"

"Yes," she answered, firmly.

"How?"

"You just do." I told her it was a disappointing answer, but thank you anyway, and I left her alone. I found the Committee for What We Have and Where We Have It doing their dawn mapping in the bakery. I pulled them outside into an abandoned shed. "Quickly," I said. The shed still held a few rusted old spades. Mice and bugs must have happily lived in the walls, but they did not skitter or scratch. The wood smelled rich and ripe, full of the sweet butter of near-collapse.

"Measure me," I demanded, knowing that the next new moon, the next measuring day, was weeks away.

"Okay, okay, no need to be rude," the greengrocer said. This was a dutiful committee and they began at the bottom. Toes, feet, ankle to knee, knee to hip, hip to shoulder.

"That looked like more than one and a half fingers to me," the greengrocer's wife nagged. The barber inchwormed his finger along my forearm again.

"It's exactly one and a half," the greengrocer said.

"I wouldn't say *exactly*." The greengrocer's wife scrunched her nose.

I asked, "Am I bigger than before? Am I smaller than before?"

"It's the first time we've measured you," the baker said. "How old are you?" I shook my head. "Sure, kid, you're bigger. You're growing, just like you should be."

The greengrocer's wife whispered into my ear, "Let me know if you need help with how to fasten a brassiere. We also sell other items."

My heart fluttered its wings, but did not manage to escape my chest. It was contained in the prison of my body. "Am I supposed to be older or younger?" I asked the greengrocer. "Am I supposed to be thinner or fatter? Am I supposed to remember or forget?" He put his hand on my cheek.

"You're a sweet girl," he said. "What you're doing is not easy. Growing up never is."

I looked at the committee members with begging eyes.

"Look," the greengrocer's wife said. "You'll grow for a while and then you'll shrink again. I used to be able to see over the fence in the yard, now I have to look through the slats. Your size doesn't really matter." The promise of this comforted me and I saw a tiny, frail, shaky-legged version of myself—either very old or very young—toddling down a wide street, going unnoticed by the world around me.

I took the barber's warm palm and placed it over my heart. "Count," I commanded.

"Your heartbeats?" he asked. I nodded. The two of us closed our eyes and concentrated. The greengrocer and his wife were quiet. "That was twenty beats," the barber said, and then, because my face must still have been full of questions, he added, "Very strong. Very healthy. You are doing fine."

The shed seemed to lean a little to the left, like a sleeping person shifting for comfort. I opened the squeaking door and released the committee back into the light of that day. I imagined not just stepping out of the shed, but stepping out of my own skin layer by layer, leaving shells of myself everywhere, crisp and translucent, until I was just a tiny pink snake of a girl, hidden in the shade of a small stone.

The widow never became a better voice teacher. She came and she sat and she drank her glass of vodka and she scolded and then she fell asleep.

After the teacher left, Kayla said, "Let me hear you sing."

I hedged. "Later. I don't want to ruin the surprise."

So Kayla said, "What a fabulous idea, a surprise concert! We will invite everyone." Then a look of stunned excitement passed over her face. "Your coming-of-age ceremony!" she said, staring at the wall. Kayla saw a vision of me in a starched dress with flushed cheeks, and around me a roomful of admirers, their complete attention on the young woman. "Young *woman!*" Kayla squealed. In the crowd of admirers there would be young men, appreciative young men, hopeful young men, potential husbands. "A husband. A *wedding.*" Kayla sighed.

"A what?"

"Don't act like you aren't ready for a husband soon. It's only natural," Kayla snapped. She got a faraway look in her eye. "Oh, oh, yes," she cooed.

I tilted my head down, headed out into a strong wind.

That weekend, everyone gathered in our sitting room. The baker, the doctor, the sheep farmer, the chicken farmer, the weaver, the banker, his wife and their small army with Igor at the head, the stranger and the jeweler, who insisted on sitting close to her and unwrapping candies for her to suck on, the gossips, the mothers and the fathers, the man with no left eye, the healer, the children, the butcher, the axe maker, the sheep shearer, the grandparents and the babies, the wives and husbands, everyone. It was pouring outside and the kitchen held a dozen stacks of heavy coats, puddles forming beneath them.

Sitting in the front were Perl, Vlad, Regina and Moishe. I had anticipated this meeting. I had torn my list of known objects into four pieces. They were secreted away in my pocket, waiting.

"This is a celebration of Lena's life," Kayla announced, everyone's fingers dusty with sugar from the plates of cookies. "Our little Lena, who is a woman now."

They looked at me as if they did not exactly see a woman, though they did not see a girl, either.

"Kayla," Hersh said quietly. "Do we know what we think we know?"

"My husband the philosopher," Kayla joked. "Lena is a woman now. I raised her myself, of course I know." No one said anything different. "Think of your sons. Will they be looking for a good wife?" She passed around a dish of Linzer torte baked by me and asked that everyone please be silent while they enjoyed the confection. "Focus," she told them, "focus on the cookie." Then Kayla told me to demonstrate my horse-riding skills by trotting around the living room.

"Trot?" I asked. "You want me to pretend I have a horse?" I looked for the stranger, who knew how to become what others needed. She was waiting for my eyes to find hers. Her signal was a short, decisive nod. She was trying to offer a fact: you are you. You still are. I was red with embarrassment, but I trotted. Hersh tried not to look upset. He loved his wife and I knew he wanted her to feel supported. And me, too, prancing as if I were a horse, as if I were a girl and a horse at the same time. Was this right? Kayla stopped me and everyone clapped. My next trick was to count to ten in all of my languages. This was the thing I was actually proud of.

Kayla stood up next to me and said, "The widow, where is the widow?"

Everyone looked around the room. None of the faces belonged to our large, frowning widow. "She isn't here," I said.

"How could she not be here? It doesn't matter. You are the star. Sing for us, Lena. Sing us your song." She turned to the audience and said, "Lena is learning to be a star on the opera stage. Are you ready to see what that looks like?" The audience clapped, looking as if they did very much want to see what that looked like.

"Presenting! Lena!" She sat down to applause, like a burst of thunder.

I did not start singing, because I did not know how to sing.

The room became sticky with silence. Outside, rain wanted in. I vibrated with fear at the center of our circle. With quiet crawling all over everyone's skin, making us itch, and with quiet seeping into our ears, the barber caught my eye and put his hand over his heart. He patted it, ba-bump, ba-bump, to remind me that I was alive, that I was all right. I opened my mouth, and what I did was I howled. I howled like a lost dog. I howled and I howled and I howled, filling my lungs with air and howling again. My voice cracked but I still howled. Dogs all around began to sing with me. They joined in and in until the whole neighborhood was an eruption of music. Every ear in the room was stuffed full of howl.

It was clear that people were confused. People were worried. They might have thought that maybe I was not a girl anymore. What could I be? Could I be a wolf? But I howled with such happiness, with such completeness, with the wild hillside dogs and the tame village dogs in full appreciation, full agreement, that the villagers' faces began to crack and joy replaced concern.

"Listen to that girl go," they said to one another.

"She is really howling now," the jeweler whispered.

"Have you ever heard anything like this?" the greengrocer asked, shaking his head. Kayla stood up and put her hand on my shoulder. She was breathing like a bird, small huffs of air. But I did not stop. I did not care that Kayla was there, huffing at me. Kayla looked at Hersh, her eyes desirous of any help at all, but Hersh stayed put.

Perl smiled. Perl looked at the girl she had given birth to, standing in the center of all the people in the village, making my very loud noise. She and Vlad held hands tightly.

The stranger began to laugh. Not the laugh of mocking but the laugh of total enjoyment. The jeweler joined. Pretty soon everyone was laughing, everyone was shaking, everyone's eyes were spilling out. Igor and his gang clapped and hooted. Then they started to join me in my howl. They opened their dark mouths and like the pack that we were, we sounded our collective call. We are all here, our voices said. This is our home, our turf, our valley. We have peed all over it, slept all over it, dreamed all over it, renamed it. No one is here except all of us. I howled and we howled and the dogs sang back to all of us.

The widow was the only person in town who was not there. She was asleep in her chair with her stick and her bottle. She had thought this would be the end of her. I would sing terribly, she would lose her job and she would have no choice but to slowly eat her own arms and legs. Despite the rules in place to look out for one another, the widow was prepared for the very worst she could imagine. Our howling must have seeped into her drunken sleep and hushed her up—the whole world singing at the same time like that, not a learned song but a known song, the long, shrill note of simple existence.

When I finally stopped, the dogs went on. We ate the rest of the Linzer torte. We milled and we chatted.

"That felt great," people said to me. "Thank you for leading us in such a tremendous howl."

"You can be our official town howler," they added. The dogs kept up, the dogs celebrated on into the night, after people had started to go home, after the streets echoed with footsteps.

The stranger put her hands on my shoulders, and her face, always so unmoved, spread in a wide smile. "That's how," the stranger said to me. "That's how you survive it."

I caught sight of Regina sneaking Moishe away. I followed them, unnoticed. She showed him the bedroom where I lived, where Regina herself had lived for one very dark night. I stood outside the door to listen.

"It could have been me up there," Regina said. I could hear the music box begin in the middle of a phrase.

"I'm the only one who never lived here," Moishe said. "Is she still our sister?"

"I think so," Regina told him. I smiled.

"Let's leave her a note," he said. They rooted around in the drawers and then Moishe dictated, *Dear Lena, Good job. We liked the sweets. You are getting to be an excellent howler. Love, Sister and Brother.*

Regina recounted her one night in the house, playing daughter to her aunt and uncle. She remembered how Kayla had stood next to her before bed, both of them in their nightgowns, and measured Regina's height against her own. "What have they been feeding you?" she had asked.

"Cabbage," Regina said.

"No more of that, then." Regina said she could hear, through her wall, her aunt and uncle talking all night. She could not make out words, but their talk was never punctuated with laughter, no sign of the joy of being new parents in their voices. In the morning, Kayla came in and began to fold Regina's clothes back up. "Time to go home," Kayla said.

"Can I have the music box?" Regina asked.

"No, dear, that belongs to our daughter."

My old family was the last to leave. Kayla, Hersh, Perl and Vlad and I stood in an open circle. "Your daughter is wonderful," Vlad said. I could tell he wanted to put his hand on my head, maybe bury his fingers in my hair, pick me up and hold me like his very own child. Instead he said, "Congratulations." One of the world's most inadequate words.

"Thank you," Kayla said, stealing the praise for herself. I wished I could take myself apart, distribute the pieces around. A leg for my old parents, an arm for each of the new. I imagined myself rolling on the floor, limbless, making my noise.

"Thank you for everything," Perl said. Regina and Moishe put their faces up to my ears, one on each side. "We miss you," they whispered together. I smiled and slipped each of them a note. I hugged Perl and Vlad. Their arms around me were so familiar, the exact scent of their necks, that I grew dizzy and my vision filled with stars. I managed to feed notes into their pockets.

I opened the door of my new house and let my old family out into the cold, star-spattered world. The rain had quieted. The streets, the moon, the bugs and the clouds received the old family. Four notes, four treasures, waited in their pockets.

Kayla and Hersh bustled around the house, cleaning up, not knowing exactly what to say to me. I had been a hit, but it had not been the debut they had meant to host. Despite all their best efforts, they had raised a different kind of animal.

Moishe would find his note that night when he took his jacket off and hung it by the door. *Moishe, This is how I love you—sweat, spit, hoof, home, mother, face. I almost remember who you are.* Regina would find hers next, when her brother sent her looking. *Regina, This is how I love you—cut, basket, cabbage, God, marble, big, less. I almost remember who you are.* Vlad discovered his note in the morning, trying to keep his hands warm on his way to work, his boots and the mud kissing sloppily as he went. *Vlad, This is how I love you—mouse, bed, fingernail, missing, hot, fire, lie. I almost remember who you are.* Perl stayed inside all day, did not put her coat on, did not stick her hands in the pockets, and so the note stayed there until that evening when she went to stand outside to look at the world, just to smell the wet bark of the trees and listen to the birds peck and sing. My words were louder than any of the world's other songs. *Perl, This is how I love you*—as she held the worn piece of paper in her trembling hands—*dog, pillow, mask, cabbage, kiss, shovel.* Perl imagined each item as a creature at her feet, an army her daughter had summoned to look after her. *I almost remember who you are,* the note read. "I almost remember who I am, too," Perl said, and the sky answered her with a yellow lip of sunlight at the edge of the mountains, and the trees answered her with leaves, and the birds answered her with short, warbling calls while they shook their wings out and took flight.

· III ·

THE BOOK OF THE RIVER

Igor's face was ragged with pimples and his voice had only barely settled into itself. As he had done many times before—when each of his siblings came into the world—he sat at the edge of his mother's labor bed and fed her carefully cut bites of steak, spoonfuls of potato stew and glistening candies. He read to her from the Book of Children—adventure stories written by little brothers, where toad heroes caught in the talons of hawks were saved only by the smallest, most nimble of frogs. He read the rules for every marble game and the lists of names for dolls. Anna, Muffin, Leaf. Igor's mother did not thank him or squeeze his hand back. She had come to expect his kindness, to rely upon it. The suggestion that he did not owe it to her would have been absurd.

When Igor's mother yelped with the worst of the contractions, her husband did not come crashing up the stairs. She asked where he was, but no one knew. Probably lost in the glory of an account book's perfect columns, a tower of stacked coins. The banker's wife was cared for all the same. Igor rubbed his mother's scalp and hummed while his ten sisters and brothers sprawled on the bed, on the floor, their eyes half closed. Igor wetted his mother's forehead with cloths. The girls kissed her face. Two middle children went to get their father and the healer, while the youngest ones held their mother's feet in their cupped hands.

After a while, the banker threw the door open and yelled, "You are having a baby!" He had bread crumbs stuck in his mustache. The healer, following behind, told the banker they had nearly missed the birth of his child.

"*That* is the head of my son!"

"We have not determined the sex yet," the healer corrected.

"My son!"

The banker's wife yelled and spat and the healer yelled and spat and everybody pushed, even though only one of them really needed to. The baby, sure enough, became not just head but shoulders, arms, gut and legs. He became he. He became entire. He hardly cried at all, and only moved his fingers and toes. Before anyone else had even held him, he fell asleep on his mother's chest, exhausted by his entry into the world. She was nursed with squares of chocolate hand-fed to her by her eldest son. Her lips on Igor's fingertips were warm and soft.

Igor fell asleep at the foot of his parents' bed like a dog. He dreamed of being the only child in a houseful of mothers.

The following day, Igor and his family went out for a walk, for a victory lap. They wore their best boots. The baby slept through the whole adventure, while everyone gathered around him to greet the first new person to enter our world. Even the widow cooed when he came by.

"I do tatting lessons now," she said. "You know, lace."

"This baby is a son," the banker corrected her.

"Oh, well, I do shooting lessons, too." She cocked an imagined rifle.

Igor said, "I would like to learn to shoot." But his father brushed the idea away, saying, "She can't teach you, you're too old. She would have needed to start when you were a baby."

"To shoot?" Igor asked.

"To anything," the banker replied.

The baby looked like a little old man with his crinkled face. People were certain that a baby born a little ugly in an old man sort of way would grow up to do great things. It was a story we could not remember. Something about already having his father's soul, or about how ugly is really beautiful turned inside out, or wrinkles are lucky.

When the baby was set to celebrate his four-day birthday, the banker's wife opened her eyes and she stretched out her arm and she tried to remember the dream she was having. There were fruit trees and there were rivers, but the rest was lost. She looked over at her husband and smiled at the pillow lines on his cheek. She looked down at her son, and she screamed. He was just sticking out from under his father's body, and he was blue. Sometime in the night, there had been rolling and turning and the little, perfect, slightly-ugly-in-a-good-way baby had been suffocated by the weight of his father.

Igor heard the scream and came running. Fault—he had left the baby, he had not kept watch—tapped him on the back. The banker woke up and saw what he had done. Igor's mother pulled the baby out from under her husband and she put his dead mouth on her breast and watched as the milk drained down her body, purposeless. Igor had no way to help. His hands were hunks of flesh, his eyes were marbles rolling away, his heart was a rhythmless drum. The unbidden wish for a warm hand, a steady hand, placed quietly on his back, made his eyes sting.

"Wake up, wake up. You're four days old today. You are the baby I had. Wake up," his mother said. She seemed certain that if she could say enough, if she could construct the argument, God would change his mind. There was no shortage of reasons—the baby's size, his future entirely unchipped, pristine. Igor's father put his hands on the baby's back while it did not nurse. He cried himself out. He tried to hold his breath and die but he kept gasping. His body kept him alive despite all his best efforts.

Igor felt God close his curtains and leave the banker's family alone on the earth's crust. Igor felt everything slow down. His blood, his breath, his thoughts. He felt like he was melting. "Am I awake?" he asked, which made his father cry yet harder. When his mother looked at him, her eyes were churned pools, silt and mud rising from the bottom. She looked away, disgusted by herself, by being seen that way.

Slowly, the other living children gathered in a circle around their parents. They were a wall keeping the world out of this moment. No birdsong, no blown wind, no water dropped from the sky, no evidence of life. They said the prayers they knew and the prayers they did not. Igor closed his eyes and told his parents, "I am so tired," and he lay down on the floor.

And outside in the world, people kept trading money for fruit and fruit for hammers, knowing nothing of the death of the first new life or what would occur because of it. In everyone's root cellars were congratulatory canned apples and sympathetic canned potatoes, and we would need every jar.

Kayla sent Hersh, uncertain, uneasy, but obedient Hersh, door-to-door, measuring, inspecting, trying to win over any marriageable young man inside. He brought hard candies in foil wrappers, cookies in wax paper. Small sculptures of horses for the boys, nice wooden spoons for the mothers and strong tea for the fathers. He remarked on the beauty his girl was turning into.

The fathers of sons said, "She's a lovely girl."

Hersh said, "Lovelier every day."

The mothers of sons said, "It wouldn't be so bad to let her grow up a little."

Hersh said, "She grows so much we can hardly keep up. Growing is *not* the problem." The mothers and fathers of sons accepted the chocolates and the teas and the wooden spoons.

They chatted about the progress of our existence, the state of this and that. The beets were on the soft side, but the potatoes were delicious; money was not as plentiful as anyone had hoped; the weather, the weather, the weather. When could we look forward to some sun? "We will become aquatic soon," Hersh joked.

When he left, the fathers of sons said, "Thank you for the gifts. Your daughter will no doubt find a good husband, in time."

"I am trying to do the right thing. I'm trying to do as my wife asks," Hersh said, wanting to explain, to apologize, to find a way of loving simultaneously everything he loved: me in my growing, Kayla in her mothering, the new world asking questions no one knew how to answer yet.

"In this, the beginning of the world, I think we're all trying to do as our wives ask," the fathers of sons assured.

Hersh kicked a rock down the cobbles, enjoying the tink it made against each set stone. Free rock on caught rock, showing off. At the banker's house, the windows were draped in black fabric, which caused Hersh's heart to fall in his chest. He knew what black fabric over the windows meant. Death, the idea of death, struck him across the head like a punch. No one had died yet in the new world. We had lost nothing we ourselves had not pushed out. He stood on the stoop's reed mat, cleaned his boots but did not knock. A loss so final seemed nearly impossible to him, almost absurd. The End, he said to himself, and it did not make sense. He examined the hair on the backs of his hands, considered how air felt in his nose. Hersh was alive, every bit of him was so alive. Losing one part made sense—his arms could die, his skin could fall off—but not everything. Not at once.

The door was cold and solid when Hersh leaned his forehead against it. What was lost was locked inside—everything beyond was blind and dumb to the fact of it. All it took was a door, and the day cooed along without sadness. Hersh imagined the banker's family in the dark, inside—which person he should erase from the picture he did not know—standing around a nest of eggs, incubating the hot yellow yolks of sorrow within. Soon, the eggs would hatch, and whatever creature sadness had made would fly out through the opened door.

Am I the one to let them out? Hersh asked. He knocked, curiosity enough to propel his knuckles. The stranger opened a seam in the door, her white face framed like a portrait. "I saw the curtains," Hersh said.

"Thank you for your concern. It's the baby. He died in his sleep." The eggs cracked. Our beautiful world waited to meet grief for the very first time. The wind changed, moved through Hersh's clothes like a ghost. His skin cooled.

I was supposed to be ready at any moment to become a screeching infant or a dying old woman, a wife. Except I was not ready for any of that, not ready or prepared. Aware of the possibility. Alert at best.

When Hersh's husband-finding mission had commenced, I escaped through the drizzling world to the river. I took my wash and my books and I went to a bend where the willows grew up high and the mud was red. On the opposite bank, I could almost make out the shapes of two deer drinking. I soaked and wrung my dresses and my uncle's underwear. I soaked and wrung Kayla's stockings. I let the sweat of their bodies wash downstream. I took my clothes off and got into the river, which was cold and smooth with silt. As I washed, I felt the new shapes my body made. Little hills on my chest, my waist deeper than before. How did it know what to do? My skin tightened in the cold.

I held on to an underwater branch to keep from drifting downstream, and I floated. The river did not ask my age or my purpose but kissed me blindly, the same as if I were an old man, a fish or a discarded chair. I thanked it for this.

On the bank the mud was mounded, curled around rocks, matted in the roots of the trees. The mud was full of small, hardshelled beetles. The mud was full of the sucking roots. The trunks of the trees rose out of the river as arms for the mud, ways for the mud to catch birds. Wind flashed over the mud's skin.

I hung the bodiless sacks of clothing over the branches and lay down, covered myself in muck, stained my skin the color of earth. I let the sky come down and the earth come up and press me between them.

"Can you tell who I am?" I asked. "What do you think, mud?"

The mud pulled at my fine hairs as it dried. The splitting felt deeper, like I might break down, pieces departing from pieces, until I was a shattered thing and the bugs could carry me away. But I was as whole as ever. The only thing I started to lose were tears, unreasonable, unspecific tears. I did not know if I was crying for the loss of something or for the weight of what I had gained. The mud did not care one way or another, it drank my sorrow up. I was a baby, then I was a teenager, and no one had ever asked me what it felt like. I could not have answered, but I would not have minded the question. Here I was, in the sloppy, thick muck, and it seemed to know how to make a place for me, to mold itself around my body. It was meeting me at all my edges. It was cold, but I did not want to move.

My hair lost its hope of being strands and instead became a mash of fibers. I sank down a little. The hands of the mud held my own hands, the arms of the mud held mine. My ears filled with the dark meat of the earth. It said, "We haven't forgotten you." Whispered, "You're home." Whispered, "We do, we do, we do remember who you are."

Hersh found Kayla working her knife over the skin of a potato until she had a tiny, naked globe in her hand. "The new baby," he started to say.

"Yes, I know. He's very cute," Kayla snapped, as surprised as Hersh was by her own jealousy.

"No," he told her, "not that. The baby is dead." Hersh looked away from his wife because he thought he might see a flush of relief in her cheeks.

"Dead?" she asked.

"Suffocated." Kayla put the potato down on the counter and stabbed the knife into it for safekeeping.

"Why?" she asked, and looked at her husband with the clear eyes of a child who has come upon a piece of nonsense everyone else takes as fact. Hersh had neither a sufficient answer nor an insufficient one. Wisdom ran away from him, comfort with it. "Lena!" Kayla burst out, desperate. My ears were far from there and I did not come running. "Lena!" she yelled louder.

"Maybe she's not here," he said.

"Oh, oh, oh!" Kayla picked up and put down the stabbed potato. She picked up and put down the chair she had been sitting in. Hersh recognized these as the movements of someone who has lost something, but their girl was too big to be discovered in the vague condensation under a skinned vegetable, or the footprint of a chair's skinny leg.

"What are you doing?" husband asked wife. He had not moved yet—he was waiting for the scene to make sense or come to a quiet stop.

"She's gone!" Kayla yelled. "She's gone!" She took from the shelf an iron soup pot and a wooden spoon, and ran outside, slamming wood against metal, shouting, "Help! Lena is missing! Lena is lost!"

When Kayla came to the banker's door, ringing her alarm pot, the stranger opened it and begged her to be quiet.

"What are you doing?" the stranger asked.

"Lena is missing!" Kayla shrieked.

"Please," the stranger said. "Please be quiet. The banker and his wife lost a baby today."

"And what of my grief?" Kayla wailed. She swung the spoon once, hard, on the pot. Sense, reason, were clearly going to melt like snow on the hot surface of Kayla's panic. "All right," the stranger whispered. "You stay here for a minute. We're going to find your daughter, but please. Please be quiet."

The stranger left the others with the banker's family, where the low ceiling pressed their grief back down each time it drifted for a moment. Igor had fallen asleep on the floor by the fire. Peace was a distant thing, but the truth of what happened had also fallen far away. His dreams were dim and chaotic. Ravens, wind, closed doors.

Kayla and Hersh were worried about whatever it was they were going to see—nothing, probably. The absence of their daughter. The places, hundreds of them, thousands, where I was not. The crooks of the trees, the trunks of the trees, the tall grass, the tall grass, the tall grass, the shelves where the chickens nested, their warm round forms atop a bed of possible kin, willing and warming them into existence, all empty of me.

"Maybe the Golem has her," Hersh said. "What's that story again?"

"I don't think we've written it yet," our stranger told him. "How should it go?"

"Well," he began, "the monster is made of mud and bugs and sticks. The monster is born out of the earth itself." He paused. "Is that a good start?"

"That's a very good start," our stranger assured him.

"Okay. So the monster is born out of the mud and he lives peacefully on worms and fish and small rodents."

"I don't think he lives peacefully at all," said Kayla. "I think he terrorizes the villagers and chews on their toes and steals their potatoes right out from under their knives. I think he falls in love with all the daughters and takes them away to live in the mud with him." She looked up at her husband, terror renewed. "Oh, dear! He's stolen Lena!"

My parents sped up, shined their lights on any dark thing. The row of lanterns along the riverbank bobbed. They dipped close to the water, scanned the bushes. Webs of branches came into relief in the light, then faded back into the darkness.

I unearthed myself, sat cobbled with mud, my complete arms around my complete knees, watching someone come to me. I had traced their approach, the giveaway of their lights making a line through the fields. I knew I would be found, would be washed, would be taken to bed. I knew I would be scolded and loved.

When the chain of lights came close, when the voices with *Lena* in them were in my ears, I stood up. I was myself, but crusted over and thicker. Rougher. My hair was one solid brown mass, my eyebrows and my eyelashes.

"Another stranger," the stranger whispered to herself. It was as if she were discovering herself on the shore, rescuing her own cold body from the water.

Hersh and Kayla came to the mudded person, ready to demand their daughter back. They saw my eyes and reached out together, scraped my arm and watched the brown crust fall off. Their lamps lit up their faces from below, making them look like masks, their cheekbones sunken, their chins jutting out.

The stranger recognized me, which meant she was still alone. She was still the only stranger. She turned her back to us so we would not see her face twist up.

"It's you," Hersh said.

"It's me," I answered.

"What were you doing?" Kayla wanted to know. Her voice was smoke, dissipating. The thing she was sure of—tragedy—disappeared.

"I was here. I am here."

"Why did you leave me?" Kayla whimpered.

"I didn't," I said. "I just came to do the laundry and stayed on awhile."

Kayla draped a still-wet bedsheet over me, saying, "It's indecent. You're not a child anymore." They began to lead me home, but paused when the stranger did not follow. "Hey," Kayla said, "we found her. Time to go home. Everything is fine." The stranger, her back still turned to us, waved us away. "I'll come back soon," she said quietly. "I'm going to . . . stand here for a while."

"Thank you for finding me," I told her, not wanting to leave her alone.

"Thank you for finding me, too," she answered. There was a little rain, which was so light we could not feel it falling. Hersh and Kayla had our clean laundry slung over their arms, and I, coated in mud, followed behind. I felt like a flower bulb they had just dug up, hopeful that they might plant me in the garden, where, after the long, frozen stillness of winter, a spray of irises might emerge as if from nowhere.

THE BOOK OF HOPE,
LOST AND GAINED

We gathered under the swinging branches of a cottonwood at the northern edge of the village in the middle of the cemetery, where the road, grown over with hungry vines, once led out and away. Igor stood with his brothers and sisters while his parents were shoulder to shoulder. His mother had not spoken to him since the baby's death. She would not meet his eye. That morning, his father had said, "She will forgive you someday," and Igor had said, "Forgive me for what?" His father had shrugged his shoulders, as if his were not the weight that had ended the fragile life. "Forgive me for what?" Igor had asked again.

"For seeing her like that. For being disgusted by her."

"Disgusted?"

The rain was heavier that day but we were dry under the tree, all the water falling in a ring around us. We remembered in great detail the four days when the baby had been alive. Igor asked our stranger to explain what had happened and she said, "He was conceived in a different world—he was not meant for this one." She blessed his cold body and washed him off with river water carried here in a flowerpot. We each took a turn putting our fingers on his forehead, wishing him a safe journey and thanking him for visiting us here. But more than anything else, we stood in silence, because death lived with us too now and always would. The sweet months were over when no one had ever left us.

And was it true that he came from another world? Was it true that his death was right? Or was this the first curse, the first shining ring in a chain? We offered our sadness to the banker and his wife and the eleven siblings—who stood together in a group just failing to add up to a complete dozen—but we did so from a few feet away. We did so with our hands hidden in our pockets. We did so without once kissing any of them on the cheek or offering our own clean handkerchiefs for their miserable eyes. We each threw handfuls of dirt into the baby's hole, and placed small pebbles on his gravestone, which read simply, The First Birth, The First Death.

Later, Kayla polished her wooden spoons. She kept looking into them, waiting for the moment when her rag had worked enough circles for a mirror to appear in the birch. I was transfixed by her hopeless determination. Kayla always felt the electricity of her own belief crackle and spark so ferociously that she was sure she could light the world. At the door, three questioning knocks.

Kayla lined her wooden spoons, ungleaming, on the table. It was the banker, dressed in black. Kayla stood in the doorway, blocking the entrance while she offered him tea, a sweet and her condolences for his tragic loss.

"Can I?" he said, motioning inside.

"Oh, certainly, yes of course, certainly, yes," Kayla said while she stood in his way. The banker took a step and forced her to move. "I cannot imagine," she told him. "None of us can imagine." He shook his wet hat out on the floor. She eyed the water like something contaminated.

"That's not what I'm here about," he said. "I know there is talk of a curse and maybe it's true. I'm here about your daughter."

"My daughter?"

I looked at both of them. "Me?" I asked.

"I have settled on the story," he said. "Are you ready? May I sit?"

"Okay," Kayla told him. "Certainly. I'm sorry, yes. We like stories." The banker arranged himself in the chair slowly, crossing and uncrossing his feet, folding his hands on his lap.

"Once upon a time, there was a quiet village at the edge of a river," the banker started. His voice was measured and low. "For a long time, the village was innocent and nothing very bad had happened there. But then, a baby was crushed by the weight of his father's love. Crushed. And the people in the village understood that sadness waited for them ahead."

The banker picked one of Kayla's wooden spoons, stirred an invisible pot. "But there was a beautiful young girl. The Girl Who Retold the Story. No matter how afraid the others were, she could tell the next chapter of the story, and they were always safe in it."

He had been watching; I had been seen.

"Now, once upon the same time there was a young man who needed to find a new home, and a new family. He was a little bit greedy with his parents and asked to have a hand in everything, but he would grow out of that. He wanted to change and he wanted to marry. He had waited patiently for the perfect, magical wife who could cancel out any family curse. Who could turn the story into something happy. When the boy's father came to the girl and asked for her help, she gave it."

He paused, watched me, a silent girl sitting across the table from him. I looked at my hands, which were utterly ordinary, as was everything else. Somehow, other people kept seeing something they thought could save them, when all I saw was dry skin, chipped nails. I felt like a vessel, the container itself meaningless, yet into it people kept pouring ashes, tears, blood, and calling me holy. As much as I wanted to explain the mistake, I knew they would brush me aside. A person who wants to believe lives in a world full of proof.

"We need to not have any more dead babies in our house again. Never. We need to not be the bringers of the first curse in the world. And my wife needs Igor to move along. The only one who can ensure those things is Lena."

"My daughter is the best girl in the village, is that what you're saying? Because she was raised so well? Because she has such an outstanding mother?" The banker didn't have a chance to agree before she said, "It's a good arrangement. When?"

"Right away. He's ready. She's ready?"

"She could be ready."

"Wait, how old am I?" I asked.

"Old," Kayla told me, and she shook the banker's hand.

In the evening, while we all three forked beets into our mouths, Kayla said, "Exciting news. Lena's getting married." Hersh opened his mouth and he left it open. His long face was the side of a cliff with a gaping cave in the middle. I half expected leather bat wings to begin flapping out. When he looked at me, I shook my head. I had nothing.

"You are making this up," he said, knowing that he had made no agreement with any father of a son.

"Nope."

"We can't lose her," he said.

"We have to lose her, it's our only chance."

"How did this happen? You didn't even ask me?"

Kayla shook her head and chewed her food. I tried to pay attention to the warm slide of a potato down my throat. I felt like a weed in the river, having no say which direction it was pulled. My throat closed up, my heart closed up, my fists closed up.

"There was this nice story about how our daughter is some kind of sage, and how she is the only person who can turn a sad story into a happy one. The whole point is that the banker doesn't want any more bad luck. No more dead babies, right? Plus, there aren't very many worthy boys around, and plus, Lena is a woman now."

Kayla smiled then and squinched her eyes shut. When she

spoke again, her voice was higher. "I get to be the mother of the bride." She laughed, the last word stretched out into a long whine. "I get to plan a whole wedding!"

Hersh poured a glass of vodka from the dusty bottle he kept hidden behind the special occasion teacups, went outside and sat down on the ground and called God's name. Hersh said he hoped God was paying attention and not throwing curses and blessings around just to keep busy. "Look, can you just do what is right?" It was what he always asked for. Kayla, watching from the window, swore she saw God roll his eyes and take a big gulp of Hersh's drink.

"You have to ask him for something in particular," she said to her husband through the open pane. She had always complained that Hersh did not know how to pray right. There were plenty of worthwhile requests: to come upon a store of gold coins, a fat cow, a spring in the forest that washed the years away. Why did Hersh always have to be so abstract, so trusting?

"I want him to do what's right," he told her.

"You have to tell the man what you need. Don't give him some whatever-you-think-is-best crap," Kayla scolded. "He's busy, he needs you to do the research for him and recommend a course of action. Tell him your daughter ought to be blessed and that even if the boy is cursed could they at least even out? And could there be many new grandbabies very quickly?"

"If he is God, he knows more than I do."

"Apparently he makes mistakes. That innocent baby. Oops," she said.

"I'm going to get *married?*" I interrupted from the chair where I had been frozen.

"What happy news!" Kayla exclaimed.

"Now?"

"Soon."

"How *old* am I?" I asked for the second time.

"You have grown a lot," Kayla said. "You're even older than when you asked that earlier."

Cold air swooped inside when Hersh opened the door, and disappeared just as quickly when he closed it. He stood over me. He put his hands on my head and came in close to whisper, "Everyone knows you'll be okay—it's me missing you that I'm worried about."

And for the second time in my life, I prepared to be passed on. The feeling I had was of hovering above my own life. As if I were the shed skin of an insect, and the body I used to hold had simply walked out. Even the word *marriage* sounded gravelly in my mouth. Mangled, half chewed. I understood nothing. But there were my hands, my fingers, and thank goodness for them, because they remembered, as always, how to do the next task. I went to my room and began to go through my things, fold and flatten, shake and stack, as if this small preparation would be enough. That was how my hands and I prayed that night. I touched everything in the room so that in the end my dirty fingerprints were on all of it. Proof that time had passed, evidence of my existence. I took out the note from my first mother to my old sister. *This is how I love you*, it said to her again, and again she was not there to see it. I am here, I prayed. I am real.

✦ ✦ ✦

Igor fainted the moment he saw me enter the room. His eyes rolled back in his head and he collapsed, not onto the hard floor of his kitchen where we stood, not into the sharp corner of the table, but precisely and theatrically, into the arms of his mother. She looked at him, shock wrinkling her nose, trying to figure out how she came to be holding her grown son. He shuddered for a moment and then his eyelids opened to the world around him. Igor's mouth widened into a gawky smile when he saw that I was still there—not dreamed but flesh—and he stood straight up, brushed his hands over his clean, pressed wool pants. To him, I looked like an exactly right young lady.

Sweat burst from the foreheads of his parents, but not from Igor's. He weakened in all the right places, and got strong in all the right places as well. This was the story he had been told his whole life. The story of becoming a man in his own town with a nice girl. There would be little Igors soon, and the butcher would sell him nice cuts of meat, and the baker would sell him the best loaves of bread, and his wife would be capable in the kitchen (and in the bedroom, praise God who art good to me, amen). Igor was being offered a door leading out of the tragic house where no one looked him in the eye anymore. His new life appeared just like that, detailed and populated, at his feet. He had done nothing other than come downstairs in the morning wearing the clothes his father had laid out, and there it was: his future, blessed, alive and, most important, now.

The wedding was planned for a week hence, and everyone

helped clean the barn for the big event. "What happens at a wedding?" the greengrocer asked while he washed windows.

"Two people turn into one," his wife said. "Sometimes it's a loss and sometimes it's a gain."

"In your case?" he asked. She shrugged and he pinched her on the back of the hand.

"A wedding can be whatever we want," the stranger said. "Any ideas?"

"We should light candles," the baker's wife said.

"We should throw soft things," two of the banker's youngest daughters suggested. "We should dance."

"We should break something," Perl suggested.

"Break something?" the stranger asked.

"Yes. Because brokenness is the truth of life." People squinted at her, drawing away. "It's not a bad thing," she said, defending herself. "There are more pieces to share."

"Should we read our prayers?" the stranger wondered. Like a lullaby, this quieted us. Long before we could hear the words, we were comforted by them. The jeweler, who appeared at all times near the stranger like an attendant, a maid-in-waiting, made it official by handing her a book and pen to record the decree.

Some people brushed the sheep and some people culled dirty feathers from the hens. Some people hung garlands of flowers on rusted nails, and some took turns climbing our tallest ladder in order to clean the cobwebs and cement the tiles of our first complete constellation up on the ceiling: the Constellation of Hope, Lost and Gained, which had three stars—the star of Lena, the star of Igor and the star of the dead baby, all in a line.

The villagers put on the nicest clothes they had and men slapped their faces with alcohol and felt cleaner because of it. Everyone carried their own chairs from their own houses and set them up in rows. The barn smelled of earth and dust, of waiting. The low chatter of anticipation hovered like fog. Would today be beautiful and joyous? Would nothing disrupt the union we were trying, like magicians, to summon from thin air?

The villagers placed gifts on a table near the horses. They talked about the beauty of this, the first marriage in the new world and the joys it would bring. They talked about the first baby, which was also the first death, and decided that our stranger was right—he had not been able to live because he was conceived before the world began. What was he supposed to do? He was the last breath of the old world, and now we were truly free. The next baby would be the real first baby.

In the sunken eyes of the banker's wife, Perl saw the bruises of loss; a mother, pecked at by a flock of justifications for her son's death. Perl went to her, said, "It never goes away. You will always hurt." The banker's wife wanted to scream in the face of this woman who had come to further salt her tears. But then she looked at Perl and saw she too had a swollen heart. Waterlogged, soaked, engorged with loss and love.

"I hope Igor doesn't ruin everything," the banker's wife said.

Perl had known Igor only as a kind, gentle herding dog for the flock of siblings following behind. She had a hard time imagining him ruining anything. "He's going to be a friend to Lena. And a fine husband," she added, though the idea still sounded like a dress-up game. The banker's wife hid her face when tears started to pour.

"I'm afraid I will lose the baby again when the wound heals over," the banker's wife managed.

"It never does. It never heals."

"Swear it," the banker's wife said.

The villagers took their seats. The stranger stood between the animals and the people, under a heavy quilt stretched tight across its corners by four long wooden poles. Both audiences, furry and bald, waited. The healer sat at the piano and pressed his fingers on the keys, which only breathed. We imagined a solemn, lifting song for me to walk by. Kayla had cinched me into a tight corset, which made the tiny breasts I had look much bigger than they were, while my waist was squeezed into a channel just wide enough for the blood to flow through. Kayla had also sewn me a long white skirt and white blouse with a lacy collar, which she buttoned all the way up, her hot breath leaving a film of wet on my neck. "Yes," Kayla had said, a gust of wind blowing across my legs while she fluffed my skirt. I felt twenty-five years older than I was, or might have been. "You really look like a bride." I was a convincing doll.

Igor, skinny and awkward, his voice high and creaky but kind, his eyes alight with the turns his life had taken, wore a black suit, a new top hat, glasses and a cane. He only looked ten years older than he was. He and I stood in front of our stranger, keeping as still as we could, and did not smile. Above us was the canopy, a symbol of our home together, where we were meant to share all the nights of our lives.

"We are gathered to celebrate a new family," our stranger said. "A new family in a new world. We are here to celebrate life, which persists in spite of everything. We are here to celebrate the joining of Lena and Igor, the saddlemaker's daughter and the banker's son, who are really everyone's children. We wish all our prayers on them." She asked us to take each other's hands. Igor's were warm and bony. He gripped my fingers so tightly the blood took leave. The villagers took hold of one another. Our stranger began to read from the Book of Prayers, half singing, half swaying. Here, for the first time, we were hearing the history of our world. We had deposited, but never withdrawn, our prayers. Around us, dust drifted downward in the yellow window-light, horses were quiet and attentive, hens puttered, bats and swallows kept to the eaves.

"We pray for everything we can think to pray for. We pray, of course, for food, and if we have enough we pray that it will always be so. The washed potatoes boiling in a pot are prayed over. The cabbages, severed and pickled, are prayed on. We pray for the lives we know to go on. We pray that everyone has a job to do. We pray that our mothers will live forever. We pray that our fathers will stand up strong until the day when they lie down and rest. We pray that we are smarter than our brothers and that our brothers are kinder than we are. We pray that when we go to count the money hidden under the floorboards it will have grown. We pray that the rain does not wash us away. We pray that the sun will one day heat us again."

Perl's glowing head was the brightest spot in the temple-barn. She put her palm up to me and I smiled for her. I wanted to tell her I forgave her, except I was not sure if I did. Vlad cried into his sleeve, left it shimmering with the tracks from his nose. Regina, who had only grown larger since having been traded in for being too large, sat, certain that she would never be the one under that wedding canopy. By the time anyone asked her to marry, she would be taller than the roof, her legs would be trees, her arms would be trees, her head would be who knows what. She was prepared to outgrow everything.

Kayla's crying was that of an actress, all gasps and whimpers. Hersh offered her his handkerchief, but she had brought her own, a brown lace square so delicate it looked like it would melt with her tears. She remembered the days when I was a baby in her arms. She tried to remember the moment of my birth, the first look I had given her, but she could not. Her time as a mother seemed so short, but she guessed it was always that way. Was it not just last month that those fingers were no thicker than string beans? She looked up at me, at the girl, who really was still a girl, and hoped that I was going to be enough. Hersh knew I would be enough—it was himself and his wife he worried about. It was going to be back to the two of them in the house, and he hoped that Kayla would not take up residence on the floor again, and he would not have to buy anyone else's children from them. That he would get a saddle or two made every month, and that the rain would one day go and snow would cover them, melt away and cover them back up again.

And me? What did I feel? Thinking of that day, it is as if I were not there. As if someone told me what happened later. I must have made each required movement, passing through the wheels that turned me from a girl to a wife. If there was a transformation, I did not witness it. Still, I was no more afraid of one made-up version of my life than another. I was already far away from anything that had ever been true, and somewhere in this was a surprising sense of peace. I had nothing left to lose.

"I have a question," Igor said. The stranger looked surprised. "Can you promise that there will be more good than bad in the world, overall? Can we make a rule that I will be happy?"

The stranger studied this boy, this nearly husband. He was standing on the very border between his childhood and his adulthood. She saw Igor as a boy at the window looking out at freshly fallen snow—all the broken branches and thornbushes covered up with sparkling, pure white. "I promise that I will help you try. But it's your story to tell." He smiled at me with satisfaction. He was negotiating for both of us.

The stranger resumed her prayer. "We pray that the grandmothers will not die suffering and punish us as ghosts, demanding the sweets we have baked and asking for the only soft bed in the house and scolding us for the things we have left undone. We pray for Lena and Igor and their life together, and for all of our new lives. We pray for the river to stay holy and for any snazzy trick you feel like throwing us: a terrific growing season, a man whose body is made of gold, a girl who bears children weekly. We pray for whatever you have in store, but better, if you can."

The jeweler handed Igor two gold rings, engraved with vines twisted together. In his head he said his own prayer—May love be mine too someday.

"Do we know about rings?" Igor whispered.

"Definitely," the jeweler said. "We know about forever, and they are the same thing." Igor slid one onto my finger, and I slipped the other onto his.

Igor smashed a perfectly good wineglass under his foot and we put our dry lips together for a very short second. Later, the shards of glass would be pressed to the wall in a constellation invisible except when hit by the sun.

The village toasted and celebrated, dancing, singing and wishing for beautiful things under our very own sky. It felt like we might be safe from unhappiness here in the barn. We almost believed it was possible the rain had stopped. The healer sat at the piano, and though it was mute, you never would have known it from his exuberant playing.

Our dream of a dry world had not come true, but we tried not to be too disappointed. In the glimmering dark, their bellies full of food and their heads full of prayers, the village sent Igor and me to our new house to make good on our new marriage. The house had always been there, but no one had lived in it. Vlad had quietly fixed it up, working for a few hours each day, imagining my face while he replaced rotten beams, plastered holes and sanded the floor. He had offered it as a found object, not a made one. To Hersh and Kayla he said, "Maybe Lena and Igor could live in that little house between the two big oaks and the cabbage field?"

"Isn't it a wreck?" Hersh had asked.

"It's in surprisingly good shape," Vlad had told him.

It was a clean, dry, square room with a stove and a wash bin. I looked around at the little place. Someone had lain a woven rug down, and there was a rocking chair. This was the second time since the world began that I was going to sleep as part of a new family. Without asking if he should, Igor made me a cup of tea. I wondered if he knew that, as the wife, I was supposed to be the boiler of water. But he was a boy with a mother who knew how to ask for what she wanted. If I was smart, I might be able to make a few requests, rather than dancing only the steps I was taught. We sat on the floor because neither of us wanted to take the one chair. We looked out at the rain. The dancing feet, the applause, our own celebration, was too far away for us to hear. The world was empty of any sounds but our own.

Igor touched my hand. "Do you like chocolate?" he asked.

"Sure," I said.

"Me too. Do you like hot milk?"

"I've never had it."

"Never?"

I shook my head. "Do you like cabbage?" I asked.

"Yes, of course," he answered, which made me feel safer. "Do you know what we are supposed to do now?" he asked.

"We are supposed to be married. You are the husband and I am the wife." He laid a sheet down over the rug, laid himself down, and asked me to join him. I sat there, and it felt like a strange picnic. Igor pulled me to him. We were side by side, and close.

"How old are you?" I asked while Igor touched the smooth ridge of my arm.

"I'm fifteen," Igor said. "How old are you?"

"I don't know," I told him.

"You don't know?"

"First I was nearly twelve, then I was someone's new little baby, then I was married." My voice sounded very far away. A speck in the huge silence of the night.

"You can be my age if you want," he whispered. He put his palm out to me, open, as if it contained the thing I needed to be grown. I lowered my face into that cup and lapped.

"Thank you," I said, and kissed him on the forehead, as if he were my child, while I tried to hide my tears of relief. He kissed me on the forehead as if I were his child too, as if we were each other's. "I would like that very much," I said. In the morning we would open many wedding gifts, but this was the only one I would remember.

"We could even have the same birthday, if you want, so it's easier to keep track."

And as a new couple with our matching ages and matching birthdays, Igor and I kissed badly and wetly and sweetly all over our young faces to the call of an owl outside asking the question again and again, "Who? Who?" to which we tried the answer, "Us, Us."

· IV ·

THE BOOK OF SLEEP

I do not wonder so much why we were left alone as long as we were. Why our village was skipped by marching Romanian soldiers with orders to send all the Jews and Gypsies to the other side of the border for the Germans to deal with. What aches in every part of my body is that we did not hear their cries, the lives ending. Death by machine gun, death by starvation, death by sadness. Along we went, our lives day to day, morning to night. A million mothers, a million fathers, a million sons and daughters screamed at once, and all we heard was the good wind shake the trees out.

The villagers gathered under umbrellas in that clean, glassy air outside my door and waited to meet the first baby, the real first baby, in the whole world. Dawn sprawled out across the sky, a woman waking up. Inside, I howled and the healer let a slow river of encouragement wash me down. Pacing from oak tree to rain barrel, Igor beat a nervous path in front of the house. He looked determined to get where he was going, which was nowhere. His father stood in his way, but Igor made a detour and persevered. The stranger coaxed him quiet, saying, "The baby will find his place. Trust him."

"And Lena?"

"She is finding her place, too."

Up and back and back and up he marched, the soggy grass under his feet trampled. The villagers watched Igor clear a path, counting off his wait for fatherhood. This made Perl dizzy, so she approached Igor, the husband of her daughter-niece, with a big bag of birdseed. She reached inside and flung the handful out to show him. From the oak tree, two ravens came to investigate the seeds. Their black was almost blue, their eyes like polished amber. Perl tossed another handful and the ravens pecked the ground. Igor looked at Perl, his own eyes big and hollow. "She's going to be fine," Perl said.

"What have I done to her?" he asked. In his hand, the seeds were smooth and light. They made a very faint splash on the ground and floated on the surface of a puddle. A sparrow ate what Igor offered. Squirrels, their claws ticking, climbed down from the tree.

In the hours while I worked to introduce the baby to the world outside my body, Igor drew all the creatures to him. Jays, magpies, starlings and sparrows. Woodpeckers, wrens and swallows.

Pigeons. He was surrounded, an island in a sea of feathers. They flapped at each other, fought for his kind attention, followed the arc of his arm. Birds stood on Igor's shoes, they brushed him with their wings. They beat the air back, dove, squawked. The man disappeared inside the flock. Igor had become a seed-giving tree, a nest. Through the wings, the villagers could see Igor's smile.

Nothing winged tried to carry me away. I was vaguely aware of the wet cloths Kayla swept over my forehead, saying, "Oh, dear, oh dear," unable to hide her surprise at the pain I was in. Water dripped down my cheeks, or was it sweat, or blood, or rain? I could not remember if I was indoors or out, if I was held by loam and shaded by tall pines, or a child in my first home, weak with fever.

"Where am I?" I asked.

"You are home. You are having my grandchild," Kayla said, impatiently. In the next wave of pain I wondered if she was talking about me—was I myself about to be born?

The weeks and months that had passed since Igor and I were married floated past me like clouds. The first morning: boiling two eggs, browning two pieces of bread, Igor talking about his mother. He hummed the song she used to sing him before she had moved on to the next baby and left him songless.

The day Igor came home from working at the bank and looked like he was bursting: "Is something wrong?" I asked.

"I had a whole day, and I want you to know about it. I missed you."

"Tell me," I said, and, beginning from the moment he opened his eyes until the moment he walked in the door, he did. There was no climax, no event to speak of, but he had lived it, and I had not.

"It doesn't seem fair," Igor said, "that I can't be in your head and you can't be in mine." He asked me to tell him what it had felt like to split the potatoes with my knife. What it had smelled like when they had first begun to soften.

I remembered the night we took our clothes off and tried various configurations: I felt bald and blind in the dark, but our bodies, still equipped with the full memory of our species, guided us through. I had expected this to feel very grown-up, maybe even a test of whether I was such a person. It did not. It felt like being ageless, just a slippery combination of limbs and instincts, neither young nor old. We laughed after, for hardly any reason at all.

One afternoon, thunder cracking outside: at the table, I laid napkins, spoons and bowls for Kayla and Hersh, Igor and myself. We lit a candle, we said an old prayer. The conversation was simple— the everyday of our lives. They were at my table, and they could not change the rules here. Kayla did not and could not ask me to sit on her lap. Even her suggestion that next time I add more marjoram to the soup was met with a scold from Hersh. "I think it's just wonderful," he said. "It's your own recipe."

Later: I got up the courage to ask my real parents and my siblings over. We stood in the threshold, dumb. Words were useless to us.

"How are you?" we asked one another.

"Well, thank you."

"The weather," we started, but had nothing more to say about it. It was the saddest room in the world. These were not my parents or my siblings now, and any other friendship felt pitifully inadequate. We pulled our chairs close together, our knees touching.

We closed our eyes, and we sat like that while the rain gained speed and lost it, the wind gusted and hushed. It was not enough, not nearly. When they left, we promised, in the friendly way guests and hosts always do, to visit again soon, but all of us knew in our hearts we were too weak to withstand another moment like that, pretending to be a family when we no longer were. It was better to love one another from a safe distance than to cantilever ourselves out over the chasm, always barely failing to touch fingertips.

Each day I had visited the stranger in the barn. She had two chairs set up back-to-back, and several thick volumes to record our prayers. The chair she sat in was big and soft, while the one for the visitor was a straight, ladder-backed chair, because we had decided a person praying should not be too comfortable. He should not want to settle in and take a nap, but should sit straight and remain serious. A prayer, in our minds, was like the turn of a wrench or the pounding of a nail—it fastened, sturdily, our lives together. I remembered looking at the constellations around me. We had covered all the easy parts—from the floor to the height of our shoulders. The background colors were everything from light blue to black, and sometimes had shocks of red or deep brown. The stars were always white, though some had the soft pink-flowered pattern of another world's wedding china. The Constellation of Hope, Lost and Gained, was the only one on the ceiling. It was the fixed point in our universe, our guide. Looking up at it, I prayed for everyone I loved. I prayed for food and sleep and patience, all around. When I stood up to go, the stranger always said the same thing: You are you. Each time, it felt a little bit more true.

Late at night: I woke up and was pummeled with the feeling

that everything was fine. With the feeling that I was a person in my own bed, in my own home. I was so shocked by this that I lay there until daybreak, only trying to memorize the sensation.

Igor opened his eyes. "How old are we now?" he asked.

"Older," I said.

"Have I deserted you?" he asked.

"You have always been right here," I told him. "You have been steady."

"I suddenly got scared that you were alone and I was far away." He reached out to me, rubbed his hand over my body. He turned me dark and infinite. He pressed the stars of his own constellation onto me: here and here and here and here. I let the rest of me go away into darkness and only those spots, those pins of light, remain and shine holes into him. Drill him through with my brilliance. We connected the stars with lines, drew a map of our heavens.

Inside me, the dust of a new planet began to gather.

For the next forty weeks, everything made me cry, whether it was beautiful or sad, grand or meaningless. A pile of beets, a swarm of ants covering a dead bird, the falling sun turning our whole village gold—I stood there in awe, facing all of it with a pair of salt-wet eyes.

The light the day of the baby's birth was white, and the villagers shaded their eyes against it. They shifted on their feet, passed hunks of cheese, made a few laps around the usual topics of conversation: When would the rain stop? How much caraway makes the perfect sauerkraut? How long before the sky was complete in the barn? How much lazier were men than women? Meanwhile, my husband was giving the world's birds the feast of their lives. They might have picked him up in their beaks, carried him to a high, avian throne. I would have told my baby the story again and again that his father was a bird king who had been taken to the top of the highest tree and, flightless, would remain there to live the lonely life of the worshipped.

But as the seeds ran out, the birds began to depart. Igor was filled with fear that there would be nothing left of him, that he would find himself a picked-clean skeleton. Back to the tree went the ravens and woodpeckers, back to the square went the pigeons. Igor examined his arms and legs and found them uneaten. But he could still feel the points of the birds' feet and hear their feathers against one another, against the wind.

And just then, from inside: the cry of a brand-new life. Into my arms the healer placed a creature small and slippery. It was complete, I marveled. And I was complete—neither of us had to be undone for the other to exist. "A boy," Kayla said. "Isn't that amazing? A boy!" She threw the door open, spread the news.

Igor smelled like birds when he kneeled at my bedside, his eyes pooling. His hair was wild from clawings and his black wool coat was streaked with the tears of droppings.

"What became of you?" Kayla asked, using the same cloth she had mopped my forehead with to clean Igor's sleeves.

"You look like how I feel," I said. Igor brought his face to his son and took a long whiff. This made me laugh. "How does he smell?" I asked.

"Warm," Igor said. "Extremely warm."

◆ ◆ ◆

The boy cried wildly, throwing himself completely into the sadness of being alive. "Cry all you want," I whispered to him. "You have been born into this new, strange place." But he did not keep it up. He learned in a few days that the milk was warm and sweet and the touch of his mother's hand on his head was as soft as anything, and each pair of hands was safe.

When I put my son to my breast, and when I felt that there would be warm liquid for him to drink, I closed my eyes and I did not need to open them for a long time. Whatever else was there—the chair holding my back, a table, the rugs and windows, a jar full of spoons, onion skin like a piece of stained glass in the sunlight, and outside, birds and the shadows of birds, oak trees and their pinky-brown lost leaves, the approaching night—it did not need to exist in order for me to go on feeding the one I had made.

Igor sat in another chair, thumbing the hem of the tablecloth.

"I will show you everything," I said to the baby. "Don't worry."

Igor jolted his head up and stared at his son—his son! This person in my arms who would absolutely not exist without he himself. Igor examined his own fingers and his own arms and found them bald and inadequate. "Do you know how to be a mother?" he asked.

"I hope so," I said. "I have never known how to be what I was, but the next thing always came anyway."

"But this baby has *nothing* without us. He's completely helpless without us. He would die in a matter of hours without us. You *hope* you know how to be a mother?"

"I have been someone's child, twice," I said. "I just have to do the other side of the job this time."

Igor put his head in his hands. "I have no, no, no idea what I am doing. The last baby I knew died under the weight of his own father," he said into the sweaty trunks of his wrists. "He is ours. *I* am the father." I gathered the baby and sat on the floor at my husband's feet. "Oh, dear," Igor kept saying.

"Let's say the world is beautiful and safe," I began. "Let's say that the new world we are all making together is a fair one, and that everything turns out all right. Let's believe that you are a good father and I am a good mother, and this baby is a healthy boy who will live long enough to tell the story again and again that he was the first baby in a brand-new world where there was always enough food, always enough warmth and always enough love."

Igor pulled the blanket away from his sleeping son's cheek and poked it very gently. "He looks happy," he said.

"He is." I smiled. The baby was warm on my shoulder. He was perfect, absolutely perfect, right then.

Igor said, "I am the father. That makes me feel very, very tired."

I patted my thigh. "You want to put your head on my lap?" Igor found his own place on my leg. I felt like a tree with two birds nesting.

"Let's name the baby for the son of a king," Igor said. I asked if there had ever been such a person. "Well," he said, "in the story of another world, at least. Maybe it will come true in this one."

"That you will be a king?" I asked. Igor blushed.

"Solomon," he said, "both the son of a king and a king himself."

"Go to sleep," I whispered. "I'll take care of you."

◆ ◆ ◆

Igor talked more and more about being tired. Not the tired of a long day's work or the tired of an uphill climb or even the tired of too many hours in the sun. He was tired from the idea of his own fatherhood—the simple fact that he had passed himself on to another, entirely separate being. He had been an older brother for a long time, but this was something very different. His whole life hit him at once. He had been witness to his parents' elation and grief, and somehow because of this, he had been married off. Now he was himself a father with a son. He kept himself awake to eat, to stretch, to rearrange the blankets, and then he went back to sleep, saying, "Just a few more minutes."

The more he slept, the more Igor talked of it as a job: his purpose was to rest for all of us. To absorb the sounds and smells of what occurred around him—not to participate, simply to take it in—and spin the threads into wispy, drifting dreams. He still went to work at the bank for a few hours in the morning, but that was a duty, not a purpose. Igor's true calling was to sleep off the pressures of existence, the unknowable meaning of life, like a hangover he was trying to lose.

He slept through the afternoons, the wind knocking gently at the windows. He opened his eyes for a few moments, drank a glass of water, scratched his back against the doorframe like a bear, wrapped himself in a blanket, tucked a pillow between his legs. He waved away the birds that lit on the windowsill.

"I am that baby's father," he said, reaching out toward

Solomon. "I can't believe it. I'm going back to bed." I did not mind his being around, but I didn't mind his not being around, either. For me, the quiet house felt like a sigh of relief. No one was asking me to be their baby. My job was as simple as chopping vegetables, starting the fire, washing the floor, sorting the socks and sitting at the table with my son. I did not know how old I really was, but it did not matter so much anymore. I was a mother and a wife, and that was all anyone needed to know.

I liked having someone in the house, an appreciative mouth to feed, and when Igor's eyes fluttered open and he came to me, I was happy to listen to the dreams he had had, that parallel life he was living in which he could jump from the tops of trees and take flight.

"Do you remember," he yawned, "the time when we built a boat out of reeds and sailed to the other side of the river and ate cheese?"

"I think you dreamed that," I said.

"No, I remember it. You were there. You wore a yellow dress."

"All right, I'll remember," I agreed. "Was that the same time that Solomon was a bear cub and he kept scratching us by accident and we had to very carefully trim his claws with a knife in his sleep?"

"That was another time. But I remember that, too. I'm glad he's a boy again." The tone of his voice changed. "Remember the time my mother did not run away every time she saw me approaching? Remember the time I was her son?"

"I remember that," I said, wrapping my fingers in a bracelet around his wrist.

❖   ❖   ❖

Kayla entered first, knocked second. Stomped her muddy boots on the mat. "Are you unwell?" she asked. "You didn't answer."

"I'm very, very well," I said, and I let out a small howl.

"We thought you had stopped that," Kayla said.

"I hadn't." I took a sip of cold, dusty-tasting water and did not look her in the eye. I did not not love her. I understood that she had to invent being a mother just as I had to invent being a baby. I knew that she loved the person she imagined me to be, and maybe even, a little bit, the person I actually was. Still, the quieter the little room was, the more I could hear the sound, like the faint ringing of a tuning fork, of my own, real mind.

"Here are the potatoes, and here is the chicken. Here is some extra money. When are you coming to our house for supper?" Kayla asked.

"Not for a while." I pointed to the baby. "I don't want to disrupt him."

"It's just a few doors away," she whined.

"And yet," I said, smiling. "It feels very far." Kayla scrubbed ferociously at a potato. She had not realized that by finding me a husband and releasing me to the course of events, she would lose her grip on my life.

"You are still my daughter," she scolded. "I'm still taking care of you."

I said, "As you know, being a mother is the most important thing. The baby won't survive without me."

"Just you wait," she huffed. "Before you know it, he'll be gone."

Solomon sucked and spit and sucked and spit. Milk ran down my chest, my belly. I dipped my finger in and tasted. "Me and you," I said, squeezing my son.

"What did you say?" Kayla asked.

"I was talking to Solomon," I said.

"He's just a baby, he doesn't know anything yet."

"He knows what he knows."

When Kayla left, I checked on my husband, disguised as a worm in his blanket, and whispered to him, "Remember the time all the trees sprouted cakes and we lay in the sun on our backs eating them and nobody had to worry about whether there would be enough later on?" His eyelids flickered.

I took my baby outside. "This is the street," I said, "which we use to get places. Right now I feel the round stones under my feet. When you walk you'll know what I mean. What's falling is called rain. Sometimes it's heavy and sometimes it's light, but it hardly ever stops completely. It's what makes the plants and the trees grow, so we can be grateful. Your real grandfather is a cabbage farmer. I'll cook them for you so you know the smell. Your other grandfather makes saddles to ride horses. Your third grandfather keeps other people's money safe. They will all love you, and you don't have to do anything special for them. Just do what you do."

And what was I supposed to do? I had no job in the village. Maybe I had helped tell our story once, but the need for that had disappeared—the story was telling itself now. I was Solomon's mother, and maybe that was enough. My husband had completely stopped showing up for work at the bank. Igor's father still dropped his weekly pay off at our doorstep, though it was unearned. I picked it up and poured the coins into the bread jar at the back of our cupboard. Igor never asked where I got the money to buy flour or eggs and I did not explain it to him. He was tired enough without the weight of taking charity. If the banker stopped paying his son for nothing, I was not sure what we would do. Still, in the history of this world, no one had gone hungry. No one had withered away. I surveyed the land around me and saw plenty. "All we need is enough," I said to Solomon. "No more."

The next thing I knew, my son would be running around and I would be pregnant again. I would cry every time I cut Solomon's soft brown hair, those beautiful silks dead on the floor. His legs would become too long for each pair of pants. Solomon's arms would soon wallow at his sides, and his feet and hands would become knuckled and workable. He would turn one, two, three. He would learn to walk. Then he would learn to talk. He would learn to read and to write and I would find notes on scraps of paper. *My name is Solomon. I like to eat fruit. My father is asleep. I love my mother. I am tall.* Though he would be precocious, he would learn everything in the right order, and even while his mother would sometimes wish she could have another day with him as a baby, she—I—would never, ever ask. I would watch him stack boxes, chew carrots and make friends with ants. I would watch him chase a ball and bury a stone. "Today it was a monsoon. Tomorrow there will be a shower," he would sing. "Drizzle, deluge, cloudburst."

For what would seem like a very brief moment, he was still my baby. I looked down at Solomon, his eyes open to whatever we passed. "These are the fields where we grow our food. This is wheat for bread." Explaining the world to my son, I noticed things I had not before. Our houses were creeping with moss, greening from the ground up. The window trim was no longer the brown of wood but bright emerald. The houses appeared to be sinking slowly into the soft earth. Birds bathed in the mud puddles, which were everywhere. "These are the paths between the stalks we walk to get to the river. This is the river. I'm going to put you in it, let the water wash you clean. Are you ready?" I said, unwrapping him. "I'm coming in with you." And I unwrapped myself too, my coat and dress and shoes, and we waded in together, Solomon pressed to me, until I dipped us down so that his tiny, complete body was as wet as mine and our skin was pushed by the rushing current and the reeds scraping on the shore cried out to us and the moon was white in the gray sky, and the river was a different gray, and I watched it slide off around the curve where it hugged the village and disappeared into another place and time.

Solomon did not cry. The river made all the sound we needed.

THE BOOK OF LOVE
AND SECRETS

Three years passed under us. Three sweet, regular years. The tiled stars had spread out over the walls of the barn, white constellations against blue and black sky; they made us feel at home and safe. These days, we had many things to celebrate. My once-brother had fallen in love with the tailor's delicate daughter, and they were to be married, Solomon would celebrate his fourth birthday soon, and I was due to give birth to my second baby. The heavens joined in the festivities by offering the best weather we could ever remember. It was a moment of mercy, of joy. It was also a farewell party, though we did not know it at the time.

This sun was full, complete, not just the clouded-over orb we had grown used to. We emerged with trepidation, carrying our umbrellas out of habit. We shed coats. We closed our eyes. We were made warm. I took Solomon to the greengrocer, where I picked carrots, a beet, a handful of pearl onions. The greengrocer put my basket down by the wooden cash drawer, where a slim stack of greasy bills looked deceased, coffined. Wordlessly, he reached out and patted my huge belly, then he placed his hand on my heart and closed his eyes. I started to step back, but he hushed and pressed. "I'm counting," he said, his eyes unopened. "We haven't measured you in a long time."

"Sixty-five beats per minute," the greengrocer finally said. "Very nice, excellent. You are just as you should be." His statement surprised me by being true. Out of the muck, something green had sprouted. I paid quickly, the bell clinked, the door closed and I went around to the back of the shop, where I leaned against the mud wall and cried.

"What's wrong?" Solomon asked.

"That's the thing—nothing is wrong." I was fine, I was big. I was just as I should be. If only it could have lasted longer.

On an evening full of the last gray light of a halfhearted sun, the stranger found herself alone in the barn with no prayers to record. She decided to sweep the floors and wash the windows with vinegar. She did not reach out the back window and prune the apple tree, because she liked the sound the leaves made when the wind pulled them across the pane. Where the wall and floor met, she found a dried-up lily of the valley. The stranger put it behind her ear. She admired the stars our village had made so far. She felt a kind of lightness—almost faith—when she looked at them. A universe was being constructed, even though there had been too many losses to write them out of the story. It was not the purity of this world that the stranger loved—it was how hard everyone had worked to believe in it.

In the corner still reserved for animals, the stranger swept under the sheep, who bleated and mewled. She put the scuffled-out hay back in the chickens' nests. The chickens pecked at it. The stranger picked up a bowlful of feed and swept where it had been. The floorboard moved under her broom. She pressed it back into place but the other end came up. She pulled at that other end, and it opened like the top of a box. Underneath there was a dark hole and the scent of cold earth. She kneeled, pressed her hand to the dirt. She lowered her arm in, deeper and deeper until she touched a square object. The stranger pulled her empty hand back out quickly and looked at it, questioning, as if it might be able to tell her what it had found. The hand was mute.

The stranger closed her eyes and lowered her arm in again, this time waiting for the shape she knew she would find. She wrapped her fingers around it and pulled it slowly out. In the light, it became a radio. Speakers, dials and an antenna. It was not dirty, as it should have been if it were buried long ago. Her fingers grazed the dials, but did not turn them. "Do I?" she asked herself. The loss of her old, real life began to thrum in her temples, in her chest. She remembered the letter she had read, and how meager it had seemed. The old world's failed attempt to matter. Here it was again, ready to make another plea.

Never forgotten, but never remembered completely either, the truth of what once was began to bubble up. The stranger remembered the smell of her husband's neck after he had worked all day. She remembered the shoes by the door, and the heat of her daughter's forehead when she had been sick in bed. She remembered the day everything exploded in flames. Belief, the way the villagers worked to hold up the misty walls of the reborn world, was what made the stranger love them. Still, she wondered what would happen if she put her arm through one of those walls; if she opened her hand to another world, what might she find? Quickly, she put the radio in the hole and laid the board back down. She waited for someone to bring her a prayer. The forbidden world stirred.

All of us migrated to the square, where we sat or stood, faces up, adoring the warmth. We could not believe how wonderful it felt or how big the world seemed—our entire village was flooded with light. We had had moments of sun over the years, glimpses, sometimes even whole afternoons, but this was something different. We were utterly saturated.

Solomon was pale from sitting in the dark all day. His skin looked so thin it might tear. With his face to the sky, he began to thank God for the sun, but I stopped him. "God hears you in your own head. He knows you're thinking of him."

"I have to thank him for each thing," Solomon said.

Igor and Solomon had been spending whole afternoons in the temple, making little groups of blue progress. After a new space of sky had been made, Igor would let the sound of the prayers and the color of the artificial night lay him down and rest him. Solomon would keep working and kept listening, memorizing the incantations. There were prayers by now that we always sang the same way. *Blessed are you who made us, blessed are we who praise you.* Solomon had made a list of the blessings he could give and the blessings he could receive. When he and his father came home in the evening, he had prayed over everything he could: the bread, the water, the soup, the chairs, the table, the beds, the windows, the lights outside and the lights inside. Igor would fall right to sleep, but I would stay awake listening to my son chant to himself for a long time, the room breathing with his prayer. *I bless this moment and this moment and this moment.*

We sat quietly while Solomon said words in his head and I tried to let the warmth soak through to my second baby, who should have come days before. I watched a group of boys playing at the other end of the square. I knew Solomon did not play like that, did not tumble and build the way the others did. Had I made my little four-year-old into an adult before his time, even though all I wanted was for him to be exactly his own age, every day of his life? Had I kept him to myself, and now he only knew how to be like me?

"Do you know those boys?" I asked.

"I know who they are," he said.

"Go play with them," I said, giving Solomon a push. He shook his head, uneasy with people his own size. "Go," I said, and watched him walk carefully across the sea of shining stones, polished under the feet of endless walkers. I looked the other way, tried to give my son a little privacy in which to make new friends.

I noticed Regina and the widow talking by the statue. I felt a rush of affection for the girl who used to be my sister. Regina and

I had each experienced the other's alternate life. I wanted things to work out for her, not only because I loved her, but because it was the same as their working out for another version of me. The story was like a comforting, worn-in old fairy tale, and all I had to do to keep it alive was tell it to myself. I had rag-doll versions of us to play with and hold.

Regina had remained unmarried. She thought of herself as another species, like the unwanted child of a forest-dwelling giant dropped off at the cabbage picker's doorstep in what must have been a huge basket. To the rest of us, she did not look especially large. But Regina's reflection in the mirror was balloonish. Like someone had stuck a straw up her nose and inflated all her features. The day Moishe first brought the tailor's daughter home, that elf of a girl, Regina had left the room without saying hello. Her brother, with whom she had felt a clear and wordless understanding of life, with whom she had survived the loss of a sister, the beginning of the world and the aches of growing, had stood in front of her and said, "I want your opposite."

Regina had left the house with a satchel of clean underwear over her shoulder. She had gotten as far as the center of the village before losing her nerve. She sat there, hating her brother, hating his bride, the sausages of her fingers clenched in a fist with nothing but her satchel to punch. The underwear inside took more of a beating than they deserved.

"Bad news?" someone said. Regina thought, Great, now the statue is talking. Best of luck to crazy me. Off I go. "This world is

shit," the voice said. Regina turned around to find the widow leaning against the statue.

"I don't want to learn to howl," Regina said.

"Me either. But I do want a drink. Come on." The widow took
Regina's hand and, miracle of miracles, in that truly giant palm,
Regina's fist looked delicate, demure, ladylike. Regina could have
hugged her right there, pressing her face into those abundant breasts.

The widow's house had an earthen floor and a baby bassinet
full of empty jars. "I'm an inventor now," she said to Regina. "I have
invented something wonderful."

"Not enough money in singing?"

"No one in this town has any talent. It's a waste of my time on
earth." Everything smelled like vinegar. Burlap sacks of mustard
seed lined the walls and a vat of brown sauce bubbled on the woodstove. Garlic skins hovered like spirits. The widow put her big finger into the pot and offered the gleaming sauce to Regina. "Can I
trust you? With my secret?" Regina opened her lips and licked.

"Ouch, that's hot." She sucked air in to cool her tongue.

"Tasty?"

"Sour. Hot. Delicious."

"I'm calling it mustard," the widow said. "After the seed. In the
future, it will be in every house on earth."

"We haven't already invented that?" Regina asked, trying to be
gentle. "Are you sure you made it up?"

"Ha! It's so good you can't believe it ever didn't exist."

Regina decided it did not hurt anyone for the widow to credit
herself with this invention.

"Yes," the older woman said, drinking, "yes, yes." Regina had

had wine before but never this, and it felt like she had released a small, burning snake down her throat. She coughed. There was a narrow bed Regina could not believe her new friend fit into. She imagined the widow's bedtime routine: washing her face, putting on her nightgown, tying her legs in a knot.

"Were you ever married?" Regina asked, knowing a widow must have once been a wife.

"I was married for about five minutes when I was eighteen. In the naked part afterward, his heart stopped." Regina had a rare feeling of appreciation for her own lot. The widow refilled their glasses from a foggy, corked bottle. What was there to say? "This world, like I said, is shit." She looked at the girl next to her, her uneven hair, her unfitting clothes. "You're not so bad," she said. "You'll be fine. Love is not the only road to happiness. I'll show you around the mustard business."

In the sunshiny square, Solomon reached the boys and the boys said, "Get out of here, you're cursed."

Solomon prayed over them, saying, "I bless you, God bless you, I bless you."

And the boys said, "Your grandfather is a murderer."

Solomon said, "I bless you, I bless you, I bless you."

"Prove that you're not cursed," the boys said, pointing at the highest branch of the tree.

Solomon put his foot in a crook between branches.

"Your father is the brother of a dead baby!"

"Your grandparents are murderers!"

Solomon went branch by branch into the sky. His little body outdid itself. The branches became shaky. They shook with the wind. They snapped back. The boys quieted below and watched with their arms folded together. It might have taken him five minutes or ten to make it to the top. No one was even aware of time, only watching and waiting.

Solomon turned around and waved from the top. He looked down, triumphant. I opened my eyes just for a second to see if Solomon was playing with the other children, and I saw him up in the weakest branches of the tree. I screamed his name, and everyone's eyes opened to look at me, then at him. Solomon waved to me, waved to celebrate. He waved until his feet slipped out of their crooks.

He did not fall all the way down. He just tipped over and was wedged into a space between the branches.

Other people were much faster than I was in getting there. My legs felt dream-heavy and I snapped at them to move faster. It felt as though the space between my son and me kept stretching and each step took two to cross. By the time I arrived the new baby wanted out, and Solomon had a thin trickle of blood headed down his face.

"Are you . . . ?" I tried to ask.

"As long as you are." He was completely unhurt, except for a twig that had stuck into his forehead. At the healer's orders, and all at once, the village split into two groups. One carried me above their heads to my house, like a war hero. The others helped Solomon out of the tree. He was carried home in the arms of the quiet man whose name many people could not remember.

My people stood in a clump outside the house in the sun listening to the sounds of birth—my wailing, the gentle words of the healer, and my wailing again.

"Is Solomon all right?" I kept asking, and the healer told me again and again that he was perfectly fine.

"He is excited to meet his little brother or sister," he said.

Igor came running through the front door, his arms flying at his sides. "Another baby?" he yelled, as if this were the first he had heard of it. He tripped on his way over the threshold, falling onto his knees, then nervously turned to wave. "I'm fine!" he yelled to the well-wishers. "Another baby!" And he closed the heavy door.

Igor did not come to my bedside. He went into the closet, took out his best suit, black and pristine, and he put it on. He polished his shoes. Igor put on a sharp hat. He wanted the baby to believe that his father was a strong and capable man, a strong and capable father. The outfit, he seemed to believe, would be the first indication. He sat down on a chair outside the room where I could see his back and the rim of the hat. He held his hands on his lap. I like to imagine he was thinking of ways to impress the baby right away, prove that it had been worth the journey.

Solomon sat down next to his father and mimicked the folded hands. He had no top hat, nor did he have a fresh black suit. He crossed his feet at the ankles and tried to be very patient.

"I was just trying to play," he said. Igor nodded, unclear what the boy was talking about. "Dad?" Solomon asked. "I liked playing, even though I got hurt. I had fun." Igor smoothed his son's hair and leaned his own head on that warm globe.

"You are delightful," Igor said, and he began to doze happily off. Solomon stayed as still as he could while his father snored softly, head on head.

The crowd outside dwindled as the hours passed. Around the little house, there was the glow of a cluster of candles, shaded by the hands of the stranger and a few of our most faithful old ladies. And then a voice never before heard in the world called out.

"Hey," said Solomon to wake his father, "it happened. Time to go meet the baby."

He gently rubbed the sand out of his father's eyes and took his hand.

Inside, the new eyes were wide open.

"You see the world, don't you?" I asked the squirming boy. I was spread flat out on the bed in my nightclothes, sweaty. My veins felt like they were ringing.

Igor put his hand out and said, "I am your father." The baby did not reach for him but I took the tiny hand and placed it in his larger one. Igor smiled and shook. He sat down at the bedside where he patted his new son and me alternately.

Solomon came to the foot of the bed, saying, "I bless you, I bless you, I bless you."

"Come here," I said to my first son. "Are you all right?" He nodded. He looked perfect except for the small hole in his forehead, which had, at the healer's direction, been filled with cobwebs.

The stranger awoke suddenly that night. In the corner of the moonlit barn she saw a dark shape. Immediately, her dream-heavy body was sure that the ghosts of the past had found her, and she prepared to be taken back to the old, burned-out world.

"All right, I'll go," she called. Her voice bounced from the hardwood of the walls. The shape jumped and scrambled. "Hello?" the stranger asked.

"What did you say?" the shape asked.

"I'll come with you."

"Oh, I was just checking for leaks," the shape stammered.

"Leaks?" the stranger asked. Sleep softened, melted away, and the shape stood up from the place in the floorboards where the radio was hidden.

The jeweler came out from the corner and into the moonlight of the dusty window.

"I know about the hole in the floor," she said quickly. "I know about the radio."

"No. Oh, dear. Have you listened?" He fidgeted with the buttons of his jacket. He rubbed the back of his neck.

"No."

"I am terrible. How could I have?" he asked. "I'm so sorry. I never meant you to know. No, no, no." He punched himself in the temple. The stranger shook her head. Her outstretched hand was an invitation. Wordless, she opened the creaking barn door. The question of what she was doing appeared like a bubble. She popped it with an answer—loneliness. She knew the weight of knowing. Of feeling like the only one who knew, standing guard alone at the gate. Wind flapped the stranger's white nightgown against her legs. They were an unlikely pair—she in her bedclothes kneeling in a patch of bloomless flower plants, digging—he, dressed for the day, his hair blown on end, crouched and waiting to see what she would unearth. Mudded, decomposed paper was born from the hole. Whatever words it had recorded were erased by the dirt and water.

"What is it?" the jeweler whispered, holding in his palm a handful of paper shreds, torn roots, earth.

"The mail," the stranger told him. He pressed his thumb into the hand-warmed dirt.

"It never even occurred to me." He trailed off.

"You wanted to believe." The stranger picked bits of paper out, seeds from a lost species. She squeezed them together in a ball, tossed it back and forth between her hands.

"What did they say?" the jeweler asked.

"I wanted to believe, too. I never read them." The stranger felt a sting for the single exception she had set sail, which she did not want to admit. The jeweler felt a sting, too: an orphan who finds himself full of questions about the past that have no answers in the living world. The other story was lost in the ground. The stranger placed the ball of paper back where it came from, then offered her empty, cupped palms, and the jeweler poured his burden in. She put the dark earth into the hole and began to fill it back up. The stranger patted the sealed wound. She scattered a few loose stones over it, and the jeweler thought how like a faraway graveyard it looked, the bodies of another place so distant their markers appeared no larger than pebbles.

Inside, the stranger lit a dozen candles by the side of her bed. Their light made the barn walls come alive with stars. She patted the spot on the bed next to her, which relaxed under the jeweler's weight. The stranger felt her children, her husband, her own village reach out to her. Their memory filled her up—the empty space in her chest felt clogged and she coughed to clear it. She waited for a second before she asked the question she knew could unravel her life—all our lives. "What's left of the old world?" The jeweler took her two hands into his. He held them to his chest and shook his head. His face was white, but the face of the moon outside the window was whiter still. She put her head on his shoulder and cried the names of everyone she had loved before into his shirt. Regret for allowing this sadness rolled through her chest. All the work, all the fierce belief, all the help the world had offered by sealing this land off, by keeping the sky clear of airplanes, by trusting the villagers in their invention—the stranger's tears were a thousand promises broken.

"I don't know if the other world is there," the jeweler whispered. "I haven't listened yet. I was so lonely at night I couldn't stand it anymore. I just wanted some music."

"You don't know if there are terrible things?" He could not tell the stranger if there were or not. The soft moon and candlelight in the barn was so full of dust it was almost solid. The stranger swept her hand through it and watched the tiny particles fly away. She blew her nose into the handkerchief the jeweler offered to her. Sorrow sprouted leaves in the jeweler's chest. Now that his secret was shared and he saw what it could do to another person, he regretted having saved this object.

"I should never have come back for it. I should never have saved it."

"What if I want to listen?" she asked. He did not answer. His chest filled until it was tight, and he held that breath to make time stop.

"Why?" he asked finally.

"I could give you reasons. Because it might be the truth. Because it might not mean anything. Because I can protect us better if I know what's coming. To test what we've made." She paused. "Or none of those. Because here it is. Curiosity. Look at those dials, waiting to be turned."

The jeweler did not try to convince her that he had truly only been wishing for music, that he was entirely unprepared for the possibility of news. "Can I say no?"

She shook her head. "Please don't."

In the darkest part of the night, when the owls and the wolves were the only animals looking for food, the stranger and the jeweler made a small nest of blankets and they turned on the dial that brought one world into another, that made a window in the wall the villagers had worked so hard to build. Before the sounds made any sense yet, the jeweler turned the radio off again. "I have something to say first," he said, cracking his knuckles. "I love you. I have always loved you."

"But I am nothing. I am a space, a hole."

"And yet, you manage to fill me to bursting. I overflow."

The stranger ran her hand over her arm, her legs, feeling for more than she thought existed. In her chest, something very much alive was pounding.

"You are so good to me," she said.

The jeweler's shaking fingers turned the dial.

The radio sounded like a whimper at first, and then a man's words formed in the air of the barn. The language came rumbling through the stranger like an old train down overgrown tracks. "Do you understand English?" the jeweler asked. "Do you need me to translate?" She was surprised that she did understand. Her father had taught the language to her. So surreal was it to hear another man speak these words that it took a moment for their meaning to sink in.

This is the BBC Home and Forces program. This is Bruce Bellfridge. Here's some excellent news, which has come during the past hour from a communiqué from Cairo. It says the Axis powers in the western desert after twelve days of ceaseless land and air attacks are now in full retreat. It's known that the enemy's losses are extraordinary.

The sound changed and became crackly. Another man's voice came through the radio.

I'm lying in a cornfield. I can see many men around me taking shelter behind the banks, wearing their steel helmets while the terrific barrage goes on around us. The shells are whistling overhead. Now just listen to them.

There was a sound of pops, shots and then the crackly noise went away and the first man's voice came back.

We're interrupting this program to bring you a news flash. This is a news flash from the BBC in London. American forces have crossed the Rhine at a point north of Cologne and established a bridgehead on the far side. And that's the end of this news flash from the BBC in London.

Voices were replaced by a violin, rising, falling, the notes so sharp they could have cut skin. The stranger and the jeweler were absorbed. The names of places, rivers, were not supposed to mean anything, but the jeweler and the stranger remembered them like part of a dream, almost as a taste or smell more than a fact. They drew closer together.

The stranger asked the jeweler what the man had meant. Who was fighting? Where? But the jeweler did not know. They waited for the man's voice to come back. The violin played on. "Who are the men speaking?" the stranger asked.

The jeweler knew only one thing: He had not been so close to another body for this long since he was a child.

We shall fight on the beaches, we shall fight on the landing grounds, we shall fight in the fields and in the streets, we shall fight in the hills; we shall never surrender.

The strains of the violin formed, crested, fell.

They waited all night for more, but none came. In the short fits of sleep the stranger found, she dreamed of swimming in an ocean whose tides kept washing her back to shore, even as she swam farther and farther out. And the jeweler? What did he dream? He did not, because he did not sleep. He lay awake all night, not because he was worried about a great fight, but because he was feeling the soft heat of the stranger's body while music filled the big, dusty room.

In the morning, the stranger felt upside down. The world we had left behind was no clearer or more understandable than this one. Here, stars were populating the barn, people were going about their business and history only had to manage a few years of complexity. In the old world the names of hundreds of generals, borders of a thousand countries, territories, pacts, and everyone who had ever been were all trying to crowd onto the same little globe. It was impossible, she felt in a rush—too big to be real. Instead of what she would have expected, the new facts presented overwhelming evidence that the old world was the make-believe one.

"I have a wedding to perform today," she said, glad to have work to do.

The jeweler set off for the day feeling surprisingly light and free. No film of dishonesty or sneakiness was on his skin. The radio was not a danger but a prop, like a warm fire around which to gather, an excuse to allow two people's knees to touch.

The stranger went to wash in the river, but she never entered the water, because on the bank she found a man's shirt, which had come down the river so full of rotten leaves it looked as if the man was still in it. Out loud she said, "This might have been my husband's shirt. This might have been my father's shirt." She shook the leaves out onto the muddy bank. She looked around her. Green and sure, the mountains were the same as always on the river's opposite bank. Every tree grew slowly and patiently toward the sky. The stranger slapped herself on the face, as surprised as if someone else had done it. "But it could also be no one's shirt," her own voice reminded her. "It could mean nothing at all." The stranger dug a hole and buried the shirt. "Nothing, nothing, nothing," the voice in her own mouth told her. The mud went soft and shaky when she patted it. She wanted no one else to know. She believed the story. No—the story was true, indisputable.

That afternoon, the man who used to be my brother stood under the canopy, his sweet, chosen bride next to him. "We pray for this family, this new family," the stranger said. "We pray for everything you have in store, but better, if you can." She did not meet the jeweler's eye.

"We pray for this glorious sun to shine on!" the butcher hollered, to a blaze of cheers. This moment was transposed on top of my own wedding, and they felt like the same instant. Time was a dazzling lie, a magician with a bird in his hat. The truth, I felt certain, was that everything happened at once. How old was I? I was every age, at the same time. All the days of all our lives were today.

For the second time, Regina sat in the barn while the wedding taking place was not hers. She felt again that her limbs were enormous and as old and dry as thick-barked pine. But at her side, her friend was bigger still. The widow blew her nose into a piece of burlap that once held mustard seeds, but Regina knew that if anyone had asked, the widow would have insisted she was not crying;

it was only a bit of dust, caught in her nose. Handing the rings over, the jeweler said his private prayer again—May love be mine someday.

Perl and Vlad felt a rustle in their branches as their son took flight.

"Love," the stranger said, "is the single absolutely true thing in the world. It cannot be argued away, it cannot be crushed, it cannot be killed."

Everyone around me hooted and I looked up to see Moishe's shined shoe come down on a glass wrapped in a napkin that I recognized from my first childhood. I clapped and shifted my new baby into one arm so that I could put my other hand out into the aisle to try and touch the blessed pair as they passed, running as fast as they could into their good lives.

The villagers, wine-drunk and tired from dancing, drifted home. I fell asleep with my family warm around me. Moishe felt like mine again, just a little bit mine, now that we were both part of new families. I could imagine our lives becoming more and more similar as we went on, until we were two ancient bodies, deaf and blind, crooked and weak, remembering only the brightest flashes of our lives.

At home, Kayla spread butter, thick as her jealousy of the mother-of-the-bride, on a piece of brown bread. Hersh ate his butter with a spoon, and sprinkled a little sugar on top. In the space of a few years he had a baby, a teenager, a bride, and two grandchildren. He loved that his life tomorrow would not be transformed—the new world had made him grateful every time the milestone took place behind someone else's door. Kayla wanted every celebration to be hers. Hersh leaned his head on her shoulder and in the joy and sadness of their momentousless home, they put their heads on the table and fell asleep.

Regina went to the widow's house, where they drank vodka surrounded by the reckless scent of vinegar. While she drank, Regina carefully wrote labels for the mustard jars. The widow had jagged, fearsome handwriting that would have led any potential customers to believe they were about to be poisoned, while Regina's was a lilting script. Good Mustard with Seeds. Good Mustard without Seeds. The widow believed names should be direct and never tricky.

"It's hard to believe we ever weren't friends," Regina said, eating a deep yellow glob out of a jar with her finger. She offered a taste to the widow, whose mouth was warm and slick. By the grace of God, both women, still in their wedding clothes, fit into the small bed and slept as soundly as they ever had or ever would, their legs and arms finding rest like the tangled roots of two trees.

And for the first time since Regina was born, Perl and Vlad came home alone. The fire was still going and the house was warm. Vlad stoked the coals; Perl picked up a rag but found nothing to dry or clean. No one asked for a song or a prayer. "I don't know what to do with myself," Perl said. Vlad opened his arms.

"Just us two and no one else." He placed, like seeds in the earth, a hundred kisses on his wife's smooth scalp. Anything could grow there, but my first parents were in no hurry. They liked the offer this empty room made, all the dark quiet filling it like deep, rich, unknowable soil.

✦ ✦ ✦

The jeweler came to the barn with a box of cakes and a new part in his very combed hair, and he drew the radio out of the hole. The stranger said, "Let's wait to turn it on until some more of that beautiful music is on." The jeweler was confused, but he wanted her to be happy. They tucked themselves into the nest of blankets.

"Cake?" he said, opening the box.

"I have to tell you something," the stranger said. "I remember the other world," she said, biting into a chocolate square. "I remember all of it." This secret blossomed in the silence around them. "But I don't know if I believe in it."

"What does remembering mean, then?"

"The only true thing is what's in front of you, right now. We listened to the radio and nothing changed. It's Once Upon a Time. A fairy tale," she added.

"Tell me a story from before," he told her. "As a test." She let the old, forbidden images rise out of the ground where she had buried them.

"Once upon a time a girl lay on her back in the sunshine with a stomachache from eating too many plums off the tree," the stranger said. "She was proud of that pain because it had been such a joy to earn it."

"Once upon a time there was a boy whose father would stalk off to his jewelry desk whenever he was mad at the boy," the jeweler said. "He would always put the loupe over his eye. When he looked up at the boy, he had one small eye and one giant, magnified one and the boy thought he could see his insides with it. He thought his father was watching his mad little heart beat."

The stranger looked at the jeweler and smiled. "You had a father?"

The jeweler reached both hands around to the back of his neck and unclipped the necklace he was wearing, a gold chain with a delicate pearl pendant. "And a mother. This was hers," he said. "My real, actual mother. She wore it in the last world, but I want you to wear it in this one." The stranger closed her eyes as he brought the two ends around her neck. He moved her hair and it sent waves of goose bumps down her arms. "Listen," he said. And it was true— the barn was still the barn.

"This is the nicest thing, after reinventing the world, that any-one has ever done for me," she said, laughing, and she pulled his head to hers, and their lips together were the warmest, softest thing that any universe had ever seen.

In between kisses, the jeweler turned the little knob on the radio and the violin joined them in their loving. But that night they hardly heard it. They buried themselves under the stranger's blankets and held their bodies so close that there was no point in trying to tell one from the other. Their laughter and the small notes of their voices rose up with the radio's, and in the barn there was room for every version of the story—there was room for a hundred thousand beginnings and a hundred thousand endings. There was a place for everything that had ever been, because there was a place for the most infinite, indescribable future, too.

"I was wrong," the jeweler whispered into a small puddle of sweat in the stranger's clavicle.

"What about?"

"Something did change." The jeweler kissed his lover up and down her shoulder. That line, which had never existed before, now felt seared, tattooed.

"What's your name?" the stranger asked, her scalp itching with a sudden desire for this forgotten fact.

"Mordecai," the jeweler said. The name, floating down the river on that tiny white boat. It seemed so long ago that she had wondered which of her beloveds it might be. "Your brother is well," she said. "He misses you. Isaac, isn't it?" Shock did not register on the jeweler's face. He did not gasp. The jeweler did not even ask so simple a question as how she knew this. A kernel of laughter slipped from his mouth as he turned to look at her. To him, it seemed natural and perfect and glorious that the woman he loved would know his family, though she had never met them. As if they were distilled in him, and she had drunk them all up.

"Tell him I'm very well. Tell him I'm wonderful." He rolled the fat of her earlobe gently in his teeth. She unfastened every button, snap and tie the world had asked her to enclose herself in. Naked, the stranger felt like a specimen, and she wanted the jeweler to examine her, to discover the reason for every warm offering. He wet the dry riverbed of her spine with his mouth, he measured and weighed her breasts in his hands. He made an end-to-end journey.

I woke up before it was light out. I had dreamed about being chased by something fast. I wanted not to disturb my family so I tiptoed out of bed, slipped into my boots and coat and went outside. The stars were resplendent in the softening blue, and rain had brought the smell of sky down to earth. All our trees were dark and wet. I thought of the nocturnal animals making their last chase of the night as I walked toward the barn and thought about what prayer to log. I had nothing specific that day—everything seemed to be looking after itself—so I decided to pray for mothers, all of us.

The barn door was cracked, and I put my head inside. The stranger's bed was empty and I heard the sound of a man I did not recognize. "Hello?" I whispered. I went inside. A big shape in the middle of the floor caught my attention. As I approached, the sound of the foreign man grew louder. I found myself standing over the stranger and the jeweler, whose bare shoulders stuck out from inside the blankets. The stranger opened her eyes and gasped, shook the jeweler's shoulder. I was not looking at the lovers—I was looking at and listening to a radio, tipped over next to them, the man's voice coming out of it, clear and sure. I understood most of what he said, though it took me a little while to name which language he was speaking and realize it was the jeweler who had taught it to me.

The Battle of France is over. The Battle of Britain is about to begin. Upon this battle depends the survival of Christian civilization. Upon it depends our own British life and the long continuity of our institutions, and our empire. The whole fury and might of the enemy must very soon be turned on us. The enemy knows that he will have to break us in this island or lose the war. If we can stand up to him, all Europe may be free, and the life of the world may move forward into broad and sunlit uplands. But if we fail, then the whole world, including the United States, and all that we have known and cared for, will sink into the abyss of a new Dark Age made more sinister, and perhaps more protracted by the lights of perverted Science. Let us therefore brace ourselves to our duty, and so bear ourselves that if the British Empire and Commonwealth lasts for a thousand years, men will still say, "*This* was their finest hour."

I dropped my head. As simply as that, everything was unmade—a single crack and the silent darkness was flooded with fierce light. One sun shuts all the stars up. A bubble rose in my throat and I thought I might be sick. The stranger pulled the blankets over her body. The jeweler put his shirt on. I straightened silently up. "We tried to save you," I said to the stranger. "All you had to do was let us."

"You did save me. Look at me—I am saved."

I was thinking of my children and their lives ahead, and I was thinking of the terrors surrounding us, and I was thinking of my own two pale hands. Now that the story had been snipped, those hands were all I had left to protect my family with. I would fail, I would watch them die, they would suffer and all I would be able to do was reach out toward them with my blind fingers. I had been there at the beginning of the world, and now I knew what it felt like to be there when it crumbled. I took the radio outside. The last sound it made was of bursting open on a rock when I threw it.

The stranger, naked under the blanket on the floor of the temple-barn, her home, did not record, but prayed. "Bless Lena and Igor and Solomon and the beautiful, nameless baby. Bless the people upstream and the people downstream. Bless the clothed and the naked. The night is ahead as the day is ahead. We pray the bodies that know each other keep on knowing each other. We pray that the bread rises. We pray that we keep believing."

I stood at the doorway looking in, too angry to speak to God. Too angry with myself for believing in the protection of a new world. Too angry with the others for trusting the story. I touched what was within my reach, looking for something real. The wooden barn door, a rusted nailhead, my cheeks, my teeth, the spring my eyes tried to feed me with. It was as if the whole earth had gone soft under me.

Without being summoned, others came. They saw the radio. Without hearing it, they knew what it had said. I could hear a few old women inside join our stranger in her prayer. Then a few younger women started. Then the boys. They talked over the stranger. It was two, then three, then four, then all. Everyone had a prayer. If I could have found the steadiness to speak, I would have asked, begged, that the future—the only land my sons had to live on—would be longer than the past. That we had not found the ending to what had only just begun. *We pray that the night is longer than the day. We pray that the saddles survive until horses walk under them. We pray that the horses have someplace to carry us. We pray that there are a few cookies left someplace. We pray that sleep will rinse us all out. We pray that our stomachs make themselves full. We pray that there is a reason for everything. We pray that we do not die, do not ever die and leave only scraps of our clothing—silent, torn flags.*

These prayers were not one and then the next, these prayers climbed on one another, ground their heels into the shoulders of the others. The sayers of them started to shout, to yell their prayers in order to be heard. They put their necks back and screamed their hopes to the built sky. *We pray, we pray, we pray.* The sound of the prayers came smacking back from the walls. The walls yelled to everyone at once, and they voiced again their demands and wishes. It felt like being tumbled by a sudden torrent of water, a flash flood. I gasped, coughed. The prayers did not let up.

The people fell to their knees in the din of noise. They covered their ears and prayed louder, their own voices rattling in the cavities of their noses. They pounded their fists on the hollow drum of the barn floor. They stomped their feet. They jumped to get higher than the rest. And from above them, from the Constellation of Hope, Lost and Gained, one piece of one star was loosed and fell down to the floor, breaking into dust. When it hit, every single person stopped praying. They uncovered their ears and covered their mouths instead. The people looked at the broken piece of sky.

Now even hope wanted to bring the walls down around us.

"We will crush each other," the stranger said. "We will crumble this place."

"There will be no point in speaking if we don't pray," others argued.

"We will have no world left," she told us.

"What if we already have no world left?" I asked from the

doorway. The stranger made a sweep of her hand, pointing out the evidence, the facts, the furnishings that said our place was something solid.

"You pulled me from the river and we told a story. We just keep doing that."

Everyone squinched their eyelids and clenched their fists and asked and asked and asked as hard as they could in their own rusted brains, and the room sagged with silence. In my mind there was no clear prayer—just the words *please* and *help*, asked of no one in particular because there was no one I trusted would hear me. The villagers filed out into a lawless place, a penetrable place, a breakable place.

I sat down by the rock where the radio had burst open. I held my head.

The stranger came and sat on the ground next to me. "I'm sorry," she said. "I'm really sorry to have hurt you like this."

"Did you really believe in the new world? At first?"

"No. I knew I could learn to. I wanted to." She paused. "I have been working very hard to protect it by keeping everything out." She told me about the mail, the odd bits she threw back into the river. She was trying to calm me, to say that the only threat was our own disbelief. I was not reassured.

"It's all a lie then," I said. "And we are idiots."

"No," she pleaded. "It's just a day, another day, after hundreds of others before. Nothing has changed."

"I don't know what to do." My boys appeared in my mind, ungrown, their faces sticky, questions on their lips. I was sure I would not have the answer they needed.

"Just as we have been doing. Waking, sleeping, loving, praying."

"Except the story doesn't make any sense. What happens without the story?"

She was quiet. The metallic scent of love was on her skin. "There is always a story. No matter what we do, it can't help but unfold."

"I'm afraid," I said.

"Yes," she told me.

We watched sparrows flutter up, leaves quaking when the birds lit again on the branches. Even those small bodies were enough to set the trees shivering.

That night, the ghosts dragged the old world into our dreams. They whirred like huge fans, blowing all our good work around until it hardly made sense anymore. The butcher dreamed of giant metal birds. The baker dreamed of black huffing trains that rolled through the valleys, full of grain and passengers. The banker's wife dreamed of speaking to her sister through wires stretched across the mountains. All of us dreamed of villages bursting into flame, of running, the sound of boots hitting the earth behind us.

"Are you doing okay?" I asked the ghosts, who had once been people—grandparents and uncles—I knew and loved.

"We're dead, if that's what you mean," they answered. We asked questions we had always wondered about—the chicken farmer wanted to know which child was his mother's favorite, and the butcher asked his grandmother what it felt like to die and the butcher's wife asked her sister what year it had been that the trees were so full of apples their limbs broke. The ghosts shrugged us off.

"We thought you were starting over," they said. "We thought you were done with that old boring world we made."

We tried to explain. "Your world was starting to erode."

"Sure," they said. "We understand. We don't mind that we did it all for nothing."

All the ghosts wanted to do was bicker. "The new world," they scoffed, while they noted the holes in the baker's socks and the spiky slept-on hair of the banker's children. "Doesn't look like anything's changed to us." The ghost mothers sat at the bottoms of their living children's beds and cleaned their nails. "Are you going to do those dishes in the morning, or is that unnecessary now in the new world?" they asked while their offspring tossed in their sleep.

"At least we realized when it was time for a new beginning," we whispered. The ghosts were silent and, we were certain, smug. "Stop acting like you know something!" we said. We felt them smile down at us. "Ugh!" we cried.

The stranger waited for her own ghosts to arrive. Her children, a hundred times over. Each version of themselves—three days old, two years, three and a half, six. She imagined them all standing over her, their porcelain skin broken only by the flush in their cheeks. They would be peaceful-looking, a kind of patience fallen around their shoulders like a shawl. "Hello," they might say. "Hello Goodbye. Hello Goodbye." They did not come, those ghosts. Were they angry for being invented out of the world? Did they want to help their mother survive, which was the hardest job of all? Much harder than dying? While the rest of the village was haunted and nagged, the stranger was left alone, stirred into the dark batter of night.

But the dream every single one of us had, and the one that broke our hearts, was not about death or destruction or anything momentous. It was this: a normal day, no new world, no new rules, just an unremarkable day. Nothing floated down the river. We drank some tea with our bread. Birds were singing, but we did not notice. Time was a river we were carried upon and neither the spring nor the mouth was visible. We had no reason to appreciate every single second of the day—we had no reason to do anything but sit and breathe.

In that dream, the world did not require us to turn it.

THE BOOK OF
THE SECOND FLOOD

We were drenched, soaked, full of dirty water. As if the radio had made a hole in the roof of the world, and everything we had kept out for a time flooded back, a torrent. The streets were puddles. The puddles were ponds, the river was a gnash of toothy froth. And in the tall grass: frogs. As if they had been seeded there, as if the wheat had dropped these four-leggeds. The frogs were a thick, slimy lather over everything, and their song was so loud we could not hear one another's words.

The chickens proved themselves tireless hunters of frogs. Soon the barn was empty of those slippery things and we took refuge there, gathering each evening to construct the heavens. The sky grew to cover everything we could reach while standing on chairs, and then, bit by bit, the places a ladder could take us.

As we worked, the butcher suddenly burst out, "The world was supposed to be designed to work perfectly. We made it *exactly how we wanted it*, and now it's malfunctioning right under our noses!" The butcher's face was splotchy and sweating.

Kayla threw her plaster spade onto the floor. "He's right," she said. "We wanted a new place, a quiet and safe and clean place. What was so difficult about that? Have we not earned it, have we not given up absolutely everything we had to make it possible?"

The stranger bit her lip. "It's not going to be easy. You are doing your best, but you have to be patient."

"But are you doing your best?" Kayla sniffed. Depending on how you looked at it, the stranger had either given up or gained more than anyone else. At first I had thought of her like a blown-egg shell, delicate and empty, but then I came to see that she was not breakable like that. She withstood storms, bowed in the wind. She was a weathervane, twisting in gusts and in breezes. I did not know if I admired her, or wanted to send her spinning in circles.

"Why did you bring that forbidden object into our barn?" the widow asked.

"She didn't. I did," the jeweler said.

The widow sulked in the corner with the goats, scraping their food around with her spade. The goats and the woman were a temperamental match. Regina ground a dry pile of anonymous poop into the floor with her boot.

The stranger praised the beautiful starry night we had created. She praised our efforts to make a bright place in darkness. "You have done so much," she said.

The stranger had tried so hard to keep us from all the confusion, the unfairness, the sadness. "You are a mother, too," I said, remembering it as the words left my mouth. Her eyes fell closed, sails losing their wind. "I mean to say that you are our mother," but her dead children had already been invoked.

"You won't be surprised by this, but I'm tired," Igor said. He sat down cross-legged and held his head.

While our minds bit and spit, our hands were busy cementing pieces of broken plates to the wall of the barn, and our sky grew around us, each neighborhood of stars, each tile, a dream of peace and silence. Our hands believed in heaven even while our minds panned for catastrophes. Our hands were first to forgive.

"It was belief in, not against, something—that made the world new," the stranger said, reminding herself as much as anyone. She suggested we go around and say the names of the constellations we were working on—the sheep, the goat—to each of which we had given a meaning: the horse, which oversees the birth of babies; the pine tree, which keeps watch over men who can't sleep; the potato, which looks after those who fear being alone. The frog, which must have *some* purpose, and the chicken, which pecks the frog.

We told the stories of our lives and made stars for each of the parts: a star for the day we saw our wives first; a star for the first day we held our mother's hand for her sake and not our own; a star for the day the rain came under the doors and each man in each house thought he was going to be the hero, that when he went to his window he would find the rest of the buildings gone, having floated away, and only his own turned into a boat.

The greengrocer's wife opened several jars of fruit canned many summers ago. We ate it by the light of our lanterns, the apricots sweet and slippery on our tongues.

While we licked the juice off our fingers, people suggested many honorable names for my baby. Saul and David. Strong-sounding names like Gregor and Ivan and Radu. I did not like any of these. I said I already had one king, and two only meant fights. I said strong was fine, but I wanted better than that. So they suggested beautiful names like Florian for *flower* and Aster for *star*. But I told them to be patient—surely he would tell us his name when he was ready. "Call him whatever you like, he will still be himself," I said. The villagers looked to Igor in case he was more logical, but he had ceded all authority to me by falling asleep at my feet.

Every family I had ever been part of was in that room. It made my skin itch. The Lena I was when I was six in a houseful of cabbages and the Lena I was when I was growing at the rate of a year every few weeks with Kayla and Hersh and the Lena I was when I became a mother were people who might not have easily understood each other.

Time outside crashed away, beating the earth and emptying the sky.

And then, just like that, the seal of quiet broke and we heard a series of huge crashes outside the barn. We heard knocking on doors of the houses nearby. We went quiet. I wished I had more hands, enough to hold my boys and Igor, who slept soundly by my side. We all opened our eyes wider, as if we might be able to see through the walls. A group of three men in uniform threw the heavy doors open and looked around. For a long moment, the soldiers scanned the room, face by face, a black pistol in each of their hands. They looked in my direction and began to laugh, which was a language we understood.

The soldiers, dressed in torn green uniforms, spread out across the room, stumbling, pinching women's cheeks and whispering greasy words. They smelled like someone was trying to preserve them in alcohol. Husbands raised their hands to slap the men away but the open mouths of guns talked them down. The biggest of the soldiers walked straight toward me, though he did not meet my eye. My heart crashed into my chest. Solomon cowered in a ball behind my back. I hoped I was big enough to hide him. The soldier kneeled in front of me and tucked a fallen lock of hair behind my ear. His breath was wretched. His eye sockets were deep pits and he smelled like alcohol, dirty hair and marsh water. At the slime of his touch, I reached up to wipe my face. "*Brutta*," he cursed.

The soldier turned to Igor who, incredibly, slept on. "*Prezioso*," he said, the word slithering out of his mouth like a snake hatching. He slid his big arms around Igor and picked him up. I screamed, put the baby, his cry like a saw, on the floor and tried to wrestle Igor back. The soldiers just laughed. The thought that Igor was going to wake up in some horrible man's arms was like sharp glass being dragged through my chest. The big soldier, my husband in his arms like a child, spat at the floor by my feet and stumbled right through the door. The two smaller soldiers squeezed in a last assault. One punched the baker in the neck, kicked over the stranger's stack of prayer books. The other knocked Vlad's hat off his head. Then he fired a single bullet through the wall.

I started to run after them but the barber blocked my path.

"That's my husband," I said, my voice full of hills and valleys. The barber made the shape of a pistol with his fingers because this was enough to quiet any fight he might have had in him. "Where are they taking him?" I asked.

The barber shook his head. "We don't know who they are," he said. "We don't know anything."

"That's Igor," I kept saying.

I looked to the stranger, because she was supposed to be the one who understood the horrors we were here to avoid. She shook her head and put a hand on her chest.

"They were from Italy!" Kayla announced. "I remember that language! Hersh had a grandmother who was from that seaside country, she was a silk trader, nice stuff that silk. Maybe we are related to that man!" She kept chattering, nervous and hysterical. I saw a flash of Igor wrapped up in a fabric so soft he might never wake up again.

"Where are they taking my husband?" I asked no one. All the no ones shook their heads. Solomon cried and was tackled by a pile of women, where he was met with so much comfort, so much soft singing, so many shushing bosoms, that his cries were snuffed out.

"We're sure he will be returned," everyone said, not at all sure.

"No one is going to help him?" I cried. "No one, no one?" My eyes ran around the room, but nobody stood up. We had become a fearful people, living on an island where we forgot how to defend ourselves. I had known the ache of a growing family—of adding mothers and fathers, husbands and sons; now the first subtraction bit me with jagged teeth.

I gathered my babies in my arms. The stranger followed me out under the eaves, beyond which waterfalls of rain were sheeting. "You are you. You still are," she yelled over the downpour. At that moment, I was not comforted by the idea. I might happily have fallen out of my life and into someone else's. I did not respond or turn to the stranger. She grabbed me hard on the shoulder. "Now say it to me," she said. Solomon looked up at her and wrinkled his brow.

"What?" I asked.

"Tell me that I am myself. Tell me that I still am." I had grown used to the stranger existing as an empty case. We all had. The city where she used to live, burned and tortured, returned to the world. Grass had grown over it. The children, the husband, the friends, walked that rubble as ghosts. They remembered the woman who was the opposite of a stranger to them. She was the opposite of a stranger to me too now. She was as familiar to me as my own reflection, showing me my own existence each time I questioned it. Until now, I had not considered that I might have the privilege of doing the same for her. "You still are," I told her, and she closed her eyes.

"You have to survive to tell what happens," the stranger said. "That's your job now."

I ran home through a torrent with my babies in my arms. Solomon said nothing. His eyelashes were studded with tears or rain. The wetted stones underfoot reflected a sluggish moon. My heels clicked and echoed—my path was no secret. From each corner, each crack between shops, I expected, almost hoped for, a pair of long arms, reaching for us. "Where are you?" I asked my husband. "Be here," I pleaded. "Be home."

At my door, our door, I could not turn the knob unless I put one of my children down, which I would not do. Solomon untucked his little hand from his coat pocket. He tried to reach the knob, but his arm was too short. "Put me closer," he said. I leaned us down, the knob turned, the door opened. Igor was not inside. Somehow, that felt like the final answer. His not being in the house was the same thing as his being gone from existence. Off the face of the earth.

My heartbeat was incomplete, an unanswered question rising again and again in my chest. I understood how precious the last years had been, how still the surface of my life had become. Now the world was rotted and full of holes. Igor had been plucked as easily as an apple. Solomon and the new baby were even smaller, even more grabbable, and I knew that I myself could be traded. Igor's space was open, and any man might decide he wanted to fill it, to save me, to do me the favor. War was a sick dog, teeth bared, the rope around his neck unraveling. A need began to rise up in me, and that need was to run.

Suddenly, someone tapped on my window. I jumped up to open it before I thought to be afraid. "Igor?" I asked. But it was not him. Fear knocked me across the head as the figure there reached bony fingers up to push its hood away. I slammed the window closed, but the latch was slippery and I could not get it in my grip. The figure tapped again. The window creaked open.

The hood fell away and the face came into the light. It was my real mother. My heart would not still—I had to lean against the wall to keep from falling. Perl drew her face close to mine and said, "Sometimes you think you've lost something but you've only shared it."

"You scared me," I panted. She put her hand on her heart. "But sometimes you really have lost it," I whispered back.

"You'll see," she said. Her hand, when she touched mine, was cracked and rough. She had not held it since I was a child, since I was her child. Her fingers were warm, in spite of the cold outside, and strong. I was still tremoring.

"Are we dying?" I asked Perl. She did not answer me. "Is the war coming? Is it here?" She did not answer again. "Why did you give me away?" I asked. "Why did you lock the door so I couldn't come home?" I could have stood there asking questions without running out until the flood carried us all away.

"I never stopped being your mother."

Together, we felt the weight of our small tribe lessen. We felt subtraction. "There is so much more to lose," I said.

Perl reached into her pocket and took out a forbidden old object: a silver compass with a black face and a bright red needle. "I am always going to be in one of these directions," she said. "No matter how big the map is, I'm on it somewhere." As soon as she placed the compass in my hand, I realized the process of my leaving had already begun. Away. Our village was found, it was known and it was mapped. The only way to protect my children was to make us disappear. A person who does not exist cannot be tracked and she cannot be traded.

"Come with me," I said to her. "All of you."

"It's better if you are few."

"I can't rescue Igor," I said, praying for forgiveness. "If I found him, there would be nothing I could do. My children, they are mine to save."

We both wanted to say we were sure Igor was going to be fine, he was going to come back, something was looking out for him, but neither of us had the strength to lie right then.

Away, away. My brain started clacking out a list: sweaters, bread, water, socks. Elsewhere, that forbidden place, trickled closer. I looked at the compass. No matter which way I turned it, the needle righted itself. I decided to follow it—something that steady should not be taken for granted.

I said to the woman who was once my mother and might have been so again, "Please do not forget us." Her hat was stuck to her head with rainwater.

She said, "I know it doesn't always make sense, how you go about loving someone. Sometimes loving someone means gathering them back, sometimes it means sending them away." She had already forgiven me for breaking her heart. "Include us in your story and we will include you in ours. That is the job of a family."

"Take care of Igor, if he comes back," I said. She turned away from me. Neither of us said goodbye.

And then, the world froze over, the rain turned to snow and the fields at dawn were crisp and shimmering, and the frogs were flat, dry disks—their toes spread open, their eye sockets empty caverns and their mouths frozen silent.

· V ·

THE BOOK OF THE SEA

Igor's head throbbed at the same time that it felt cottony and slow. What dream is this? he wondered, as he opened his eyes. Latches clicked, gravel crunched under the boots of the men who would likely slit Igor's throat. All at once there were voices everywhere. Men and women talking to each other, the high-pitched plea of a little girl begging for something sweet. The language was a singsongy jumble. He was pulled through the door, led up a creaking walk and seated on a bench. Salty wind teased at Igor's hair. Birds called mournfully overhead. The sound of water everywhere, sloshing and churning, bubbling up. A man leaned in close to Igor, ruffled his hair and said, "Almost home." Russian was a language Igor did understand.

Igor waited to be shot from behind. He waited to be kicked into whatever body of water was below, to sink to the bottom. He waited to see God, the whole hulking bright light of him. The word *alone* knocked around his brain. For hours, no one came, no one killed him, no one set him free. The voices were far away and chirping. The craft he was on rolled up and down, tossed back and forth. Igor was sick, and the smell of it taunted him.

Igor tried to make sense. Where and why and who. Scenes from his journey rose like bubbles: The snap of a latch and Igor was pushed onto a cold seat. He was blindfolded and his legs were tied, trussed like a broiler hen. An engine came to life. An engine? he thought, and in that rumble Igor became a traitor, the world he helped make turning to foam. He begged; the soldiers laughed, and then one of them knocked him hard on the head with the butt of his rifle. Igor had felt everything go soft around him as they began to move. The direction they went was away.

He remembered waking up with his back against a tree and an argument going on around him. He tried to plead but his brain was mushy. In the tall trees a hundred feet above Igor wind had been caught; not even the wind was free to go. He could not stay awake for more than a few minutes at a time.

He remembered being back in the automobile, bumping farther along, the three men laughing and chattering like schoolboys. When they stopped moving, the scent of urine came at Igor. He needed to pee too, which made him furious. His body had dumbly continued its machinations. Then a man came up close to Igor, close enough that the smell of him, which was stale alcohol and burning wood, saturated everything. The soldier leaned in and placed his hands under Igor's arms as if he was picking up a baby. He stood his prisoner up, feet on the ground outside, and gently unzipped Igor's pants, held him. It was the sort of kindness that made a person feel ill. They were there for a long time, the soldier kicking rocks, before Igor's muscles relaxed and let go the liquid. In the car, he cried.

There had been nights on the ground and days driving. In this dream, there was an endless supply of land to cover. Away, away, away they went.

Footfalls again, this time toward Igor. And then light, a flood of it. He saw stars, though it was daytime. Here was an entire ocean, a thing he had never seen. It became bluer the farther out he looked. His vision widened to take in the scene. He was on a passenger ferry. There were huge curls of rope like dredged-up sea serpents, salt-eaten wooden benches and churning smokestacks. Scattered around the deck were men and women in the middle of a regular day. There were soldiers, too, uniforms and weapons marking them. The language they spoke was long lost, like a song remembered somewhere in the body's hidden cells. He could not understand the words but the tune began to make sense. Italian, Igor thought. From Italy. He almost laughed because it seemed so silly, this sudden insistence on the existence of Italy. Of all things, that was what had fought its way back in?

Igor's attention came back to his own body. He was tied to a bench by his wrists and ankles. He couldn't see anyone else tied up and no one seemed to want to look him in the eye. He felt dirty and sorry and foggy. A soldier, seeing that he was awake, came and stood over Igor. The man was small and he looked tired.

"Please," was the only word Igor could say. The soldier sat down next to him. He began the job of untying the ropes around wrists and ankles without explaining why. Igor listened for the sound of explosions, of guns, of airplanes. Only the sea splashing the ship's side sang back.

"Can you understand me? I don't know your language, but can you speak Russian?" the man asked in a rough accent. He paused. Igor nodded. "You are our prisoner," the soldier said. "If you cooperate, we won't hurt you." He put his hand to his brow to shield the sun and his eyes turned a soft gray in the shade.

The light felt like needles piercing Igor's brain.

It would not have mattered if Authority Himself had walked up, bespectacled and with a ream of evidence to support his case: Everywhere, atrocities and battles. Bombs dropped on the innocent by dozens of different kinds of men, all of them believing that that particular explosion was worthy, those deaths justified. Newspapers, military orders, radio broadcasts, blood-soaked uniforms and wailing widows would have confirmed the story. But Igor, a career sleeper, was sure he knew how to spot a dream.

Someone on shore caught the giant rope a person on board had thrown to him. The ship rubbed against the wooden pilings like a neglected dog. A crowd gathered on the dock, sobbed for the boys who had survived the war so far and the boys who had not. Three mothers nearly suffocated, in pillowy bosoms, their returned sons. Mothers whose sons did not disembark collapsed on the ground and had to be carried home. The crowd asked about this prisoner the boys had brought, how dangerous he was, how deranged. By

now, the soldiers had grown bored with their trophy. "Not dangerous at all," they said. "He sleeps most of the time. He's like a
housecat. He might even be good luck. We didn't break down once
after we took him."

"Can I keep him?" a young man, the jailer, asked the soldiers.

"He's all yours," the soldiers said, wanting to think about anything but the war.

Igor's dream took absurd turns of loveliness. He and his personal guard went for the tour. Igor was shown the taverna where he
could have his wine, the market where he could buy his cheese and
the bakery where he could buy his bread. All the people in town
shook his hand, because he was their prisoner.

The guard showed him which bench was best for watching the
girls coming out of the place where they did the wash, which bench
was nicest in the morning to drink your coffee. "I was thinking
about it, and it's likely that we've saved your life," the guard said.
"You are a very lucky man."

Here he was in the most foreign of foreign lands, a place filled
with outlandish sunshine. A place with its own ocean. A place
where there was a man in charge of one thing—making sure Igor
was taken care of. And somehow Igor was supposed to believe that
this was because of a devastating war? Because millions of people
were dying? Because he was a prisoner of war?

Igor decided to wait patiently to wake back up into his old, gray
life. A person does not get lifted to salvation this easily.

The guard showed Igor to the jail where he would sleep.

"Will anyone else come?" Igor asked, looking at the six bunk beds.

"No, not that we know of."

Igor had thought of a sure way to reveal the guard's kind exterior as false, to stretch the membrane of the dream until it burst. "I hate to say, but is there a larger bed someplace?"

"A larger bed?"

"I love to sleep. It's what I'm best at. Usually, and I hope I don't sound ungrateful, I like more room so I can spread my legs out."

The guard looked at the cot. "I will see what I can do."

Igor felt a strange hum in his head, disbelief rumbling like the engines that brought him here.

Within a day Igor was helping several men carry the bunks out and carry in the four-poster of a recently dead old woman. The guard borrowed blue sheets and white cotton blankets from his mother, which he and Igor tucked in around the mattress, snug. The pillow remained—a pillow is the same size no matter the bed it lives on.

Each night, the guard came and locked Igor into the cell and each morning he came and released him. They went for their coffee and they sat on the rocks by the sea, where the guard taught Igor his spiking, giggling language.

"Tell me again how I am here? Why I am here?"

The guard told the story the same way it had been told to him.

The island boys had fought a losing battle far in the north. Their side had sustained hundreds of thousands of casualties, and three of the island boys, just three, walked out on their own feet. For months, they hid in a fallen-down building and gathered parts to fix their car so they could get home. They had no radio, no idea what was going on anywhere. They could not get their heads back after so much death. Finally, the motor turned over and they drove for two days without sleeping, without speaking. At the foot of a mountain range, exhausted and filled with the rabid, manic combination of the elation and guilt of survivors, they bought two jugs of vodka from a band of Gypsies, and that night, as they made camp, the boys emptied them.

Drunker and drunker, they replayed the deaths of their friends, the rotted bodies they had seen, the enemies they had drained of blood. We must deserve something, they said. A little honor. A small trophy. Somewhere in that stupor, it made sense to go looking for one.

Morning slipped in too early and revealed a man tied to a tree, blindfolded, with blood dripping down his face. The soldiers remembered only vaguely how he had come to be there and disagreed about what to do with him. It was the war itself that made the best case: life is disposable, nearly meaningless. Every day, thousands more are extinguished, captured, maimed. Everyone on this continent is marked for death. How much could it hurt to take a single little prisoner?

Sometimes it happens that two very different stories, two distant lives, come crashing together. Once, there was a sleepy man who had lived in a brand-new world until he was reeled out like a caught fish. And once, very, very far away, on a scrubby island floating in the black-blue sea, there lived a lonely young jailer who had no prisoners, had never locked the door on a murderer, an adulteress, even a petty thief.

All through the winter and spring, the summer and fall, the jailer had swept and paced the cell. He had washed the walls, which were already clean. He had polished the stone floor. All through the winter and spring, the summer and fall, the other island boys had inched closer to the night they would seek a reward. All through the winter and spring, the summer and fall, Igor had practiced being sound asleep.

Perhaps Igor and the jailer's fate was an answer from God. Perhaps the entire architecture of the war was built to land a single body in a single cell. Or perhaps fate is nothing more than an accident—two ships lost in the dark, running aground on the same windward beach.

Igor thought about what the scene of his capture had looked like: the villagers cementing stars in place, the room turning slowly into the heavens, no talking, only the scrape of tile. Enter soldiers, exit soldiers, Igor, just awake, in tow.

"Was I asleep in the story?"

The guard squinted at him.

"All right, then," Igor said, deciding he liked his portrayal better in the soldiers' version of the story. "But if I am supposed to be your enemy, then will you kill me?"

"No, certainly not. Maybe a life sentence with no possibility of parole. You are useless to me dead." Even the guard's eyebrows were thin and unthreatening. "Anyway, why would you want to leave?" He gestured around them at the thyme-dry hills and the blue and bluer sea.

"I have a family. I have a home." Igor thought for a moment. "When you say there is a war, do you mean a real war? Horror and all that? Death?"

"You haven't seen the pictures? Hitler, Churchill? Mussolini? Stalin?" Igor was quiet. He rolled his sleeve up and examined the rope burns on his wrist. They stung at his own touch. "I knew your village was far away, but I didn't know it was that far away."

"It doesn't look like war here," Igor said, and put his face up to the dry, warm day.

"Of course. This is the best place on earth," the guard said.

"I have a new baby boy. And a wife, and a bigger son."

The wind brushed a little of the heat off their bare arms. The guard looked ashamed. Small beads of sweat popped and trickled down his forehead, which made Igor inexplicably sad. "That's a nice breeze," Igor said, surprised by his sudden desire to be kind.

"Is there anything you aren't satisfied with? About your experience? It must have been a bumpy ride."

"I am asleep," Igor reassured himself. "I am asleep and I am dreaming."

In the afternoon they ate a large lunch at the guard's mother's house. She fed them bean soup, pasta, baked chicken and a custardy dessert. She told Igor, "If you can tell me you eat better at home you can go back. You will be freed."

"Mother," the guard scolded, "he is our prisoner, you can't go freeing him."

"He won't go anywhere, because there is no way he eats better at home," she assured her son.

They both looked at Igor, whose chest was covered in crumbs, a trail of fallen soup leading the way to his lap. He shook his head. "It would be a lie," he confessed, spooning another bite into his hole of a mouth. "I have never eaten such a meal."

"Then he stays," the guard's mother said. "I told you." To Igor, she said, "This is what I can do with wartime rations. Just imagine my table in better times."

The guard's mother told Igor that her son was all right but a little bit of a sissy. She told him that his guarding of Igor was the best thing he had done so far. She told him how his brothers all lived in big cities where they fought for important things—the holiest of churches, the most beautiful of paintings, the most important politicians—but not this one. This one guarded a jail with no one in it. "You can't leave us," the mother said. "You're the only thing that makes my son here not look like a total idiot."

When they had eaten the last of their desserts, the guard's mother told them to go sleep in her bed. "I'll do the dishes," she said. "You have a nap."

Igor nodded enthusiastically at this idea, but the guard said, "No, thanks, Mother, we have to get him back to jail."

"I really am tired," Igor said when they got outside.

The guard looked puzzled. "What else would we do with our afternoon? This country is nothing without its nap. We'll sleep in the jail. That woman makes me crazy."

"I had a mother." Igor remembered, quite suddenly. "A lot of us had the same one. We were eleven, plus one who died when he was a baby. She cooked nothing but beef. She loved beef." He remembered being utterly devoted to her, following her around without acknowledgment. After he was married, he could not recall his mother ever having come to visit him and his family, not one single time. She had avoided him in the market and averted her eyes in temple. As if he were disgusting to her, as if she could see through his skin and bones to the hairy, blistered soul within.

"Did she make you feel like swimming out to sea and never coming back?" the guard asked.

The two men walked the path through the dusky green olive grove. The ground was raised raucous with rocks and branches. A lot of chickens wandered around, aimless and pecking. Goats clanged their bells without meaning to, tearing the grass from its roots. There were no sounds of voices. No bubble of laughing washerwomen, no scramble of children, no gruff of men smoking in the plaza. Just chickens and goats and the rustle of horses' manes in the wind.

"Everyone is asleep?" Igor asked.

"Certainly," the guard replied.

"This place is incredible. If only my family was here with me."

The guard opened the jail door to let Igor in first. "Home sweet home," he said. The guard opened the gate into the barred cage and Igor flopped onto the bed. "May I join you?" the guard asked.

"Please, guard, make yourself at home."

"Maybe you should stop calling me guard and start calling me Francesco," the guard said. "Since you're staying around awhile." Francesco went to one side of the bed and Igor to the other.

As he was falling asleep, Francesco asked Igor, not unlike a marriage proposal, to be his friend. Igor was not sure how to answer. Francesco gave him a pat on the back and, lying as hard as he had ever lied, he said, "I didn't realize how lonely I'd been."

As he drifted off, Igor saw my face and the faces of our boys. The angle of our noses, the smell of our hair, the way we moved. The deeper that Igor fell, my face, Solomon's and the new baby's faces, turned to mist. We hovered still, cloudlike, around him, but we had no hands he could hold, no ears he could speak to. *I almost remember you*, he thought, but then he did not again. He caught his family in whiffs, as faint and drifting as the scent of a flower. Home had been taken away as easily as it had been invented. A new place lapped at Igor's feet.

THE BOOK OF
THE DISTANCE AHEAD

In the pink of dawn, the border was clogged with blackberry thorns and brush. I wrapped my shawl around the baby and tied him to my chest. As if diving into water, I held my breath. We had to tear the branches apart, untangle their talons, duck and overstep, and still we emerged with bleeding arms. I had thorns stuck in my dress. The baby had a scratch across his little cheek and he grimaced at me when I peeked into his cocoon. We walked out of the village, just like that, out of the world. We did not fall off a cliff, nor were we swept into the sky by a tremendous gust of wind. The earth went on as if we had not crossed any border.

The old road was shabby and overgrown but obvious. We were going one foot, then the other into the past. Or was it the future? Had the lands outside our borders zipped ahead of us or slipped behind? What assembled itself along our path offered little evidence either way. Short, soft-needled pines, weeds, a bloomless crocus. Endless rolls of wheat, planted by knobbled human hands. A thousand worlds' worth of sky, and the singular sun coming to give us our turn at daytime. Light poured over fields and the way ahead of us was open and long.

The compass pointed us toward the mountains. I had no idea which direction was safest and which was most dangerous, but it felt better to follow something than not to. All I could do was go on. We came into a dense birch forest, thousands of white fingers of trees reaching out of the ground. A stream ran through the trees, and the rocks were mossy. Sticks stuck on the rocks, then came loose and twirled as they floated away. Solomon climbed into one of the birches, stood like a new branch.

"Are we looking for Father?" Solomon asked.

"We're staying safe," I told him. "It's better to be alone and quiet. We can be quiet, right?" We lay down under a huge tree whose branches cut the sky up. Fallen leaves under us crushed themselves soft. The tree smelled full and sweet and dropped only a few jeweled raindrops down to us, one at a time.

We listened to the sound of water hitting leaves. We could see only the gray of mist around us. We were wrapped in it, clothed. I took in the rich smells of leaves decomposing, of wet bark and turned dirt. The baby was warm on my chest. What does it feel like, I asked myself, to be away? Even though my back was against the earth, I felt as if I were floating above.

"Come to me," I said to Solomon, who was drawing the shape of a house in the loam with his finger. "Let me have you." Solomon put his face to my chest. He listened to what transpired inside, the gathering and sending out of blood. He listened to his brother taking liquid into his mouth.

"Can I taste it?" Solomon asked.

"What?"

"The milk."

The baby's suckling sounds matched the rolling of water over waxy leaves.

"You can if you want to. Do you?"

"Please." I pulled away the shawl I was wearing, pulled myself out from inside of it.

"What do I do?" he asked me.

"Just suck a little, it will come." Solomon's mouth was warm, now both breasts held in the soft of my children's lips. I felt the milk leave me. I knew that I was allowing one brother to steal food from the other, but I wanted to be enough for both of them. I felt Solomon stop for a moment, then start again. He laughed and drank. He was gentler than the baby was, more persuasive. I put my head back against the tree. I tried to feel its roots under me, the net of them holding everything up. I watched the leaves shake in the wind and the rain, the rain, which was slowing, which was quieting, which was loosening its hold on us. Solomon fell asleep and so did his brother. I held them to me, felt them against my skin. The breath turned wet and cold. They were heavy but I did not put them down.

At this moment, what was real mated with what was dreamed. I want to be able to say exactly where we walked and how we survived out there, for how long. We went north, unless we came to a wide river, or it looked like a town might be ahead, in which case we went east. In my palm, the compass was warm. Facts about how much food the body needs and my memory of what we found to eat do not match up. And time? As if time had ever made sense to me? What followed was one long night.

In the morning Solomon went out into the wheat and gathered stalks of it, brought it back to me. Together we opened the shells to pull impossibly small bodies of meat. We did not eat them one by one, but saved them in a pile, waited until we had enough, so when we ate it actually felt like eating. We chewed every bite until it was nothing. We worked and our fingers were striped with cuts. Today this was enough.

In the afternoon we tried to sleep. The baby talked noise into the canopy of whatever trees we found. Oak, maple, pine, beech. He seemed happy. He was with his mother and his brother, and his father still loved him someplace, of course.

In the evening we peeled sheets of bark off the tree and soaked them in caught water. Once soft, we ate the bark, dark tasting and sponged.

"We are doing fine," I whispered into the dark.

"I know," Solomon said.

"We are doing fine," I said again.

"I know," he repeated.

"We are doing fine," we said together.

I laid the baby, asleep now and wrapped in a blanket, on the leafed ground.

"Let's look at the stars," I told Solomon, and we walked out into a treeless place, out into the tall whispers of grass. We tipped our heads back and tried to find ourselves on that map. "Which ones do you know?" I asked.

"I don't recognize these," he said. "These stars are different."

Above us, the stars of another season rolled along. What was slapped here was unrecognizable, the work of a different God.

"Let's name them then," I said. "Let's get to know them."

"But they aren't our stars. Our stars are the ones on the barn."

"These are ours too now. This is our temple."

We traced a horse constellation, a river, a house. We traced a tree and a leaf. "There's a rabbit whose job it is to look after the birds," Solomon said, and I nodded though I did not see.

"What about this one as a man holding a sack?" I asked.

"No, not that. It's a woman holding a sack."

"All right, a woman. Where is she going?"

"She's going home," he said. "God will take care of her there."

"What if God is busy doing something else and forgets?" He did not take notice of my faithless question. Little believer, unbending. "What does she have in the sack?" I asked.

"It's her children in there, asleep. They were tired of walking."

"How far do they have?"

"Not far. They are almost there."

I tried to point out a row of stars that reminded me of an arrow but Solomon did not answer me. I tried to show him one that looked like a face but he did not answer.

"Are you asleep?" I asked him.

"Of course not. Where did we come from?"

"We came from our village, Zalischik. We lived in a house near a well. We had two sturdy pots, three stable chairs, a woodstove, beds, more families than we could have hoped for."

"What else?"

"We had your father. He will be back. We will be back."

"Tell me about everything," Solomon said.

"There was a river where the mud was thick and dark. Willows lived at its edges. In winter it was quiet and cold, in summer it was loud and cold. You had to walk through a field of wheat like this and a field of cabbage to get there. Your grandfather Vlad worked in the cabbage field. He was a very fast picker. He loved us."

"Remember the time Father and I discovered a cave on the bank of the river and it was filled with magic foods that replaced themselves whenever we ate one?"

"Sure, I will remember that."

"I want to nurse," he said, "just a little bit."

I opened my dress up, brought him close. I knew the milk would quiet if I did not eat enough, but I let him suck it away, let him drink what belonged to his brother. He drank me down. I felt the mechanism of his swallow against me. I felt the warmth of his cheek against me. I felt a drop of milk slipper down along the curve of my breast and fall off.

"Remember the time we forgave each other for everything?" I asked. Against my chest, Solomon nodded yes.

The birds had no idea that it was time to be quiet. They exploded the mornings with their music. They had so much to ask for. I, awake before my boys, waited while a sparrow hopped along, pecking. I waited until it crossed in front of me, but when I went to grab it, it flew. Its wings had it high and safe above me.

Already, time was losing us. It felt as if we had never had a home and also as if we had left it only in the last moments. It felt as if each sleep lasted weeks, leaving us with colder and colder mornings. Our feet wept with blisters and the corners of our eyes were scabbed with dirt. Our bones, tucked under threadbare blankets of muscle, rattled and shook. Above my sons and me, the stars slid along and the moon returned a new shape each night, and no one came looking for us. No one caught us or saved us. The days did not count themselves off but circled, dizzy and lost. It made sense to keep track of time only if there was a known end to the journey, which there was not. We might have been on day twelve of twelve thousand, or day thirty of one million. I let go of the idea of time, of progress, of beginnings and endings, and tried to pay attention only to one fact: We were alive, we were alive, we were alive. We were alive, and the little red needle kept pointing us onward.

Not one drop of rain fell from the sky. The earth and the sky and the trees and the stones and the path were dead dry.

THE BOOK OF HOME

There was a kind of stillness in the days after my family and I were gone. The villagers washed the dishes in warm water and fed the animals scraped-off leftovers.

Clouds poured forth and fear curdled all other emotions, but there was bread because the baker made it, there was water because the wives drew it up from wells, and there was meat because the animals were still killable—the animals were drained of blood if someone drained them. There were many things for the villagers to be grateful for.

Now no one liked to be outside in the day's revealing light. The street felt as exposed as a sliced-open wound. The man who captured

Igor became a giant. The villagers imagined that I was lost now in a hot, dry desert, my flesh burning away. Who knew what was next for the people, what curses remained? Just to press tiles on the ceiling—to eat something each day, to keep track of the dangers and hopes—was almost more than they could bear. They hated to leave the barn.

Both sets of my parents recounted my birth and childhood, two separate stories. Perl remembered that it was a bright morning when I was born and I had opened my eyes to look around. Kayla remembered that it was a wet, shimmering evening and I had cried so hard my throat must have been torn up.

"Has she told herself into a better story?" they kept asking.

The banker's children reminded the others about their brother Igor and the villagers remembered him, too. "He was an amazing sleeper," an old man said. No one denied this.

The wives touched the arms of their husbands and tried to tell them in this way that they were watching. Sunlight through that single bullet hole in the wall of the barn drew a bright, dusty line across the room. The villagers ducked to cross it, as if it might be sharp enough to slice them.

The baker recruited hands for kneading. In the bakery, the air was yeasty and alive. Did they discuss what they imagined was coming? Did they wonder if it would be better to run or to stay? When they kneaded the bread, and their hands were warmed by the motion of pressing and rolling and the dough was warmed by their hands, were they trying to remember what it was their grand-mothers looked like long ago, before any of these people were alive? Before this world existed?

Vlad took a wheelbarrow and some men with him to where the cabbages were still growing, paler and softer. He wanted to pile up whatever there was and watch over it.

The villagers said their prayers in their heads, a tiny orchestra, but did not let them get out. Nothing crumbled because of the people's prayers.

The stranger's life was the same as before, except now the jew-eler slept next to her, and into each other's ears in the dark of night, they laughed and they whispered and they pinched. When they were together, their bodies were entirely uncrushable, even by fear, that most invisible—and heaviest—of weights.

The weather grew colder and still everyone waited for the terrible end. Fat arms of vines scrawled out of the ground and choked trees. They wound themselves into windows like thieves. And then there was the sinking. At first it was dismissible. People felt a little taller than they had, that was all. They had to stoop farther to get through the door. When Vlad smacked his head on the lintel, he knew the house was outshrinking him. Some houses declined faster than others. Some slumped on one side, others descended evenly, like ships whose hulls were heavy with bilge-water.

Buttery morning light brought the stranger out of the barn to find the two best milk cows lying dead on the ground. She examined them and found no wounds. This was not the work of a fox. They were facing each other, as if a pact had been made, as if they had decided to go together to a better place. The stranger petted each on the head. "I understand," she whispered, wishing she could give the cows her blessing but knowing how much the villagers needed them. "I'm sorry to do this," she told them as she kneeled down, milk bucket in hand, and pulled at the cool udders until they were empty. She prayed for forgiveness for draining these corpses dry. When she announced the loss to the others, fear of shortage swept through like a sandstorm. Everyone looked at the flock of goats, who backed away, bleated. They were doing what they could. They had no more to give. No one did.

Instinct told them to condense, to stay close. Without discussion, all the villagers left their capsizing homes and moved into the barn. People brought their favorite sweaters and best pots. They went for their wrenches and fur shawls. Then for their meat tenderizers, their butter churns and, of course, the sacks of coins buried under the rosebushes. They rationed flour, butter, eggs. Everyone wore two words on their lips: Not Enough.

The villagers remembered sitting down with their children and eating supper, watching the fire in the stove tongue the air dry, discussing one thing or another and even playing a game of marbles on the floor before the husband and wife stood together over their young ones and sang a song to put them away. Their old lives had gone on so regularly it made them feel sick.

And frost started to form and the earth got its crust of ice. In preparation for the moment when everyone might freeze to death in one solid mass, as now seemed likely, and wanting nothing of their lives left behind, the villagers ventured out to take even the things they had always wished to get rid of. The whole drawerful of broken things—cups, eyeglasses, dolls waiting to be fixed whose eyes rolled around in their sockets, floppy and loose. The constellations on the walls became blocked by towers of objects. No one wanted to let go of anything they used to touch back when touching it meant nothing.

And the stranger and the jeweler held each other close. They learned—ever so quietly—every ridge, every slope of each other's bodies. The fact of one ankle held between two calves, four arms like a lock keeping everything good inside. He wanted her to be anything and everything she possibly could be. The biggest wallop of desperation, the brightest sweep of joy. If the stranger were burning hot, the jeweler would have become a lick of fire. If she were freezing cold, he would have become the spear of an icicle. If she was a swamp, he would be algae, growing over the entire surface of her.

If the people had been put out to sea, would their odd cargo have sustained them? On their lost ark of a world, floating alone, unpulled by the moon, unwarmed by the sun, the people waited to be dragged up onto some dry shore, some island where flowering trees might drop petals into their salty hair, and not long after, globes of waxy fruit.

THE BOOK OF
THE SEA AND THE SUN

When Igor passed by, the headlines all but walked off the yellowed newspapers and forced him to read them. German troops occupy Hungary. USSR retakes Odessa. Allies invade Rome. Tens of thousands killed on the beaches of France. USSR retakes Minsk. U.S. takes Guam. USSR invades German-occupied Romania. Allies liberate Paris. Soviet troops capture Warsaw. No story appeared about a miniature world discovered in the crook of a wide river. Igor scolded himself for even considering that the newspapers might have meant something. "Stupid Igor, stupid brain," he said to himself. "Never forget that this is all in your head."

For Francesco, there was only one fact of the war that truly scared him: Italy had joined the Allied forces. Technically, he suspected that his prisoner, captured for the now opposing side, ought to have been freed. But his island had been floating on the same deep blue sea for thousands upon thousands of years. It had not only seen empires rise and fall, but witnessed their relics dug up out of the soil and sold to museums. No one on the island labored under the delusion that politics meant anything. It did not matter to them if their sons switched sides, only if they came home alive. Their ability to continue living was the only real stake the island had ever had in this war. So far, no one had questioned the prisoner's fate, and Francesco planned to enjoy the company as long as it lasted.

Igor and Francesco went to the sea each morning and swam. They dove under the water so their hair went flying back behind. They stood on rocks and jumped in, judging each other's dives based on the lack of splash. They learned flips. When they got cold it was to the rocks with them, where the flat heat would leave red rounds on their backs. Even Igor turned a nice toasted brown. He shared bread crumbs with the yellow-legged gulls, who failed at their attempts to appear cold and ungrateful.

"It still isn't raining," Igor said.

"No, no rain today."

"At home it was raining. It was flooding. I wonder if it stopped there, too."

Whenever Igor mentioned anything about home, Francesco's muscles tightened. He tried to change the subject, to draw Igor's attention back to the spectacular glory of the island. "In the springtime, this whole hillside will be covered in tiny purple flowers," he said. "It looks like a painting. You will love it so much."

✦ ✦ ✦

Francesco's mother had them for lunches. They ate all the things she could make. They were filled up with food in such large deposits that it made them stupid for the rest of the day. They looked around fogged and dreamy. So much bean soup and stewed tomatoes and roasted meat that the world seemed practically motionless.

Full and clean, Igor brought the only part of the newspaper he loved—the advertisements—into bed. Dark-eyed men squinted from underneath crisp straw fedoras.

"I would wear that hat," Igor said.

"It would look great on you."

In the evening Igor and Francesco went to the square and played checkers with the other men, drank wine and flirted with the girls who strolled around and around, their arms hooked. The men ate things pulled from the sea and fried. They smoked the thin fingers of cigarettes. They talked halfheartedly about the war and who would win and which dictator was a bigger snake, and how much better it would be if their little island could secede and float peacefully away. Igor thought to himself that this was getting to be a very long dream. He looked forward to telling his family everything he had seen; he also hoped not to wake up just yet.

Igor shared his bread crusts with the pigeons, who gathered around him as dedicated as pilgrims. The girls came around, made a second of eye contact and then continued on. The checkers jumped one another and piled up. The wine stained everyone's teeth red, and they all smiled bloody smiles. The men commented on the girls: which one had the nicest eyes, the nicest bosoms, the nicest whatever else. The sea licked and went back, tasted and went back. The pigeons begged for forgiveness and love, promised devotion for the rest of their humble lives.

"You think anyone is left?" one of the men asked Igor.

Francesco reached out and put his hand on the man's shoulder, gripped it hard.

"Never mind," the man said, his words a syrup of insincerity. "I'm sure everyone is just fine. I'm sure nothing bad has happened since you left."

"Do you know something?" Igor asked the man.

"We're perfectly safe here," Francesco told him. Igor felt stung on his chest. It was a satisfying, hot, spreading pain. That's how concerned I am for my family, he thought. His body was burning with it. His hand went to the hurt, and crushed a wasp. Igor was flooded with disappointment—he had not felt his heart's big ache, but an ordinary, earthly bite.

Waking from a nap, Igor said to Francesco, "Did the soldiers mention anything about where I was?" Francesco opened his eyes and looked at his friend, propped up on his elbow. Francesco shook his head.

"I was in the temple. We were putting the constellations up all over, the entire night sky. They didn't mention that? It was the most beautiful thing."

"What was the purpose?"

"It was the beginning of the world. We were making the heavens for ourselves. Do you remember the beginning of the world?"

"The Garden of Eden?" Francesco asked.

"No, that was just a story." Igor drew the shape of a star on his palm. "It was the best sleep I have ever had in that barn."

"And you are a connoisseur." What Francesco had stolen from Igor—home and family—pulled at his ankles. To love Igor, he had to hurt him. He had to take Igor's past away to make a place for himself. What a miserable organ the heart was. Francesco said, "When I was young, my brothers were already grown. They pretended to be nice to me, because girls liked boys with cute little brothers, but after they got what they wanted with the girls, they'd be back to throwing sticks at me."

"When I got married and my son was born, I felt so exhausted, just the idea of it put me flat on my back. I could hardly stand up. Life is so huge, so impossible-seeming."

"I don't feel lonely now," Francesco said. Igor still felt tired.

Igor tried to walk the streets of our home in his mind. He tried to make the turns from one street onto the next. What was that shop there? What was the name of the woman who hulked around, always grumpy? And the petite girl who sewed all the men's pants? He walked the route to the river, despite the fact that it had been me who most often made the journey there, with my wash and our babies. He walked from his father's house to his own house over and over, trying to get the number of steps right. Did I never work? he wondered, and panning through his memory it seemed to him that he hardly had. Where did we get the money to survive? Had I nothing to do with that? he wondered.

Igor did not tell Francesco that his family appeared to him, his parents, his wife, his children, all. Why did he omit this? Because Igor did not want Francesco to feel guilty for taking him away? Perhaps even guilty enough to return him to that wet, gray place?

THE BOOK OF
THE DISTANCE BEHIND
AND THE DISTANCE AHEAD

The beautiful baby grew and shrank at the same time. His bones insisted on lengthening. They extended themselves out in every direction, but on top of them the flesh thinned, leaving the shape of his optimistic skeleton exposed.

Solomon did not grow any new inches. His body had nothing to hold on to. I felt my rivers dry up when the boys went to drink from them.

"We have to keep moving," I said, "we have to find something to eat."

Solomon and I took turns holding the baby. The earth was either dry and dusty or wet and sucking—all the puddles thick with tadpoles. We took roads sometimes if the compass pointed that way, but worried that we would be seen. We took paths through the woods where pine needles made a thick perfume. We followed streams, valleys, ridges. We had come to and crossed the first mountain range. We had descended and snaked the valley. Always, there was a new landscape through which to draw a path. Always, the tiny red arrow. Never did we know where we were. Dirt stuck to our legs, to our hair, buried itself in the pores of our skin. It attached itself to us as if we could save it, take it somewhere better. When we came to a river we held on to reeds and floated in it, tried to be at home. When we came to a forest, we ate the bark of the trees and the meat of the grass and sometimes the bodies of rabbits caught and discarded by birds. Some rabbits were undressed, skinless and small. We passed farmhouses hidden behind groves of trees, farmhouses with doors to keep the cold out and windows to let the light in. Life busied itself inside, knowing nothing of the mother and sons tangled together under an abandoned appleless apple tree.

Solomon made fires, but only in nighttime to keep the giveaway smoke out of the air. Warming ourselves, I asked, "What do you think they are doing at home?"

"Sitting in the barn," Solomon said, rocking the baby on his lap. He was as dutiful as a father.

"You are only four years old," I said to him, which I meant as an apology. He squinted at me. To Solomon, this is what it felt like to be a little boy. A stolen father, a long escape, the outcome still unknown.

I wanted to ask if everyone's throats were slit open. I wanted to ask if they had their own kitchen knives in their chests. I wanted to ask if they had all been led to the river and drowned together. I had a small wish for one of these stories to be true, the smallest wish, only for the sake of knowing I had not picked my children out of the rich earth for nothing.

"What else have we forgotten?" Solomon asked.

"When I was young I wrote a list of everything I knew," I told him and this made him feel better. He wanted another of the lists but since we had no paper we had to try and remember it.

"River, rain, leaves, bark, dress, scarf, sun, dirt, mud, mother, son, son," I started.

"Father, house, temple, stars, stars, stars," Solomon continued. "God," he said.

"Where?" I asked.

"God," he said again. He started to talk about the weeks before we left, a time that seemed as if it belonged to other people. He tried to remember the prayers, blessed a loaf of bread he did not have, a glass of wine he did not have, a candle he did not have, a day of rest he did not have.

"I used to know how to pray," Solomon remembered.

"You still do. Bless the path," I said, "ahead of us." Solomon put the name of God all over the path, paved it with that name, so that every place we put our feet would be soft with it.

"Bless the wheat," I said, and he blessed it, hung prayers from all its blowing leaves.

"Bless us," I told him and he put his hands on the baby's head, his hands on his mother's head, which I bent to meet him.

"I can't remember anything else," he said.

"Horse, street, lamb, baby, day, night, day."

"Wheat," he said, looking around him at the dark fields, "wheat, wheat, wheat, wheat."

Each night Solomon slept a little less. At first he woke up suddenly from terrible dreams, but soon sleep was such a thin membrane that all it took to break it was a gust of wind, an animal crackling in the branches, his empty stomach.

We dried the tears rolling out of our blistered feet. I chewed leaves and grass to make a paste for our cuts. I licked the bruises on Solomon's knees like a mother cat, clearing in this way the rotten dirt that seemed to be growing out of his skin.

We soaked more bark of trees in rainwater caught and saved.

We relieved rabbits of their skin, roasted them. We dug roots from the musky ground and ate them whether they looked familiar or not.

We stole potatoes if we found them, carrying as many as we could in my shawl. The baby sucked on his fingers, which were chapped and pitted things. His length increased alone.

With a spine of mountains blue in the distance ahead and a low roll of hills gray with cold behind, the compass pointed us into a pine forest, where we came upon the carcass of a horse. Everything was gone from it, eaten by another animal. It was a sheet of skin and the eyes, yet we knew it unmistakably as a horse. We tore the skin up with rocks, put it over a fire. It did not break up in our mouths. The skin was leather, it was fur, and we ate it.

The baby waved his arms and I praised him.

When we tried to sleep hidden in the heavy brush of the forest, a thick but sharp layer of pine needles to hold us, Solomon rubbed my back. He hushed me the way I should have hushed him.

"You should sleep," I said.

He told me, "You're doing great, we're doing great. We had meat today. The baby is still the baby." He drew pictures on my back with his finger. "What's this?" he asked. I shrugged and he said, "Guess."

I said, "A mouse?"

"No, it's me."

"Do it again," I told him.

"How old am I?" Solomon asked.

"You're big. You're growing," I said. "How old am I?"

"You are all the way grown."

All through the lit parts and the darkened parts, I asked myself, "Where am I?" I asked myself, "Where should I be?" I wondered if our village was safe, warm, completely normal, and only I was lost and battered. Or maybe everyone was sliced through and the whole village was full only of ghosts. Was Igor home now? Was Igor dead? Were the blankets still stretched tight over our beds, waiting patiently to be dreamed in?

The air started to ache with cold and I knew we had to find a place to be warm. Solomon put a sharp rock in his pocket and stood up to go. He tried to carry the baby but he was heavy. I tried to carry the baby but he was heavy. Solomon took him, held him close, the baby put his hand to Solomon's chest, felt for a breast.

"No," Solomon said, "I'm not your mother." The baby started to cry.

"You can't cry," I said, kneeling on the ground, my face to his. "You cannot cry. It is *impossible*. Do you understand me?" The baby stopped mid-phrase, he did not finish even one more shriek. "Close your eyes and be light," I told him. "See if you can make yourself weigh nothing at all."

THE BOOK OF
THE SEA AND THE NIGHT

E ventually some of the girls came to watch the checkers
game, even drank the wine. They were named things like
Mariza and Mila and Francesca. They tossed their hair.

"You have so much hair," Igor said to Carolina, sitting next
to him.

She looked at him with her head aslant. Igor felt something
related to delight. He touched her hair and she bent her head to let
him. "Nice," he said, not thinking of anything else to call it. "Very
nice." The men laughed at him.

"You can touch it all you want," Carolina whispered into his ear.

"Very nice," Igor repeated.

"I can wrap you up in it," she whispered.

"Okay." He smiled.

"You can kiss it," she said.

But when he kissed, the hair disappeared from under his lips and was replaced with other lips. The two pairs of lips adored each other. They matched and they knew it. Everyone around clapped and cheered but Igor pulled away. He could not believe how different those lips were from his wife's, lips he could absolutely not kiss now, so impossible was that kiss that it made his stomach hurt. He could not describe the difference, like trying to explain the scent of apple blossoms against the scent of lilacs. "I have a wife," Igor said. The men laughed. "I was only planning to kiss the hair."

"Okay," Carolina said, offering the side of her head. "Have it your way."

Later, standing in the doorstep of the jail under a yellow bug-fluttered light, Francesco said, "You're not in charge of your fate. Your wife cannot be upset."

"My *wife*," Igor said.

"It is not for you to decide. Here on the island, when someone wants to love you, what choice do you have?"

"If I sent a letter, would my wife get it?"

"A letter, to your wife?"

"I want that. I think I should tell her that I am all right. Alive. What if she marries someone else?"

"Not possible." Francesco knew all about the German soldiers, the emptied-out villages, the bodies smashed into train cars, cells.

"How long have I been here?"

Francesco tried to count on his fingers but gave up. "You have been here for many weeks," he finally answered. "Many."

"That's many weeklong chances for her to forget me. She does not know that I'm alive."

"Is *she* even alive?" Francesco asked. He realized his coldness right away. "She's fine, I know she is."

"She could not be?" Igor asked back, betraying his shock.

"They are fine, maybe they really are."

"We have no idea. We do not know if we are alive," he fumbled.

"I am alive and you are alive," Francesco said. "We know that much. Carolina is alive." The bugs crashed and crashed into the light, so certain they had found something worth finding, if only they could get closer to it.

"Stay here tonight with me," Igor said. "It seems I have lost everything."

Francesco was light-headed. "Yes, please," he said.

"Did you hear me? How big is my firstborn?"

Francesco put his hand out at hip level. "Maybe like this?" He was still thinking of sleeping the night away with Igor by his side.

Igor went into the cage, where he washed his face in the small sink at the wall. Francesco closed the gate and locked the two of them inside. He curled up on his side of Igor's bed. "I'm sorry we took you away," he said. "But thank you, too." Francesco had gone from doing his duty to imprisoning someone for his own benefit. He did not pray for guidance, only forgiveness.

Igor began a letter.

> *Dear L,*
> *Things are pretty good with me. How are you? I hope you are well. I am being held captive in a town by the sea by a nice man named Francesco who is also my friend. Maybe someday*

*he will come and get you too and you can live in my jail with
me. It is actually very nice. I have a comfortable bed and a
sink and toilet and they give me money to buy food. I am
allowed out during the day. Francesco and I swim and I like
to drink coffee in the square. I am learning the language.*

*Solomon must be big. And even the baby must be big. Do
you remember me? Do you? Are you alive? Are you going to
marry someone else? If you wanted to come and live here I am
sure they would take you prisoner, too. There are girls here but
you are my wife. Today, one of them told me she'd wrap me
up in her hair, but instead I am here, writing to you. Do you
even appreciate this? I have a bed from an old woman, a big
old bed. I am getting to be a fast swimmer. I did not know
how to swim before, any more than to hold on to the reeds in
the river when we used to go together. Are you still lucky? Do
you look the same? I have a new suit. Francesco and me like to
lie on the warm rocks by the sea. Do you know what the sea
looks like? It is very beautiful and I think you would like to go
into it. I would like to show you how to swim along the shore.
We could eat cheese after and walk in the sun. Do you want to
see me again? Do you want me to be your husband? Does
Solomon like to practice arithmetic? Is the baby as high as
your knee, as high as your hip? Which of them looks more like
me? Which of them looks more like you? Which of them
remembers my name? Are all of our parents alive? Do you
sleep alone in the bed? How are the constellations coming? Is
the whole sky there now, over everyone? I would like to sleep
there again. Please tell me you are alive. Please tell Solomon*

*and the baby that I am their father. Please send a letter saying
they know. I almost remember who you are.*

Sincerely, I

In the morning, as Francesco was going to get his pastry and
coffee, a small boat pulled up to the dock, and out of it came two
soldiers, older and full-cheeked, no one Francesco knew. They
wore Italian uniforms, and as they approached, they drew their
hats down to their hearts. Francesco thought, They have come to
take my friend. Solemnly, he met them on the wooden-planked
dock. "There have been some losses," the older of the two men said.
"Giuseppe Carbone." The face coalesced in Francesco's mind. A
younger boy, thorny and uneven, commanding a game of tag on
the beach. "And Bianco," the man said.

"But that's me," Francesco objected, instinct prompting him to
check his own hands to see that he was alive.

"Luca Bianco." Francesco's oldest brother, so confident the air
swirled around him, drawing everyone nearer, so much what the
world had dreamed a son could be.

"He can't die," Francesco said, sure of this. Like that part of
the contract had been renegotiated, this man too good for the
world to lose.

"We're very sorry for your loss," the younger of the two soldiers
said. "It was an ambush, in Rome. They were both brave."

The soldiers saluted, and then they turned around and left.

For a moment, the tears in Francesco's eyes were made of relief
and thanks. Francesco had been granted a pardon. No one wanted

to take Igor from him, not yet. And then, Francesco saw Luca's shadow collapse at his feet. He, the ever-disappointing son, would have to walk this news to his mother's doorstep, he would have to be the one to throw her heaving to the floor with it. Francesco sat down on the dock and put his head in his hands, and for a long time, nothing breathed. God was benevolent and he was cruel.

THE BOOK OF
THE DISTANCE AND THE
FUTURE, WHICH IS NOW

The mountains, deep green and fully alive, were high around my bony children and me. We did not ascend or descend, but walked straight across the low valley of this revolving earth. On the coldest nights we slept in barns, if we found them, with the pigs and goats. The animals did not seem to feel heroic, sharing their house with refugees. They moaned and grunted and grudgingly allowed us a little corner. We whispered about our own barn and how well we had made it into a place to pray. We sneaked eggs and animal feed, chewed on the same hay the pigs slept on, but as soon as the idea of light peeked through the cracks in the walls, we left to let the new day shake us, tackle us, wring us out.

On a clear and blue afternoon in which the branches on the trees were naked but not shy for it, we came to a spectacular and strange thing—a mattress in the middle of a cleared field. The grass was dry and cut short, whatever it had been grown for gone into cooking pots and bellies. But there was this old and moldy thing, a thing once slept on by people, loved on by people. It had grass growing through it. It was a nest for new baby grasses. For this family, who had survived on whatever was found, this seemed like a gift. Solomon, slow, weak and broken-in, did not lie down but began to jump.

He was a beautiful, enthusiastic jumper. He used his whole body to propel himself upward. When he came down, the springs of his legs sent him up again. The good ground, hanging on to his ankles, did not stand a chance against all that sky.

I held the baby on my lap so we could be bounced by Solomon's jumping. The baby laughed, a sharp and definite laugh. Maybe his first. "How long since we laughed?" I asked. We tried to keep quiet, because we never knew who was going to steal us away just for existing, but in this moment it was not easy. In this moment Solomon's muscles began to ache from his laughter. I collapsed in my own joy, watched my son go up and down, his hair bouncing, his arms flapping, flightless.

"What are you?" I called to Solomon.

"A boy!" Solomon called back.

"No, you are jumping!" I laughed.

"I am both!" Solomon shrieked, dizzy.

I lay down in the grass beside the mattress. I put my head on a rock and covered my eyes with my hands. The sun was lost light. The sound of my shrieking and laughing boy was unmuffled. I listened to every beat of it, every landing and takeoff, every collapse and resolution to continue. Solomon slowed down, said, "I see the stars," then collapsed on the mattress in dry heaves. He had nothing to vomit up.

My hand ran the ridge of Solomon's spine. It hurt to cry—I had no water to spare, but my eyes had waited long enough. Solomon tried to stand, but it was too much. His legs were soft and bendy. Beaten, he lay down and wept. I told him the story of the very day we were in—once upon a time we were a family who came upon an amazing mattress in a field just like every other field and how the older brother had jumped so high he saw the stars while his mother and brother listened to the sound of his laughter with the sun on their faces.

"Don't you remember how wonderful?" I asked.

He repeated just the last word, but it collapsed on his tongue.

The sun stopped being worth shading ourselves from. The cut field was a pincushion of interrupted growth. The baby fell asleep on the bed, and Solomon lay next to him. I went to find food and came back with a rabbit, a baby, already dead but undiscovered by birds. I skinned it, put it on a small fire and waited for the smell to wake my baby up.

We tried to sleep on the bed, all of us, but I could feel Solomon turning back and forth, awake. The stars were hidden behind a cover of gray—even though I knew the stars were there still, arranged and held, I could not believe it was true. There seemed to be another world over me, a flat gray place, just as hard and true as this one. A world where you could walk for months having no idea where you were, then walk some more.

I woke up when Solomon started to jump around me. Dawn

was a luminous bruise on the horizon, the rest of the sky dark. I felt the surface under me go soft and shifty. I felt the spring of his feet against it, their insistence on high and higher.

I started to gather the baby into my arms, and at the first touch I understood that he was not going to wake up. He was cold, and he was still.

"Stop," I said, "stop jumping."

"We are boys," he whispered to himself, "two boys. We are jumping."

I took the baby into my arms. In the dark, only his shining eyes were easy to see. I laid him on the bed. I listened for his breath. I listened for his heart. On the mattress, the grass-sprung mattress, here in this field after one harvest and before another, the baby's little spirit was caught on the wind and carried absolutely everywhere.

"This is my baby who is lost," I kept whispering. I remember saying that so many times it turned into one word.

I opened my dress to put the baby onto my long-dry breast. "What if this?" I said. "What if you are new?" Solomon opened his shirt too and tried to offer the breast that he had never had, not even for a moment of his short life.

"What if this?" he echoed. We held the boy together against us while he did not drink. I wondered how long he had been waiting to slip away. How hard he had tried to hold on. "All right," I whispered, further than I wished from forgiving him. "You chose to go."

"My brother who is lost. I bless him. May His great Name be exalted and sanctified in the world that He created as He willed."

The prayer split me, the way only the sight of blood makes a wound begin to sear with pain. Years from now, a thousand or more, I might be ready to dress in black and mourn. For as long as I could imagine, for the whole crooked duration of my life, I tasted the metallic desire for misery in my entire body.

"I'm not ready for the prayer," I whispered. I pressed the baby hard to my chest, and for a second I thought he might slip right inside. Rejoin.

"We are supposed to say the prayer. That's the prayer we say."

I covered my ears and wept. I had never wanted to hit my son before. "No one is listening, don't you see?"

The baby's skin turned rubbery. His body became less and less. The heartless compass pointed away: always, farther and farther away. The sun rose to show us how beaten we were. The wind started to gather itself and throw our hair around, toss our spit and tears back at us, slapping our grief onto our skin. *We have no use for this*, the wind said of our tears, *this is yours*.

When the light had us pink and orange and looking like we were on fire, Solomon said, "We have to put him someplace. He needs a home."

"And you? A home?"

"Not yet," he told me, faith hanging on to its overwhelming opposite.

I carried my smallest boy away from the mattress. His legs were stiff and unmoving. We had no shovel with us in the field. We dug with our hands, cupping the clumps of dry dirt and moving them aside.

We did not get very deep. The earth turned us away, dry and

unbreakable. We hit it with rocks, trying to make a crack but only freed a little dust. It was a long time before a small boat floated there, in which the baby could drift away. We laid the baby down, tucked just below the surface of the world.

"He never had a name," Solomon said.

"He never told us what he wanted to be called."

"Should we name him now? Should we call him Star or Wheat or Field?"

"None of those would be enough."

So the baby went away the same as he had come: himself and nothing else. No name, no debts, no winnings. He had no road in front of him to walk, no food to find, no tears to lose, no mother and brother to pray for. He had only to sleep, and maybe dream, for as long as the earth kept turning.

That was the last night we lived as three, and all through it Solomon and I stayed as still as we could, though we did not sleep. We wanted to move no more than our third companion, to be like him, for us all to be like each other, lying still, as is natural to do, under the dark heavens and the uncountable stars.

THE BOOK OF HOME
AND THE FUTURE,
WHICH IS NOW

It began with a far-off yelling, the sound of voices loud enough to pound the grass flat.

Guns were shot.

The far-off yelling became less far off.

The villagers pulled in close to one another. Sleep still sat with them. One person, they did not know who, lit a lantern. All of them were mountainous piles with jagged faces. Someone else whispered to blow the lantern out, at least in the darkness they were invisible. The jagged faces went dark again but when everyone closed their eyes they could still see one another printed on the backs of their eyelids.

The stranger said, "Yes, I remember this. I remember all of this." People shushed her, pleaded with their silent eyes. The jeweler met her gaze. He wanted to say that he remembered too, except that he did not—he had never lost everything at once before. Still, he wanted the stranger to know he believed her, and he also wanted her to assure him someone new would be there to gather them out of the river just as she had been gathered. That forever, no matter how many times they were washed away, another world would always meet them a little farther downstream.

"I remember my daughter. Her hair was scratchy on my shoulder. I remember my son's laugh and how he curled his lip when he played," the stranger said. Perl leaned closer to the stranger and reached her hand out, as if she was trying to tame a stray animal, quiet its yowling. The stranger shook her head. "I'm so sorry," she said. "You have been very kind to me. You saved my life, but I remember the old world. I remember it perfectly. I remember every single thing I lost, and how each one smelled."

The far-off yelling was close yelling. The guns were close guns. Boots broke whatever they came across. The people heard every snap. They watched the stranger nod at each sound. This was a symphony she had heard before.

"What happens next?" the banker asked her.

"Everything happens next," the stranger said, and she clamped her eyelids shut.

Windows turned to water splashing back on itself. Doors slammed against walls. Unfamiliar voices shouted in the abandoned houses, *Come out, you filthy creatures. Where are you? The moment has arrived.*

And if the people could have seen the cavities of one another's eyes? Would they have been so afraid that they would have fallen to the ground in piles of loose bones? Fear seemed hot enough to melt them.

Perl reached for her family—my family—took Vlad and Moishe and the tailor's daughter close, their arms tangled together, holding firm. Regina and the widow were not in the room with everyone else—the only time Perl saw them anymore was through a prism of mustard jars. Perl ached to touch her daughters, but hoped hard that we were hidden someplace, and safe.

"Is this the end?" Moishe asked. He was old enough to be able to see both ahead and behind himself now, the clearing he had come through and the forest grown suddenly wild at his feet. His question was posed slowly, deliberately—a child trying to sound unafraid, as he supposed an adult would. Perl wanted to tell him how scared she was, how scared he was allowed to be.

"Stay close to me," Vlad said. "Just do not go away from me."

"If we get separated, send a letter here with your whereabouts," Perl whispered. Vlad's eyes were swarming with fear. Perl felt stung, as if by bees, when he looked at her. "Never ending," she said, and pointed to her heart. The flutter of terrified wings did not calm in Vlad's eyes. He squeezed her so tightly that both hands numbed and neither could tell which fingers stemmed from which palm. Vlad hummed very faintly through his nose, making a river of sound just big enough for his family to drift on. Moishe added his own soft hum, and Perl and the tailor's daughter held on and on.

The banker's wife saw the same ugliness of her heart after the baby's death reflected in everyone else. Fear had eaten their eyes, it had caved their cheeks in. This was a strange comfort to her.

The stranger said, "Most of us are going to die, but not everyone. We will begin again, as many times as we need to. The end is the same thing as the beginning. Exactly the same. Lena will tell our story."

"How will she know it?" Kayla asked.

"She will know," the stranger said, sure. The jeweler memorized his lover's words, wished the words were solid, were coins or pebbles he could squeeze in his fist. She opened her empty hands and said, "Thank you for being my family. It has been an honor. I remember who all of you are."

The greengrocer thought about the census he and the rest of the Committee for What We Have and Where We Have It had so carefully written over months and years. *What do we have now?* he asked himself. *If we die, every single one of us?* The story, he thought, remained. Once told, it does not ever go completely away. It has no throat to slit. The greengrocer wanted to tell this theory to his wife, who was crying silently next to him, but when their eyes met he thought she might already know.

Kayla and Hersh quietly slipped out the door. Those inside could see them break through the trees but did not watch, averted their eyes, drawing no attention to the escape. Others did not try to join them and they did not throw the lines of their voices after Kayla and Hersh and reel them back into the struggle. The village simply let them disappear. Would they climb into a tree and nest there, a pair of unusually large crows?

Perl, Vlad, Moishe and the tailor's daughter were so close together they felt fused. If one of their hearts had stopped it would not have mattered because the others would have pumped for that body, too.

The people heard two voices outside, just there, and then a tap on the window. The single bullet hole in the wall went dark. The villagers heard the men outside laugh.

For several seconds they heard the exact and complete sound of nothing.

Then the door opened and the moonlight was slapped down on the villagers, their bodies returned to being mountains and their faces returned to being jagged and no matter what they did, they did not become planks of wooden floor.

"Everyone's together!" the men shouted. "How kind of you, to have gathered for us. You must have been waiting." They were very tall and stood so straight as to look like statues. They wore pale green from helmet to boot, and the guns in their hands were shiny and animated, alive-looking. Nothing felt real. Yet now that the moment had arrived, it seemed inevitable. Almost a relief. When is it over? It is over now.

The children did not break first. The children kept their silence the longest. It was the fathers who went right away, trying to wrap their two pathetic arms around everything they loved. The arms seemed so short, so thin. Why were the arms not twice their length?

The sound in the room was of the fathers struggling to hold.

The mothers went next. When one began to cry loud enough to be heard, the room cracked. The children and the grandmothers and the uncles and the cousins. They cried because they cried.

They cried because across the room and next to them, there was the sound of begging.

One of the men in uniform approached Perl. "This one is already bald, no lice on this one." He slapped the shiny skin of her scalp.

The other man in uniform laughed. "Are you trying to steal from us?" he asked her. Perl looked hard at the floor. "Are you trying to steal from us?" the guard repeated.

No, she shook her head.

"Are you bald *and* dumb?"

Perl shook her head and the first man smacked it. "We wanted your hair," he told her. "Didn't you think we might want that?"

"What will you do to apologize?"

"She will shave the heads of the others," the first man said. "She will get their dirty lice all over her."

The people did all the possible things to do. They fought back. They were hit on their heads with the butts of guns. They hid behind shelves. They were dragged by their hair back out. They stood up, put their hands over their heads and waited to be shown the way. People put themselves in front of the ones they loved, saying, Take me, take me.

Stacks of things began to fall, and my people heard only the sound of them crashing down. The pots rang when they hit the floor. The books, the silverware, the saddles—all of it tumbled. The people were swallowed. The soldiers kicked the piles, listening for the yelp of a person underneath. The sound of their voices, once shrill and stabbing, became like the hiss of a fire—behind, around, but not central. The prayers in the villagers' own heads were rumbling and thunderous. A silent cacophony. They all prayed the same prayer.

Please exist. We want to believe in You.

People had stopped asking for particulars. No requests for safety, no more hopes of a hole in the floor to hold them, no more wishes to replace one person with the other. They only said, as many times as they could: *We are here. We want to trust You. We are here. Please exist. You will certainly watch us today. Won't You? We are here.*

The village began to come apart under its own hope. People felt as if their arms would snap off, their heads would roll and rest with the cabbages, their hearts would stick to the floor. When the butcher was taken by one man who held his wrists together, no one could believe that even now the butcher's arms did not come gently off. *We trust You. We trust You.* Still, the shoulders hung on. All the knobbed ends of all the bones stayed cupped in their sockets.

The stranger said to no one in particular, "My daughter had long fingers and short toes. Her ears were like shells. Her brother followed her around asking her opinion on everything, and her father trusted her with his tools. I used to like to watch the crows hop across the woodpile. I can smell that wood right now. But I also remember the way the cabbage picker's wife's fingers felt as they cleaned the mud from between my toes on the day I washed up on this shore. I remember the taste of toasted bread in the jeweler's house, and the smell of the butcher's roasts. I remember the long, peaceful rainstorm of all our days since the beginning of the world. I remember, I remember, I remember." She smiled, a

wide and honest smile. The banker's wife looked at her in confusion. "No," said the stranger. "It is a privilege to remember. I am
not afraid of it anymore. Absolutely everything is true."

As the stranger's words attached our two worlds back together,
Perl saw a flash of my face at age five, before she could have imagined giving me away. She saw my uneven teeth, none of them yet
fallen out. She saw the game I was inventing—a pencil-drawn maze
that began in the cabbage field and ended at our big blue door,
where the family was waiting with sloppy smiles on. Wherever
you are, my mother said to me in her head, I hope you are home. I
hope I am still yours. And for Regina she found two words clacking together: *alive* and *love*.

The first man in uniform dumped a basket of cabbages out
onto the floor. "They love these things," he said to one of the other
men. "They should be grateful that we'll dump their ashes over a
cabbage field." The man in uniform drew his fingers under my
mother's chin. "You'll make excellent fertilizer."

The men began to shoot at the ceiling and the chips of sky fell
down on them, sharp rain, and the villagers put themselves in lines
and waited their turn to follow the men out the door.

They went two by two, not cabbage pickers or tailor's daughters or weavers or bankers or the wives of bankers or the strangers
anymore. Vlad and Perl and Moishe? Just bodies among bodies,
just animals, rattling out of their temple into the captured world.

The villagers were one body, each of them losing individual
characteristics, their minds beginning to melt into a note of utter
fear and utter hope, which were one feeling and not two as they
might have believed before.

Outside, the rain had gathered its strength and pelted them all. The old stars, too far away to be shot down by bullets, greeted the line of people. "Let there be lights in the firmament of the heaven to divide the day from the night. And let them be for signs, and for seasons, and for days, and years," the jeweler said.

"And by them, may we find our way," the stranger whispered. Each person was given a new star, too. Their upper arms were wrapped with yellow bands, and on each band: one star. The soldiers had not tied the villagers' hands together, expecting fear would be enough to bind the people.

The water was running away, it was beckoning. It was as if the sky, practicing all this time, was finally ready to wash the people to safety, to carry them. *And the water prevailed upon the earth, and it bore them and lifted them up.* The stranger took her lover's hand and began to run. The others did not have to be told to follow. As if commanded by a single voice, which echoed at once in everyone's heads: We are the stars, we are the heavens, let us spread out across the darkness. They ran and the water ran with them, everything moving together. Some people died quickly, from the hundreds of bullets fired at their backs. Some of them were injured, some captured. Perl felt the heat of her husband's hand in hers, their fingers making a knot. In the other hand, Moishe's palm was sweating and slippery. She felt like one part of a bigger body. Her arm and Vlad's arm—her arm and Moishe's—could not be prized apart. The blood flowed between them, the life they had shared. Perl became less and less herself and more and more everyone, everything, as she ran. Her heart thundered so loudly she knew the beating she heard was not hers alone. The people's names did not matter—the difference between the banker's body and the butcher's body meant nothing now. Survival was not an individual pursuit, but a collective one. They were all of us. The air was thick with ghosts—every life lived on that land, every life lived in that story. Through the wheat, through the empty cabbage field, through the rain, across arteries they had made for themselves on the earth, the sound of their heart was one drum, all the chambers in all the chests, commanding, Let there be morning and evening, another day.

Before the small group of villagers who had survived dove into the river, they looked at one another. They were all strangers who had known one another a long time ago. Oh, hello, they thought. You look so familiar to me. I think we were friends when we were children. Didn't I used to pick cabbages? Weren't you my wife? I think I might love you. They let themselves fall, and the surface of the earth was liquid, and they could pass through it. The people gasped with the shock of the water's cold; it felt like coming home.

The water was moving fast, and my people, all of them strangers and all of them family, were carried away.

Ahead of the others in the tumbling water, each of Hersh's and Kayla's pumping organs pumped hard. Like the men before, they had crushed what had fallen in their path. The mud had slapped their feet. They had parted the grass like a curtain and passed through it. The rain got in their eyes as they rounded the corner to the river. They had jumped into the cold, rushing water. They took each other's hands and Kayla held on to a reed to keep them still. The water chewed them with its cold teeth, made all their short hairs stand and their skin harden.

They looked back at the barn and could see the dark ink of movement inside. They could hear as well as they had ever been able to hear in their lives: the begging and screaming was needle sharp. The river was another kind of music, rain falling softly into it. Kayla and Hersh listened to the melody of the two sounds together.

"The real stars," Kayla said, looking up.

"We will have to let go," Hersh said. "They will eventually find us here."

Kayla's shoes fell off, one and then the other. They rushed away.

"My shoes are gone," she told her husband.

Hersh reached down to untie his but did not remove them, he let the river do the removing. Their skin was numb now, just a casing for their insides.

Their socks stayed a few moments and then snaked themselves off, slithered away. Kayla's dress was heavy on her shoulders. She turned to Hersh and without her asking him to, he unbuttoned it and they waited while it slipped down the length of her body. It surfaced, a white bubble, which they watched until it turned the corner. She was in her underwear now, the weedy, soft grass fanning against her skin.

"I am not a young woman anymore," Kayla said.

"I am not a young man."

"I never swam well. We should have gone to the woods."

"We do not need to swim. We only need to float," Hersh said.

"Let me take the weight of your clothes away so you are a lighter boat," she said while she unbuttoned his vest, his black woolen vest, and then his white shirt. He put one arm out at a time while she held the other and his clothing was caught in the current and slipped away.

They took turns holding the strong reeds and each other while they removed the last of the cloth. Their skin, loose now after all the years of hanging on to their bones, flapped softly.

"It was a nice place to raise our daughter," Hersh whispered.

"She's fine," Kayla said. "Someplace in the world, our daughter is fine."

"We have passed ourselves along," Hersh told his wife. His face was white with moon and cold.

"We couldn't have done anything to help the others," Kayla said.

"No one could have done anything."

"I'm happy we finished the sky."

"Do you remember the beginning of the world?" Hersh asked. "What a lucky time to have been alive."

"I wish it hadn't gone so fast. Here we are, old and swimming away."

"But I'm glad we're old and swimming away together," Hersh said, and he laid his cold lips on her forehead.

On the bank, in the tangle of dark willows, something small scratched in the branches. Something else slapped at the water. In the distance, Hersh and Kayla could hear the march of hundreds of feet. The entire earth rumbled under the migration. They could see the black line of the villagers leaving the village.

"The river is cold."

"Should we be getting on?" he asked.

Kayla let go of the reeds. The two of them began their bobbing journey. Their naked bodies floated to the top of the water and they put their heads back and held their breath. Their fingers were twisted together.

They did not say the names of the constellations out loud but they knew them all. The sky was a cloth with enough holes to breathe through.

After a long time, Hersh said, "Tell me you're here."

Kayla made a small and caught noise.

"Say your name," he told her.

She made the same small and caught noise.

"My name is Hersh," he said. "I am yours."

He floated with her cold hand for a long time. The river turned and turned back. The banks narrowed and the water grew faster, then the banks widened out and he could hardly feel the water's movement.

"I'm yours," Hersh said again to his floating bride but she did not answer him with a squeeze of her fingers or a word.

"You're mine," he said, and he opened his fingers up and let her go.

Kayla whirled in an eddy. He closed his eyes even though the darkness was already a sheet over everything. "I'm yours," he said again, and kicked against the drift, trying to stay close. He gave her a final push, sent her coasting toward the edge. "Bring good luck to the riverbanks."

The weeds would be the ones to catch Kayla, the long arms of the willows taking her close. They would spiral around each of her parts. They would grow into her, under and through. Short green leaves would not be far behind.

Hersh floated away under the shameless beauty of the heavens. "Let the waters swarm with swarms of living creatures, and let fowl fly above the earth in the open firmament of heaven," he said to himself, remembering when he had read the passage as a young man and the idea that life could be invented had seemed like a fairy tale. Now, floating alone in the river, far away from the known world, he was hopeful that someone had thought to conjure up places downstream from here. "Let there be a village not far away," Hersh said quietly to the night. The stars winked back, as if to prove they heard him. "And let those villagers be out on the bank gathering glinting fish from a flood," he said. "And let them be there when a stranger washes up on their shores, and let the villagers wrap him in wool blankets and take him home where a new world waits. And let there be someone, somewhere, to tell his story. Our story."

THE BOOK OF THE SEA
AND THE FUTURE,
WHICH IS NOW

Igor slept alone in the windowless dark of his cell. For the first time he wanted to punch the walls out himself. For the first time the cage made him feel kept. For the first time he did not sleep well in his four-poster bed, even with his legs spread wide, his arms out and the blanket pulled up to his chin.

"I'm by the ocean!" he yelled, and the walls sent his words back. "I don't know where that is!" He stood up and jumped on the bed. He sprang up high and yelled, "I'm a prisoner in a foreign land!" He jumped and he called, "I have a wife and two sons someplace!" He landed, bent his knees and flew again. "I have everything I need! Where is it all?"

Later, Francesco took Igor by the arm and walked the scrabbled path to the post office. The letter went addressed to *Lena, My*

Wife, Zalischik. Igor touched the envelope to his cheek before handing it over.

"A swim?" Francesco asked.

"I'll come and sit on the rocks and watch you. I will be waiting for my wife to write back."

"It will take weeks, I think."

"Then I'll write another one."

"There is no point in being angry. You're a prisoner, you have no choice. You might as well enjoy it." Francesco had felt easy knowing that his friend could not leave him, trapped as he was. Yet he had not considered the troublesome and unkeepable mind, free to remember, to imagine, to roam. Francesco flung his arms down as hard as he could onto the surface of the deep blue sea. It stung his skin, and salt splashed into his eyes. Igor did not recognize it as one man's great display of heartsickness.

Francesco hauled himself out of the sea and sat down on the rocks. "Once," he said, "when I was little, I was playing on the beach while my eldest brother talked the bathing suit off a girl. My job was to keep watch and yell if someone came. I spied on them and saw my brother's hand slip up the girl's salty, cold flanks while she stared at the sky with a profoundly bored look on her face. My brother did not look heroic, as I would have expected, but pathetic. Cross-eyed and drooling. I wished I had never seen it. I wished I could have known only my brother's elaborate tale of conquest, and not the fumbling truth." He looked at Igor. "Love looked so sad. So humiliating." Igor patted Francesco on the knee.

"That wasn't love," Igor said. Francesco's face brightened.

Francesco felt as if a bird were flapping its wings in his chest.

He felt as if he could fly. He stood tall, reached his arms up. Francesco dove into the sea, soared right through the surface of the world.

Igor sat on the rocks and wrote several more notes while Francesco swam laps, looking like he was having the most wonderful, the most completely terrific time.

> Dear L,
>
> I am alive, did you know? I am getting to be a very, very fast swimmer. I can swim from the big rock all the way to the sandy beach in a matter of seconds. I learned how to make lasagna. Do you know what that is? My friend Francesco taught it to me, actually his mother did. How are my sons? Are you alive? What is the weather like where you are? Remember the time we climbed to the top of the apple tree and fell asleep in the branches? I hope you are alive.
>
> Love, I

> Dear L,
>
> I still don't know if you are alive. Please write back. Please don't forget. Please tell Solomon that he is my son and that I am his father. Please send something of yours that I can keep.
>
> Love, I

> Dear L,
>
> I am sitting by the sea. I am waiting. I am not swimming because you are far away.
>
> Love, I

Dear L,

I might like to go swimming sometime but it's not because I have forgotten you. I suffer if you suffer.

Love, I

Dear L,

I am hungry. Should I eat something? You would have fed me if I were home.

Love, I

Dear L,

I am going to put my feet in the water but not my knees. You never told me, is the baby taller than my knees? Does he like to go swimming?

Love, I

Dear L,

We are going to have lunch now. I am going to eat but I am also being punished, you have to remember. I am going to eat less than I want to. Maybe I should eat more, enough for you, too? Which do you prefer? I'll do whatever you want.

Dear L,

Lunch was not very good. Is that what I should say? Is it better if I am unhappy? I will try to be.

Dear L,

I still sleep whenever I can. Is Solomon a sound sleeper? Will you be bringing him with you when you come? He is not an adult yet, right? What size is the baby? What qualities has he inherited from me?

Dear L,

I will try to win at checkers tonight in your honor. I will declare that I dedicate my game to you. When I look at any girl I will replace her face with your face. I will begin to make a list of all the things to teach Solomon and the baby when I see them again so that I should not forget. I am a father today, tomorrow. I am still alive, so that you know.

When Igor woke up, he waited with his letters, all the time writing more. He used to sleep until Francesco unlocked him, the morning sunlight on the other side of the windowless wall unable to alert him of day or later day or evening or full night. But now he woke up himself and waited. Now he sat with his back against the bars and his lamp on, reading the mail he wanted to send off into the waiting world. He thought of me, his wife, sitting in a comfortable chair with a blanket over my knees, reading his letters, both boys at my side. What would I do in between deliveries? Eat some fresh preserves on toast? Did I wait all day, all the next day? And when would my replies make it over the mountains and mountains and mountains?

Igor put his lamp out when Francesco left for the night. The dark of his cell smacked at his open eyeballs. He blinked and tried to make shapes in it but the darkness came at him. He swatted and it hit him back. He was soaked through with it, and he curled up and felt the dark crawling over him and lapping at him and filling up his lungs and his ears and his mouth and his eyes.

Igor made Francesco escort him to the post office again and again. He wrote a note and wanted to go take it in. At first, Francesco obliged, guilt souring everything. After a few days, he told Igor to collect all the notes of the day into a pile and they would take them after lunch. And then he told Igor to collect all the notes in a pile and keep collecting until the week was up. Then he told Igor that until they got a reply there would be no more notes.

"What kind of jail is this?" Igor yelled.

Francesco shook his head. "We cannot afford the postage," he replied. "There is a war on, and I'm pretty sure we're losing it. We all have to make sacrifices." He did not include the ultimatum: if you promise to be my best friend for the rest of time, I will send your mail, even if every general in the army finds out about it.

"My wife is busy forgetting about me *right now*," Igor said.

"Who could ever forget about you? Maybe not Carolina. Certainly not me."

"Keep that exquisite woman away from me," Igor said, "before she tries to kiss me again. Can we go for a swim?"

"I thought you were punishing yourself."

"I need to swim in order to teach my sons to swim. I have to be very accomplished to be a role model. Don't worry," he added, "I won't put it in a letter—I'll put it in a book so when I see them again I can teach them everything."

Igor tried to keep exact track of each of his movements. The muscle-by-muscle motions he made in order to transport himself through liquid. He touched the undersides of his arms and the sides of his waist, hunting for the stringy mechanisms of movement. He listened to his breathing, the scratch of air in his lungs. Francesco climbed out and warmed up on the rocks but Igor kept swimming. He kept sweeping his arms out over himself, a fan of water falling from them. He kept kicking his feet in the straightest lines he could make. His hands were flat paddles. Igor came up and stood on a rock, called up to Francesco on shore.

"Write this down!" he called. "Make your hands into cups!" He dove in again and came back a few strokes later. "Kick with your whole leg!" He swam more, rose up dripping. "Think of your arms as wheels!" Francesco transcribed Igor's instructions, and by the time Igor got out of the water all the way he was blue and shaking. He went flat on the rock and said, "Thank you. My sons will be great swimmers." He closed his eyes. "I'm going to fall asleep. Here is how I do that: I close my eyes. I let my toes sink down, I let my legs sink down, I let my back sink down." Francesco did not fill in the rest of the list, but lay there listening to the sea rolling over every rounded thing, every jagged thing.

· VI ·

THE BOOK OF THE INDOORS

I said to Solomon, "Can I carry you?"

"I'm too big," he told me, sorry for it.

"Just to that turn in the road," I promised. I bent down and scooped him up, carried him beyond the bend where, on either side of us, flat fields of grass aspired to be endless. My throat was hard and dry. He did not point out the distance we had come or the difference between his own weight and the weight of a baby. He willed himself lighter, as I had asked the little one to do. "Be a baby," he whispered.

"Be a baby," I whispered back, not to him, but to myself, both of us wanting to start over again, new and unknowing.

In the tall grass: a white farmhouse with a barn next to it. Not a temple, just a barn. This time, instead of passing by in the trees, hidden, I began to walk toward its wide brown door. It was due west—every rule broken at once.

"We are hiding," Solomon reminded me. "We should wait until night to sneak into the barn."

"We are going inside," I said. "Today we are going inside."

Solomon's voice cracked—a clean fissure down the middle—when he asked if there might be food inside. When I had turned off the road, I thought I would walk to the barn, and we might steal some eggs, sleep in the hay. When the word "food" fell out of Solomon's mouth, he looked at me, startled, apologetic for having admitted a deficit, as if this made him a traitor to our little army. In an instant, I adjusted my aim to the door of the farmhouse. Before us was a path, marked for human feet by white stones laid in lines. It was meant to be followed, but not by us.

"But what if it isn't safe? What if they hate us? Should I run? Should I hide?"

There was a silver knocker in the shape of a fist. I shut out Solomon's river of questions, held that hand and asked to be let inside. A man answered, looked at us and closed the door back to a crack. I flinched away from the smack I might receive. "What are you?" he asked in Russian.

"This is my son, I'm his mother," I said, trying to make sense. The man looked Solomon up and down, studying his every inch. He kneeled down and took Solomon's arm, measuring it with the bracelet of his fingers.

"What are you doing still alive?" he asked. There wasn't answer for that question, so I said nothing. "Are you lost?"

Certainly we were not found, I thought. We had no idea where we were, but neither did we have any idea where we wanted to be. Must a lost person have a destination in mind? I gave no answer to the farmer's question. He looked at me and he must have seen something hopeless because the man opened the door into a kitchen with a heavy table and chairs, pots hanging on nails on the wall, an enamel washbasin and a cutting board with the orange fingers of carrots waiting to be sliced. There were walls, high and flat, made of wood. There was a floor, low and flat. A pile of folded clothes, all bright white, sat on the table, clean and waiting to be put away. On the black stove was a big silver pot, steam escaping. The smell made even my marrow ache. A woman stood over the carrots with her hand on her hip, looking at the broken people entering her life.

Solomon pushed close to me and said, "We are inside a house."

"That's right." The farmer gave Solomon a warm smile.

"You let them in?" the woman asked.

Shame slipped her fingers around my neck and squeezed. My face felt hot. I wanted to apologize for bothering them and leave. Not back to the bruised world this time, but a day-to-day place, the decades ahead, Solomon's future unfolding one unnotable hour at a time. I wanted that possibility to exist.

"I'm sorry, I don't want to put you in danger. We should go," I said.

"In danger?" the farmer's wife said, and squinted.

I did not know the real stories, only the fear of what they might be. Only the banished, threadbare memories. Only the radio's babble. "We shouldn't have come."

"Yes," the farmer said, something between a grimace and a grin on his face. The owner of a gruesome tale, he cracked his knuckles while the audience waited.

"They will never manage it," the farmer's wife said. "It is not possible to do what they say they will do." Someone, somewhere sharpened his dagger. He put his hands into long black gloves, unrolled a map of his expanding territory.

"Maybe." The farmer shrugged. "So far, they are managing."

"What do they say they will do?" Solomon asked.

"They say they will kill certain kinds of people," he told us. "All of you. In the name of improvement."

The farmer's wife shushed him. "But you are safe here," she said, opening the lid of the big silver pot and letting the smell saturate the room. "For now," the farmer said. I saw that Solomon's eyes were watering. The farmer's wife spooned soup into bowls. "Sit down and eat. Eat as much as you can." Chairs were beneath us, a floor, the table's surface made itself available to our arms and our bowls. "Look at how skinny you are," the farmer said. "You poor, poor boy." He shook his head at me, scolding.

The soup was unbearably warm. It made me feel faint. The world slowed down. My heart was a throng of people, fists raised in the air. There was butter to put on the bread. Solomon was silent. He did nothing but deliver himself food. He delivered and delivered and delivered, sucking and chewing and sucking. The farmer could not take his eyes off my son, who was filling his little body with the man's salvation. His wife trained her eyes on her own supper. No one spoke.

And then Solomon turned to his side and threw everything— absolutely everything—back up. The soup looked the same on the floor as it had in the bowl. I started to cry. I knelt down and began to scoop it into my shawl. "I'm sorry. I'm sorry," I kept saying, "he didn't mean it."

Solomon looked stunned. "I didn't mean it," he said. "I can eat it again."

The wife came around the table and said, "No, stop right now. Do not save that." The farmer blotted the corners of his mouth before placing his spoon carefully on the table. He had ceased to enjoy his supper.

I said, "I'm sorry. I'm so sorry. We won't waste it." Solomon picked up his bowl again and began to eat. He ate even while he watched me try to gather the bits of potato together.

"Stop right away," the wife said. "Please stop. There is more food. Please." I lay down on the floor and cried. I shook myself out. I was stupid and useless at trying to stop myself.

"What should we do?" the farmer whispered. In the question was a story that did not end well—the dirty woman come in from the war, sick, dying, the whole house stinking like her rotting body, her rotting soul.

The farmer's wife filled Solomon's bowl with fresh soup. She brought warm water from the stove and cleaned the floor, took my shawl away. From the corner of my eye I saw her open the front door and throw it outside. Garbage.

"Eat," she said to the boy, "try again. Your body didn't know what to do." Solomon ate slowly this time, smoothed the soup into his mouth and sucked it through his teeth. In each mouthful I heard the weeks I had allowed him to nearly starve. Solomon watched me but he kept eating.

I felt the farmer's and his wife's eyes on me. Is she insane? Is she sick? The boy is all right, handsome even, but what will we do with his mother?

Only after my son had eaten his second dinner, his eyes heavy and low, did the farmer kneel at my side, slip his arms under my back and lift. I could have stopped him, gone rigid, kicked. I could have made it clear that I was operating under my own power. But I let him take me from the floor in his arms, a body folded in on itself. I was soft, blind, compassless. My lids slipped open for a second and the farmer's eyes were waiting for mine, full of light and lightning. They told me I had one chance to deny a series of facts: You are weak and confused, ill-equipped. You are potentially crazy. You are in danger and in need of charity. You belong to a dangerous tribe. Your life, as far as it still exists, is owed to my kindness. You will do what I want.

I shut my eyes again, and let my head roll back.

The farmer's hands, one on my shoulder and the other on my leg, felt huge. I could already tell the tips of his fingers would leave bruises. But was this because he pushed them down hard? No, my own weight was to blame, crushing itself into those gentle pink pads. The farmer carried me to a bed made on the floor, where he lit and then blew out a candle. Solomon climbed in next to me. The wife pulled the wool up to the necks of her strangers. The journey from the floor near the table to the floor on the other side of the room was no more than a few paces, nothing like the hundreds of miles we had come. Yet in these last yards, a border had been crossed. The farmer had carried me like his innocent bride over the threshold. I listened to the fire spark and whine until it died and the coals left only the faintest halo of light for me to pray by.

In the next days, Solomon learned how to stack wood, churn butter and dig up only those potatoes whose bushes had begun to wither. I was given socks to mend by the farmer's wife. Her face looked like it was made of dough that had risen. Her lips puffed out around her teeth when she smiled, and enclosed them like a well-packed crate of eggs when she stopped. The farmer did not like to talk, at least not to me. He surveyed me and measured my son, like a banker wondering over an investment. His eyes were milky and his beard thin. "He's nothing like what I would have expected. He's a natural outdoorsman," the farmer said, bragging like a father. I could not think of something to glory about that would make sense to someone who had lived on the solid earth all along. My son is a natural constellation maker, a natural escaper, a natural mourner.

I ate and slept and our hosts knew by watching that these acts were as much as I could bear. Meanwhile, my son got himself back. It happened so fast. His legs were legs again, rejoined by the hopeful wrap of muscle. His hands were not a web of bone anymore. His feet. His toes. His spine—all of them were covered by a thin layer of new flesh. I still felt weak and wrung-out. My body did not build itself back up so quickly. I stared at myself in the mirror hanging beside the washbasin. "You're me," I said to it. "Hello." I waved and the person waved back. "I almost remember you. Remember me?" The woman repeated it with me, not waiting until I was done with the question to ask it back.

"Remember me?"

"Remember me?"

"Remember me?"

I watched my son out the window with the farmer, gathering, separating, hulling and seeding barley. They sat on stumps and worked. They walked and worked. They came inside, put their feet up and talked about the work that was done. They scrubbed the potatoes and they brought eggs inside, fed the chickens. There were some early apples, small and bumpy. Solomon liked to suck on them and let the sour juice sting his mouth.

As the weeks passed, my jealousy bubbled over. I imagined that Solomon and I were alone in a field somewhere, telling each other the story of what once was. His skeleton arms, his skeleton legs mine alone to hold on to, to provide just enough for, to love. I had taught him to be adaptable, to put his hands up and catch, like a tree, whatever moisture blew past. And I had knocked on this door. All Solomon had done was not say no. I missed him now in this foreign house. I missed being alone with him.

The farmer's wife had Solomon help bake the bread. She had him churning and boiling. She gave him candies to suck on and bread to eat between meals. He liked what he was asked to do—he liked working for the sake of something.

Each time the farmer saw me, disappointment scribbled over his eyes. He seemed to be patiently waiting for the day when I would quietly and respectfully disappear. I moved less and less.

The farmer ignored me more and more. The farmer's wife gave me things to chop, which took me all day. Three potatoes were hours of work, slicing them in half was enough. Cutting their starchy bodies, cutting them again. The farmer's wife worked quickly, gathering everything together and cooking it.

"We used to be three," I said, my knife resting at the edge of the board.

"Your husband?"

"If you count him we used to be four."

"Your husband and who else?"

"The baby. He was Solomon's little brother."

"Your son?"

The farmer's wife came and put her hand on my head. She brushed the hair that fell there. "Did they kill them, your husband and your baby?"

"My son fell asleep and did not wake up again." Out the window: everything else. It looked like home to me sometimes, the big emptiness of it, the unknown.

"And your husband?"

I explained Igor's kidnapping, how he was the only one taken and no one knew why or what it meant. Chosen like an egg out of a basket.

"Was that the end of it?"

"We left that night. I have no idea if our village has been burned up or if it's the same as always. No one knows where I am. Even I don't know where I am."

"That is . . ." the farmer's wife began, but she never told me what.

◆ ◆ ◆

A few days later, the farmer came home from a trip to town with a newspaper curled under his arm. I saw it and the air fell out of my body. That there might be a fact, a truth about where I was and whether I had been in danger at all. Whether I had lost my son for a reason. Whether I had starved us all for a reason. Whether the winter would come again and trees would hang themselves over me while the stones made pits of my back.

The farmer did not open the newspaper up. He put down a brick of cheese, a wreath of garlic, some meat wrapped in paper, blood seeping through.

"You have a newspaper," I said.

The farmer did not answer me.

"You bought a newspaper in town," I said.

The farmer did not answer me.

"Does that newspaper tell us how we might die?" I asked.

The farmer looked at me. His eyes were sorrowful holes in his head. His cheeks were hot red from walking and the wind had mangled his hair. He smoothed it down. "Not how I will die," he said, finally. For a second, punishment flashed in his eyes. My punishment. Truth shining like a weapon in his hands.

"You don't have to read it if you don't want to," the farmer's wife told me.

"I thought you might feel better knowing," he said, his words hot enough to burn.

He put it down, opened it flat. The picture was of a temple, exploded. A symbol like a bent cross was laid over the rubble, a flag. I imagined that he had written this paper especially for me. If I wanted to develop a theory of a crumbling world, he was going to prove it. Watch what thoughts your imagination conjures up, the farmer and his newspaper seemed to scold.

"It's possible it will end soon," the farmer's wife said.

"End," I repeated.

Solomon came in from outside, from running or rolling or building. He was alive and warm and his skin was washed with wind.

"Everything is fine," I told him, taking the newspaper away. He smiled and nodded.

"I know," he said, "everything is great."

Silently, we set to work making and then serving dinner. I ate a piece of bread. The farmer asked Solomon what he had done in the afternoon and Solomon told him about the house he had built for a beetle out of sticks. He told about the windows and the door, the bug-sized trees he had planted around it. The soft grass bed and the hidden shelter behind it. He hoped to make a pond for the bug to swim in once it got warm enough, he said. If he made it nice enough, more bugs might come. Pretty soon a whole family, a whole village would be his to take care of.

In the dark, Solomon wrapped his leg around my leg. He hit me without knowing it or meaning it. He slept so soundly now, as soundly as his father ever had. He did not wake from a nightmare or from hunger or cold. Solomon was somewhere far away from me, his sleep a thick, safe net around him. I put my hand on his cheek and whispered, "Hello," but he did not flicker. I felt like a firefly, dimming. Soon, I would be too dark to see anymore; the night and my small body the same color.

Next door, the farmer and his wife imagined it was themselves in bed with the boy. I was incidental in my own life—I could be explained right out.

"She doesn't realize that she isn't behind enemy lines anymore," the farmer whispered. "She thinks she is still in grave danger."

The farmer's wife needed a crutch of justification to lean on. "It could always change, though. The Germans could suddenly take control, and then she would be right."

"We could name him," the farmer whispered.

"He could be named for you," his wife said, thinking it charming before guilt burned her face.

"He could be ours. Saved from a terrible fate. Saved from his own life."

The farmer's wife let the story lull her. She let righteousness rinse away shame. She let saving overshadow stealing. She closed her puffy eyelids over her puffy eyes and untied the strings of the day.

"We will take him to meet my mother and father," he went on. "He will eat whatever he is given, he will be a very appreciative eater. We will baptize him. He will love roasted pork the best. He'll want to get a pet later. He'll want to get his own duckling, at least, and I'll buy him three or four. It will be his job to collect the eggs every morning. He will carry them in a basket so carefully, never breaking any of them. He'll pet the chickens. He'll fluff their hay."

The farmer's wife was asleep completely, gone from the world. Crickets scratched their song out and the leaves of the trees rubbed against each other. There was no moon, no cool light. The farmer spoke into the complete darkness.

"Whatever is bad, he will resist it. He will know what is right."

He kept himself up all night, trying to keep track of everything that would be. "I don't want to forget this," he said to himself, "there is a lot to remember. I treasure it already."

When the orange beams of morning streaked the window, the farmer came to where Solomon and I were sleeping. He picked Solomon up and took him to the bed where his wife was snoring. "This is your home now," he whispered to the boy, who did not awaken. "This is the part where we save you."

Then he got into bed with me. I came awake to his fingers petting my head the same way his wife had earlier. His fingers were like snakes nesting on my scalp. They twisted through my hair. "He is going to be happy with us, we will keep him safe," the farmer said. I heard the words but I did not open my eyes. "He is safer here than anywhere."

I listened. Wind kicked up outside. It squeezed itself between the cracks of the house and wailed in pain.

"You can tell me about him later," the farmer said. "Before you go."

"Where am I going?" I felt myself dimming.

"The farmer can't have two wives. You'll give us all away."

"Where am I going?" I asked again. Any heat I might have generated cooled to embers.

"Home, maybe. A new home, maybe. We have money—you

don't have to worry. You can take my wife's papers as if you were her. You will be my wife from now on, and she will be you. I will make all the arrangements."

"But she will stay and I will go," I said.

The farmer tried to add up the numbers to get another answer. A piece of my hair caught in his wedding ring and pulled. "What else?" he asked. "You stay and she goes? No. Certainly no."

"I will not be anyone, then," I said into the coming daylight. Even my body's weight lessened.

"Exactly, it will be perfect." The daylight invaded, making the handles on the chest of drawers stand up and the cracks and canyons in the floorboards fill with shadow.

"Where will I go?" I asked.

"Where do you want to go?" the farmer asked back. "As long as you leave, it doesn't matter to me where." I could see in his milky eyes he meant that as a kindness—all I had to do was name a peaceful, warm place and he would buy me the ticket. That Solomon was my place, he had not considered. There was frustration in his face, childlike frustration at my blindness to the logic he saw so clearly accumulated.

"I don't know if I can live without him."

"Wouldn't you rather live without him than have him die? He will live and you will live. It's the only way."

"Where will I go?" My fingers bent and straightened. Fisted, spread wide. Is this what dying feels like? I wondered.

"We have said enough," the farmer whispered into my ear. What began to rattle in my chest had not been named before—I was not laughing and my eyes were dry. I shook as soundlessly as an empty jar. If this were my moment for a crushing rebuttal, what came out of my mouth was as disappointing as a dry heave. The snakes of the farmer's fingers retreated and, disgusted with me but pleased with himself, he left me alone on his floor.

Here, Solomon would live and live and live. I did not say yes, but I did not say no. The question: How long does it take to not be me anymore? The answer: A few days. I watched the farmer add items to a small pile near my bed. He went out each day to work on the details of my departure. His wife no longer looked me in the eye. She bent her big head, let her neck fold in on itself. She served me as if I were a wolf who might bite her if she withheld the soup bones.

At night the wind kicked up and screamed. It was a language that made sense to me. Howling, whimpering. Solomon was my son, but for how many more nights I did not know. When I turned away from him he put his face into my back where his breath out was hot, his breath in, cold. I took the compass out and watched that sure little arrow point, as if it were just that easy. I shook it as hard as I could, but it bobbed dumbly back into place. The wind blew and blew, clattering the windowpanes, knocking the rakes and shovels over. And then the windows blew open and snow flew inside. I turned onto my back to see giant white flakes whirl into the house. I was not cold, I noticed, and I thought it was because I had changed from a warm-blooded animal to a snake. Flurries of snow gathered around our bed and I did not get up to close the windows. I hoped we would be buried, hidden. Blanked out. Erased. On the back of this storm, may we be carried away.

Morning quieted the wind. I sat up to discover that what last night had been a snowstorm, today was apple blossoms blown off the tree. Pinkish, slightly bruised. They were banked against Solomon's still sleeping back, and in his hair. Like a baby born out of the stamen of a flower, he was pink himself. Spring's own child, bursting with new life, nothing but warm days ahead. At the other end of the room, the farmer was fastening the buckles on a suitcase.

My first mother, that cabbage picker's wife, that hairless crystal ball, that ghost, put her hand out to this lost daughter. We are the clan of women who love their dearests by giving them away. We are the same mother. The metronome of my heart, working to be whoever each person needed me to be—daughter, daughter, mother, mother—now came to center. Absolutely still. My children were not mine. In the same instant I passed my boy on, my mother took me back. As if the difference in our hearts—mine managing to stay whole and hers broken—had separated us. The instant when the earth's continents, drifted asunder, vast oceans between them, remember they are made of the same stone. Hardened lava, granite. And then, with tremendous force, mountains are thrown up when two plates crash back together.

When we are born, we do not belong to any tribe. We earn membership over our lives—the clan of the first people in the world, of adopted children, of heavy sleepers, of foreigners, of cabbage lovers, of lost mothers.

The four of us stood in the sunshine and said little. The new parents repeated to Solomon everything. His life was being saved. He would have his mother's love with him and plus his new mother's love with him—double. He would have a father now, and always the old father wherever he was would love him, too. He could hardly escape his fortune, so much bounty. The bready face of the farmer's wife looked toasted. Any baker would have been proud of that honey brown, egged and glistening.

"And you'll be near your brother," the farmer's wife told him.

"My brother is dead," Solomon said.

"Don't fight with your mother," the farmer said.

"I'm not," Solomon said, looking at me. "My mother hasn't said anything."

"Your other mother. Your new mother. Don't fight with her."

Solomon moved closer to me. "This is just a story. I will always be your mother," I said. "In this chapter Natalya is your mother. Nothing is changing except what we say."

"Everything is changing," he corrected. "Where I live."

"Which is also where your brother lives," the farmer added.

"My brother does not live," Solomon said.

I nodded for him. "He would miss you if you left," I said, smiling the most honest smile I could invent.

"You're leaving," he said. "Don't."

"I'm leaving because I have to. There can't be two wives. But there can be a son."

I thought he might break down and scream. I thought he might grab on to me and swear that he would never let go for the rest of his life. He did not. He had learned something about survival. He had grown up, I knew that much, because he looked into my eyes and said, "You'll look after yourself for me." I could not speak, but I drew a smile on my face as a promise.

"You'll look after yourself for me," I finally managed, the croak of an afraid but obedient girl.

The farmer nodded. Done, his nod said: All said, all set. "We have thought of everything," he said out loud. "You have your papers and you'll be Natalya. You have your extra clothes and your money. You have your memories. We have our lunch and our dinner."

"I have all of those things," I confirmed. "Wait," I said, taking the papers out of their leather envelope and unfolding them. "How old am I?"

"Twenty years old," the farmer's wife said.

I looked for a birth date. "Nineteen twenty-five," I said, "June sixth. Twenty years old." That number did not seem big enough to hold even part of what I was carrying.

Solomon's eyes started to soften up and fill with water. "I'm not leaving you," he said.

"No, I'm leaving you," I told him. "You are not doing anything wrong."

"Where will you go?" Solomon asked, suddenly realizing he did not know which direction to picture his mother walking in. Would I be in the high, snowy mountains? Would I huddle in the wheat and make myself flat and easy to overlook? I took the compass out of my pocket and gave it to him. "I will always be in one of these directions. No matter how big the map is, I'm some-where on it."

"Don't ask her when she will be back," the farmer scolded, though Solomon had not said the dangerous thing.

"What is your name?" the farmer's wife asked.

"My name is Natalya Volkov."

"Go on, Natalya. The world waits for you." She gave me a pat on the head.

I put a piece of paper in Solomon's hand. He did not open it right away but let it warm in his palm.

"You are my love," I whispered in his ear.

"We are our love," he whispered back.

The farmer shepherded me down to the path. I imagined Solomon watching each of our footsteps, each of the impressions we left in the dirt. The cloud we kicked up hung in the air before falling back down. He watched until we went around the corner and he could hear us more than see us. He listened then, trying to amplify the sound of his mother's body crossing over the earth.

"Time to go inside," the farmer's wife said.

"I'm listening to her go," he replied.

"You can't hear her. She's gone."

"I'm listening."

The farmer's wife stood there beside him until the sun changed the color of the grass. Every so often she prodded him, "Now we can go inside."

My son continued to stand there when the night was smeared

everywhere. There was a sliver of a moon, a cut in the solid black, and three stars, which would disappear when he looked too hard at them.

"I see you, stars," he said to them. "Why don't you go on inside?" he suggested to the farmer's wife.

"I'm not going to leave you. I'm your mother." So they stood together and the farmer's wife tried to hear but heard nothing and Solomon tried to hear and heard something and the stars pecked their way out, breaking the darkness everywhere. Solomon did not point out the now familiar formations.

They did not go inside again and again. A hundred times over they stayed exactly where they were.

In Solomon's palm, the compass warmed and the note softened. *Solomon*, it said, *Milk, Wheat, Baby, Farmer, Home, Stars, Stars. You survive this. I know for a fact. Mother, Remember.*

"What are you looking at?" the farmer's wife asked.

"A note," he said.

"It's too dark to read anything. We're standing outside in total blackness."

"I know what it says," he told her.

"I'm ready to go inside," she prodded.

"Wheat, wheat, mud," he said.

"What?"

"Stars, stars, stars."

"I do not know how to talk to you."

"Mother," he said.

"That's me," she pleaded.

"Mother, mother," he said.

"Me, me," she answered.

"No. Only one you."

They did not go inside at all that night. They did not go inside but instead made themselves warm by huddling together on the ground. Solomon kept hearing me make my way. He heard me kick rocks and swing my arms. He heard the sound of my suitcase brushing up against my leg. Both of them listened to the breathing earth.

THE BOOK OF SKELETONS

The farmer and I walked silently; even our feet whispered with the ground. I was the one leading us, and we were not going to the train yet. The farmer was confused, fidgety. The woman he had bargained so easily with, who had gone limp in his very arms, now demanded to be followed. I could not feel the specifics of my own body—my hair caught in the button of my dress, my feet tired, my face cold. My brain felt like a beehive. All I knew was that I was walking away from my only known relative and I was doing it as a favor. The only gift I could give my son was the absence of myself.

"Are you angry?" the farmer asked, suddenly.

"What?"

"You haven't spoken to me since we left."

"Angry?" As if I could know, as if it could change anything.

"You don't care how I feel." I said this as fact. Not something I was sorry about, or something I wished to change.

"But I have been very nice to you. I have been nicer than you probably deserve," the farmer said. His clear eyes told me he meant this. I looked away. The farmer's voice sounded higher to me. It was the voice of a boy with a question he could not figure out how to ask. He told me I was making his wife happy. I was generous. The choice I had made was the only sensible one.

"My son will not die because he is related to me. That's a gift and you're the ones who gave it to us. I'll spend my life being grateful for that. I'll spend my life trying to forgive it."

Fear, that dependable dog, would not be fed out of my hand anymore. Everything worth losing had already been lost.

I remembered the way back, remembered the line of pines at the edge of the field, the vein of granite, the small hill and the dip on the other side. We walked in tight circles, looking for what was left. I did not panic. I knew my boy would have waited for me to kiss him goodbye.

"I don't think you should come over here," the farmer said through the wind.

"My son is there," I said.

"It's not a good way to see him."

I came and stood over the pile. "His bones," I said.

The farmer was not looking at the bones. He saw matted old muscles, dry, chewed sinew. He saw rot. He saw a body feasted on by birds and worms.

The farmer fell to the ground. "He could have been my son."

I picked up a long, thin bone. "He *was* my son," I said. He was my baby, my real, true boy, and this was my chance to touch him one last time.

I went to the mattress and jumped. I jumped and I held the long leg bone. "You are my love," I said to the bone. The mattress made sucking sounds as the grass that grew there was squashed under my feet. I said, "I absolutely remember who you are."

"How can this happen? How can we go on? There is so much to lose," the farmer said. And lose it you will, I thought. The process of living is to surrender what, for a few glimmering days or years, you have been allowed to hold. But there is no such place as gone. The next thought I had hit me hard: I hoped the baby died with a patched-up heart. Please, I thought. Let us be broken together. Years from now, when Solomon's heart finally breaks and all the beautiful rivers of hope and sorrow have canyons to run in, he will be my son again. In some sea, under a fury of stars, far away from any named place, my sons and I will collide.

"How can we leave the baby?" the farmer asked.

"That is *my* baby, *my* son," I said.

"But from now on, I love him. He is my son's brother." God, in his endless generosity, had found yet another thing for me to share.

I looked up at the heavens. The stars began and continued. The moon made a lazy attempt to exist. The story of my life, of the whole world, was encoded in those lights. They were the only things that had never left me. I gathered strength because my job as a mother was not over.

"Do you see those stars there? Those are the dog stars," I said. "Solomon found them."

The farmer puzzled at the shape, tried to make a dog of it.

"What else?" he asked. He could not hide his relief that I was speaking to him kindly.

"That one is a cart. Over here is a fish." He studied the sky.

"I can't find anything," he said.

"It doesn't matter if you see it or not. It's there."

"I have taken your son," he said.

"I am letting you borrow him," I answered.

"What will you have?" he asked. Everything that ever blew into my arms had blown back out again. But snow turned to blossoms. Beneath the apple tree, the shawl I survived under now warmed the rotted core of a fallen piece of a fruit, coaxing a green shoot.

"Your promise that you will be very kind to my son."

"I promise."

"Is there anything you need to know about being a father?"

The farmer thought about it. He said, "I don't know anything about being a father."

"Do you know what to do when Solomon gets sick?"

"No. But we're calling him Johan. He is a Christian now."

I took a sharp gasp. A new pain: a lost bit of healthy flesh, stabbed. Just keep being the mother, I said to myself. Let my arms grow so long I can wipe his tears from the other side of the earth. "When Johan, your son, gets sick, a cool cloth is the most important thing. And water to drink. But he's going to tell you he's dying even when he isn't. If it's winter, give him packed snow to suck on. If it's summer, find him a place in the shade."

"But what if he *is* dying?"

"You'll have to learn the difference between when he's dying and when he isn't."

"Is there anything more I can give you?" the farmer asked.

I listened to whatever made sound: the squish of the mattress, wet and unwell. The sound of the crying insects. The sound of my son's bones rattling. The sound of the man and the heat of the man traveling across the baby's leftovers.

"I have my life," I said finally. Even this—life—felt weightless. Some invisible string must have kept me tethered. When I found it, I planned to cut it and let myself float away.

"I could give you more life," he said. "Not because I love you."

"I have more life than I need for just myself," I said.

The farmer pulled up my dress. He did not smooth his hand over me, not even a gentle stroke. He did not come to me with any warm part of him, but one. I closed my eyes to the covered world. Nothing tried to be seen in that darkness, everything was happy to hide from me. I did not move my body away, or turn my head or say words that would have changed what happened. The farmer's body was a body and my body was another body and the bones of my dead son rested against us both. The farmer wrestled himself in. His beard was full of dew, bright seeds, which dropped onto my face. His movements were simple and unadorned.

A flock of ravens crossed over the farmer and me but we saw nothing of the birds. The birds were the same as the sky that night. There was a sound of flying, but only for a second, and then a sound of calling back to the ones behind. The followers answered back, *Yes*, they said. *We are all here together.*

"For the baby," the farmer said, when he had climbed back down and moved the scattered bones from under him.

The ravens went on. The ravens crossed over whatever was below but did not stop to rest there. Did not stop to acknowledge the world laid low around them.

From then on, the road was new to me. It took only hours this time, the walk an actual, measurable distance instead of an endless journey away. I kept trying to count the steps, knowing that there would be a final one, a total number. The place I walked through was a perfect reenactment of a real world. These bushes looked exactly like real bushes. All the details had been thought of—birds of different colors and size, needles spilling out from the skirts of pine trees. Only the air was wrong. It was thin and tinny, cheaply made. Too bad, I thought, they almost got it right.

In the afternoon the farmer said, "I'm sorry."

"Yes," I answered.

"*Should* I be sorry for what I did?" the farmer asked, wanting me, instead of being angry, to tell him how grateful I was.

"Life is not replaceable," I told him. The proof was all around me: the made-up bluebird drinking from a puddle of newly melted snow, as if something that precious could be real. The real bird, mangy and cold, was hidden away somewhere.

The farmer's voice went up, "Forgive the approximation. Life is life. I tried my hardest."

I did not answer.

"No!" the farmer suddenly yelled. "Say thank you! Tell me thank you for saving your son! I'm doing *everything* I can *think* to do for you," he growled. "You have our money and our passport and I'm even trying to give you a companion. I'm trying to make you a family."

He pushed me into the tall trees along the road.

"You have done enough," I said. "Please stop trying to help me."

"We have to be grateful for what we can offer each other," he said, deflating me. I punched his back and slammed my feet against his anklebones. I fought. I remember twisting beneath him, but he did not have to struggle hard. I was weak. I posed no threat to him. I was a source, that was all, a well for him to draw upon.

The sticks cracked with every push and the leaves broke into a thousand crushed squares and none of the birds watched us. The moment was quick and over.

"You don't know what this does to me. I do not love you."

I did not have enough matter in me to hate him with.

"I don't mean any of this," he said. "I have a family at home. A wife and a son," he said. "I'm just trying to do what's right." I held my breath until my lungs prickled. I let out one long howl until my chest was sore and empty. The fake forest was mawkish around me. Greens too green, sky too crystalline to be possible. Not on a day like this. The poor rabbit burying his nose in the underbrush would surely starve by nightfall, finding nothing but pieces of wood someone had carved to look like seeds.

A buzzing, rolling, mechanical city met us soon. This invention had outgrown its creator. Hammer together scraps of wood into the shape of legs and in the morning the body is up and walking. By midday, your tools are missing and the roads are battered by wheels. The farmer and I stood on the very edge of the road while people passed us in cars. The cars spit out gray smoke, hot and thick.

The town was full of people, walking, driving, riding bicycles, yelling, wearing hats and carrying large leather bags, reading the newspaper, smoking and standing there with the sun in their eyes, waiting for whatever came next.

"Where have I always been?" I asked. The farmer put his hand on my shoulder.

"This is the world," he said. "This is the regular, loud world." The cars spit dust up at children poking their heads out of second-story windows. The children called to other children on the street, broke down in giggles. The scene unfolded in slow motion. A gray cat tore at a liver, which turned his face dark red. One of the children tripped over the cat and fell into a puddle and the liver rolled and the cat squawked and the other children's faces burned up with laughter. No one laughed harder than the boy in the puddle, who was on his knees, holding his belly. His friends came to him, took him by the elbows and picked him up. These boys on this street had just lived one of the stories they would tell and tell, a story whose medicine would be strong enough to draw laughter for all the years of their lives. One of the boys kicked the liver back to the cat, who resumed his feasting.

"So many people are still alive," I said.

"These people are different from yours. No one's trying to kill these ones," the farmer said. He led me slowly through the streets. The windows in the cars winked light at us. Small pieces of trash were ground into the sidewalk. A pair of dogs approached us, looked up with polished and hopeful eyes, waited to be saved. The farmer tossed them nothing and I had nothing to toss.

"Your train," the farmer said, gesturing.

The machine was churning and soot-black. I studied its huge and numerous wheels, its doors and windows and platforms and chains. The farmer gave me a ticket for the Black Sea port city. He gave me the name of the office where I should buy passage on a ship to the New World—that's what he called it.

"I already lived in a new world," I told him. "I'm not sure I can manage another."

"I don't know what you're talking about," he said, "but this is a nice place where you'll live your life out. Your entry papers are all set. Everything is prepared." He was talking quickly, anxious to get to the part where I was gone and he was free to be the father he had dreamed of being. He said he did not know what had happened to me out there in the fields, or before, but that he was sure the world would make sense to me again soon. He wrote my name in his dirty arm with his fingernail: *Natalya*. I nodded. He added: *Live*. I nodded again. On the other arm he wrote: *Sorry*. I nodded a third time. I scratched two words back: *Good Father*. He smiled. His whole face rose up. He did not pay me the same compliment, and I was glad because I would not have deserved it.

The farmer waited alone on the platform. I watched two women run to each other and exclaim utter delight with their arms wrapped around each other. One handed the other a round box, which popped open to reveal a light purple hat with a small robin perched on its brim. The hatted woman looked at me and I looked at her. We observed each other, probably misunderstanding everything. To her, the farmer could have been my brother, missing me already, the next visit years away. We could have been lovers whose parents had forbidden our union. We could have been a mother and a father, doing all the heroic and vicious things we knew to protect the child we each claimed. The train cried and began to drag itself out of the station. Every single person on the platform, absolutely all of them, waved. They had practiced, and they performed beautifully. The farmer waved, looked at the ground and then waved again. I wept into my cupped palms, where a pool collected, salty and warm, which I lapped up like the gray cat.

I tasted the dead and I tasted the living.

THE BOOK OF
THE LOCKED-AWAY HEAVENS

When a warship appeared on the horizon, Francesco brought more paper but no more envelopes. Igor said, "Aren't we going swimming?"

"We're staying here."

"How long to ride even a slow, crippled horse to my home?"

"We're staying here."

"I'm talking about the mail. What is the slowest possible time?"

"Nothing leaves this room from now on. You are a prisoner of war and I am your guard. Those are the only orders I have ever been given."

"No reason to be defensive," Igor said. "It's just that I was planning to go swimming."

Francesco punched Igor once, hard, in the face. It was a

terrible, exhilarating feeling. His fist came back bloody with hero-ism. "No one asked what you wanted."

The islanders tracked the warship as it came ever closer. Francesco paced, practicing for the arrival. He would play the just and righteous guard, carrying out his duties with a firm but fair hand. No one had given him orders to empty his prison.

Igor spent the wait writing furiously in a notebook whose pages he did not tear out and send away. It was a manual to his sons on how to live, as best he could tell them.

> *Open your eyes to wake up. It is possible to be awake*
> *with your eyes closed, but you will not be able to see*
> *anything around you.*
> *When you are given bread, try to enjoy it right away.*
> *Bread right away is better than bread later.*
> *If you can't remember the stars' shapes, make more up.*
> *Sometimes you have to make your own heavens.*
> *If you have children, which I hope you do, do not get taken*
> *prisoner so that you cannot see them when they are five, six,*
> *eight. Do not fall asleep in the barn and get taken away in a*
> *car, even if the island is warm and beautiful where you are*
> *going. If your children are boys, name them for kings. If your*
> *children are girls, name them for mothers.*
> *You must already know everything I know. What can*
> *I teach you? I know how to eat and I know how to play*

checkers. This is a game played on the diagonal. One of us will win.

Do whatever your mother tells you to. She is probably right. She will be thinking of what will be best. If you see me again, I will try to tell you what is best, too. I hope your mother and I will agree. We will try to. You should try to agree with people, too.

Solomon used to know some of the prayers. Do you still know them? I know the sound of them, but not the words. Try practicing them so you do not forget. Roll them around in your mouth. This is one thing that I do with your names so that you feel close to me all the time. Your names, Lena, Solomon and Beautiful Baby, are in my mouth. Your names go down my throat when I swallow. I carry you everywhere.

"What have I missed?" Igor asked through the bars.

"Cooking. Cleaning up. Walking. Serving of tea. Staying dry in the rain," Francesco said.

"Help me remember."

Dear Igor, Francesco thought, I can survive anything with you.

In the afternoon, the huge warship docked, and a hundred men disembarked.

"Are you with Mussolini or the Allies?" the biggest man yelled in badly accented Italian. The old man who ran the taverna shrugged and told them, "We're for whoever you are. We just want to live."

"Good. We need supplies."

The soldiers took food from people's cellars and medicine from their cupboards. They gathered rope from people's boats and shoes from their closets. They came to the jail where Francesco was sitting at his desk with his feet up looking as much in control as he could. Igor was cowering in the corner of the cell. Three soldiers came to the prison door and said in unison, "Is that it? One prisoner?" Francesco, so consumed with his duty to Igor, had forgotten to think of his jail as deficient.

A prayer slipped out of Igor's mouth. It was the first time he had prayed since his arrival on the island and the long-lost taste of those words was dusty and sweet.

One soldier came to the bars, studied Igor. "Wait, are you Jewish?" he asked softly. Igor looked up at him. He did not know the answer to this question. Once, in another place and time, he had been a Jew in a world full of Jews. "Why are you still holding this man?" the soldier asked Francesco. "You should have freed him long ago."

"What?" Francesco and Igor both asked at the same time. Francesco squeezed his fist, but this did not stop the feeling that everything he loved was slipping away. And for the prisoner, freedom was a sharp word. Free to go where? Igor thought.

The soldier kicked the bars of the cage, making it rattle. "Italy has joined the Allies, or hadn't you heard?" he mocked. He moved into the light and Igor could read the name embroidered on his uniform: Weinberg. "Do it now!" the soldier yelled, and Francesco took the key from around his neck and unlocked the door. Igor stood up, came to the opening. Igor watched Francesco's shaking hands turn the key over and over.

"He's been good to me. Please don't hurt him," Igor said.

Weinberg turned to Francesco and said, "I'm watching you." The soldiers began to leave.

"Excuse me," Igor said, "free to go where?"

The soldier's gaze fell to the floor. "I wouldn't go home, I wouldn't go looking for my family, if I were you." The soldier looked out the open door where the day was bright and windless. "You'll find a new life. Bless you."

THE BOOK OF
THE MOVING WORLD

I looked out at the spinning grass, knitting itself into a blur next to me, the early spring trees behind standing defined. I thought of the number of steps it would take to make this same journey. The number of times I would swing my arms. Out there I would be able to close my eyes for a few strokes without tripping, I would be able to memorize the ground and move over it blind. Outside, the number of gusts, rustles and shrieking birds. The number of beetles making a slow track across the path. All the bees roving for sweet juices. The clouds sometimes a single drift. Inside the train, everything was constant. The movement was not in added-up single steps but one long thrust forward. So decisive, so sure.

When the conductor came to check my ticket, I said, "I need to go home."

"I don't know where that is," he said carefully.

"I don't either."

"Which direction?"

"I don't know where I am."

"You're in Russia. You are headed southeast toward Odessa."

"I'm in a country?" I asked. This idea seeming unthinkable.

"Where else?"

"The grass. The fields. The mountains."

"Do you know where you want to go?" the conductor asked.

"I want to go home."

He tore a corner off my ticket and shook his head. "Tell me if you can get a better idea than that." Outside it started to rain. The windows became foggy. The trees looked weighed down and ashamed, the same as me.

The train had a car to eat in where they made cups of coffee for anyone who asked. They dropped leaves of tea into baskets. At each table two or three men relaxed, feet crossed, cups steaming. They were enjoying their journey. I wanted to ask them where they were going and where they had been. What they had survived. Which side they were on. They looked like men whose wives were preparing, at this moment, for their arrival. Pinning long hair, ironing dresses, wrestling sons into clean shirts.

I sat alone at a table and let the relaxed men relax. "Sir," I said to the white-coated waiter, trying to sound like someone else, someone sane, someone with one name, one family, one story. "Do you know where a village called Zalischik is?"

He shook his head, not understanding me. Why did nothing I said make sense to anyone?

"Home," I said.

He said, "We have tea, we have coffee, we have cake."

"All right," I said, pressing a gold coin between my fingers. "I'll have those things, if that's all you can offer." Perhaps home was simply gone—a concept done away with.

I dipped my finger in the coffee and then touched it to my lips. "Do I like coffee?" I whispered to the stranger of myself. I dipped my finger in the tea and then touched it to my lips. "Is tea better?" I ate the cake quickly. I knew I liked cake. I sucked the cubes of sugar the waiter brought. I felt the coffee, milky brown, and the tea, clear and precise, roll down my throat and land warm. I watched the surface shake rhythmically with the rocking train. The objects in front of me seemed solid and real, it was the ones not in front of me that kept shifting.

The waiter came back to take my empty cups away. "Would you like to look at a map?" he asked. "I could bring you a map."

"A map?" I asked.

"Maps are supposed to have all the places."

"Thank you, yes, please, yes." I had made sense to him and he to me. I wanted to shake his hand, but I stopped myself. I brushed the crumbs off the table and into my hand. I shook them into my mouth. The waiter spread the map out on my table.

"This is where we are," he said, pointing to a line with little crosses over it. "Train tracks." He moved his finger along the line.

"This is everything?" I asked.

The map showed so many names. Smolensk. Kursk. Stalingrad. The names were pasted to the earth. The mountains were jagged lines, the rivers were curling blue.

"Has all this always been here?"

"The names have changed. Things move around, I'm sure. But for our purposes, I'd say so."

"Even in the beginning of the world?" He looked at me blankly.

"There's a list on the back," the waiter said, "arranged by spelling." And there it was, right between Zalim and Zalizyki. In real life it had been a small island with the river curled around it. On the map it was the same.

"That's the place I'm from. That is home," I said, and my finger covered it completely. The river was squashed. "Show me again where we are now. And show me where we came from."

The waiter pointed and pointed. "The train stops nearby. You could walk there." I was still thinking about the journey my sons and I had made over all this land. I began at the place where the river curled and walked my fingers over the in-between. "That's what happened," I said. I could say this, and the map acted as proof. To start the world over, upturn everything we knew, had I hammered and nailed and rallied and campaigned? No. I had spoken it. Told a story. Still, when I looked at the map—the lines, the differing greens, the tiny etchings of rivers—I could not see what had really happened.

By the time the long white light of the afternoon had tired itself out and lay splattered orange on each rain-wet surface, I was on my way home. Riding in a warm cave inside me, unknown to me then, was the stew of a person. Nothing sensible yet. No specifics. Not even in miniature. But if left alone, the being would do the dance it had to do. Its body would freight in the needed supplies. The blood would stay thick and protective. Divisions and additions.

What I could feel were the wheels of the train heating up the tracks, and the distance closing in between my home and myself.

The first to greet me were our sheep, which floated dead on top of a lake that used to be their pen. The wool was beaded with water. The eyes of the sheep were rotted-out pits—anything could have made its way inside. The smell caught in my throat and made me gag.

Our streets were soaked with mud and our stones were turned on their sides, making the path unsmooth. It was no longer a street but a pile of jagged rocks. The windows in all our houses were smashed and vacant, eaten away like the sheep's eyes. Everything was blinded. Was this a real place?

"You are the house where I had my babies," I said at my own rotted door. When I pulled it open I was flooded by water. Free now, the water spread wide. I walked through the slush of the house, which was empty. No pots remained in the kitchen. No pillows remained on the beds. No books. No spoons. No people. "No one is here?" I asked the soggy house. No table, no rocking chair, no poker to stir the coals in the fire. Someone had moved us out. The water had made boats of the few items left inside: one broken chair floated, one wooden bowl floated. My sons' mattress remained, draped like a dead animal over the sink. It was green with mold.

Water had driven in and my house had dutifully held it. Fill it with rugs and chairs, fill it with children and baking bread, fill it with cabbage. Fill it with all the water in the world.

My walls were a crawl of mold, turned bright green, eaten down by moss. "How long has it been like this?" I asked the ghosts I could not see. "When did you go?"

If the ghosts tried to answer, their mouths were useless. I wished they would try to rustle my clothes, cool my skin or warm it, put their hands in my hair. Did they want to tell me they waited as long as they could? That they had taken care of my mothers and fathers and grandparents and siblings? Had they tried to remember me even after I left? They were empty wind by then. They were sucking mud at my feet. They were flaking bark on the trunks of fallen-down trees. Crushed rocks, clods of dirt, dried water, blown air.

At the first house I was raised in I stood in front of the door. I remembered the night I had tried to come home, and, of all the huge and complicated things that might have stood in my way, what had kept me out was a simple lock. I could not bear that again, so I left the big blue door out of it. I hung my clothes on the branches of an apple tree ravenous with white blossoms and climbed through the window where the water was ankle-deep and muddy. The smell was rich and dark. "No one is here? Was I right to leave when I did? Is anyone alive?" I called. My voice echoed off the water. I felt as if I were in an ancient cave.

I waded to the counter where I had watched my first mother chop cabbages every day for the first eleven years of my life. I splashed to the far wall where the fireplace was a dark pit, then to the place where my first mother and my first father had slept, had made me, had made my sister and brother. This was the first time I had been in the house since I was traded away. I scoured the bottom for cabbages but found none, dragging up handfuls of mud. I pulled up a marble and a soaked handkerchief. I wiped my face on the cloth, which only left me dirtier.

The second house I was raised in had fallen to one side and lost one of its walls. It held no pond inside—it was an empty skeleton. "No one is here?" I called, my skin cold but dried now by my clothes, my hair still dripping. "No one at all is anywhere? Anywhere here?" None of Kayla and Hersh's beautiful things were displayed on the mantel. No soft Persian rugs were at my feet. The story of their lives was silent. I wanted to say something for them, some prayer, but I realized I hardly knew them. Bless Kayla and her desires. Bless Hersh and his attempts to fill them. May someone somewhere adopt you both.

I went into houses I had never entered before. Everything had sunk into softened ground. All the windows were too low, some of the doors buried enough to be sealed shut.

The barber's was tiny and dark, all four walls tipped toward each other, a single pair of scissors, shining as if just polished, hanging from a nail on the wall. To the people who had lived there, no place would have mattered more.

Outside, the square was more beautiful than I remembered. Even destroyed, the windows had careful scrolls framing them, the roofs were pointed and red tiled, the doorways arched. The greengrocer's was painted yellow, the butcher's was pale blue, the jeweler's little sliver of a shop was pink with white trim. This place was new to me, and yet completely familiar. It was as if I, a girl, were meeting myself as an old woman. The same body, the same place. Except.

The widow's house was a graveyard of jars. I kicked them around so that something in the world would talk to me. They clattered but made no sense. Yet something revealed itself: I saw a small piece of yellow paper lying on the ground with a tack stuck in it. The ink had run, but I could still read the words. *Dear Ones, We did not know what to do but hide when the soldiers arrived. There was a lot of shouting, then running toward the river and gunshots, then quiet. We waited for weeks, but none of you came home. We will not forget to include you in our story, which in spite of everything has a happy ending: we have been swept up by handsome Russian giants. If anyone is alive, write to us in Krasnograd. Love, Regina and Zelda.* And there it was: my sister was saved. It was almost as good as being saved myself—my shadow had made it. Good news tasted like food to me. I folded the letter up and held it tightly. What else would I find? I said, "Thank you," out loud to the roomful of jars, listening to me like a hundred ears.

The barn, I discovered, was where all our belongings had gone. I had to jump from desk to dresser to table to saddle horse.

The room was a swimming pool stacked with towers of belongings. It smelled like mold and rotting wood and urine. I looked up and saw, complete but for one shattered bullet wound, the summer sky. Around me toys, mittens, boots and chair legs floated. Stacks of dish towels, hammers, worn wool coats, boxes of rusted jewelry, and rolling pins would have to wait a long time for this town to come alive, to need tools again. The piano, which had arrived along with our stranger, washed up on the shores of the old world, did not stand upright—it kneeled with its broken smile in the water.

I looked for but did not find a body to carry out and put in the ground. I did find the bones of some chickens, gathered nicely in the highest shelf of empty nests. I imagined them, wings folded, waiting to be saved.

Standing on the pedestal that used to live in the square and had been host to the long-dead war hero, now missing, I reached up and dragged my hand along the constelled wall. "Solomon would have known your name," I said to the stars. One white tile was loose so I pulled it off and put it into my small bag. "This is the Solomon star," I said. "Whatever it was called before, now it's called Solomon." I had nothing, and since I did not know what I needed, I decided to take whatever was being offered.

At the top of a stack of books I found the soft underfeathers of chickens and geese, gathered in an old sack. They even smelled soft. I tied a knot at the top of the sack and put it into my bag.

And there was one more thing tacked to a floating island of wood. It was a letter, and the letter was addressed to *Lena, My Wife, Zalischik*.

"Do not joke with me," I said to the room and I listened for its reply. "Is this another letter for me?" The room echoed and dropped water down. I took the letter with my name on it. On the back was written: Igor, Jail, Sardinia, Italy. Inside, one piece of paper.

> Dear L,
>
> I am alive, did you know? I am getting to be a very, very fast swimmer. I can swim from the big rock all the way to the sandy beach in a matter of seconds. I learned how to make lasagna. Do you know what that is? My friend Francesco taught it to me, actually his mother did. How are my sons? Are you alive? What is the weather like where you are? Remember the time we climbed to the top of the apple tree and fell asleep in the branches? I hope you are alive.
>
> Love, I

"This letter is for me," I said, holding it up. "Am I alive?"

"This letter is for me!" I yelled as loud as I could, loud enough that my throat hurt. "Nobody is here! The Beautiful Baby is dead! Solomon is saved! I went northeast! The world is full of trains! Have I been gone a hundred years? Igor has become a very, very fast swimmer!"

I looked at the letter again, tore my name off—*Dear L*—and shredded it into a fine snow. "You left me completely alone!" I screamed to Igor. "Our boys are gone. What am I doing here? Why am I not dead?" I threw the snow of my name up into the air. "What am I going to do now?"

I listened, but heard no one answer. I put the bag of feathers down on a dry shelf and waved the muddy handkerchief and the letter in surrender. I tossed some chicken bones up like confetti and they splashed down, a sad, sinking music.

On the back of the note with a pencil that floated beneath a desk, I wrote:

> Dear I,
> Why is everyone always leaving each other? I almost remember who you are, but I don't remember who I am.
> Do you?
>
> Love, L

"Take me away! I'm yours!" I yelled. "I'm ready to die here!" The temple's dumb eyes stared past me, did not acknowledge me or wink in camaraderie. The trees outside did not wave their branches.

Even though it might have been a relief to see a group of men in tall black boots come out of the fields and take me away, they did not. No one arrested me or shot me in the chest or dragged me away by my feet. No one whispered in my ear or brushed my hair. No one told me to be careful since I was going to be a mother for the third time. No one sat down nearby and opened a newspaper. No one ate an apricot and spit the pit at my feet. No one blew his nose or scratched his cheek or sighed. In a world filled with millions of people, I was left absolutely alone.

I looked at the pool around me. "Will I be a very fast swimmer like my husband?" I asked it. "Is that what I'm supposed to find out?"

The surface was a shimmering thing. Above: air; objects that used to matter; the stars; the new world. Below: mud, rot; everything buried, everything lost.

I reached my arms up over my head and stood tall. I pictured myself a champion diver on a very tall board with the entire ocean around me. I imagined myself in a bathing suit and a cap. I filled the shore with cheerers. Each man had a hat he was waving. Each woman had a handkerchief. Each child, a banner with my name on it. It was not water I would dive into. It was another world— someplace I had never been. I believed, and that was a feeling I had forgotten. The flutter of wings in my chest.

The surface of the world was permeable—a line meant to be broken. All I had to do was jump through.

My arms made a sweep and my toes pushed off the edge of the pedestal and my dive was in motion. I cut through the air like a huge bird, the noises and the colors disappeared around me as if it were all one great arc of sky.

The lake took me in, clothes and all. The water was enough. It took my head and belly—my bones—gently down, all our prayers, turned now to water. I sunk down to the bottom of the lake and let all the air out of my lungs. I sat there as long as I could, as heavy as I could, and listened. It felt like the moment before I was born, and I did not want to rush it. I was beneath, below, under, beyond. The water held me completely, tight. It got into my ears and nose, between my toes and fingers. There were almost no sounds: only the pop of bubbles that escaped my nose and floated to the surface. Only the water sealing my ears. I opened my mouth and let the dirty water in. I felt my hair lift up and float. In front of me, my hands were hardly visible, just ghosts. "I am alone beneath the earth," I said into the water, which muted my words and carried them up as air.

I heard the sound of my heart, as always. When my lungs prickled, I had a choice: breathe water, or breathe air. I let my mouth flood, but could not make myself take the water deeper. I pushed myself up, and filled my chest.

The pool sang when I wrung my hair out onto the surface, returning what I had taken.

· VII ·

THE BOOK OF
THE DISTANCE, AWAY

The miles back to the train were marked by water dripped from my hair and clothes. I left trails on the path and shivered with cold. I had my two small bags—one with my papers, a chip of the Solomon star, a muddy handkerchief that might have belonged to my first mother and a letter from my husband who was having a fun time down south. I wanted not to be angry with him, to feel only the relief of a wife who discovers her husband is safe and happy, and I did feel that, but there I was in my wracked body, in my empty village, alone. If I could have summoned him back at that instant, had someone to walk those miles to the train with me, I would have forgiven him all the comfort of his months away.

In the second bag were goose feathers, packed tight but even still, weighing very little. My feet made pools in the mud and all along my path were the twisted bodies of worms. Rain had drawn them out and then left them stranded. Some were balled up, some were stretched so long and thin they looked like the beginnings of snakes. Some were in the shape of letters. An S, a P, an O. I tried to read their message as I walked but found nothing but random deformations.

"Stop talking to me," I said to the worms. "I'm not listening."

I stood under the yellow lights of the station platform, holding everything I had not lost, while a herd of moths crashed again and again into the lightbulbs. Banging their heads against something so promising.

I was asked six times in the first hour for my papers, which I gave easily, looking out the window, thinking, *Do I die here? Is this the end?*

"Natalya Volkov," I told them each time. "My sister is sick in Odessa. I'll be with her when she dies."

"Tell me your husband's name. Tell me the names of your children."

"Volkov. Johan. I have no children."

The train stopped and hissed. People walked through the corridor, spoke words muffled by the walls. In my compartment, I sat up with the bag of feathers behind my head and the bag of treasures on my lap. Outside my window: the sea, tall snowy mountains, a lake filled with geese.

I thought about getting out at the goose lake and staying there to collect all of their softest feathers. It would be an agreeable life, my feet dangling in what would surely be clean and cool water, with a goose on my lap, gently pulling the down from its belly. I would sing to the goose, if the goose wanted. I would smooth its top feathers down and clean any dried muck off its beak. When it waddled away it would be happier. I would stuff pillows for everyone. People would come from all towns nearby to buy my feathers. They would send them to their relatives, who, far away in some new world, would rejoice at the packages. Who would tear open their old pillows and pour the rough old down out their windows onto the streets, where the people below would be covered. Snowbound.

An old woman snapped the door to my compartment open. She carried two bags and a cane that she did not walk with but held at the ready like a well-used weapon. Her face was an oiled hide. She said, "Don't talk to me while I eat," and unpacked a piece of chicken, a piece of bread and an ironed napkin. I nodded. The world slipped past. She reminded me of my old music teacher, the widow, and I wondered what this woman could teach me before our paths divided. Games of chance? Fistfighting?

"What are you looking at?" she asked. I apologized and turned away. She slathered at the mouth while she chewed. Her hair, I was surprised to notice, was impeccably twisted into a complicated, youthful brown chignon. It was shiny. Her hair could have been going to a fancy party, if only the rest of her would leave it alone. It occurred to me that this woman had probably been alive all along—all that time when I was living in an infant world, inventing rules to live by, she had been tearing meat off bones and wiping the grease from her leathery face with a starched white napkin. She might have been beautiful. She might have had children and grandchildren. Her memory of the last few decades would be absolutely different from mine. Unrecognizable.

Her eyes tunneled into mine, trying to root me out. "You want to know what I think?" She paused, sucking at her chicken bone. "God is a spineless pansy. Bless him." The woman shook her napkin out. Grease had made it almost transparent. With it she polished her cane. I could not figure out what to do with my hands. I scratched my cheek, rolled my sleeve and made a fist within the space of a few seconds. The woman glared at me, angry that I appeared to be a worthless pupil. Still, she continued, "I know he exists, because—look around. Only God could think of a place as deranged and gorgeous as this. But the problem is that he won't tell us yes or no. He's very impressionable. We say, Everyone has to wear a fancy hat and pray on Sunday and he says, All right, let's see it. We say, No one can eat meat from a pig and he says, Good idea. Someone else says, Everyone has to eat meat from a pig and he says, Fine with me. Someone says, Let's kill everyone with brown hair and he says, Sure, why don't you try it out."

The woman examined the sheen of her cane. The handle bore the shape of a rabbit's head, long ears pointed back. It looked like it was sniffing the air for a predator. I waited for her to give me some kind of answer. Tell me what to believe in. "God just likes a good story," she grunted, and then her head fell forward and she went to sleep. Her cane rolled back and forth.

The woman snored. Her cane fell onto the floor and I picked it up to pet the rabbit. I could practically feel it tremble at my strange touch. "I won't hurt you or try to be your friend," I said, placing it back on the woman's lap. The rabbit rolled, looked at me, looked away.

Together with me, as the fabric of my seat, the planks of the floor, the tracks beneath and the hot, rolling wheels, was the fact of each beautiful, terrible thing. I could still feel everyone I had ever loved— the misery of their absence and joy of their lives on either side of a scale, each trying to tip it. Past the mountains a city no longer stood. A snaking river filled with blood. Yet the grass was as green as it could be, and the water as blue and the sky as clean and smokeless. Above good or bad, our God must have admired contrast.

The stations and their names were a scramble of letters. With only the occasional station light filling our compartment, we rocked through the dark. The old woman snorted awake, smoothed her hair. She searched for something in her coat pocket, scratched a match to life. Her face in the firelight was jagged and disturbed. With her free hand she tried to unlace her shoe. The match burned down, the woman yelped quietly, blew it out and lit another.

"So?" I asked.

"So?" She struggled with a knot.

"What do we do?" I took the match from her so she could use both hands.

"Thank you," she conceded. She spread her toes like a fan, rolled her ankles. "Try to be kind, try to have fun. Enjoy more chicken. That's it. On we go into the night."

Two scrub-cheeked young soldiers woke me in the morning. The old woman was gone. Had someone met her at the train station? I wondered. Had she simply disappeared into the darkness? What kitchen table or graveyard had she been journeying to? "Good morning," I said, and the soldiers studied my papers.

In the next station we had time to get out and stretch. I ate a long roll of bread. I went outside and stood on the marble steps. I could see the tops of huge buildings over the trees. Their rounded and pointed heads reflected the sun. They shot the sun back in stabs, which sliced the sky. A policeman came up to me and asked for my papers. I did as I always did: answered all the questions, tried to look Russian. *Do I die here?* I asked myself. *Is this where I die?* But the guard gave the papers back and went on. There were birds on the steps, big black birds dropping and picking up scraps. Their eyes were yellow and sharp. I tossed them part of my bread and they tore it, hopped toward me, stared at me. I saluted them but the blackbirds stood still at my feet, waiting for more of my kindness.

And inside? Inside me? The stew was a tiny form. The form nested, warm, and the form was you. You got right to work growing a heart. But I still did not know you were there. I sat, I watched the world speed past, and both our hearts rumbled away inside, clanging their cages.

You made yourself a hole of a mouth in order to say later, "What is that there, what kind of tree? The one with the shaking leaves?" You made tunnels for ears so that I could tell you, "Cottonwoods. There must be a river." I ate bread and we were both fed by it.

What mattered was not that around the train there were low green hills with yellow flowers cupped and shaking. What mattered was not that we clanked over bridges with rivers tumbling underneath, which I could almost hear. What mattered was not that there were church steeples or brick towns or even far-off mountains ahead. Instead, it was the miles behind that counted. There was a river now between my home and me. There was a brick town and a church steeple. There was a man riding a bicycle, a field full of unbloomed sunflowers. There were so many blades of sharp grass and tracks of dry dirt and puddles and trunks of decapitated trees between us. Cities erupted from the plains and craned their necks to see the growing distance between here, now here, now here and home. Even this field, even this stream, even that fallen-down wall that does not keep sheep in were between me and home. Even the sheep who jumped over it. Even the ants crawling crazy circles over the dirt, carrying it down into their rooms, standing on one another's polished backs.

Everything was between. And yet, something else kept being ahead.

THE BOOK OF LOVES

Because the night was clean and they were hidden inside it, Igor and Francesco sneaked out to the night-dark sea—past shut-up windows where the sleep of war-frightened people was being slept, past the animals whose job it was to die in time for dinner and to give milk not for their own babies but for someone else's. Igor and Francesco took their clothes off, every last scrap of the made world, and lowered themselves into the cool brine. Their bodies were surrounded by halos of glowing phosphorus. The sound of stones rolling over one another's backs at the bottom and the sound of wind shucking the surface of the sea. Igor put his head under. Francesco watched the halo of his friend below him, then looked at the real, perfect stars overhead. Each single dot was entirely distinct, alone against the black question of the sky.

"Am I really free?" Igor asked.

"You are really free."

Igor thought about the possibilities for this. He could go in search of his family, who everyone seemed to believe must be dead. Dead—it was too big a word. But when he looked around him, he could not fathom where in that dark night I could be or how, no matter his care or diligence, we would ever happen to meet on a road, in a square, under a tree. Just because a man sets out does not mean he finds. Igor thought about trying to learn to love Carolina, trying to replace my features, glue new memories over the old ones. He could be a father again. He thought about the births of his two sons, meeting those achingly small bodies for the first time, shaking their hands and promising to protect them. Had he managed to do that, to protect? Probably not, not from here, this far away. He could not bear to leave another pair of children in the early morning, their entire bitter lives waiting at the door, snarling. He and Francesco could move into Francesco's mother's house and eat themselves fat, eat until they had to be rolled out into their graves. Or he could stay where he was, his own bed and his own sink and his own window. Bars to keep him in and bars to keep everything else out. His own personal guard. He kicked his legs in the cool water, watched them light up.

"It's as decent a place to wait as any," Igor said. "I am a very bad father and a very bad husband and probably very bad at lots of other things, too. No one has asked for me to come home. It's true, right, that I have received no mail?"

"It's a letter you're waiting for? An invitation to come back?"

"I suppose so. I don't know if anyone is alive. If my house is still standing." Igor looked at his palms, which were cracked simply from being alive. "I guess I'm waiting for word that the world has itself figured out. That we're through capturing. I would rather not go until I know it's safe out there. Or until someone misses me so much they come for me."

"You want to be safe. And loved."

"And home. Is that so much to ask?"

"I can promise that I will do everything to protect you here. I'll hire you, to work in the jail. We can swim at night," Francesco said. "We'll sleep the day away. I doubt you'll get the same promise from anyone else."

Igor looked at Francesco. "For a long time," he said, "I was waiting for you to kill me. I thought you were biding your time until I was fat enough, like a goose. No matter how I added it up, there was no way the story ended without me being dead."

"I suppose you will be dead in the end, as we all will, but only when there's nothing else I can do to keep you alive."

The world did not beg for Igor to put his armor on and head out to fight. He heard the sea swish and spit back out onto the shore. He heard the trees shake with wind and coax soft, thin blades of grass out of the dirt. *There are enough of us fighting,* the world seemed to say. *Why don't you stay home and sleep? Eat something tasty for the rest of us. Keep track of your dreams. Try to pay attention to the smell of thyme in the morning. Scratch the salt from your hair and watch it shine as it falls to the ground.*

Igor said, "I think my job in the world is not to do anything. Nothing particularly good and nothing particularly bad. It's not a very important job, and no one cares how well I do, but I'm not in it for recognition."

"A job is a job," Francesco said. "You know your talents."

"What's your job?" Igor asked.

"My job is to look after you and my mother. My job is to admire her soup and make sure you have what you need to sleep soundly."

"We shouldn't try to do more?"

Francesco thought about this. He thought about the men all over the world dropping bombs on one another, cocking a gun and firing—each one of these people thought they were doing the best thing. "I think we might be helping the world by *not* doing anything. We hurt no one. Maybe no one is helped, but at least no one is hurt." He put his head underwater and slicked his hair back when he surfaced. "If I were a woman and you were a man. Or the other way around." Francesco stumbled. "And if we fell in love and got married and had children . . ."

Igor looked at him with suspicion. "Okay," he said, waiting for the rest.

"Then our children would say that if it hadn't been for the war, they never would have existed. That family would be thanks to someone else's fight. Nothing is as simple as it seems. Good things are born from bad things."

"Our friendship is thanks to the war," Igor said. "It's kind of like a family. In a way, I guess."

Francesco smiled brightly, took Igor's hand and said, "One . . . two . . . three!" And they dove headfirst into the moon-flickered surface of the sea. Bombs of green light exploded around them.

They laughed and kicked and dove. They met at the bottom, where they opened their eyes, everything completely black except for the stirred-up glow they made by moving. What was still was invisible; what moved was a light to follow, and within that: a warm hand, a warm leg, a prisoner or a protector, just there, in the darkness.

THE BOOK OF
THE DISTANCE, AWAY, AWAY

Even when I had to change trains, and a circle of soldiers surrounded me, and I easily handed over the same worn papers and gave them the answers to all their questions, I was not scared. *Is this where I die?* I thought, saying the names of someone else's parents and the town where I was not born. *Where will it be? Where is the place where I will die?* And then it happened: one soldier took me by the arm, squeezed my flesh. He shook his head and led me away.

The soldier led me through the station. I noticed everything around me—this place perhaps the last I would see. Pigeons roosted in the high eaves. Their gurgled song was a constant echo. Sausage was for sale, newspapers, sweet cakes in small boxes. Men wore hats and coats, women wore hats and coats. Everyone watched me being taken away. There was something like relief in this scene—the answer to a question as long as my journey to the farmhouse, as long as my journey on the train, as long as my life. Where will the end come? The end will come here.

You, the life inside me, scrambling to put together the cells of guts and toenails and the follicles with which to grow the long shine of hair, could not have seen the soldiers and their boots. Could not see that behind their eyes were so many deaths that there was no sense in memorizing all of them. Just to name the names would have taken them all the nights of their lives.

The soldiers stopped at a stand in the middle of the station. The soldier paid for and received a roll of bread. He put it into a bag and handed it to me. My eyes were questions. *You*, he said. *Bread.* He wrapped his fingers around my wrist. The other words were lost in my shock, but the word *bread* kept landing, clear as a dropped coin. I nodded. *Bread. For you.*

The soldier put the package in my hand, led me to my platform, bowed his head and left. I could not find him in the crowd through my window, though I still felt the ring of fingers around my arm and wrist. *I do not die here?* I asked the bread, which revealed its soft white heart.

"I'm going to the New World," I told the agent at the dock. He curled his lip and narrowed his eyes.

"America?" he asked.

"Is that its name?" I wondered aloud. "Was the new world always named that?"

"Is it just you?" the agent asked, already writing my name on the ticket. I did not know that I was lying to him when I said yes.

Inside, the tunnels of your ears became more precise. The one single tube began to make itself into an entire network of intestines. Bulbs of arms and legs began to blossom out. No bones yet. No increments of spine. Nothing hard, only soft parts first. Your veins reached out to other veins and opened their mouths to kiss each other.

My cabin was full of Russian women and their children. Hair was combed, clothes were put away in shelves, armpits were splashed with water. Everyone was talking so fast I had a hard time figuring out which words came out of which mouth.

"Maksim is the lowliest of scum," one young woman said, trying to jam a pin into her blond hair.

"You're lucky compared to me. My husband doesn't even remember my name."

"Mother, I want," a little boy said.

"What's that, Vovochka?"

"Find me an American with money and a straight nose and I'll do all your laundry," a teenage girl said, laughing.

"Candy. And where's my water gun?" the little boy whined.

All at once, they noticed me. The room turned silent.

"Hi there, scaredy," the first girl said to me. "You staying with us? You got your life rafts there?" I saw myself, hugging my bags to my chest. I felt dirty and despicable; pathetic, lonesome, lost. I was no one to nobody, alive without reason to be. I wanted to be invisible, to be air or water, anything but a human body and soul.

I said, "A mistake," and walked away fast. I felt like I was going crazy, caught in a crawl of biting ants. Down the length of the hallway, each bunk bursting with men or women, kids crashing into each other and laughing hard. "Where are my slippers?" a woman shrieked.

"You expect me to keep track of those disgusting old things?" a man bellowed.

"Superhero!" a little boy screamed, and ran in front of me, his arms out. The air felt sticky at the same time that it was cold. I ran up the metal stairs where the wind, the salty wind, blew my hair. I drank it in. Everything around me was either gray or blue. It was cold outside. I was cold inside. I was tired.

On the bench nearby a man in a black hat was sitting with a radio on his lap. When he saw me, recognition flashed across his face. As if he had been waiting for me to fly through the door. The man's eyes were filled with sadness. He put his hand out to me. The hand was a beggar, destitute and hungry. "Sit, please. I can't listen alone," he said in English. English, I thought. The same language as the radio. That language that brought it all back. He did not ask me who I was—our names, the facts, had nothing to do with this moment. The hum in my body settled, the women and children downstairs in the bowels of the ship hushed up. I sat at his side, my parcels on my lap. Our shoulders touched. The radio filled my ears.

Here, on over an acre of land lay dead and dying people. You could not see which was which except perhaps by a convulsive movement or a convulsive sigh from a living skeleton too weak to move. The living lay with their heads against the corpses and around them moved the awful, ghostly procession of emaciated people with nothing to do and no hope of life. There was no privacy, nor did men and women ask it any longer. Women stood and squatted stock naked in the dust trying to wash themselves and to catch the lice on their bodies. Babies have been born here, tiny wizened things that could not live. A mother, driven mad, screamed at the British sentry to give her milk for her child. He opened the bundle and found the baby had been dead for days.

I was floating above myself. I tried to find my body. My feet were resting on wooden planks hammered down with dowels and beneath those were cabins where people prepared to sleep, dream, stand up to go to the bathroom and have a sip of water because their mouths were dry. Girls were in love with boys. Boys were mean to girls. Children wanted sweets, toys. I felt so lonely it almost seemed unbelievable that I myself was there. That emptiness should not be possible in a living body.

"It's over," the man in the black hat said. "Hitler is dead. The camps are being liberated."

"I don't know what those things are," I admitted. He studied me, the clear state of disrepair, of despair.

"You are safe, that's all you need to know. You survived."

The man in the black hat opened a newspaper with a picture of a man with a square of a mustache. The headline read: HITLER AND HIS BRIDE KILL THEMSELVES. "He married his mistress at midnight and they were dead by afternoon. You can read it." I put my hand around Solomon's star in my pocket. *I do not die there? I asked. Do I die at sea? Is it a matter of a cleaner, better world?* Though you had no bones yet, you sloshed and rocked inside me. You sent waves out until I had to run and throw up over the side of the ship. The froth swallowed it; I could not even see what I had lost.

The man in the black hat came over and offered me a hand and a handkerchief. "Would you like to sit down?" he asked, his accent flat and songless.

"Do I die here?" I asked him.

"It's seasickness," he said. "It's perfectly normal."

"Is it a better world now that we are all dead?"

He patted my face with the little white cloth. "No one here is dead. You have made it."

"I had four parents. I thought it would be enough to last." I started to cry into the cloth, I cried until the thing was limp and useless. I tore my throat with air. My feet were weak with loss—so were my knees, my earlobes, my fingernails. My hair and dry, stretched skin cried. The tiny bones in my hands cried. The sea of my belly was a storm. You must have felt dizzy, washing back and forth, but your new heart did not stop pumping. *We are alive,* you said, *we are alive, we are alive, we are alive, we are alive.*

The man put his hand on my head awkwardly and patted it. "We are going to be all right," he said. "We are on our way home."

"Do you know me?" I asked.

"I know you now." The man in the black hat smiled. "And it's a pleasure. My name is Edward."

"Are you one of my people?" I felt as if I knew him, as if he belonged to me and always had. And why wouldn't he? Here we were in the endlessness and God had not offered a good explanation. I was alive with hands, a mouth—this story was mine to tell. I imagined the villagers running away, leaping into the river, gathered by the loving arms of the water, washed to sea, transformed. I began, "And the people turned into the boards, nails, the passengers. In the ship's depths they became fires great enough to push this whole floating city across the world. They became the entire, unbreakable ocean."

Edward was not afraid of me, of where I had come from. Somehow, I seemed to make perfect sense to him. In those clear eyes I saw a place to rest, a small, safe corner. Yes, you are one of my people, I thought. Of course you are. We began to move. The ship rocked on the sea, the sea which counted all the blues as its own, the sea which rolled over itself and sprayed across the bow, landing white and thick on itself.

The motion of the sea felt the same as the motion inside. Everything swam and floated. "Who are you?" I asked my middle.

I looked out and memorized the shoreline, the shape of the way back. I did not have to try hard to memorize the shape of the water because it was so flat, so deep, so endless. Against it the land looked tiny and harmless—a miniature, floating island.

Edward and I spent the whole journey together, yet I hardly remember speaking to each other. We shared food, watched each other's things when one wanted to stand up and go for a walk. We made a small bed on deck and slept under a cloudy sky. "Good night, new friend," Edward said each night. I do not know if I slept peacefully or wildly. If I snored or howled. In the morning, Edward handed me tea and we took our place on the bench, where before us the sea was vast and generous—she hid her treasures and her misery; only the tumbled waves were ours to see, only the surface. Ahead of us: This sea, another. The great big ocean. For weeks, our whole world was blue.

THE BOOK OF
EXPLANATIONS
AND ENDINGS

Curled up on the salt-sprayed deck, my head on the bag of feathers, I dreamed of the dictator's wedding.

There were no balloons. No ribbons. There were no flags for miles along the road and no procession of shining cars. The dictator wore his green suit, of course and as always. His bride wore a green dress and green shoes and a green hat. Did she call up and order this from a shop in the city where she was born? Did she tell them it was for her wedding? Did she put her right arm up even though the person on the other end of the phone would never have known if she did?

At the moment of their nuptials, our earth was heavy over them. Many feet of ground between the wedding and any daylight. Ants and ant holes. Worms and wormholes. Gophers, rabbits, snakes, spiders and the green backs of beetles. Rainwater did its best to make it down inside their cave and drown them there.

In the cave, the dictator had had a floor installed. There were pastel-colored telephones and beds for sleeping with fresh goose feathers to fill them. The tapestry from his former living room was hung now over the wall, moist with groundwater. Ants made their way along its silken strands.

"You have been true to me all this time," he said to his bride. "This, finally, is your reward."

"I have followed along behind."

"Exactly right."

On all sides, deep and shallow, the dictator and his bride heard the four-leggeds hunkered down, feeding their bald babies, licking the blood off.

There were two other men in the room, officials. One was the witness and one was the officiant. The dictator had not known either of them long. They had been called upon only recently, as the land got smaller and the only breathable air was underground.

"Everything is going great," the men lied. "We are sure of it. How could it go any other way?"

The dictator combed his fingers through his mustache. His companion looked down at the brought-down wood floor. She did not say to him that this was no wedding: her mother was not there with a hat on. Her sister had no new dress. Her father would not give her a new silver knife with which to divide the vegetables along their spines.

"We are supposed to be getting married," she said. "I have been following along."

"The lady is right," he said. "Tell us what to do."

"Stand near each other. Stand so you're touching," the official told them.

They moved shoulder to shoulder but the dictator took a step away when his head came up shorter than her head.

"Friends," the official began, "we are gathered here today to witness the union of this man and this woman in the eyes of all that is pure."

The walls crumbled slightly under the feet of living things inside them. Powder fell in soft piles. The hundreds of feet came closer.

"The earth is cleaner now than it was. The world is new and better. We move ahead cleansed," the officiant continued.

Centipedes, millipedes and carpenter ants devoured the sandy ground. Their legs needled and pinned the path.

"Do you take this woman to be your wedded wife until the day that you die?"

"I will do that."

"And do you take this man?"

"I will."

"For the rest of your life?"

"For the rest."

The walls simmered with the bodies of the living things.

"I now pronounce you man and wife," the official said. "Kiss."

The dictator leaned down and scratched his new wife's cheek with his lips. "Is that what you wanted?" he asked. "Are you satisfied?"

"Do you love me?"

"You're a pure woman."

Champagne was enjoyed out of crystal flutes. The bubbles stung the faces of the celebrants when they sipped. By the time the toasts had been toasted, the floor was dotted with insects. The four humans stomped as many dead as they could but the supply was quickly renewed by the bountiful, plentiful earth.

The new wife lay naked all night long, waiting. Her skin was cold. He did not press against her. He did not spank her in the midst. He did not kiss her with his open and dripping mouth. He did not collapse and whisper a few words into her ear. He slept right through the night, though the creatures made the turn from floor to bedposts and found the two large bodies under the covers. The dictator's wife was walked upon by tiny feet, pricked by them on her pale skin, but she did not scream because she did not want to disturb her fair, sleeping husband.

And in the morning, when the officials came back with the news that the enemy was closing in, that the space of their territory had become very slight, the dictator handed his wife a terrible, beautiful pill and took one for himself. "Thank you very much," he said to the official. "We will be in our room."

"Cheers," the wife said, ever hopeful, while she tapped his pill with her own.

"Bite, then swallow," he told her.

But after the stuff spilled out over their tongues, and before it worked to end their lives, the dictator took a gun out of his belt and put it to his head, giving his new wife the opportunity to watch him die. She fell over him and watched his blood roll down into a river in which the bugs swam. In the time it took her to die, the river had reached the wall and begun to soak into it, the wall was reddened and rich. What was alive inside rejoiced.

The officials wrapped the two bodies in a cloth, carried them through the tunnels and out into the spinning world where spring tulips lost one waxy petal at a time. The dictator and his new bride were tossed into a hole, where they became inseparable, indistinguishable in death—bones were bones, insides were slippery and rich—and the tiniest of creatures began to eat.

THE BOOK OF
THE DISTANCE,
CLOSER, CLOSER

The buildings were giants and the trees were small. Our boat rolled into the muddy slip, the ghosts wrapped themselves around mussel-ringed pilings, mossy concrete and the soft, wet wood of the dock. They climbed onto shore and wiped themselves clean.

They rubbed the salt out of their eyes and shook their hair out.

All along the shore, men in beige grabbed ropes and yelled. In front of me was a city huge and prickling. It smelled of rotting wood. Edward and I tried to hold hands while people pushed down the gangplank, braying like horses. Our fingers slipped apart in slow motion, centimeter by centimeter, in the crush of bodies. I was mashed and had to tip my head up to the sky to find air. Had I died right then and there, the mob would have carried me without meaning to or wanting to.

I descended from that ship carrying nothing but the feathered makings of warmth and broken pieces of home. At the bottom of the gangplank, we were funneled into lines. A man sat me on a cold metal stool and stuck something into my ears without asking if he could. In my chest, the old fear pumped. "Name?" the man asked in my language.

"Natalya," I started to say, but then shook my head. "I'm safe here?"

Prideful, full-chested, he said, "You are safe here." I wanted to start my life with my good name. With this first stitch, I attached two new worlds together.

"Lena," I said, and it was like shaking hands with an old friend.

After that, he was gentle and careful. I had offered him the position of my savior, offered this country whose name still felt jagged in my mouth the chance to rescue me.

I looked at the man's blond hair, oiled into a sharp part. It was a mirror for the vain, bright lights hanging from the ceiling. At other stools, other dirty boat people. In front of them, other slick-headed men in gray wool trousers and shirts. Their belt buckles, the whole row of them, looked like a chain. Then the man stuck his tongue out and I stuck my tongue out. In went and out came the thermometers from under the tongues of the boat people, and numbers were added to the record books of the clean boys. He handed me my bag and motioned to the row of doors. Outside, everything waited.

"Welcome home."

"I don't know where I'm going. This is as far as anyone told me."

He handed me a small map. "You'll be fine. You have nice

American eyes." The man clicked the button on his flashlight, preparing to shine it into the ears of another lost soul, as if, diligent and practical, he would search in the least likely of places, in case what we all were looking for was hidden there.

Some streets smelled like flowers because that was what was sold there, and some streets smelled like rotted flesh for no reason I could see. The map was meaningless no matter which direction I turned it. I put it in my pocket and walked. The streets were tightly cobbled, the sidewalks full of walkers. People, like a swarm, like an infestation. This must be where all the ghosts have come, I thought. Everyone who has ever lived—this is where God has decided to keep us.

"Excuse me, sweet cheeks," said a man with a table full of oranges.

"Give me six of those," a woman in a blue dress cooed.

"I'd give you six of anything you wanted," he told her. "I'd give you twelve."

Women wore skirts that left their legs out and men had small cases in their hands. Unquestionably, it was spring: trees were hot with blossoms and people carried their coats, kept putting their faces up to the sun, offering their appreciation to the earth for turning around again. I was bumped and stumbled over and my bag of feathers was almost knocked out of my hand.

"I'd like to show you," a deep voice said.

A higher one giggled. "Marty is handsome five times over."

"You want to put money on it?" grumbled one kid to another.

"Hey, lady, buy a paper?" a boy yelled. Above me on wooden tracks a train shook the earth and I ducked and covered my head. People walked on, unafraid. I felt a hand on my shoulder and I looked up to find Edward, tipping his brim. He was thatched by light coming through the tracks. I grabbed him in case he slipped away again. "It's you," I stammered. I wished I could lock our arms together.

"Follow me," he said. "Let's take you home."

"Everyone keeps using that word."

"Isn't that the whole point?" Edward led me through the crowds of people waiting for cars to pass, over holes in the street that smelled like everything awful had died at once, and to a tall brick building no different from the others on the street. Why this one? I wanted to ask. It had a door, which the man knocked on. Hearing the sound of wings, I looked up to see pigeons dive off the roof, their feathers blue in the light.

A woman opened the door and let us in without asking who we were. The apartment was all beds, tightly made up and stacked. Two girls and a boy were flicking marbles toward a tipped-over cup. I suddenly felt dizzy. I thought I was looking at myself, on the second day of the world, before everything had changed. The shock flickered across my skin. "Who are those children?"

"Tra-la-la," all the ghosts sang. "No one is here except all of us."

The woman answered my question without concern. "These are Rosa and Isaac Stoneberg's children. Rachel, Frida and Abe. Stand up and say hello," she told the three.

"We're not supposed to talk to strangers," Frida said.

The woman laughed. "She's not a stranger. Well, she is, but

she's our stranger." She tried to make sense. "This is Lena, who will be living here."

I was dizzy. I was the stranger and this was my home. They had been waiting for me. Meat was cooking, and tea was placed in my hand.

"Edward says you escaped to Russia? You are lucky to have made it to safety."

"I was safe?"

"Behind Soviet lines, I mean."

"We were safe?" My vision tunneled. "Does that mean . . . Solomon, could I have kept him?"

"Three points!" yelled one of the girls.

"War is so complicated," the woman said.

"It's five dollars a month," Edward told me, saying much more with those kind eyes. "Can you sew? There is work nearby."

"I think I'm pregnant," I said. The man and woman whispered back and forth and I did not try to listen in. The teacup in my hand was too hot to hold, but I held it anyway.

"Re-do," claimed the boy. "That was a bad roll."

"Nothing of the sort!" one of the girls argued.

"Abe, Abe, can't get a . . . Nothing rhymes with Abe!" The other girl laughed.

"You can take some time when the baby is born, for free," the woman said. Her voice and the pale light of her neck, the brown curl tucked behind her ear, were too familiar. Here, I thought, is where the blood fills our veins again, where our bodies resume their work, where our skin is warm to the touch. That part we took for an ending? In the next instant the girl walks out from the forest into a valley where everyone is alive—boundlessly, feverishly alive—and the earth is raucous with flowers and the day is not at all cold, and the wind picks up a gust full of apple blossoms—the petals every spring has offered up, exactly the same, identical—and the next thing the tree gives away will be red fruits with white hearts, seeds in the shape of a star.

Stars, indeed, I thought, because I was completely surrounded by white flashes, falling in the sky of that room. From my hand, the teacup fell and the sound of it breaking was muffled static. "Out of bounds," the boy said. And the next thing I remember is waking up on the floor, Edward fanning me with his black hat, the woman whispering and my lap wet. "The baby," I called, my voice too loud in my ears, my hand on the wet spot.

"Your tea spilled is all," the woman said. "Did it burn you?"

They did not sit me up, ask me my name or rush me to a doctor. Maybe because they saw the way my sadness had spilled out over the edges of my cupped palms, maybe because they knew the stories that kept arriving with each new shipment of people from the old world, maybe because they remembered all the ways they too were tired—whatever the reason, the man and the woman wordlessly lay down on either side of me. We stared at the cracked ceiling, we ignored the three children asking what was wrong with us, and we wept.

THE BOOK OF
THE BEGINNING, AGAIN

It was only women in the room—for the birth, the husbands and children were sent out into the canyons of streets where buildings were walls and even the outdoors was indoors.

On the floor, under my head, was the bag of feathers I had carried here from the temple. I was stretched over a sheet, and at my sides were many warm hands. The women had cloths wetted with warm water, chips of ice for me to suck, pieces of torn fabric for me to bite, and hands, just smooth uninterrupted skin, stroking my forehead and cheeks.

I howled until the room shook and our small glass mourning candles fell off the table. They were unlit and so rolled along, posing no threat, coming to rest on a shoe or the leg of a chair. We could not afford to buy enough candles to mourn all the dead. Instead, before bed each night in this new world we had gathered around the five glass cups, held a match into them where another flame was made, burning with the Reginas, Aarons, Adams and Esthers. The names smoked over us and hovered in the room. I had not heard those prayers since Solomon had said them over the tree bark we peeled off in paper sheets.

The unburning candles rolled and I howled. The women mopped me, dried me, mopped me again. A window was opened to the cold of winter, which whipped us until our skin was tight. A group of boys tossed their voices around on the street below like snowballs. They called each other names and laughed. Inside, we said prayers quietly. My new family laid their hands on my belly. "Beautiful baby, beautiful baby," they said, "come on out into the world. Today is the day for you to be born. Beautiful American baby."

"Do you remember the time the whole world was new?" I asked.

"That time is now," the women said. "That time is always now."

"Teach me the prayer," I said. "Tell me what to say."

Together we made the words, syllable by syllable. "Ba-ruch," we said, "A-ta," we said, "A-do-nay," we said.

"What does it mean?" I asked.

"Blessed are You, God, Lord of the Universe, Who has kept me alive, and sustained me, and made me arrive at this day."

"Do I mean that?" I asked.

"Of course. It's what we say," they answered.

"But was it God who kept me alive? Was it not the farmer? The potato fields? The enemy soldier who gave me bread? Was it myself?"

"God is also what we all are. Anything is God. There is no way to say God without saying Everything."

I howled again and someone closed the window. One woman rubbed my feet with oil and another rubbed my hands with milk. Someone spooned a little cooked cabbage into my mouth.

"May it be that You will provide food for Your servant, this child, with plentiful milk sufficient for her needs, and make us aware of the appropriate time to nurse her, and make us sleep lightly so that if she cries out our ears should hear her immediately," the women said.

"May You never ask me to give this baby away," I begged, between pain. And again, "May You never ask me to give this baby away."

Into the cold room came this slippery girl. You tossed your fists around and made as much noise as you could. You looked baked, stewed, boiled, but in fact, you were healthy and very alive.

Two younger women brought me a basin to wash you in. The older women all put their hands together on a pair of sharp scissors and cut the cord that connected us. You were cleaned and dried. I was cleaned and dried. Someone gathered the sheets from the floor and wrapped them into a ball. The woman who worked at the greengrocer's downstairs dug a hole in the frozen earth of the window flower-box, planted the birth matter there.

It was when I put you to my breast that you went silent, and I cried. I felt less like I had given birth to this creature than you had been dropped from the sky into this room, and my entire journey, every turn I made in the fields and forests, every instant I spent looking at the sun-blistered skies, every sleep, mistake—all of it was timed precisely so that I would be in this room here in this city when you, this wrinkled pink girl, fell from the sky, my arms perfectly aligned to catch you. And all the questions about what was lost and what was found, the beginnings and the endings, my doubt following me like a shadow, all of that was silent. "So here you are," I said. "May I always have enough for you. May you be awake before you are asleep. May the fields never take you. May the dead keep their hands to themselves. May the stars be stars."

I called to two young women who were planting, "Bring a little dirt over to me." I took the soil from their cupped hands and rubbed it on my forehead and yours. I named you right away, easily and certainly: Chaya, which meant *life* in a language that might not have mattered anymore.

"Does the dirt mean something?" the women asked.

"It might mean protection," I told them. "We used to think so."

No one ever asked me who the father of the child was. Instead of a name they said, Father of Lena's Baby, Father of Chaya, Father of Life, when we lit the candles. The lost names hardly mattered anymore. It would have taken years to say what was gone—the only thing small enough to describe was that which remained.

To celebrate the birth of the baby, Edward came over with dozens of new candles for mourning.

"Look what you found," he said to me, his finger in your tight grip.

"Look what found me," I corrected. Wicks caught and danced. It was a treat to get to mourn well, to get to say the prayers by the light of many fires. Around me, all these new people were very familiar. They said, "Out of the desert, we walked. Through the split sea, we walked. Across the oceans, across the mountains, we walked. By the rain and the rivers, we were carried." That is how, in a new city, in a new country, in a new world, I was surrounded by my family.

You fell asleep under a blanket of chants. You were alive, each second that I checked, you were alive again. Again, you lived. Even still, you were alive. Edward said good-night and asked me if I would like chicken or beef next time he came. "You are a good friend," I told him.

"And you are a good stranger," he said.

It was by the light of the dead, after the rest of the house had gone to sleep, that I wrote my letters. There were enough candles to generate real heat, and I pushed my sleeves up while I worked.

On the Solomon star I wrote in tiny, careful letters:

> *Dear Igor,*
>
> *I am alive. I think you may be alive, too. Once, long ago, I was your wife. Remember the time we dove to the bottom of the river and the monster had us for tea? Remember the time we tried on gray-haired wigs and pretended to be old?*

Remember the time we were children, and then we were married, and then we became parents together?

I have a daughter, and if you wanted to be her father I would like that. She is just born. She is alive. Solomon is someone new. The beautiful baby did not survive. I am so sorry, Igor. Since you were taken away, everything in the world has happened and I don't know what to say first. I am here. What else is there to say but I am here.

Love, Lena

On a small piece of paper I wrote:

Dear S,

I am alive. You have a sister. You are always my son. Your brother is always my son. The farmer and the farmer's wife are also your parents. I am alive. Your sister is an American girl. I don't know if I saved you or destroyed you. Nothing makes sense, but I remember you anyway. I wish I could wrap my arms around your head and smell your hair. If you are safe, then everything was worth it.

Love, Lena, Mother

On another:

Dear Regina,

May your life be huge. May you never be able to contain the bigness of it.

Love, your sister

Then I unfolded the handkerchief, which had been carefully washed and pressed. On it I wrote:

> Dear Everyone,
> I think you might be here with me. I think we might be together again. I have a baby. She came to me a strange way, but she is beautiful. At the end of all that death: life.
>
> Love, Lena

On a piece of bright white paper, I began a letter for you—the story of the world before you existed.

> Dear Chaya,
> I am sitting with you on my lap, by the window. There are ice crystals on the glass. If I put my ear close enough I can almost hear them cracking and growing. It's not snowing now, but it has been all morning. Even though you have only been alive a few days, your story, our story, started a long time ago. Ours is a story I know, both the parts I saw with my eyes and the parts I did not. This kind of knowing comes from some-where in my bones, somewhere in my heart. Someday, your children will ask what happened, and you will tell a new version, and this way, the story will keep living. Truth is not in facts. The truth is in the telling. . . .
> You started crying tonight and would not stop. I pressed you to my chest and I hummed, but you still cried so hard your face turned red and swollen. I started to cry, too. I knew what you meant, the world so dark at night and only the cool

moonlight to help us see. We both cried for half an hour, and during this time, no new stars appeared in the sky. But then, as if the bell had rung on your hour of grief, you stopped all at once, and you started to smile right away. You pulled at the buttons on my blouse like they were sweet blackberries. You sucked your knuckles. Your world presented you yet again with bounty, yours to enjoy. I marveled at this—the distance between sadness and joy so short.

Now you are asleep in your basket. You are wearing a hat the same color gray as the sky today. You could be dreaming about anything, just anything.

Mother

I stuffed a few feathers into the envelopes. On one, the very exact address the farmer had given me. On another, the name of my town and the name of the country. On the third, *Igor, Jail, Sardinia, Italy*. On the fourth I wrote, *Krasnograd*. Beautiful sister, beautiful city. On the fifth I wrote no address. I just pressed the paper to your heart.

Solomon was twice his old size, and his name, like his new father's, was Johan. He chopped enough wood to keep two families warm. He washed his face in nearly boiling water and ran back and forth across the fields, tearing a path. He kissed his parents good-night and good-morning. At the arrival of the letter he read the words and said, "I remember everything."

Johan opened a drawer where he kept his brother's remains,

brought to him by the farmer, who returned without me from the train, saying, "If you swear to love me, I will allow you the memory of your old life."

With string and nails, Johan built his brother back. He came out short and there were small bones that he did not know what to do with, so he put these in a pouch and hung it around the wrist of the puppet. The baby's skull was never found, but instead of leaving him headless, Johan attached the small skull of a bird he had discovered one morning on the floor in the kitchen. The puppet hung from strings in the light of the late morning. His beak was yellow and his skeleton was bright white. When he was moved, everything clanged and rattled.

Johan made him dance. He made him jump.

He took the note I had written to him when I left, the note he tucked into the cave of his hand and held there until it got warm and soft, the note he had read so many times each word felt like a part of his own body.

Solomon, it said, *Milk, Wheat, Baby, Farmer, Home, Stars, Stars. You survive this. I know for a fact. Mother, Remember.* Johan added some new words. *I am all right. I am alive. I do not remember the prayers but I pray them anyway. Mother, mother. Solomon.*

He tucked the note into the pouch. "Beautiful Baby," Johan said. "You have an American sister. I have more parents. I know how to multiply one number by another. I have so many stories to tell you."

He went to the farmer and said, "I have a new sister in America."

"Just now?"

"Just now."

The farmer counted the months back in his head. "I have a new daughter in America." He grinned.

"You do?" Johan asked, uncertain.

"She's alive?"

"She's alive."

"Good Father," the farmer said.

Johan and his father walked outside to chop wood. Here, the puddles left by rain, which put mud on boots. Here, a patch of snow shaded by enough heavy brush to have missed any sunlight. The trees were unburdened by greenery, just smooth, naked arms, no waxed leaves to hang in one another's eyes. The wheat was shaved, making the distances visible. Everything, even the farthest-off places, existed. The view ahead was endless.

The dutiful postman arrived at the thorny place where the stranger used to wait. Her stump was empty and there were no boot prints in the sloppy ground. The thorny bushes had been cut away and a road led onto the spit of land. Here was a line the postman had not crossed in years, a barrier that had kept two elements from meeting. What fizz, what explosion might occur now that they were mixed? Curiosity mashed around in his chest, and duty allowed him to follow it without admitting his reason.

There was disappointment as the postman watched houses—plainly built of wood and stone—arrange themselves as a village. He realized now he had expected something stranger. Caves, tree houses, a village in miniature. This place did not seem like a secret worth keeping—it was the same as all the other towns he delivered mail to, only sunken. And just as in hundreds of other villages, the end had come. The postman could see the doors hanging from their hinges, the windows smashed in. At one house, he peeked through the broken pane at an empty room. Moved out of, evacuated. The smell of mold made him gag, and he found the same thing in other houses. Like the secret the village's mysterious people had been keeping was that they could disappear. Close their eyes, tuck their chins and be gone. Everything they had ever touched, any evidence that they had walked or slept, vanished. Maybe, he thought, they had been ghosts all along.

The postman dropped the envelope with the folded handkerchief at the doorstep of the cabbage picker's house, though there was no doorstep and neither was there a door, nor did those people inhabit bodies able to turn knobs and let the daylight in. The house was a wrecked ship. The walls were devoured. The package sat where it was placed and waited for the mud and the mold. It waited to be greened and browned. It waited for the ghosts to take it back into the earth.

The letter in Regina's hands trembled with her. "Lena's alive!" she croaked. All at once, the memory of those last days swelled in her.

When the screaming had risen up, and doors were pounded upon, the two women had looked at each other and blown out their lanterns. They had crawled into the little bed, wound themselves together and pulled a blanket over. The air was wooly and hot. Regina understood that her family was not going to be there when or if she came out. She understood that her trade had finally been negotiated: she belonged to this oak-limbed woman now, this mustard queen, in life or in death. She understood too that there were parts of her that were her parents, Moishe, me. Not similar to, but of. All that matter, traded over a life, was stuck.

The widow had been afraid, and she had grabbed Regina's hand. There they had stayed, through the sound of yelling, quiet, then a sudden thunder of footfalls, gunshots, and yelling, and finally: endless, petrifying silence. All night, and on after.

Venturing out of bed only to open another jar and slice another loaf, Regina and the widow had inhabited the bed as two castaways on a remote island. For days, they had lived on their stored-up creation, their tongues dimpled and puckered from the sour. They had begun to be sure they would live the rest of their lives like that, growing old imperceptibly, until one day when they died, their memories one unbroken day of waiting.

But one afternoon, a pair of giant Russians had kicked open their door and thrown light onto two women surrounded by empty, finger-scraped jars. The Russians had been thrilled, having come to liberate the village but believing until now that they were too late. Regina and the widow had had no way to know that this was not their end, but their salvation. They had cowered. The Russians had been tremendous, gargantuan, colossal—bigger than any dreamed-of men—and they were hungry. The very last jar of mustard had been eaten with their huge fingers and delighted mouths. "Beautiful mustard," the Russians kept saying. "Gorgeous. We came to save you, but you saved us."

"You need a bath," one of the men had said. They had picked the women up in their arms as easily as a pair of babies. At the river's edge, Regina and the widow had kept their underclothes on while, with an old enamel pitcher, the men had run water and their enormous fingers through the two women's hair. The cool liquid had felt like a new life. Like they were being born.

"Pretty girls," the Russians had said, clearly a little surprised at what the dirt had hidden. "Shall we go home?" they had asked.

"Home?" Regina had asked.

"If we are going to rescue you, you will have to come with us."

Dried and in clean dresses, Regina and the widow had packed a bag of coins and surveyed the room for anything else they wanted. Spoons, blankets, rags of clothes? They had had no idea where they were going, what life was waiting to be lived there. They had left it all. The widow had had her one friend and her memorized recipe. She had cleared her throat, preparing to speak, which was not something she was sure she still knew how to do. "Please call me Zelda," she had said to Regina and the two giants.

"Zelda?" Regina had croaked.

"My real name."

Then, Regina had scratched down the note that would stitch her past and her future together. "Where are we going?" she had asked.

"Krasnograd," one of the Russians had said. "It means 'beautiful city,' but that will only come true once you are there."

In Krasnograd, my letter in hand, Regina went into her house, where her large husband sat at a large table eating a large plate of potatoes. She kissed him on the cheek. "My sister is alive," she said, tears tracking her face. She could not wait to write back, to tell me that her life was enormous. Utterly overflowing.

On the island, on the day that package arrived, Francesco carried it in his palm from the post office to the jail as if it were a sick bird. He knew what was inside was either an invitation home or word that there was no such place. He watched as Igor read my words with pooling eyes. "She exists," Igor said.

"Do you want to go to her?" Francesco asked, unbreathing, waiting to be torn in two.

Igor paused, looked at his friend, at his bed, out his window. "Think of the years it took just to send and receive *one letter.* Do I have to remind you that I am far away in a foreign land? I am not in charge of my own fate."

"Who knows if the distances are even passable? The walk between your bed and the sea is a long enough journey?"

"As you say," Igor told Francesco. Francesco went to the sink and splashed his face with cool water to cover any evidence of his relief. Igor's wife had been saved, and so had Francesco.

"You could write letters with her," Francesco said.

"Yes, a wife-in-letters might be possible. A paper wife."

Francesco did not ask what Igor thought about the idea that he had a new daughter, despite what he knew about the time between conception and birth and what he knew about how long Igor had been with him. He wanted Igor to find the silvery threads of joy wherever he could. And maybe in this dream, this daylight waking dream, children could wander in and out and as they pleased and someone would always be there to love them. Maybe Francesco would even be allowed to love this daughter, too. The way he loved the man who was and was not her father.

They fell asleep in the sun, which cut through the one wonderful window. Bars interrupted the light and left stripes of shade across their faces, but their blood was warm and coursing. Telling the story of the warm day was a riot of songbirds. Igor's dream included an enormous fish carrying him through the weedy deep, where the hands of many children were fat and healthy. He would tell Francesco of this later when they swam and Francesco would swish his own fingertips over Igor's legs. But for now, life was patient and let Igor and Francesco sleep, peaceful and warm all afternoon with the Solomon star unlit between them.

And the sheep outside scratched their backs against the rough trees. The real stars were hidden behind the sun's greedy light. No one came to the door, no one disturbed the men from their dreams.

The war was a long way away.

The people did not call out.

The sea did not crawl up the shore and demand to be swum in.

The day warmed and cooled and poured light out onto the water, which turned orange and glorious even though no one was looking.

In the room on the other side of the world, we lit every single one of the mourning candles. We whispered names to ourselves, whispered whole villages, whole mountain ranges, whole rivers and lakes. We watched you, the new baby among us, this life awake for the first time. Our hands found other hands and held on, our eyes met other eyes, our legs touched as we sat on the hardwood of this floor and prayed.

"Welcome to the world," we said to the baby.

"Welcome to the brand-new world," we said to each other.

We pray that the fathers sell the vegetables for more than they paid. We pray the crack in the door does not let in the cold. We pray that the snow melts into water. We pray that our feet do not turn to rooted trees. We pray the feathers keep their soft. We pray that the lost are caught by safe hands. We pray that the morning is full of birds. We pray for whatever You have in store, but better, if You can. We pray for the life of this baby, this girl, to be good and long and better as it goes. We pray that we never have to give her away.

Let there be lights in the firmament of the heaven to divide the day from the night; and let them be for signs, and for seasons, and for days, and years.

Let every ending be two beginnings.

ACKNOWLEDGMENTS

I am hugely grateful to my editor, Sarah McGrath, for the tremendous care she has taken in helping this book come into the world. And to the whole team at Riverhead, especially Geoff Kloske, Stephanie Sorensen, Kate Stark and Sarah Stein. Thanks also to Sarah Bowlin, who believed from the very first instant. This book has had the benefit of so many pairs of not just capable but brilliant hands.

Tremendous thanks to PJ Mark, my agent, for the kind of careful attention, enthusiasm and friendship every writer dreams about. And thanks to Stephanie Koven and Becky Sweren.

To my amazing teachers, especially those who read the first shaky pages of this story. They were kind and encouraging even though I'm sure that that draft made little sense. Truly, I do not know if this novel would exist without them.

My colleagues in the UC Irvine workshop taught me ten thousand good things. Special thanks to Margaux Sanchez, who read many drafts of this book, each time helping me to see the way forward when I thought I might have come to a dead end.

To the magazines and their editors who have believed in my

work, in particular *One Story* for publishing my very first story, which changed everything for me.

Thank you to the International Center for Writing and Translation at UC Irvine and Glenn Schaeffer for support at a crucial time, support that brought this from being almost-something to being a book. Thanks also to the Squaw Valley Community of Writers, the Tin House Summer Writers Workshop, and the Ragdale Foundation.

A Treasury of Jewish Folklore by Nathan Ausubel (probably a distant relative) was full of inspiration. Some stories within it are so fantastic that I hardly wanted to change them at all.

Long ago, members of my family lived in a place called Zalischik, nestled beside the crook of a river in the Carpathian Mountains. That place and the village in this book are not exactly the same, just as some history and parts of the Jewish religion have been reimagined to suit the purposes of this novel.

My parents have never, not once, faltered in their support of my writing. Their faith is overwhelming. And it doesn't stop there— my sister, grandparents, aunts, uncles, cousins, stepmother, plus my husband's family and my terrific, terrific friends—I can't believe my luck.

Finally, to my husband, Teo, who is everything. Just everything.

A NOTE FROM THE AUTHOR

My family came from a village in the Carpathian Mountains, in what was then Romania. The story of that place was told to me many times by my grandmother, who was born there in 1920. The stories were fables to me. In them, a girl—my great-grandmother—was sent by her offspring-rich, resource-poor parents to live with her rich, childless aunt and uncle. That girl grew up, married, and had children of her own. During the First World War, her husband was captured, and terrified, she fled her village under cover of night and wandered with her children through the fields and beech forests for months, surviving on tree bark and stolen potatoes. One weakened son died when he fell and hit his head while jumping on a mattress the family had come upon in the middle of a field. My great-grandmother survived it all and stepped off a ship in New York with her remaining children and one bag, full of goose down. Her adoptive parents died at ninety years of age attempting to escape Nazi guards by swimming across a river.

When I was twenty-three, I went to New York with a tape recorder and asked my grandmother to tell me everything. We went through the photo albums full of pictures of men and women who all looked the same—mothers with black skirts and square ankles, fathers with scrawny arms and bowler hats. I wrote down family trees, birth dates, wedding dates. When I got home and started to write—it was a novel I had in mind—I couldn't get anything to move. All those facts, and the story was gone. I felt far away from the village, from the mountain range, from the wars. I had never come to the edge of life, I had never had to hope simply for survival of enough relatives to keep the family name alive. This was not a story I knew how to tell. I closed the notes on my computer and did not look at what I had written again for two years.

When I began again, it was in the dark. The legends were nothing more than points of light in a night sky. My territory, my work, was the dark matter, the emptiness of what is not known, what is unthinkable yet can still be felt. My head was quiet, but something in my chest knew what to do.

This is a book about the bigness of being alive as an individual, a family member, a resident, a member of a tribe, and a participant in history. It is about the equal and powerful weight of opposing forces: faith and the loss of faith, life and the end of life, belonging and being cast out, freedom and imprisonment. It is about God, and the moments so bleak such a being seems impossible; it is about the stories we tell in order to survive, the stories we vow never to tell, and the way those tales mix with the chemistry of the world we think of as real, and change it. The way the story, told enough, becomes the truth. It is about the beginning of the world, the places where it ends, begins again. This is a story about love and the million, billion, ways it stretches.

As I wrote through deeply sad stories, I found that hope was in the telling. Hope was not an idea, but the act of continuation, of connecting the rope's two ends and making a circle. As long as the story was told, it was alive. One life began to feel like all life, enough to crawl up out of the mud, enough to continue and continue and continue.

This book is about what we pass on—cells, letters, memories, and the right of the next generation to keep telling the story long after the facts have melted away and what is left is truth, glittering in a sky deep and dark enough to hold everything lost, everything saved.

—RAMONA AUSUBEL

P.O. 0003377849